Freedman, J. F.

House of smoke.

JAN 25 1996
JAN 25 1996

$23.95

DATE			

BAKER & TAYLOR

HOUSE OF SMOKE

Also by J. F. Freedman

The Obstacle Course
Against the Wind

J. F. FREEDMAN

VIKING

HOUSE OF SMOKE

VIKING
Published by the Penguin Group
Penguin Books USA Inc., 375 Hudson Street,
New York, New York 10014, U.S.A.
Penguin Books Ltd, 27 Wrights Lane,
London W8 5TZ, England
Penguin Books Australia Ltd, Ringwood,
Victoria, Australia
Penguin Books Canada Ltd, 10 Alcorn Avenue,
Toronto, Ontario, Canada M4V 3B2
Penguin Books (N.Z.) Ltd, 182–190 Wairau Road,
Auckland 10, New Zealand

Penguin Books Ltd, Registered Offices:
Harmondsworth, Middlesex, England

First published in 1996 by Viking Penguin,
a division of Penguin Books USA Inc.

1 3 5 7 9 10 8 6 4 2

PUBLISHER'S NOTE
This is a work of fiction. Names, characters, places, and incidents either are the
product of the author's imagination or are used fictitiously, and any resemblance to
actual persons, living or dead, events, or locales is entirely coincidental.

LIBRARY OF CONGRESS CATALOGING IN PUBLICATION DATA
Freedman, J. F.
House of Smoke : a novel / by J. F. Freedman.
p. cm.
ISBN 0-670-85347-X
I. Title.
PS3556.R3833B36   1996
813'.54—dc20   95-4772

This book is printed on acid-free paper.

Printed in the United States of America
Set in Concord

TO MY MOTHER, GLADYS S. FREEDMAN (1914–1989),
AND TO MY SISTER, SARA FREEDMAN:
TWO FORMIDABLE WOMEN

HOUSE OF SMOKE

PROLOGUE
OAKLAND, CALIFORNIA, 1993

INSIDE THE HOTHOUSE

"**M**r. Losario, would you point that gun down, please?" Kate's underarms were soaking wet. "Just point it away from Loretta and Mrs. Losario, okay? Would you, please?"

For the umpteenth time already she'd made this request, trying to make it sound as reasonable as asking him to pass the goddamn butter. The screaming was all inside her head: *Put the fucking gun down, you crazy-ass fucker, you're going to kill us by fucking accident, I don't want to die from some fucking accident!* Not the kind of language that should be going on inside a proper lady's head, as if she'd ever been one. Her mother was still alive, though, and had standards that had to be met. Her mother hated that she was a cop, her dreams for this daughter had been so much grander.

The man was deranged. You have to talk respectfully, be deferential. He's the king, in his own house especially.

Her voice sounded foreign to her, distant, like it was coming out of a tinny tape recorder across the room and she was a third party listening to it. A voice belonging to a woman trying like hell not to sound like she was scared out of her mind, but not quite succeeding.

"Nobody wants you to put it down—just don't point right in her face, okay?"

That was an outrageous lie, of course, which she didn't believe and didn't expect him to, either. Putting the gun down was the entire point of all this: disarming a crazy person without anyone getting killed.

"Why don't you go fuck yourself, Dirty Harriet?" His laugh at his own childish joke was short and mirthless, a barking har-har-har.

She had her blue-wool-covered butt parked firmly on the edge of the practically brand-new-out-of-the-carton brown-tufted La-Z-Boy, trying as mightily as she could to maintain steady eye contact with Mr. Losario, who talked like a rational human being but had gone completely round the bend. A rational human being doesn't hold a locked and loaded pistol on his wife and daughter.

She was trying to apply what she'd been taught several years before in the police academy, when she'd taken the three-day training seminar in dealing with a hostage situation. Make the offender look at you, keep your look locked with his. Whatever it takes, keep that eye contact. She'd take her clothes off if she had to, to keep him looking at her.

Her own gun, a regulation-issue .40 S&W, was on the floor, in the corner. No help to her. Ray's, too. Neither of them could do a fucking thing. She hated this feeling of powerlessness. He'd blow them both away before they could take two steps. Or even worse—do the woman and kid. He was crazy. The problem was, he didn't know that and he never would, not even if—strike that, *when, if* could not be part of this equation—they somehow managed to overpower him or talk him into voluntarily giving up the gun, either way, so that the paramedics could take him out of here in a straitjacket. He could spend the rest of his life in a padded cell on the heaviest medications in the world and he'd still be crazy.

He was sweating. Flop sweat. His armpits were stained under his shirt, large moist circles. The odor permeated the room. He was overweight, flabby, way out of shape. The sparse hair on the top of his head was also wet, plastered down across his pale blotchy scalp.

"Mr. Losario?"

He was looking at her but he wasn't seeing her. She was afraid of that. Was he not hearing her as well? Was he off somewhere, in some private world of his own, shut off from her?

"Mr. Losario?"

"What?" he asked, with the petty tyrant's perpetual impatience. "What do you want?"

"To make sure we're still all here together," she answered, remembering to smile at him. Nothing suggestive, a professional smile, nonjudgmental.

"Looks like it to me." He glanced around the room, from his wife to his daughter, to Ray, who was sitting on the other chair, his hands on his knees, to her. "Looks like we're all here. One nigger cop"—Ray breathed in deeply but didn't move a muscle—"one pussy cop, Miss Teenage Prom Queen, the missus, and me, myself, and I."

He'd never use that kind of language ordinarily, she thought. "Nigger." "Pussy." He wasn't the type. Scared to death of women, yes, but not bigoted, racist. It was the time and place, his need to show mastery. And that made this worse, because he was in waters for which he had no charts.

Losario pushed back a section of the oval throw rug with his toe. "Anybody else here? No? Good." He stared at her. "All present and accounted for. Satisfied?" A sardonic sneer, a cheap knockoff from a B-movie heavy.

"Thank you," she said. Trying to keep the rage from her voice. Little Mary Sunshine, that's what she had to be. A small, powerless object; what a man like this demanded in a woman. All women, his wife and daughter most importantly.

She and Ray Burgess, her partner of five months, had only been out of the Academy six weeks when they'd been teamed up. Her old partner, Sam "The Man" Gonzalez, had retired on three-quarters disability from a car crash while on duty in the pursuit of a fleeing suspect—the fact that he'd been drunk out of his gourd and was on his way home alone was conveniently swept under the rug at the discharge hearing. Burgess and she had taken the call.

Investigate a domestic quarrel. In cop language, a 415F, the "F" for "family."

She'd handled dozens of family feuds over the years. Occasionally there would be some heavy-duty physical action, injuries from kitchen knives or blunt objects—hammers, ashtrays—that required a trip to the emergency room; but mostly it was blusters, threats. She herself had never been hurt, not a scratch, knock on wood, but still, her stomach would tie up in a knot every time a 415F came over the car's speaker, because you never knew. A family blowup could turn violent in a heartbeat. Some of the strongest passions and most tragic behavior come out of husband-wife fights.

This had been the one.

The phone rang across the room. She almost jumped out of her skin from the sudden jolt of the sound.

"May I?" she asked. Her heart was pounding like a jackhammer.

"Be my guest." He gestured towards it with the gun, his voice sour with anger and resentment. "It's for you, anyways."

This was true—all normal communication into the house had been cut. The only line to the world outside was a digital patch-in that connected them to the car phone of her captain, Phil Albright, who was standing in the street, less than fifty yards away.

She crossed the room, taking a peek at the television set in the corner. They were on TV, a live feed. The cameras were right outside the front door. Half the block was lit up like a baseball diamond, a cluster of spotlights beaming down on them. At the moment the camera was shifting from the house and was panning the street and sidewalk. Christ, she realized, there must be over a hundred people out there—cops, press, ordinary citizens behind the police lines. Ghouls. It was turning into a full-blown media circus.

"Hello?" She spoke tentatively, even though she knew who was on the other end.

"How're you holding up, Kate?" Captain Albright's voice was down-home, laconic. A cop's voice, trained to eliminate the highs and lows.

"Still here," she replied, trying to keep her voice as neutral as possible, keeping her eyes on Mr. Losario, who was watching her keenly.

"How's the squirrel? Still as squirrelly?"

"More or less." She didn't want to say anything Losario could misunderstand, use as an excuse.

"Things are getting kind of antsy out here," he said. "The damn TV people have blown this up into a first-class clusterfuck. I sure would like an opportunity to sneak a sharpshooter around the back of the house, see if we could get a shot through a side window, end it fast."

"Not a good idea, sir," she responded with alarm. "I think that would be . . ."; she didn't know what word to use that wouldn't maybe inflame the man with the gun.

"Counterproductive?" he finished for her.

"Exactly, sir. I mean *very*," she added, to make sure he fully understood her position. He was the captain and she was a patrolman, but she was in here. It was her life and her partner's and the family's on the line here, no one else's.

There was a pause from his end. She could hear the wheels turning inside his head.

"It's your call to make," he said finally. "For now. As long as it isn't going anywhere nasty." He paused. "The natives are getting restless."

She knew the debate that was going on: the press, the politicians, the police brass. All players, all with their own agendas. She glanced outside, through the crack in the curtains. Dozens of officers were lining the street, dressed in full riot gear, holding their heavy artillery at port arms. Ready to storm the house if given the command.

There were two factions out there: One wants to wait them out, the other wants to storm the place. Somewhere the powers that be were discussing the pros and cons. On the one hand was what happened when they moved on David Koresh. On the other hand, this man inside had disarmed two officers. He was crazy. He needed to be neutralized.

A broad and a rookie. That's what some of the men out there were saying to each other, she could almost hear their voices, dripping with contempt. *What did you expect?*

It looked like all of the media in the whole Bay Area was on this street. A lot of movement, cameras pointed right at this window. They couldn't see her; maybe a shadow. She didn't want to be seen. Being a celebrity wasn't her style, she was hating all this. Go away, you parasitic bastards, she thought. She knew there was no chance of that, but she wished it anyway. They were news in the making, the genuine article.

"I can believe that, sir," she answered Captain Albright, getting back to the matter at hand. A shitload more than any of you, she thought to herself, glancing at Ray, her partner, whose thoughts she was reading like they were her own.

"Check back with you in a little while."

"Good. Thank you, sir."

The phone went dead in her hand. She set it down in the cradle, moved back towards the center of the room.

"Sit your ass down, lady cop," Mr. Losario commanded her, indicating the chair she'd been in.

She sat. The gun lay heavy on the floor, drawing her attention. Five seconds of distraction, that's all she needed. Take this fucker down and walk away to tell the tale.

Don't be a hero. One of the first things they teach you. The cemetery's full of heroes.

Losario glanced over at the TV set, which had been on to *Ricki Lake* when she and Ray had arrived. At first, when the TV crews had shown up and the live feed had started, Losario had been transfixed. He was on television. A nobody all his life, now suddenly a celebrity. He had started flipping channels with the remote, finding himself on several of them.

"We're making history!" he had crowed to his wife and daughter.

"You're sick," his daughter, Loretta, had spat back at him. She was the type of kid who didn't take squat from her father, Kate knew that ten seconds after she and Ray had walked into this inferno. An admirable quality and one of the main reasons they were in this shit barrel.

Losario had smacked Loretta good for that remark, a heavy closed-fist blow across the cheekbone that had sent her reeling. Kate had winced at the sound—she knew the feeling, all too well.

That had been three hours ago. The cheek was turning blue/yellow now, the left eye closing to a slit like a boxer's. Losario wouldn't let Loretta put ice on it, he wouldn't let anyone out of the living room where he could keep his two eyes on them. He paid particular attention to his wife, "the ungrateful cunt" (which seemed to be his normal way of describing her).

"We're in here because of this ungrateful cunt," he'd told Kate and Ray shortly after the mess started seriously unraveling. "I hope you appreciate what you've caused," he'd railed at his wife, who sat cowering on the couch, her hands covering her smashed-in face with a dishtowel.

"It's not her fault," Loretta had come back at him. "It's you, it's always you, Daddy!"

"I didn't ask you, miss!" he'd screamed at her.

Shortly after this had come the exchange that had led to his daughter's getting hit upside her head.

This was not the first time, not by a long shot. Kate knew that; now. Unfortunately, the information had come too late. She wished she'd known the history before she'd walked into the middle of this. She would've done things much differently. Her own personal experience with this kind of dehumanizing behavior would have guided her, changed her approach.

Too late now. She was going to have to play the hand she'd been dealt.

She'd been suckered into it by the circumstances, the normalcy on the surface. She should have known better, because they weren't very different from her own. The banality of evil. Where had she read that? She didn't remember, but it was true.

———

It was a normal house in a normal lower-middle-class neighborhood. Small yards, most of them fenced, the lawns mowed, everything neat and clean and orderly. Nothing to indicate the danger within. She and Burgess had parked half a block away, walked up to the front door, and knocked. Hardly anyone had been on the street. It was a neighbor-

hood where wives held jobs as well as husbands. A few kids passing by on their way home from school checked the cops out. In some neighborhoods the police are part of the scenery. This wasn't that kind of neighborhood. This was a nice, middle-class, law-abiding neighborhood.

"Who is it?" A girl's voice from the other side of the door. It sounded guarded, but that hadn't registered.

"Police," Kate had answered. "We got a call there was a disturbance at this residence."

Silence after that. She heard some low voices talking, nothing distinguishable.

"You've got the wrong house," the girl's voice finally answered.

"We have to check it out," Kate said to the door. "Would you open the door for a moment so we can see that everything's all right? It'll just take a moment. We don't want to disturb you, but we have to respond whenever we get a call."

"Nobody here called you," came the reply. "It's a mistake."

"Fine. Just open the door then, we'll take a quick peek in, and we'll be on our way."

Another silence. Kate glanced at Ray. He was wetting his lips, reaching for his holster. She put up a calming hand to restrain him. You don't pull your weapon in the street unless the situation calls for it. This didn't. So far all they had was a scared kid behind a door.

"Are you alone in there?" Kate asked. "Is that why you're afraid to open the door?"

A pause. "Yes," came the reply then. "My mom doesn't want me opening the door to strangers when she and my dad aren't here."

"Okay. I can understand that. I wouldn't want my kids opening the door to strangers, either. Tell you what—you've got a peephole in your door there, I can see it. You look through that peephole so you can see I'm what I say I am, me and my partner. We're police officers. We're here to help you. But we have to check inside. So go on, look at us through that peephole. I'll hold my badge up so you can see it."

She motioned to Ray to stand next to her in front of the door, so the girl could see both of them. She waited. Longer than necessary.

"Okay," she spoke, after giving the girl the benefit of the doubt and then some. "Now you're going to have to open up, miss, or we're going to have to radio for some other policemen to help us out, and what do you want that for? All we want is to make sure you're okay, okay?"

Slowly, the door swung open. The girl stepped back, enough to al-low them to see into the empty living room past her.

"Can we come in just for a second?" Kate asked, "to make sure you're all right?"

Without waiting for a reply, she pushed by the girl. Ray followed. SOP, by the book.

The girl stood in the center of the room, looking sideways at them. About fifteen, sullen, dark-eyed pretty, dressed in the white-blouse-blue-skirt uniform of a parochial high school. A large silver cross hung around her neck.

She had two daughters of her own. The older one was almost ex-actly the same age as this girl, she realized. Given her own family dy-namic, how suspicious of authority would either of her daughters be in this kind of situation?

The room they were standing in was neat, clean. The furniture was a cut above Sears. Matched couch and chairs in pastels, dark-stained oak end and coffee tables. A new 32" Sony television set tuned to The Ricki Lake Show *stood prominent in the corner, and there was a bowl of fresh fruit on the dining-room table. A large wooden crucifix was prominently featured on one wall.*

A nice house in a decent neighborhood, nothing about it to re-mark on.

"What's your name?" Kate asked the girl.

"Loretta. Loretta Losario."

"I'm Officer Blanchard, and this is Officer Burgess. We're with the Oakland PD," she offered, stating the obvious.

The girl didn't say anything. She shifted her weight from one foot to the other. She was wearing Doc Martens over her bobby sox.

"Where's your boyfriend?" Kate asked.

"I don't have one," Loretta answered. A little too fast, to Kate's ear.

"You were talking to somebody. I heard a man's voice."

"No, I wasn't. It must've been the TV." She pointed to the corner, to the show in progress. "You must've heard the television."

"You'd better let us take a quick look around," Kate had said to the girl.

"Do you have to?" A whiny teenager's voice, but with too much fear, way beyond the normal fear kids have of cops.

They found Mrs. Losario in the bedroom lying on top of the quilted bedspread, her back to the door, all curled up in a ball. Shaking uncontrollably.

"Oh, shit!" She heard her own voice—the woman part of her, not the part that was an officer.

"Mrs. . . . Losario? Did you call us?" She crossed to the other side of the bed, so she could see the woman's face.

It was bad. Some teeth knocked out, the nose broken and flattened against both cheeks. Heavy bruises on the jaw and temple. A terrible battering, done by somebody who knew how.

Kate knelt by the bed next to the woman. "Who did this to you?" she asked, trying to keep the quiver from her voice. "Is he still here?" The shock of recognition, of empathy on a gut level, immediately turned her stomach into a clutched fist.

The woman didn't answer. Her mouth was swollen, most likely her tongue, also.

Kate turned to Ray. "Call an ambulance. And backup."

"I wouldn't do that."

She looked up, surprised, although why she should have been surprised was a mystery to her. This was a domestic quarrel, a husband beating up on a wife. Why hadn't she assumed he was still here, and taken precautions?

Because one event had led to another, and there had been no warning until it was too late.

When she and Ray hadn't called back in after the appropriate amount of time, a second car was dispatched to the scene. That's when they found out they had a madman on their hands, an armed and dangerous wife-beater who was holding his wife, daughter, and two police officers hostage. Three hours ago, already an eternity.

The first time the phone had rung, Losario had answered it. He had listened for a moment, then had hurried to the window and looked out, making sure he kept one eye on Kate and Ray. He had drawn the curtains and slammed the phone down, hard. When it rang again he let it ring: ten, twenty, thirty times, until even he couldn't stand it and picked it up.

"What the fuck do you want now?"

He listened, his eyes darting around the room, keeping everyone in sight.

"No."

He listened some more.

"Why should I?"

His brow was wrinkled in concentration he was listening so hard.

"Okay, I will," he said finally into the phone, "but no funny stuff. Any funny stuff and she'll be the first to go." He stared at Kate. "They want to talk to you." He put the receiver on the table, backed off so she couldn't get close to him. "No funny stuff," he warned her. "I'll blow your pussy brains out you try something cute."

It was Captain Albright. That's when Kate learned that Losario had been doing this to his wife for years. He had been arrested on assault charges before but never formally charged—Mrs. Losario had always backed off at the moment of truth: the typical, tragic syndrome. If Losario had been charged, the record would have been on the computer and Kate would have been forewarned for the time he'd flip out and cross the line. The time he took prisoners. This time. It was another crack in the system, which she and Ray had had the misfortune to fall into.

Albright had told Kate about Losario: a solid citizen, by all accounts. He was the assistant service manager of a Mercedes/Porsche dealership in Walnut Creek (those vehicles were out of his league; his personal car was a frugal Honda Accord), member of the Rotary and Elks clubs, a steady churchgoer. He and his wife had been married twenty-two years.

That was the bitch of it. She remembered what one of the good judges in superior court had told her once, during a trial when a kid was accused of murdering his mother and father for no discernible reason: *No one can know what goes on behind closed doors.*

"Thank you, sir," she had said into the receiver, her heart plunging to her knees. "That's good to know. I had kind of figured as much." But wished against.

"Be careful," Albright had cautioned her. "Don't take chances. Time is on our side."

"Yes, sir. Thank you." She had hung up.

How much time is enough? she thought.

On the television set an off-camera female reporter was interviewing Captain Albright.

"Is that the guy you've been talking to?" Losario asked her, turning for a moment to the screen.

"Yes."

". . . and that's all we're going to do," Albright was saying in response to an off-camera question. "We have no plans other than to wait this thing out and hope that the gentleman inside comes to his senses."

"I have my senses, you asshole!" Losario yelled at the box, spinning back away from it to point his gun at Kate.

Almost, she thought. You almost let me. Keep talking, Captain.

". . . We are not going to go in after him. Let me repeat that," Albright said, turning and looking right into the lens. "If you are watching this, Mr. Losario, let me assure you that we are not going to come in after you. We are going to wait until you calm down and come out of your own volition."

"And a bear doesn't shit in the woods. You're going to wait until hell freezes over!" Losario screamed to the television set.

Five seconds, Kate thought, watching him closely. That's all I need. Keep talking, Captain, don't stop. Piss him off royally, until he's so wound up with you he forgets about me.

The camera cut away to the broadcaster, one of the anchorwomen from Channel 8 across the Bay, who started in on how long Kate and the others had been held hostage, how many police there were outside the house—over a hundred—stupid shit like that.

They could hear a helicopter overhead. Loud, like it was hovering right over the roof.

"Mr. Losario," Kate began. She had to talk to him, engage him. She had to talk him down off this ledge he'd constructed.

"What?"

"I have to go to the bathroom." She hadn't meant to say that, the words had blurted out; she couldn't hold on any longer, she'd had two cups of coffee at lunch and iced tea later that afternoon, her molars were floating.

"So go."

She started to get up to go to the bathroom. Was it going to be this simple? She should have thought of this hours ago.

"No," he said, pointing the gun at her. "Here, you can go here."

"Are you serious?" You humiliating bastard, if—no, *when* I get out of this—I'm going to fuck you up so bad you'll wish you'd never been born.

"I have to go, too, Daddy."

He herded them all into the bathroom, even Ray.

"Go ahead if you've got to go. I've seen women go pee-pee, it doesn't turn me on."

The hell it doesn't, you piece of shit.

She had no choice. She couldn't hold it any longer, and she wasn't going to pee in her pants. Dropping her trousers and panties—pink with lace trim, incongruous with her uniform but she needed the femininity of the ladylike touch; now the vulnerable girlish gesture made her blush as much as being naked in front of this man—she let her water flow.

Ray had the decency to avert his look. Thank God for that, they couldn't have remained partners if he had looked. They wouldn't be partners anymore, anyway. He hadn't been a cop very long, he'd leave the force after this. Who could blame him?

Losario watched her. Bullshit it wasn't turning him on. What did that wife of his have to put up with? And his daughter, too.

She should know. More than she wanted to admit, she should know.

She turned her back to him to wipe, pulled up her undies and pants. Then Loretta went, and the father's eyes were as much on her as they'd been on Kate.

"What about you?" Losario asked Ray.

"I can't go when people are watching," Ray said, hangdog.

Kate almost groaned in sympathy. You poor bastard, what have I gotten you into?

"Close your eyes, ladies," Losario commanded. The women turned away from Ray; they didn't want to see this any more than the young patrolman wanted to be seen. "Go ahead, stud."

"It's when guys watch." His voice actually cracked.

"You can turn your back, but I'm not letting any of you out of my sight."

The women looked away as the young officer turned away from his tormentor and unzipped his fly. There was a slight dribbling sound.

Losario marched them back into the living room. Kate glanced at Ray, who turned away from her.

It had gotten dark outside, which meant they had been in here for at least five hours. Losario had turned on the lights.

"Mr. Losario," she began again. They had been sitting there for over an hour now, watching the television, which cut back and forth between the house and different people speaking on camera.

"Shut up."

"Let your daughter go," she begged. "You can keep my partner and me and Mrs. Losario, but let Loretta go."

"You've got to be crazy," he said.

"You're the one who's crazy!" Loretta spat at him.

"SHUT THE FUCK UP!" He grabbed her by the hair, the barrel of the gun hard against her temple.

"Please, Mr. Losario," Kate said, as calmly as she could muster, "let her go."

"And you shut the fuck up, too!"

But it worked. He shoved Loretta away from him, towards her mother. The two clung to each other.

"Keep your mouth shut," the father ordered his daughter. "And the rest of you, too."

The air escaped from Kate's lungs; she was unaware of how long she'd been holding her breath.

"Mr. Losario," she tried again. She had to get him to talk, there was no other way of them getting out of here alive.

"What did I just say?"

"I'm not talking about blame or anything else," she went on, keeping her voice low, "but please, listen to me. You don't have to do anything but listen, that's all I ask."

"Listen to what? You think you're going to talk me out of it?"

"Out of what?"

"Whatever I want."

"I don't know what you want."

"I don't either, but whatever it is, you can't get it for me, so what's the point of talking?"

"Maybe I can."

"How can you if you don't know what it is?"

"Maybe you can tell me."

"I just said I don't know."

"Well, maybe we can talk about it and figure it out together."

"I don't see that."

"Why don't we give it a try?"

"What for?"

Circles. Keep him talking, no matter how mundane and stupid. Maybe he'll bore himself to sleep.

"Because I don't want to sit here forever watching you holding a gun on your wife and daughter. Someone might get hurt. It could be you."

"I've got the gun, so I don't think it's going to be me."

"If you hurt them, it will hurt you. You know that."

"I don't know that."

She breathed in and out, deep cleansing breaths.

"Put the gun away, Daddy."

They both turned towards Loretta.

"How many times do I have to tell you to shut up before you obey me?" he asked. "Or do you want me to use this on you?"

"Put the gun down, you bastard, you lousy shit!" she screamed, tears and snot running down her face. "Nobody ever did anything to you, why don't you just leave us alone?"

Kate stepped between them, literally putting her body between father and daughter. This was ratcheting up way too high and too fast.

"It's okay, it's okay," she said quickly, soothingly. "We're all under tension here. Let me do this, please," she asked Loretta, practically begging the girl. "I'm trained for it."

"He's been doing this our whole lives, it's not fair!" the girl cried out.

"Not fair? Not fair? I'll tell what's not fair!" He too was screaming now, so loudly that his face was turning purple from the constrictions in his neck. "I'll tell you what's not fair!"

He stopped. Like a plug suddenly pulled from a wall, a dead stop.

Kate waited a moment. They were all frozen in expectation.

"What's not fair, Mr. Losario?" she ventured, keeping her own voice down, barely above a whisper.

"Ah, fuck it. Fuck the whole . . ." He stopped talking, slumped into a chair.

"What's not fair?" she repeated. Maybe she could finally get to something specific, something she could attack and defuse.

"I'm hungry," the man said, abruptly changing gears. He turned to his wife. "What've we got to eat? I'm starving."

"I could make spaghetti," she said through her cracked lips, a difficult task for a woman with a jaw that was obviously broken. "With oil and herbs."

"And salad," he said. "And garlic bread."

"I'll help," Kate volunteered quickly. Be feminine, show him he's king of the house.

"You don't know where anything is," Mrs. Losario spoke, her language slurred and slow. "Better I do it. He's picky."

That's the understatement of the evening, Kate thought.

"You're crazy," Loretta told her mother, her voice full of teenage disdainful know-it-all. "You're going to cook him dinner so he can kill us on a full stomach?"

"It won't take very long," the wife went on, looking at the cops. Despite her broken jaw she spoke in the ingrained peppy voice of a housewife in a television commercial for detergent. To Kate and Ray: "Is spaghetti all right with you? I've maybe got something in the freezer I could microwave or . . ."

"Spaghetti's fine for them," Mr. Losario said, impatiently cutting her off. "They can eat what I eat or they don't have to eat anything."

"Spaghetti's fine," Kate assured Mrs. Losario. "Spaghetti's great."

"Fine," echoed Ray. His voice was dull, no timbre, a robot's voice.

Ray had thrown in the towel. He was no longer a functioning police officer. All he wanted now was to get out alive. Kate, looking over at him—miserable, impotent, full of self-pity and fear—had known the same feeling herself, had known it much of this day, but right now she couldn't give in to it. In this immediate situation she had to find a way out, for all of them. She was the only one who could.

Maybe she could distract Losario when he was eating. He looked like the kind of person who used both hands to eat his spaghetti.

From the kitchen, Mrs. Losario blandly announced, "We're out of spaghetti."

"Oh, Jesus Christ," Losario groaned. He turned to Kate. "Can you believe that? You see the conditions I've got to live with? Every single day, it's one thing or the other."

Kate looked away. She knew this song-and-dance, she could sing all the stanzas by heart.

"I could make peanut butter and jelly sandwiches," Mrs. Losario offered. "Or tuna melts."

"For dinner? What are you, nuts?"

"I want pizza," Loretta piped up.

"We're out," her mother informed her. "You ate the last frozen one over the weekend, you and your girlfriends, when you were watching that video."

"Duh, Ma." The girl regarded her mother as a relic, a dinosaur. "We could send out. Like they do deliver, in case you didn't know."

"Pizza's a good idea," Losario declared, foreshortening the discussion. "Call Domino's."

"I *hate* Domino's," Loretta whined. "Their crust tastes like cardboard. Can't we order from Luigi's?"

"Luigi's doesn't deliver, Sis, in case you've forgotten, and right now leaving the house to pick it up is not an option." He looked over at Kate and grinned, as if he'd cracked a joke worthy of Jay Leno. "Anyway, I like Domino's, and they get it here quick."

Kate watched him, slack-jawed.

"Anybody doesn't like pepperoni?" Losario queried.

"Just cheese for me," from Mrs. Losario.

"I want Hawaiian," Loretta spoke up, her voice firm. "With Hormel bacon, not Canadian."

"You'd better write this down," Losario instructed Kate.

Kate felt like an utter fool as she spoke into the telephone. She could almost hear the derisive laughter of the troops posted outside.

"Yes, sir, that's what he wants." She glanced at Losario, who was staring at her. "What we all want," she added quickly. "Could you patch me through, please?" She paused, listening. "Yes, Captain. I appreciate that. Ray, too."

She ordered two large pizzas and a large Italian salad, no meat. Garlic bread for four and a six-pack of Pepsis, because they didn't carry Coke.

"I'm timing them," Losario announced as she hung up, glancing at his digital Seiko. "If it's more than thirty minutes we get it free."

"Duh, Daddy. Like the delivery man's gonna have it real easy getting through all those police cars blocking up the street," Loretta jibed.

"Don't worry about that," Kate assured him, thinking if Loretta didn't put a button on her mouth real quick she could fuck this up righteously. Teenage girls—she knew about them. "We're buying," she said. "The department."

"Another example of why we're paying through the nose on taxes," Losario groused.

They could hear the whap-whap-whapping sounds of the helicopters hovering overhead outside the house. One belonged to her people, its powerful light shining up and down the street, lighting up the windows like a sudden lightning storm. The others were the media's; by now this could be on CNN, live from coast to coast.

Dead or alive, they were going to be celebrities.

To Losario's chagrin, the Domino's delivery truck pulled up in front of the house exactly twenty-eight minutes and forty seconds later, accompanied by a lights-flashing-sirens-wailing police escort. As she watched this on the television set—they were all watching the tube, prisoners at their own spectacle—Kate knew this image would be the lead story on every TV news show tonight and tomorrow morning. What a revolting' mess you've landed us in this time, she thought, not knowing if she was more angry, frightened, or embarrassed.

On the screen the camera was panning the delivery man—a boy, no older than eighteen—up the front walk. He was alone; the shot was wide enough to reveal that, which had been her major demand when she'd spoken to Albright to relay the pizza request.

"No funny stuff with the pizza man," she'd told him with trembling voice.

"Not to worry," he'd assured her. Reading her thoughts: "He'll be a real pizza delivery man, and it'll be pizza in the boxes, not scatter guns."

"Get the door," Losario commanded Kate with a wave of his gun, "and no funny stuff. Open it and step back."

Kate crossed to the door, her eyes darting back and forth between the room and the television set, and as she opened the door it was like passing through a solid wall that becomes a hologram, and suddenly the force of the lights shining down on the house hit her full in the face and she was stunned. She jerked back reflexively, covering her face with a forearm.

"Here's your pizzas, ma'am," the boy told her, extending his arms towards her, two large pizza boxes balanced on his palms. His voice was shaking with fear. He stood a good three steps back from the door, as if he could get sucked in if he got too close. "The Pepsis and salad are in this bag."

They were taking her picture. The faceless mob. She'd be plastered all over the press tomorrow. She could see the cover of *Time* magazine: a disarmed woman police officer awkwardly juggling two Domino's pizza boxes in the glare of a hundred police car lights and five hundred pairs of eyes.

"How much do I owe you?" was all she could think to say.

"That's okay, ma'am, I mean officer, it's on Domino's."

"Enough of the jabbering," Losario called from inside. "Get your butt back in here."

Slowly, making no sudden movements, she backed into the house, her arms laden with food. Losario slammed the door behind her, and they were in the box again.

Mrs. Losario put dishes on the table. The salad sat in its container in the middle of the table. Kate recognized the utensils from Crate and Barrel; she had an identical set in her own kitchen. That specific irony raised the level of bile sloshing around in her stomach.

Everybody helped themselves to slices; despite the tension, they were all starving.

"I'm going to have a glass of wine," Losario stated. "There's an open bottle of chablis" (he pronounced the s, Kate noticed) "in the refrigerator," he informed his daughter. "Pour me out a glass."

"Please, don't," Kate implored him. That's all they needed, a lunatic with booze in his system.

He ignored her.

"Get it yourself," Loretta spat at him. Then she mouthed, "fuck you."

The pistol cold-cocked her across her jaw. She fell off her chair onto the floor.

"Jesus, man." Ray had found his voice, albeit involuntarily.

Losario spun on him. "You get it, houseboy. A nice tall glass."

Loretta was lying on the linoleum floor, curled up in a ball, holding her jaw, whimpering.

"You broke it! You bastard. Mean, cruel bastard!" Her legs started kicking of their own accord, like a dog scratching fleas in his sleep.

"In the cabinet above the sink," Mrs. Losario told Ray, her hand fluttering a direction, her jaw moving in opposition to her lips while her eyes were focused pityingly on her daughter.

This could be my daughter, Kate flashed, sick at the thought of it. This could be my life.

"Get the one that has the golfer on it," Losario said. "I got it down at Pebble Beach, the day I went down there to watch the golf tournament last February. You remember that?" he asked his wife. "It was crowded as hell. I saw Clint Eastwood and Bill Murray. That Murray was something, wasn't he? That guy cracks me up."

Ray doled out a healthy pour, put the glass down next to Losario's plate. Kate tried to catch his eye not to, but he deliberately wasn't looking at her.

"He was funny," his wife agreed. She was in her own time zone. That's how she's learned to cope, Kate realized. "He pulled some old lady right out of the gallery. She was standing practically right next to me. It was almost me instead."

"You would've been on TV," her husband chimed in, taking a pull from the glass. "A goddamn TV star." He scratched his forehead with the fingernails of one hand. The other hand held the gun. He was eating one-handed. "Well, you're a TV star now. I hope you appreciate what I'm doing for you." Another har-har-har. "You, too," he commented to Loretta, who had picked herself up off the floor and was slumped in her seat.

She glared at him but kept her mouth shut.

Losario drained his glass of wine and held it up. "Once again, if you please," he said to Ray.

"Please don't," Kate pleaded with him. "It's too dangerous drinking with all this happening."

"If you please, kind sir," Losario sang out, smiling at her. Clumps of pepperoni and melted cheese were stuck in the cracks of his teeth.

Ray refilled the glass, avoiding the daggers Kate was staring at him.

Losario ate another slice, drank down half his second glass of wine. All the while making sure he kept eye contact with Kate, so she wouldn't make a move on him. He'd figured out almost immediately that she was the dangerous one.

After the first surge of appetite, no one else was eating. The pizza sat coagulating on the plates.

"How come nobody's eating? This is good." He glanced over at his wife. "Eat it, you ordered it."

"I can't. My jaw hurts too much."

"For pizza? You can gum pizza." He turned to Loretta. "What's your problem with your dinner?"

"Three guesses," she shot back. "The first two don't count."

"You got a mouth on you, girl, you know that? Since when do you mouth off to me in my own house?"

"Since you went crazy, Daddy, that's when!"

He threw the glass of wine against the wall. Everyone except him ducked from the shattering shards; luckily, no one took a hit from the splinters, because the glass had no liquid in it—he'd drained it. Two eight-ounce glasses of wine in fifteen minutes, Kate thought—.12 on the Breathalyzer, maybe higher. One more drink and she could possibly make a move on him; the flip side was that the drunker he got, the more dangerous he might become.

"You see what you made me do?" he yelled at his daughter. He had come to his feet and was weaving slightly, one hand resting on the table for balance. "You made me break my favorite glass!"

"I'll get you another one," Kate volunteered, a bit hastily.

He shook his head, his eyes narrowing as he looked her over.

"Two's my limit. You wouldn't want me to get drink, drunk, would you?"

He herded them back into the living room. The curtains on the front window were bathed in light.

"Lie down on the floor," Losario commanded them. "Everybody, down. So I can see you easier."

There was a wide shot of the house on the television. It looked eerie, bathed in spotlights.

"On your stomachs, arms spread out above your heads."

Kate fell to her knees. Until that moment she hadn't realized how exhausted she was.

The phone rang, so loud it sounded like a bomb exploding.

"Oh, shit," she groaned.

"Godfuckingdamnit!" Losario cursed behind clenched teeth. "I told them not to call anymore!"

It kept ringing. The sound rang painfully in her ears, like a dentist drilling without Novocain.

"They won't stop until I answer it," Kate explained in a self-conscious whimper, as furious at the ringing as Losario was. Without waiting for his approval she crawled across the floor and picked it up. The others, Ray included, remained lying facedown on the floor.

"What?" she whispered hoarsely, wanting to scream, but afraid of freaking Losario out even more.

"What's the status?" Captain Albright asked flatly.

She could hear the impatience in his voice. The frustration.

Which was too fucking bad. He was going to have to contain it, he should know better. Lives were at stake; including hers.

"Unchanged. And what is wrong with you?" she railed at him, for a moment losing it. "Have you taken leave of your senses?"

"We can't wait forever," he informed her. "I've been given my bottom line. We've got to figure this out, come up with a plausible plan."

"A plan to get us all killed? Now listen up good. No more calls, *comprende*? I will let you know when we're ready to come out."

There was silence from his end for a moment.

"I read you, Officer Blanchard," he answered finally. He was giving ground; grudgingly, but for the moment at least he was acknowledging the situation, and not the outside pressures.

"I don't have a chance otherwise."

"You're the one at ground zero. It'll be your call from now on, that's a promise."

The line went dead. She guided the receiver back into its cradle; she hadn't realized until that moment that her hand was visibly shaking.

Losario was staring at her.

"My boss," she explained to this petty, angry man who had lost touch with basic reality, his shaking finger putting them all an accidental sneeze away from oblivion. "He's just checking in. He wants this to come out okay; like we all do."

"I'm tired, Daddy." Loretta had rolled over and was sitting up in the lotus position, staring at Losario.

"So go to sleep. What's stopping you?"

"You are. With that gun."

"This gun isn't going to interfere with your sleep. Your precious beauty sleep," he sneered. "Some sleeping beauty you are."

The girl started crying again, from anger and exhaustion.

"What's wrong with you, Dad? You've gone crazy."

"No." His face flushed. "I might be a lot of things, like angry or pissed off or angry or . . . a whole bunch of stuff," his voice started rising as it grew louder, "but I am not crazy! Not!"

"Then prove it," Kate said. She was on her feet, across the room from him. This shit had to stop: the time had come, because every minute that went by raised the unpredictability quotient beyond tolerance. If she didn't take this gun out of his hand real soon he would be forced to use it, by the power of his own warped psychology.

"Put your gun down and we'll all walk out of here." Her voice was surprisingly steady; she'd been trained to do this, and to her surprise it was paying off. "Nothing has happened yet that can't be fixed. You can walk away from this, Mr. Losario. But *you* have to do it. Now."

She took a step towards him, her legs shaking in her regulation-issue trousers. She hated wearing these pants, they were the most unflattering pants she'd ever worn. She'd been wearing them for over ten years and she still hated putting them on in the morning.

"Don't," he said. "Not any closer."

"You can put this all behind you." One foot in front of the other, treading carefully on the balls of her oxfords, like walking a tightrope in a hurricane.

"That's bullshit!" he exclaimed. "Kidnapping's a capital offense. Even I know that."

"Who have you kidnapped?" Another step, a small one. Her gun, lying on the floor, froze her mind. Five seconds of diversion and she'd have him, sewn in a shroud and hand-delivered.

"You," he answered. "And him," pointing to Ray, lying on the floor near his feet. "Two cops. You think they're going to let me walk away from kidnapping two cops?"

"If I tell them to," she said. "If I tell them we weren't being held here against our will, but that we were trying to stop you from harming your wife and daughter. It happens all the time—you'd be surprised how often incidents exactly like this happen," the syrup was coming back into her voice now, the ease, the control, this could actually work, she had a chance, "to all kinds of people, doctors and lawyers and businessmen. . . ."

"And stupid assholes like him!" Loretta screamed in his face, totally out of control. She had sprung to her feet and was right in his face, shrieking into his ears.

"Don't, Loretta!" Kate cried, "for Godsakes, don't!" Rushing at them, trying to pull her away, the girl was out her mind now, as crazy as her father.

"Who beat up their wife and daughter and play with themselves thinking about it!" The words were cascading out of Loretta's mouth as she fought Kate off with surprising strength. "And those porno magazines, too, I've seen you, Daddy, sitting out there in the garage in your crappy car where you thought nobody could see, some of the times after you beat up Mommy, you look at that garbage and play with yourself, you pervert! You bastard!"

"Shut up, you liar, you whore!" he screamed, louder than any of them, he was going to wake the dead he was so loud.

"You're going to die in hell," his daughter came back at him in a banshee voice. "Die in hell and rot!"

"You'll die before me," he swore at her, "that's a guarantee!"

And at that exact moment the high-pitched warning beeping of a truck backing up invaded their space like a rifle shot echoing in a canyon.

Losario jerked like he'd been burned, spinning at the sound and squeezing off a round, screaming *"Shut up!,"* the wild shot shattering the picture window.

That ripped it. Sirens started wailing, Albright's voice was coming over a bullhorn, he was yelling they were coming in or something like that, Kate couldn't hear it, the gun, she had to get to her gun and stop Losario, and Loretta screamed "you bastard!" again, right in his face, her spittle hitting him across the bridge of the nose, and the gun jerked in his hand and Loretta half-twisted-half-fell to the floor, the front of her blouse spreading with blood within one second, and Mrs. Losario screamed and he shot her too, twice, right in the face, and Kate was scrambling on the floor for her revolver, drawing on Losario, Ray had crawled behind the La-Z-Boy, he was useless, she raised her weapon to blow Losario away and he was jamming the barrel of his own gun into his mouth.

Kate screamed. To make him stop. So she could do it.

He ate the gun. All of the back and a big piece of the top of his head smashing into the wall, blood, bone, brains, hair, dripping down above the television set which was still broadcasting, live to the world beyond this quiet residential street, the incipient invasion that was about to commence and make everything safe.

Her gun was in her hand. She hadn't fired a shot.

SANTA BARBARA, CALIFORNIA

1995: TWO YEARS LATER

I

THE QUEEN OF THE JUNGLE

A woman is standing on a porch, looking out at the hills. She is singularly beautiful. She is fifty-one years old, and men openly gawk at her.

There is a cup of coffee in her hand which has gone cold. She doesn't notice. She is going over in her mind all the things she has to do in the next few days. She has to be strong, stronger than she has ever been in her entire life.

It is early morning—precisely dawn. The sun, a rufous shimmering Jell-O, is starting to break through the early-morning fog, a pale nimbus spreading across the low horizon.

The porch wraps halfway around a small wooden ranch house in the Santa Ynez Valley in Santa Barbara County, California. This house is one hundred fifteen years old. A functional house, no frills. The family the woman married into, her husband's family, owns all of the land she can see to the horizon, and beyond.

Their ranch is one of the largest in the county, over 20,000 acres. A working cattle ranch, the real thing, not for show. The people that do the actual work, the cowboys and their families, live in another area of the property, in houses the ranch provides for them, in close proximity to the barns, corrals, and feed pens where the livestock is kept and the tin-roof sheds where the heavy ranch machinery is stored.

Years ago the woman's husband's father had gotten it into his head that this ranch would be an ideal place to grow bananas. The location of this property situates it climatically similar to parts of South America, areas of Ecuador and Colombia; and after reading several books and pamphlets on the subject, sent to him courtesy of the Department of Agriculture, he was convinced of the viability of the idea. There are dozens of varieties of bananas grown in the world, and he was going to grow some of them in his very own backyard. They grow bananas down by the coast, in La Conchita, south of the Rincon, so why shouldn't they grow here in the valley, a mere thirty miles away as the crow flies?

His neighbors, those that were venturing into agricultural pursuits other than cattle, the production of choice in these parts for two centuries, were planting vines for table wine or laying out strawberry fields.

He was going to grow bananas.

They didn't grow. The topography was similar to that of other banana-growing regions around the world, but the climate wasn't lush enough. After ten years of trying different strains and failing with every one, the property was let go back to range.

About the only thing that came out of that enterprise, besides the family taking a considerable financial hit, was an unofficial and definitely unauthorized name for the ranch. The holding is officially titled *Rancho San Miguel de Torres:* a centuries-old name, bestowed on the property by the king of Spain in Sevilla, with his own hand. After the fiasco with the bananas, however, it became known derisively throughout Santa Barbara County as *The Banana Republic,* and although the family has striven mightily over the years to get rid of that laughable appellation, it has stuck like gum on the bottom of a shoe.

There's nothing else near this house; it can't be seen except from the hills a mile to the east. The family members don't come out here all that much anymore. Sometimes on the weekends, mostly for privacy.

Over the years the ranch has been modernized to need. The feedlots and castration-vaccination-branding pens are up-to-date, and on the plateau above the house, about a mile away, is a runway for airplanes, capable of taking jets of up to two engines. The family airplanes—a pre–World War II crop duster, a Cessna 182, and a Cessna Citation—are kept in a Quonset hangar at the edge of the tarmac, ready for business.

As the woman stares out across the horizon she thinks about all the time and energy she's put into preserving the integrity of their property, of which this ranch is only one part. When you're on top of the mountain, as visible as her husband's family is, everyone and his brother wants to take a shot at you, drag you down to their level. She will not permit that—never. She has worked too hard to get up here. She appreciates it, even if her husband and mother-in-law sometimes don't, because it's always been there for them: their position, their power, their money, their

J. F. FREEDMAN

pride. They can be forgetful that nothing lasts forever, but she won't be, never.

"Is there any coffee left?" A man's voice calls from inside somewhere.

She tosses her cold dregs into the yard.

"I'll make some more. But get up, I've got a long day ahead of me."

"I've got time," the unseen man replies.

"You don't," she reproaches him, calling back into the house, "you have to leave when I do, you can't be here by yourself."

Feet slapping the floor. The sound of piss splashing against the side of the bowl.

She goes inside, runs water from the tap into the coffee pot. Cowboy coffee is what she's making: throw the grinds in the pot and boil the water. Tastes good enough and it's fast.

"I guess a quickie is out of the question," the man calls to her from where he's finishing taking his leak.

"You guess right," she tells him, her voice nothing but serious. She pours two cups, black, and goes outside again.

The man who comes out onto the porch and stands next to her is younger than she is, about thirty-five, lean and muscular like a swimmer, with a thick head of black, Indian-straight hair, cut conservatively. He's naked, his dark body-hair covering his chest like a fur. He slips his hand under the rumpled man's shirt she slept in, runs his fingers along the ridge of her back.

"Stop," she tells him, "this can wait."

"Sure it can," he responds, the hand moving around to the front, caressing a nipple, then nonchalantly dropping to her pussy, massaging it as casually as scratching an itch. "But why?"

He drops to his knees, burying his face in her vagina, eating her. A long moan escapes from her throat, an involuntary exhaling of pleasure.

They fuck standing, his hands holding her ass to elevate her. Gripping the back of his head, the veins in her forearms throb as she comes.

In the bedroom, she gets dressed. Last night's clothes. She sits on the edge of the bed and tugs on her boots. From the adjacent bathroom comes the sound of water running in the shower. She leans her head inside the door, letting out some steam.

"I'll lock up from inside. Just make sure the door's shut when you leave."

His reply is drowned out by the running water.

"Your coffee is on the sideboard. Don't let it get cold." She can't keep the irritation and nerves from her voice. "And don't hang around. If anybody spotted you here the whole deal could blow up."

Kate Blanchard lies on her back, floating. The sun, four o'clock, August-white, cooks the water. She can feel her blood heating up in her veins, her urine bubbling in her kidneys, all that brine percolating through her pores, coating her with a musky sheen, sweat so funky it wrinkles her nose, she can smell it emanating from all the ripe sources, armpits and thigh folds and knee creases.

She hasn't washed in a tub or shower for three days—the pool is as much bathing as she can muster. The pervasive heat leaches out the accumulation of deep-fried high-caloric artery-clogging crap she's been ingesting for the past five days. Days of dropping to sleep from sheer exhaustion, sometimes going until after sunup.

It's been one long unending march, starting from the beach, tripping up under the freeway into town, up State Street and all its flowing tributaries, up into the hills, across the Riviera, segueing into Montecito, doubling back down again. Pit stops at the Biltmore, Butterfly Beach, Jimmy's, Joe's, the Paradise, climbing the stairs to Brophy's to watch the sunset.

She's been in and out of a hundred other joints, large and small, straight, gay, and mixed, the lines blurring along with every other marker, an endless Chinese-dragon procession alongside people you've never seen before and hope never to see again. Scarfing down anything and everything that passes by your mouth, greasy burgers with bacon and chili, guacamole-covered chicken enchiladas, shrimp flautas, tacos and taquitos and tostadas.

Margaritas abound: straight shots of Cuervo 1800, Commemorativa. Anything with tequila. Until a few years ago, when the proliferation of gang violence on the street finally brought a legal end to this ancient and open custom, you could legally walk the streets with a drink in your fist; even so, although that provision has been repealed, it's enforced more in the breach than in the promise: during Fiesta, all bets, by and large, are off.

She sticks to beer. Beer suits her, and a little of that; she's seen, close-up and personal, how bacchanalia can fuck you up, which is one thing she doesn't need—another element to fuck her up, she's gone through enough of them already, thank you.

It came as a surprise to her, this behavior: the socializing, the crazed, reckless partying, the simple act of being with people in large quantities at close range, because she's been reclusive for months, almost monastic, venturing out on a job (as few as necessary), get the essentials done, maybe take in a movie or go on a quiet date. She had carved this time out for personal space and solitude, as a rejuvenation and a penance both, because you can't recover unless you've known pain first. The pain she's known, longer than she wanted or expected; now she's trying to learn what it's like not to be in it. A slow, ofttimes backsliding process.

The so-called cloistered life. Which was getting to be a bore and a drag, frankly, and more than a bit self-pitying. And it's a major big deal, Fiesta, Santa Barbara's most famous tradition and defining characteristic, like the running of the bulls in Pamplona or the Palio in Siena. Last year she'd been out of town up north, cleaning up some of her loose threads, feeling guilty, way too guilty to go partying. Over the course of the present year she'd gotten over that, she was here and alone, so she went down to the beach, where there was a party happening on the sand, and she saw some fellows she knew from the Alameda County Sheriff's Department getting their horses ready. She watched them and stayed for the rest, and afterwards it felt natural to join them.

Starting tomorrow, she'll clean herself up. You can't be a complete puritan about it, you've got to lighten up once in a blue moon. All work and no play, etc. You party and you party and you party and then you go back to not partying.

The pool is uncommonly large, San Simeon–size, built at the same time as the main house, a decade before the turn of the century. An enormous place it had been, twenty-nine rooms, a monument to wealth and high living—until the 1925 earthquake leveled everything to the ground. Now it's a jungle, the entire sixteen acres.

A description of the property on an obsolete county map had caught Kate's eye last year, when she was sitting in the courthouse basement digging up information on a case, one of her first cases after she'd put up her shingle. It had intrigued her, an archaeological ruin sitting right in her backyard, so when she had some free time she set out to find it. It took some clever sleuthing—the old private road leading up to the house had been so long overgrown she'd had to hack her way in with a machete she bought at a garage sale for three dollars, and although she now can drive her car in, she deliberately keeps things pretty much in a state of neglect, to discourage other curious hikers. It's her private place, she doesn't want company.

She hasn't been in Santa Barbara very long. Maybe that's why she didn't take this old ruin for granted. She came a year and a half ago, in January, when it was cooling down, it's only been the last few months this year that the pool has gotten hot enough for her to use; she doesn't like it all that hot anyway, it makes her logy.

Now, though, logy is good. Hot is good. She needs to sweat.

The pool had been the real find. Filthy, half-filled with years of leaves and rainwater, animal scat, old hippie trash, it still worked: it held water, the earthquake and subsequent natural disasters miraculously hadn't cracked it.

She had cleaned it up, dumping countless wheelbarrow-loads of soggy detritus over the side of the hill below the decking, scrubbing the tiles and concrete bottom clean with brush and wire.

The house had been watered by its own self-contained system of wells and irrigation ditches, which she knew about from the same maps and documents which had led her up here in the first place. It had been easy to jerry-rig a water line from the old well down to the pool and fill it with fresh, bone-chilling artesian water. She had waited for the sun to warm it up, which took months, but now it is hot, almost too much, drag-onflies and hummingbirds and several species of bees fly and swarm about, resting on the palm leaves that fall in and float about the surface.

Surrounding the pool are a multitude of palm trees, wild and un-tamed now, so closely grown together their top fronds form a partial rain forest. They give the area a tropical feeling; lying on an inner tube in the middle of the pool, looking up at the trees and the sun, you could be in Hawaii, Tahiti, Bora Bora. The people who had originally built this had been to all those places.

She's never been anywhere to speak of. Mexico, primarily Baja, New York City once, the Rockies. The usual camping-tourist shit, when she and Eric were first married and not trying to kill each other. She wants to travel, she has the freedom now, if she can come up with enough money, which she plans to do, one of these days. She's read about Paris, Venice, Rome. They sound wonderful, romantic. Places to go with a man who will appreciate them, not just bitch about how much it's costing, and how dirty the people are.

She paddles over to the side of the pool and climbs out, stroking the water off her naked body. About 5'6", a tight hundred and twenty-five pounds. Olive skin (she's perpetually tanned, she's never had to worry about sunburn), dark almond-shaped eyes. She doesn't know much about her genealogy but she suspects there's something besides pure Anglo in her blood: Hawaiian, Samoan, Hispanic, at the least Italian or Greek; something to account for the pigmentation. She's comfortable in her skin; her body isn't perfect—far from it—but she isn't particularly vain that way. She's a little heavier in the butt and thighs than she'd like to be, but so is almost every woman she knows. Her legs are long and strong, and despite being the mother of two kids, and having turned forty, her breasts are still firm. Her hair, deep brown, doesn't need any coloring.

There's no reason to wear a suit, the place is completely isolated. She whiffs at her armpit. Definitely funky; time to start cleaning up her act. A nice long shower, wash her hair and pin it up with flowers, brush her teeth, dab some perfume: breasts, wrists, behind her knees, just a touch, so she smells like a girl.

Party hardy one last night, then back to the quiet life. Yoga in the morning, long walks up Tunnel Road past the Botanical Gardens, herb teas and steamed veggies, work, and sleep.

She walks to the edge of the cracked patio and looks down through an opening in the foliage. Far down, past the foothills and the Mission and the red-tiled Spanish-style houses, down to where the streets are rocking, where Fiesta is going full-bore, tonight's the last night, the spring winding tighter and tighter, one final debauchery. She stands above it all, taking in the rays; and below, way down there below her, the city is exploding.

The *Princess Bride,* a 53-foot custom-built ketch home-docked at Balboa Island, glides past the Santa Barbara breakwater, half a mile outside the buoys. Five people are aboard: Laura Sparks and Frank Bascomb and Frank's three friends from San Diego, the woman and the two men. Laura doesn't like the woman, whose name is Morgan, a made-up name if Laura has ever heard one. They haven't hit it off—the woman is an obvious social-climbing airhead, and a 24-carat name dropper to boot, all that Hollywood crap about Warren this and Kevin that, like they were among her closest personal friends. If she gave one of them a fast hand job in his motor home on some location she'd been working as an extra it would be as close as she'd come to knowing them.

The guys are fine. Surfers, surfers' mentalities. They do the job okay enough, they know how to sail and keep the boat out of trouble, which is all that matters.

It's hot out and sticky, unnaturally muggy for California. Blame it on El Niño—what happens when you drop all those bombs and release all that pollution into the air. They'd seen Styrofoam cups floating in the ocean, a steady pond-scum stream of them, from the Panama Canal (where she had joined them, flying down in her family's private Cessna Citation) up to here. You can't fool with Mother Nature. Laura fervently believes this; she's a member of Greenpeace, of Friends of the Earth, of a myriad assortment of environment organizations, all of which tap into her checkbook with continual regularity.

She wears a bikini with a thong bottom to show off her tight ass, one of her best qualities. Morgan wears one, too; half the time she actually goes topless, she has breasts to rival that giant Guess? model, which she's happy to show to one and all.

Frank can't keep his eyes off Morgan's jugs, although he tries to feign indifference.

"Pull up a stool and draw yourself a quart," Laura had commented acerbically the first time Morgan had taken off her top, less than an hour after the woman had come on board, joining them in Acapulco.

"Nothing wrong with a great set of mammaries," Frank had re-marked. "If God didn't intend for women to have big tits, babe, He wouldn't have endowed her."

"That cow turns you on?"

"Keep your panties on, Laura. She's in my line of sight."

"If that's what you want, feel free," she'd informed her lover, trying unsuccessfully not to come off peevish and bitchy. She is small up top, less than the proverbial handful; when she was a teenager it had been her chief cause of anguish, fruitlessly waiting for the buds that never did bloom, particularly since her own mother is built like a goddess (Miranda's figure, even at fifty-one, is legendary); the teenage girl's inse-curity recurring in a heartbeat, when she has to compete with the likes of a Morgan.

Laura has thought about going the plastic route, but her mother talks her out of it whenever she broaches the subject ("It's a bigger decision than getting your ears pierced, anyway, you should wait until after you've had your children, so you'll really know what you need"); on occasions such as now, though, watching Morgan parading around the deck with those cantaloupes pushed out, she wishes she'd gone ahead and done it, even if it would have incurred her mother's wrath.

Laura is twenty-five. The night before last, lying on deck somewhere off the coast south of San Diego, stoned enough to overcome her inhibitions about prying into other women's personal affairs—she has a natural shyness around people, especially people from a different social and economic status than her, which is almost everybody—Laura worked up the courage to ask Morgan how old she was, thinking with that body they had to be the same age; the answer—thirty-one, which probably meant thirty-three—was demoralizing, because Morgan's tighter all around than Laura, who's only three years out of Wellesley and already seeing the signs of age.

"What do you think?" Frank asks Rusty, the captain. "Are we gonna make it in time for the party?"

"What time's the party?" Rusty asks back. He's roughly forty, a hard forty to look at him, bleached out from all the years of living in the sun: blond hair, blond eyebrows, skin as hard as a turtle, a dozen melanomas cut off his back, he still goes shirtless almost every day. He's a pro at this, he's been doing it since he was a kid, over half his life, which would give him pause if he thought about it; he doesn't.

"Seven," Laura calls in answer. "Seven to whenever."

"We'll make some of it. The whenever part."

The party is at Laura's parents'. A major bash, a fête, one of the must-attends for the important people in town, the people who own the enormous mansions hidden in Montecito. Rich people with power. Rusty and Morgan and the other guy aren't invited, but they don't know that yet. Once they dock and secure the boat, Laura will take leave of their company. You don't socialize with the help: it's one of the family's hard-and-fast rules (Frank, as management, is excepted), and in this instance Laura is happy to comply.

"Hey, there, Kate Blanchard. Looking good."

"Thank you." Kate smiles at him, a mask of a smile that doesn't encourage. Whoever he is, she doesn't remember. She'll pick her own company, if she wants some.

Besides, she knows she looks good, she doesn't need some middle-aged married come-on artist to tell her. She knows how to put herself together. She'd shaved her legs in the shower, smoothed AnneMarie Borlind Creme du Jour on her face, the tube that costs $46 for two ounces, an indulgence she'd felt delicious about allowing herself. After slipping on her sundress and waiting for the polish to dry on her toes she walked barefoot on her heels onto her small apartment balcony, which overlooks other similar apartments and a sluggish-flowing ditch, and plucked a flower from a pot for her hair, which she had done up in a long braid down her back; the prize gardenia now sits there, pinned at the top, the way Billie Holiday, her favorite singer, used to wear her hair.

Her hair has always been her best feature—dark brown like a mink's, thick and silky. All the time she was growing up, her mother would brush it for hours while they sat with her little sister, Julie, eating dinner off trays in front of the television set. Julie's hair was naturally curly, it was allowed to grow wild and free, she never had to endure the pulling and brushing. "Your crowning glory," her mother would whisper to her as she pulled the brush through it, stroke after methodical stroke. "You must always take care of your crowning glories, Katherine Theresa." Even though she had been jealous of her sister's freedom from the brush, she still takes the time to burnish her hair, it's her one indulgence from which she doesn't slack off. Her mother had paid attention to her because of this head of hair.

She eases her way in as a spot opens at the bar, catches the bartender's eye.

"Something with bubbles," she asks him. "No sugar."

"Perrier okay?"

"Sure."

"Lime?"

"Please." A nice touch; she appreciates that.

She pays for her drink and eases away from the bar, looking around to see if there's anyone here she knows. She enjoys being alone, mostly these days she prefers it, but an unescorted woman in a bar, especially during Fiesta, is fair game. She's seen it for years from the other side, she knows where that can go—usually down, too often ugly. Before she moved to Santa Barbara, on the occasions when she was in the company of women, they would go out in groups or pairs; but she doesn't have a woman friend here close enough to do that with. In her line of work you don't easily meet other women you can relate to.

As she surveys the crowded room she sees Garrison French standing at the far end, talking and laughing with some people, loud and boisterous, a cigarette in one hand and highball glass in the other—a tall, semibalding, good-looking WASP with the beginning of love handles, dressed casually in wash pants, faded Polo shirt, Top-Siders without socks; not her type at all, even with all the changes she's gone through in the last two years. It goes through her mind that he'd be doing himself a favor by joining a gym.

Of all the people in the world she doesn't want to see right now, Garrison is at the top of the list. He's a partner at one of the big law firms in town; they'd met at some pretentious party, and had dated, on and off, for about three months; on her part, more out of boredom and convenience than anything else. Upon awakening one morning she'd come to her senses and realized he was a tiresome asshole, someone she didn't want to see anymore, but she hasn't gotten around to telling him. Big mistake; the town's too small to duck people for very long, especially people in your line of work. She should've been honest with him up front. She doesn't like him, she never did, but she hates hurting anyone's feelings.

Like radar, he spots her before she can turn away, pushes through the throng towards her.

"Kate, hi. What're you drinking?" he asks, feigning good-naturedness. The drink in his hand is not the first one.

"Club soda," she answers. Go away, please. Just go away.

"Haven't seen you lately," he informs her, his voice lawyerish with insinuation.

"I've been pretty busy."

"I called a few times. Left messages on your service."

She kind of shrugs. Do you need me to draw you a picture?

He gulps from his drinks. As casually as he can: "Who are you with, Kate? I don't mean—you know what I mean—now. This evening. You here with anyone?"

"Just myself." He's beginning to piss her off.

"Why don't we have dinner? I'm not with anyone, either—no one I can't lose," he throws in, an attempt to flatter her.

"I can't," she says, the lying coming easy, not even the slightest undercurrent of remorse, "I'm meeting up with somebody. Later, in a little while. Soon."

"Well." He's at a loss. "I thought we had fun together. . . ." He tails off.

"We did. Don't make more of it than it was."

"We've been dating half the summer," he protests, his voice gathering heat.

"I'm not dating anyone, Garrison. Don't take it personally."

"Just like that? You break off a relationship just like that?"

"I don't *want* a relationship, so yes. Besides, what we had was not a relationship."

Saying that, she drains her drink, sets it on a waitress's passing tray, and pushes past him, out onto the sidewalk.

She motors on down the street in the direction of Kris & Jerry's Bar, where she might run into one of the secretaries she knows from the courthouse. There's still plenty of light out. Men like Garrison don't set foot in bars like Kris & Jerry's. She'll have one margarita, to celebrate the end of Fiesta.

That's bullshit. The drink is to calm her nerves, Barbara Stanwyck time from the classic movie channel. Might as well fire up a Virginia Slims while she's at it, go whole hog. *Got a light, big boy?*

She'll stick to beer. A woman's drink for a real woman.

"That's it, up ahead," Frank tells Rusty, pointing. "Home sweet home."

It's not your home, it's mine, Laura thinks, but she holds the thought to herself. The trip is over now, she can bottle her resentment for the fifteen minutes it's going to take to dock and tie up. Holding on to a line, the ocean spray stinging her face, she watches the coast come at them, the old dock and the beach and the dense growth leading up the cliff. Her family's property, to the horizon and beyond.

"What time've you got?" Rusty asks Frank, squinting against the low-lying sun as he peers down into the murky water lapping at the dock, which he's never seen before. He's taken the helm from the other guy, he'll bring it in himself; this is an expensive vessel they're sailing, and their cargo's even more expensive.

"Quarter after seven."

"After we tie up we'll have to sit tight," Rusty informs him in a low voice, making sure Laura's out of earshot. He holds three fingers up between the sun and the horizon. "An hour at least."

"This is private property, man," Frank protests heatedly. "There isn't anyone around for miles. We've got a full-time security service, we don't even allow surfers."

"That's not a problem?" Rusty queries. "The security?" He's been reassured several times, from the opening conversations about this enterprise, but this is explosive shit they're sitting on.

"I've told you: no," Frank answers, exasperated. "I gave them all the day off, *ordered* them to go into town and party. Not a soul will be around—they don't question the boss's orders."

Laura would grind her teeth if she heard him talking like this, although technically they do work for him, because he works for her parents.

Actually, the real reason she never confronts him on issues like this is that he can have a vicious mouth on him, and she never knows when it's coming—he's lashed out at her before for voicing her opinion, even though he's the hired hand.

He's a man, he's older, and he's her lover. That gives him the power, and they both know it.

"I don't give a shit," Rusty answers laconically. "You hire me, you play by my rules. What's the hurry, anyway?"

"Laura's parents are expecting us."

"You said to whenever."

"But not forever."

"I hear you. We'll wait anyway." He turns his back on Frank, ending the conversation.

The reason they don't want Laura to hear them is that she doesn't know about the cargo they picked up in Ecuador, two days before she joined them. This old buddy had called him out of the blue, Frank told her, he hadn't heard from the guy in years, he was going to sail south to the Galapagos Islands for some serious scuba diving, then come back up north. He wanted Frank to join him, relive the bad old days.

Laura had wanted to make the trip with him; but that wasn't feasible. Rusty (the old friend) wanted a few days of just boys hanging out. She could fly down to the Panama Canal and meet them there, there'd be plenty of good diving as they made their way up the coast.

The first two days after she'd met up with them had been great, the diving as good as anywhere she'd ever been. Frank had been all over her, showering her with affection and passion. Then Morgan had joined them, which, as far as Laura was concerned, sent the trip south. It wasn't Morgan's body that pissed Laura off, it really wasn't. It was her brains, or lack thereof. Laura hates dumb broads. It reflects on her, on all women of intelligence.

"Rusty's horny," Frank said when she protested. "Besides, it's his boat, he's the captain."

Bringing Morgan along for the ride had been Rusty's idea, which Frank, once he understood the logic of it, had wholeheartedly embraced. Another woman, so Laura would have a member of her own sex to hang out with (that went over like tits on a boar, which Frank suspected would be the case); that was the so-called "official" reason; in reality, Morgan was a beard, a true innocent, because like Laura she really thought a cruise was a cruise was a cruise. If they ever did get busted—a one-in-a-million shot, but still, the possibility had to be acknowledged, they all knew that the risks were worth the rewards—Morgan would be an inviolable backup to Laura's claims that she, Laura, didn't have a clue about what was going on.

They secure their vessel, both bow and stern tied firmly to the dock so the boat can't bang against the pilings and make a $5,000 dent. Rusty and his helper work easily, efficiently. They're the best in the business at what they do; Rusty's been taking out charters for twenty years all up and down the Pacific Coast, he's sailed as far north as the gulf of Juneau and halfway down the Chilean coast, not to mention countless trips to Hawaii, Tahiti, and points west and south.

In all those years, Rusty had never lost a boat, either to the elements or the authorities. His hang-loose surfer looks and attitude are only surface-deep; he's conservative, cautious to a fault, which is the main reason (after months of exhaustive research) Frank hired him. That and the fact that Rusty will haul anything anywhere, if the price is right and the odds are stacked overwhelmingly in his favor, which this voyage, after a lot of careful planning, was.

Laura, having gone below while they tied up, now comes up onto the deck from the main cabin, her duffel bag slung over her shoulder, a T-shirt and plaid Big Dog bermudas pulled over her bathing suit.

"Do you have all your stuff?" Franks asks her. "You check through the lockers, bathroom, storage bins?"

"Yes, Frank," she promises, soothing his anxiety, which she doesn't understand. If she did forget something on the boat she could call the people Frank chartered it from and they could mail it to her. Sometimes he can be too much of a mother hen.

"Okay, then," he says. "I'll see you . . ."

"Whenever. Don't take too long."

"I've got to stay until they're gone," he tells her, his voice also low. "I trust Rusty, but it's your family's dock and I feel responsible."

"That's comforting."

Against her better judgment, she had given them permission to put in at her family's private dock north of Santa Barbara, because it was Fiesta, and during Fiesta the harbor's a zoo, there's no mooring for miles; with the clear understanding that they're leaving tomorrow at first light for points unknown to her. She had wanted to say "no," but she would have felt like a snob. Besides, Frank already promised them, she could feel his unspoken pressure.

He kisses her neck. "I won't be long."

She kisses him back. He can be a prick at times but she loves him, that's the way it is. He's a man, a man among the boys she's known all her life. "And keep your hands off Sheena," she adds, directing her stare at Morgan, who's striking a pose on the dock.

"If that's the best I can do, I'm pretty pathetic. I've got you, babe, and that's more than enough woman for any man."

Which is a crock of shit, but he's her man, you put up with it.

She calls out in false bonhomie to the others: "See you later, guys. It was fun. Thanks for everything." Then she starts walking the length of the dock (uttering a final "and fuck you" under her breath) towards a dusty Jeep Grand Wagoneer which is parked alongside a couple of ranch pickups, both of which are adorned with camper shells.

"Hey, wait up!" Morgan calls as she emerges from below deck, wrestling a Samsonite valpack behind her. "I'll ride in with you." She's pulled on a pair of skintight shorts over her bikini, the two-inch-wide top barely concealing her nipples.

"You're not going in till I do," Rusty informed her curtly.

"But why do I have to wait around here?" Morgan pleads. "I want a real shower, I want to wash my hair."

"Because you're with me, not her," Rusty answers with finality, putting his body between Morgan and the dock.

"Don't bother Laura," he orders her. "And get your silly suitcase out of our way."

Laura gives Morgan a bemused smile, as if to say "your *problema*, sister, not mine." Tossing her bag into the back of the Wagoneer, she starts the engine and takes off up the private hard-pack dirt access road that winds through the hilly overgrowth to the highway. After waiting a moment to let the dust settle, she gets out of the car to unlock the security gate, swings it open, then turns and looks down the bluff, at the boat.

The men are lounging on deck, drinking an end-of-the-journey beer. Morgan, apart and alone, stares up at the car. Even from this distance Laura can see the pathetic look on Morgan's face.

"*Hasta la vista*, baby," Laura sings out gaily. She shuts the gate and slams home the combination lock, twirling the dial and pulling it hard to make sure it's secure. Then she jumps back into the car and eases onto Highway 101, disappearing in the flow of the traffic as she heads south towards the Queen Mission city.

"Okay, everybody who's done this before, I want you on this side, the rest of you, over here with me."

They are in what used to be, seventy-five years ago, the gymnasium of an exclusive all-girls high school, decades defunct now. Located in the center of town (a block from the bus station, making it especially convenient to seniors), the county appropriated it by eminent domain a couple of decades ago and brought it up to speed, serving now as a multicultural center for a multitude of gatherings: "The New Woman: Empowering Her Liberty Through Non-Competitive Sexuality"; Craft Gatherings: "Pottery for Seniors"; and this evening's dance class, "Introduction to Western Swing with Ron and Gloria."

Kate is clustered with the other rank amateurs, wondering what the hell she's doing here. It seemed like a good idea a little while ago, when she spotted the poster on the bulletin board of the Venezia Cafe, a local coffeehouse where she had repaired to escape the meat-market frenzy of Kris & Jerry's. A break in the action; to sit in a quiet, comfortable spot, listen to some jazz coming over the CD system, peruse this week's issue of *The Grapevine*, the weekly alternate newspaper, while sipping a double latte, so as to better fortify the body and soul for one more plunge into public revelry before going back to blessed solitude. But no! Like a brain-damaged girl-scout she had to check out the poster, remember that she'd been wanting, on and off, to learn how to dance country; and here, a foot in front of her face like a small gift from the gods, she spies a sign promoting an absolutely introductory lesson two blocks down the street, starting in less than half an hour. How could she resist?

"Okay now," instructor Ron tells Kate and the other stags, "you and you, you and you, you and you," all down the line. Boy-girl, boy-girl, near the end running out of boys, so some of the girls become boys for now, don't worry, they're reassured, partners are changed after every few dances, everyone will have the chance to dance their own sex's part.

"I guess it's you and me," Kate's partner says to her.

"Guess so," she replies, looking up at him.

"Lucky me," he says with a grin; a nice grin, for real.

She could have done worse, she thinks. She could have done a lot worse. Fairly tall, hard and athletic; rough as a cob, that's her immediate impression, but with the kind of lived-in face that's sympathetic rather than off-putting. Dressed like a cowboy; a real one, not the drugstore kind. Jeans, old scuffed boots, short-sleeve western shirt. About her age, she guesses, give or take a few years one side of the ledger or the other. In fact, she realizes, looking around at the other men in here, this fellow is the pick of the litter.

"Have you ever done this before?" he asks her politely, as they wait for the lesson to start.

"No. You?"

"A couple times, informally. You know, in a dance bar where they're playing something by Garth Brooks or someone." He smiles. "I'm pretty much a left-footed dancer, so you'll have to be patient with me."

"I'm no great shakes myself," she tells him. Which isn't true; she dances well enough, particularly the slower ones, she likes them when she's with a man she cares about, being held close and feeling a man's body pressed up against her own.

"We should introduce ourselves," the man says with old-fashioned formality. "My name's Cecil Shugrue."

He holds his hand out. It's calloused, cracks around the nails. Maybe he is a cowboy. She's never met one.

"Kate Blanchard."

They shake hands. He knows how to shake a woman's hand; nice and strong, but not hurtful. Big hands—hers is lost in his, and she isn't petite.

"Nice to meet you, Kate."

"Let's form a big circle, people." Gloria, the female half of the dance team, claps her hands to get everyone's attention, "men on the inside, ladies to their right. No, hon, you're a boy this time, remember? Like this." She stands in the center, joining hands with Ron. "Quick-quick slow-slow, quick-quick slow-slow, quick-quick slow-slow, quick-quick slow-slow. That's all there is to it."

She nods to the band, four elderly men who have been sitting patiently on the sidelines holding their respective banjo, fiddle, guitar, and dobro.

"Watch us one time, then you all can try it."

Frank Bascomb leans against the mast, shading his eyes against the sun, which is parked on the horizon, taking its own sweet time to set. Enough of this bullshit waiting around, he thinks, as he turns to Rusty. "Let's get started."

Rusty glances to the west. The sun's sitting there, on top of the water, stubbornly refusing to sink out of sight.

"Still light out," Rusty comments.

"Not for long," Frank answers back. "We'll be fumbling around in the dark with this shit—I don't want to trip on a rope and lose a hundred grand overboard."

Rusty licks the side of his lip, as if tasting that option.

"Security's gone home? For sure?"

"I told you. More than once." Frank wants out of here. This has been a long time coming; years of letting friends of his use the Sparks family dock, always for legitimate reasons, with the same excuse to the family— the harbor's too crowded. They're not crazy about his cavalier attitude regarding their property, but they let it slide, because Frank Bascomb is the best ranch manager on the central coast. So he gets a big head at times, doesn't always remember the distinction between employee and employer. They can live with that. He gets the job done, that's their bottom line with Frank.

Now it's his turn. One time for all the chips: a million large, his share after cutting Rusty his piece (an equitable quarter-million) and splitting with his secret partner, the moneybags who fronted the buy. Their deal is equal, fifty-fifty after the money recoups the investment. This is Frank's fuck-you money, his freedom. No more ass kissing, to anyone.

Get the shit off the boat pronto and into the pickups, drive the pickups to San Marcos Self-Storage, the garage unit he rented before they set sail. Then a shower and Miranda Sparks's bash.

Rusty takes another squint at the sun.

"Okay," he concedes. "We can get started now." He calls to his partner, the other sailor. "Come on down below, let's start hauling this shit up top."

2

DEAD MEN TELL NO TALES

"**A**re we having fun yet?" the younger man mockingly asks, ineffectively wiping the sweat off his face with the front of the sodden T-shirt which lies heavy across his body, so wet he could wring a cupful of water out of it. He's a good fifty pounds overweight, he's been warned to cut down on the excesses or he could be a statistic before he's forty.

"Three degrees to the right," his partner calls out, ignoring the sarcasm. This partner, almost a generation the lard-ass's elder, has a washboard stomach and the same military flattop he acquired in the Marines forty years before. Nothing impure ever touches his lips, not even decaf coffee. It's rumored that his shit truly doesn't stink.

The surveyor standing downhill, who had asked the question, moves his pole slightly.

"Two more degrees."

The pole moves to the right again, a fractional motion.

"Stake that."

"It's getting too dark to see," the downhill man complains as he pounds a numbered wooden stick into the ground with a five-pound sledgehammer. "Let's bag it now and come back tomorrow."

The lead surveyor, who is known for his obstinacy, shakes his head. "We're behind already, the company needs to hand in this report to the planning commission by Tuesday, and we have the whole other side of the range to do yet, which'll take all day tomorrow. We only have to set two more coordinates, we can do it. Anyway, you're on overtime, so quit your bitching." He squints into his transit. "43 degrees, 12 minutes," he mutters to himself, marking the figures in his log. He shoulders his tripod and starts moving further west across the plateau.

The reasons for this survey are unknown to those doing the work in the field. This happens all the time, for numerous purposes: the Southern Pacific Railroad wants to add a spur for which the state must buy or condemn private lands through the doctrine of eminent domain; a developer wants to build a retirement community; whatever. The information these two surveyors compile will become part of a 30-page supplement to a 350-page document that will be one piece of a paper blizzard that will take years to compile and will be read, in total, by no one.

"You see that?"

"Where?"

"Down there."

"It's a sailboat."

"I know that. What are they doing?"

"I don't know. Taking stuff off."

The lead surveyor takes up his field glasses, Bausch & Lomb 10×42 Armored Elites that cost upwards of seven hundred dollars and are rated one of the best compact field glasses in the world for long-range work like birding in wide-open spaces (an extravagance for someone in his income bracket, but it's his one true passion), adjusts the eyepiece screw to the left to compensate for his nearsightedness, and looks down at the dock.

"What're you looking at?" the other man asks.

The lead man doesn't answer; he keeps staring down.

"If there's a chick down there lying naked on the deck I want to see it, too."

"Shut up for a minute."

They can see the boat clearly, but they can't be seen; the trees and growth hide them from sight. Still, the surveyor cups a hand over the top of the binoculars to make sure the sliver of sun that hasn't fallen below the horizon doesn't reflect off the lenses and reveal their position.

"Take a look," he says finally, handing the glasses over.

The second man readjusts the focus. He searches around, looking for the dock, then spots it.

"Yeah, I see what you mean," he says, smiling. "They're huge."

"Give your cock a rest. Do these people look familiar to you?"

"How the hell should I know?" The other one laughs. "No shit, with a set like that she ought to be in *Penthouse*."

"You asshole," the lead man growls, pulling the glasses off the other's face.

"Come on, man, lighten up. It's a private dock, it's none of our business." He starts to put the glasses to his face again, to get another look at Morgan.

"That's my point. Those people down there are trespassing."

His companion laughs, a donkeylike bray. "You're paranoid, man. It's probably friends or relatives."

The lead surveyor, more angry than impatient, shakes his head.

"The Sparkses don't know anything about this, I guarantee you. Someone's using their dock. Those people were sitting there on that boat for over an hour, doing nothing, like they were waiting for it to get dark. So they wouldn't be spotted," he adds ominously.

"They were?" the second man says. "So what?"

The lead surveyor squints, looking down. "So it's suspicious, is what. I spotted them an hour ago, when we were on the other side of the ridge. They were sitting there, drinking beer and hanging out."

"That's what rich people who own yachts do."

The lead surveyor shakes his head, the head shake of an experienced hand who knows trouble when he sees it.

"Those aren't rich people," he pronounces, snapping off a judgment. "Rich people don't look like that. That's a contract crew. There's supposed to be security on this property. Falstaff Security's supposed to have men patrolling this property twenty-four hours a day. Where the hell are they?"

"In town having a brew like everybody else." The other spits, exasperated. "Who the fuck knows or cares? Come on, let's finish up and go back. I don't want to miss the last night of Fiesta, my old lady's already pissed that I had to work this late."

"This is the Sparkses' private dock," the first man says, stubbornly. "Those people shouldn't be here." He pulls a cellular telephone out of his tool belt, dials a number.

"This here's Ron Ortega, I'm a contract surveyor. Listen up—I'm doing some surveying for you folks," he says into the phone. "No, not the ranch, the beach property," he barks impatiently. "It looks to me like somebody's using the Sparkses' private dock who shouldn't be." He listens for a minute, then frowns. "Because they're off-loading some suspicious-looking packages, that's why?" Another moment of impatient listening. "I thought somebody ought to know, that's all."

He punches End.

"They'll call Falstaff—maybe." It's like no one's supposed to work during Fiesta, he thinks sourly.

"You've done your good deed for the day," the second man says, hoisting the transit. "If we're going to finish, let's do it, otherwise I'm out of here. There's a cold margarita with my name on it sitting on the bar at the Tee-Off."

He starts marching across the top of the ridge. Ron Ortega glances down at the dock once more, then with a final spit into the dry dust follows him across the crest of the hill.

Cecil Shugrue stands on the deck at the edge of the dark swimming pool, looking down at the city lights far below them.

"This is very beautiful," he remarks. "Peaceful."

Kate nods, coming up behind him with an opened beer in each hand from the stash she keeps in an Igloo behind the old pump house.

"How'd you ever find this old place?" he marvels. He's the first person, man or woman, she's ever brought to her secret place.

"Finding things other people can't is what I do," she tells him. "All the way back to Girl Scouts, I always won the most badges."

"You must be damn good at what you do," he praises her. "I'll take you back-country with me anytime."

She flushes. "It gives me privacy when I need it," she says, feeling sheepish for no reason except her pride. "I live down there," she adds, pointing vaguely towards the east side of the city, an area which is eighty percent Hispanic. "In an apartment."

He smiles at her. He's a good six inches taller than her in his cowboy boots.

"Nice to have a private place to run away to," he comments.

She ducks her head so he won't notice that her face is flushing, even though it's dark out here, the only light the stars over their heads. She's attracted to him, that's undeniable, and he's a nice guy, too, at least on first impression. She thinks she would like to get to know him.

When they'd had their fill of dance lessons (he wasn't lying, he was a clumsy dancer; but willing), an internal debate started inside of her—to bring him up here or not, or to go to his place if he asked her, which he didn't, she could tell in the first ten seconds he wasn't going to, for whatever reason. They'd stood outside, a breeze coming up from the ocean cooling them, it was welcome after the sweat-producing dancing (sweaty because new, and his proximity to her), they just stood there for a minute or so, neither saying a word. He seemed comfortable with the silence; she wasn't—something wanted to happen.

"I'm Fiestaed out," she said by way of a start. She had to say something.

"I know what you mean," he replied. They watched the procession moving up and down the street, kids six wide, drinking beer in defiance of the law and passing cigarettes around. It depressed her when she saw kids smoking, even though she had at their age, younger even. "When I was a kid I was down every night," he adds, "all day and night. Now part of one night fills the bill."

So he's local. She's lived here long enough to know that's a big deal. People talk about being third generation, sixth generation. If you've got old Santa Barbara blood you have a special place in the hierarchy.

"I don't live in town," he said then, taking the initiative, "otherwise I'd ask you over for a drink, 'cause I've seen all I need to."

That was enough of a break in the ice to let her make a move.

"I know this place up Mission Canyon," she told him, "my secret garden. It's up near the top, across from the Botanical Gardens. It's not that far," she added with more haste than she would have liked; she didn't want to appear anxious.

"I'll follow you."

He walked her to her car, then she drove him to where he had parked his, an old Cadillac from the '60's, the kind back home she'd always associated with pimps. It hadn't been washed for a while.

"I love standing up here on clear nights like this and looking down at the city and the water and everything," she says now, as she turns toward the ocean to get a better look. "I can fantasize that I own it all."

The only things of value she owns outright are her car and her computer. The rest she left behind.

He's moved closer to her, his arm touching hers. It feels like a deliberate touch, but she's not certain.

"How long have you lived here?" he asks. "In Santa Barbara, I mean."

"A year and a half, approximately." She moves some hair off her face that the wind's blown over. "Before that I lived up north. Bay Area."

"I love San Francisco," he says. "San Francisco and New Orleans, those are my two favorite cities."

"I lived in Oakland," she states to him.

"Um." He pauses. Then, slightly embarrassed (her self-conscious reading of him): "I don't know Oakland, actually. Berkeley, a little. I can find my way to the Cal campus and Chez Panisse, that's about it."

She knows Chez Panisse by reputation; it's famous. She's never eaten there.

He has calluses on his hands; his fingernails are cracked. She thought he was a workingman.

"I was born in Oakland. I lived there my entire life, until under two years ago."

Now he takes a good look at her. Whatever he thought she was, she isn't—she knows that's what he's thinking.

"Jack London was from Oakland," he says diplomatically. "I'm a big fan of his, I've read everything he's ever written."

Nice try, fellow, she thinks, fighting the knee-jerk hostility and resentment towards his attitude. He meant no harm, but still she feels the sting of his initial reaction, even though that's not his fault. Anyway, she's the pot calling his kettle black, because she isn't living there anymore, either (although because of very different circumstances). Look at his good stuff, girl, she reminds herself. He's a literate, attractive guy from Santa Barbara, one of the world's true garden spots, with enough rough edges on him so that there's an edginess, a sexy element of danger. And he certainly has class, if he frequents the places he so casually mentioned. He's about as far away from the men she's known in her life as she could get, she reflects. Certainly a step up. Except for his balls, which he obviously has—the way he carries himself, the way he can comfortably joke about himself, not take himself too seriously. All the men she's seriously known in her life have been ballsy, and most of them were dangerous; in most cases, especially with Eric, way too dangerous. Ballsiness was never the problem. It was how the men in her life used it that was always wrong.

"Maybe sometime if we ever find ourselves together up there you could show me around," he says. "It's an area of California I should know more about, being the native son that I am."

"I'd like to." She feels the flush rising on her neck again. That infers a next time, the possibility of a relationship. She's standing here with a guy she doesn't know from Adam, three hours ago she was positive she didn't want a "relationship," whatever that means to her today, and yet she's thinking about showing him around her hometown. She wants the possibility to be available, so she can decide.

"And I could show you some of what's around here. Seeing's how you're new and all." He looks at her again. "You find things, huh? What does that mean?"

"It means that I'm a detective," she says, taking a hit from her Tecate.

"A detective?" He's openly incredulous.

"Yeah. Detective. As in private investigator. Sometimes I'm called a dick."

He laughs at her.

"I know. It's funny. When I first started out I called myself a dick in training, which really cracked people up. Now the training's over, so I'm just a plain, regular dick."

"How'd you get to be a detective?" he presses.

"I was a cop. It just sort of happened. Everybody's got to make a living."

"In Oakland? That's where you were a cop?"

"That's right." They're always fascinated when they find out what she does. It gives men a sexual charge or something; this one's no exception.

"Let's talk about something else, okay? Anyway, I'm the one with the job asks questions."

"Sorry," he says. "Didn't mean to pry. It's interesting. I've never met a woman detective before, not a private one."

"We're few and far between."

She's a woman, a person. A detective is what she *does*, not who she *is*. Not anymore, she doesn't have that cop mindset anymore. Thank God. She doesn't want to be a an "object" of any kind, detective or otherwise. She walked out of that life, she had the courage to take over her life, stop that from being her work, instead of her, whatever she, Kate Blanchard, is. She's in command, she isn't about to give that up, not to anyone, certainly not to some cowboy named Cecil who finds what she does interesting. Find *me* interesting. The *who*, not the *what*.

Maybe finding her interesting is too much to ask. It could imply a closeness beyond this guy's capabilities. Maybe there's another woman. Which would be why he threw out the lame excuse about not asking her over because he lives out of town. And not just any woman, that would never do. No; a specific woman: a wife. Kids. A white picket fence, roses.

Her emotions are running away with her, she can feel them as palpably as she can feel her breathing. Don't chicken out on your impulse. Life is short and maybe this can't work, but maybe, she forces herself to acknowledge, I should try it. Isn't that why she pulled up all her roots and hit the road, to start a new life, to expand her horizons, all that good shit the therapists back in Oakland, especially Dr. Whitcomb, harped on, over and over? To know how much strength, real inner courage, you have, and not to run away from it?

Give it a shot, she pep-talks herself. You can handle any cowboy.

To get to *Desierto Cielo*, the awesome (even by Montecito standards) mansion which is home to Laura's parents, you drive clear to the top of Picacho Lane, taking a left turn off the road by the huge transported saguaro cactus onto a private driveway (after calling security via the phone box and being cleared to have the gate opened), which winds serpentlike another half-mile through several acres of gardens, both tended and wild, until the compound, consisting of the main house, two guesthouses, the pool and poolhouse (and some utility buildings), all of which have sweeping, heart-stopping views of the Pacific, comes into view.

The party is a big, sprawling, outdoor gala, a couple hundred people, carefully selected and approved by Miranda Tayman Sparks, who has orchestrated this gala; even the special invitees of Miranda's mother-in-law, the great dowager Dorothy Hawthorne Sparks, have to pass Miranda's muster, although Miranda generally doesn't sweat the small stuff when it comes to dealing with Dorothy—staying on the right side of her husband's mother is something she learned to do years ago; even before she and Frederick were married she'd figured out the lay of the land.

The guest list is a mixed bag of money, old and new, other classes of important people, artists; most of them guests of Frederick, Laura's father, a fine amateur photographer and watercolorist, who is to many of this set a major patron; and a smattering of influential local leaders, like Sean Redbuck, Santa Barbara County's Third District supervisor, a Santa Ynez rancher who's one of the family's good friends and allies.

Few of these people (except the politicians, who have to) give a damn about the real Fiesta activities. That's for ordinary people. They float above it all, rarely venturing down into the heart of the city during these five days.

Miranda works the crowd, playing the charming and gracious hostess. She's dressed in a Spanish-style skirt and blouse, with her hair piled up on her head. Twelve hours ago she was fucking a lover on the front porch of her family's Santa Ynez Valley ranch house, biting his cheek so hard she almost drew blood. Now she flits from group to group, making sure everyone is having a good time, her uninhibited laughter ringing across the property.

She spots Dorothy arriving fashionably late with some of her old friends. The old guard, she thinks with disdain, the dying breed. Miranda knows she is too down-home for her mother-in-law's taste, too earthy. For all of Dorothy's liberalism, her causes—homeless shelters, AIDS hospices, dozens of such do-gooder works—she's still a Yankee WASP at heart: moderate, conservative, always self-effacing. She expects those around her to have those same qualities, and since Miranda doesn't, never has, there's always been tension between the two women, both powerful and headstrong.

The most important component in their relationship, as much an element of their world as nitrogen or oxygen, is the bottom-line truth that Dorothy was born rich while Miranda married it, married Dorothy's only child, something neither of them has ever been able to get beyond, because Dorothy has always, in a million subtle (and occasionally not-so-subtle) ways, played the caste card.

Old money doesn't matter much anymore, even in Montecito, everyone acknowledges that. What counts isn't where you got your money but that you have it. Still, there is a certain cachet to having longtime Santa Barbara roots. Frederick, like his mother and grandfather and great-grandfather before him, is classic old California money, which they got the old-fashioned way—they stole it, like everyone else did back then. Their principal source of wealth is Pacific Land and Trust, one of the biggest ranching corporations in the state for over a hundred years. They also own an immense portfolio of commercial property up and down the state.

Along with her husband's money and her own unique beauty, Miranda has the other necessary pieces of the package: cunning, intelligence, and, most importantly, awesome ambition. It's the ambition that's always bothered her mother-in-law, and at the same time impressed her. That's why, years ago, when her husband died, Dorothy made the critical decision to turn over the day-to-day financial operations of the family empire to Miranda rather than Frederick. Miranda has the drive, the energy, and the will. Frederick is too dreamy. Dorothy always loved that about him, while simultaneously fearing how it might affect the family's fortunes.

Frederick hadn't protested when his mother had told him of her decision, which took him off the court as an important financial player for the rest of his life. He had other interests, he was happy to be relieved of the responsibility.

Standing at the edge of the pond, Laura's upset, still thinking of Frank staying behind with Morgan.

"Are you okay?" her father asks as if reading her mind, handing her a glass of Perrier Jouët, tonight's house pour.

"Great." She takes a sip. Shit, that's good. There's nothing like fine champagne, it's as good as cocaine and it's legal.

"How was your cruise?" He hasn't seen her all week until an hour ago, when she drove up, alone.

"It was pretty great. You'd have appreciated it, Dad, especially some of the marine life. There were turtles swimming off Baja that must've been twenty feet across the backs of their shells."

"We'll do it together sometime," he smiles at her with that sweet smile of his.

"You'd be much better company, Dad."

He kisses her on the forehead, moves on. She watches him go. God, she loves him. Such a good father—always has been. He was the one that was always there for her, much more than her mom; the sensitive one, who knew when she was hurting almost before she was conscious of her feelings surfacing, who helped her move from under her mother's shadow and have her own life, even from early childhood. He had been happy his only child was a girl.

Laura has his looks. Thin, slightly washed out. Frederick is a tall, angular, bespectacled man, always immaculately groomed; sporting a neatly trimmed Edwardian mustache and goatee, he bears a deliberately cultivated resemblance (relishing the comparison with delight on those rare occasions it's recognized) to James Joyce, whose works, even *Finnegans Wake*, he's carefully read; his old Modern Library edition of *Ulysses* is held together with duct tape it's been thumbed through so many times, the intriguing and mystifying passages highlighted in yellow Briteliner, sitting prominently on one of the shelves of his huge library, the largest private library in the county, already willed to the Sparks Foundation after his death. Which is a good thing, because no one in this family would read them, not even his daughter, the burgeoning publisher.

She sips more champagne, checks her watch. Frank will have some bullshit excuse and she'll buy it, like she always does. Don't bring that imbecile Morgan when you come. That's all she asks.

Frank drives the lead truck up the access road, taking his time as he navigates in the dark. Rusty follows closely in the other vehicle. They've rolled the windows all the way up, to avoid the dry dust being kicked up in their faces. At least the trucks are air-conditioned, Rusty thinks with begrudging gratitude. The shit he's used to driving in Mexico, you're lucky if it's got a transmission and brakes that work.

Rusty's never been to this specific area before, and after tonight he never will be here again. His helper rides shotgun, with Morgan sandwiched between them, her firm leg pressed against his, the fingertips of her left hand resting lightly on his thigh, creating a tingle he has to disregard for the time being. Rusty's good at separating business and pleasure—it's one of the main reasons he's stayed clean as long as he has, in a line of work in which longevity is measured in months, not years.

Both trucks are driving with their lights out, an extra measure of precaution in case anyone should accidentally spot them from the highway. Frank's idea, which Rusty endorsed. Not a dumb guy, Frank. They're all going to get well off this job.

The procession stops as Frank jumps out to unlock the gate. Rusty half-watches, his mind wandering momentarily. It's done now. Stash the load, hit the Biltmore (where he's reserved a two-bedroom suite), shave, shower, go out into the world and have some fun. He'll have to keep a tight rein on Morgan, that's his only worry. She's too dumb to know how to keep her mouth shut, not that she knows anything—she thought the stuff they were off-loading into the trucks was sailing gear, that the reason the truck lights are off is so no busybody will stop and hassle them, even though Frank is legal here. You can tell her anything, she'll believe it. One of her nicer qualities. That and her performance in bed. She may be a dumb bitch, maybe the dimmest woman Rusty's ever gone around with, but no one can say she isn't a world-class piece of ass. What the hell, Rusty muses—we all have our pluses and minuses. At heart, Morgan's just a sweet little San Gabriel Valley girl.

The lights hit them from all directions, suddenly and without warning.

"Step out of your vehicles and put your hands in the air where we can see them." The voice, disembodied through a loudspeaker, cuts through the dark, the entire scene framed by half a dozen flashing lights mounted on the rooftops of police cars.

They're trapped under the halogen spots like flies stuck to honey. Fifty yards away traffic slows to a crawl on Highway 101, lookie-loos craning their necks in anticipation of something awful, a passel of road kill and twisted metal.

"Exit your vehicles, please. No sudden movements."

This wasn't supposed to happen, Rusty thinks, his mind suspended in time as he cuts the ignition and pulls the hand brake. There's always that million-to-one possibility, but not this time, goddamnit. This was supposed to be a no-brainer.

Judges have been handing down mandatory ten-to-twenty hard-time sentences for an ounce of acid, half a kilo of grass, ten grams of heroin or cocaine. They're hauling three quarters of a ton of primo marijuana in these two trucks, worth three million or more on the street, enough for a dozen lifetimes of breaking rock in the hot sun.

No way he's going to be some big-dicked motherfucker's sweetheart. Living in a cage, no surf, no sun, no air: impossible.

He slides along the driver's side of the cab, which is facing away from the cops, waiting for Morgan to exit, for their eyes to knee-jerk to her for just a second or two. That's all he needs. Crouching low like a scorpion, edging his way towards the darkness.

Now he's running, he's broken the edge of light, he'll swim all the way to Santa Cruz Island if he has to.

"Halt!" the voice is yelling at him over the loudspeaker.

Freedom is just another word for nothing left to lose. Which is the last out-of-left-field thought that goes through Rusty's mind before the sharpshooter's Steyr SSG P-II .308 explodes, driving a hole the size of a cashew in the back of his head and blowing out the entire front of his face upon exit.

* * *

Kate chickens out and stops Cecil after he gets to second base. She wants to take her time, in case there's something here, something more than glands. Timing is everything, an old detective once told her.

He nuzzles the back of her neck, his tongue licking at her ear. The nerve runs in a direct line down to her vagina.

"You've got nice lips, Kate," he says in a low murmur. "Couch lips. Good for kissing."

"So do you," she says back to him, too comfortable to come up with some snappy original repartee.

It feels good, lying back into him, his arms around her. Let it be.

"All in its own good time," he says, as if reading her mind.

"Right."

"I wouldn't want you to think I'm an easy lay," he continues.

"Me, too," she counters. "Because I'm not."

"I didn't think so."

They dangle their feet in the pool. Above their heads, fireworks signifying the end of Fiesta explode in the sky. She lies on the cool deck on her back, watching the display, and the stars. It's a clear night considering how hot it's been.

"Are you going to go back to those dance classes again?" he asks her.

"I don't know. Are you?"

"If you are."

"We could be a team," she says, feeling giddy and foolish. "We could go out on the road and give exhibitions at county fairs. I hear the fair up in Paso Robles is dying to have such an attraction."

"We'll need a few more lessons first. To refine it down."

They roll into a hot embrace, wet legs locked together.

"Where's your beau?" Miranda teases Laura, sidling up to her with a ceviche-laden cracker in hand, slipping it into her daughter's unaware mouth. Miranda doesn't like it that Frank is dating Laura; he's too old, too experienced. They've argued about it, she and Laura, she's talked with Frank as well, privately; but she's canny, she knows when to push and when not to. She knows she'll have it her way sooner or later.

"Securing the boat," Laura answers. "Or cleaning up, I don't know. He should've been here by now," she adds, unable to stuff the anxiety about Frank, and possibly Frank and Morgan.

"Why don't you give him a call," Miranda suggests, "motivate his sorry ass?" She talks street lingo sometimes, it's part of her charm.

And Miranda knows all about the anatomy of men like Frank Bascomb. They swarm her like drone bees in a honeycomb. Frank did himself, years ago—put it right on the line.

"Any time you want," he'd brazenly informed her. They were fence-riding together, up on the family ranch. He'd only come to work for them a short time before.

"Don't hold your breath," she had answered coldly, making sure there was no mixed signal given. Maybe he'd heard something; she knew men talked about her. He was a handsome man, but that was the wrong approach to use with her. And he worked for her.

He had smiled, like it was a matter of time. It was the smile that really ticked her off.

"If you ever speak like that to me again," she had warned him, "I'll inform my husband. If you want to keep on working here, you'd best keep your mouth shut around me regarding anything personal."

Frank had been assistant foreman then. He'd taken her advice, and when Frederick had nominated him for ranch foreman after Clete Willis was forced into retirement, Miranda had had no objections. He was good at his job.

"I will, good idea," Laura responds too eagerly. "If he doesn't show up in a couple minutes."

Miranda's attention is momentarily diverted as her personal maid approaches, a look of concern on her face.

"What is it, Izela?"

"There's two policemen drove up," Izela answers.

"Policemen? Don't tell me somebody called in a complaint, for godsakes. What do they want?"

"They want to talk to Laura."

––––––––

They gather in Frederick's small study: Laura, Miranda, Frederick, the two county sheriff's detectives, and Tom Calloway, the family's lawyer, who's here as a guest (which is fortunate), dressed for the occasion like one of Pancho Villa's *bandidos,* including fake crossed bandoleers and a huge leather sombrero. The other guests don't even know the police are here, since they're detectives wearing regular street clothes.

"I don't know what you're talking about," Laura tells them. She's verging on hysteria.

"Let's establish right now, is Laura a suspect in any of this?" Calloway asks, standing so he's between her and them. He glances at Miranda and Frederick, to let them know he's got this under control, or will shortly.

"We don't know yet," one of the detectives tells him evenly, "but we do need her to come down to the jail so we can ask her some questions."

"I don't want to go to any jail!" Laura cries out.

"Take it easy," Calloway instructs her. "Just take it easy." He rubs his palms together vigorously. "All right, we'll come in tomorrow morning. I can clear my calendar," he adds, both for the detectives' benefit and for the Sparkses', who are his most important clients.

"We need to do it now," the other detective informs him.

"Why, if she isn't a suspect?" Miranda asks, forcefully inserting herself into the discussion.

"I'm handling this, Miranda. Please." Calloway looks at her sharply.

"But she hasn't done anything wrong!" Miranda snaps, rising out of her chair. "You just can't come into somebody's house like this!"

"If you want us to get a court order . . ." the first detective says, turning to confront her.

"For what?" She moves a step towards him. She's taking charge now—screw the pleasantries, this is her daughter.

"We'll come in, we'll come in," Calloway tells them. Turning to Laura: "It's all right. I'll come with you. I'll be there. It's nothing. Really."

"Am I under arrest or something?" Laura asks, almost unable to speak she's so scared.

"No," the lead detective assures her. "We need information as soon as possible, that's all. Right now. Tonight." He pauses. "There shouldn't be any reason to think you're . . . involved . . . in any of this. Not now, anyway," he adds with some gravity.

The interrogation of Laura (because you can't bullshit about it, that's what it is) takes almost two hours. Morgan is at the jail when Laura and the others get there, she's been there for hours, sitting alone in a corner of the lobby; she literally throws herself at Laura when Laura first arrives, she's so out of her mind with fear. It takes a while for Laura to register the unbelievable information that Rusty is dead, shot while trying to escape, and that Frank is in custody downstairs, charged with possession of and conspiracy to sell almost a ton of marijuana.

Morgan's already been questioned. They had a hard time of it, because she was totally off the wall. If she doesn't calm down before they're finished with Laura they'll have to call in a doctor to sedate her.

"You can go," they tell her again, having already done so over an hour ago, after she gave her statement, such as it was, she was so incoherent. "Go where?" she cried.

That was her problem. She's free to go, they'd like her to leave, but she has nowhere to go: except for Laura and Frank she doesn't know a soul in town.

They sit in a small, windowless room. Laura, Calloway, the two cops. Slowly, with Calloway hand-holding her through the process, Laura regains enough of her composure to tell her story.

She was conned, pure and simple. She joined the group near the end of the voyage, they never actually put in to any port, always anchoring well offshore. Morgan had been brought out in a small powerboat piloted by a local Mexican, with nothing but her one suitcase.

Morgan told them the same thing.

"Frank didn't know about this," Laura tells the police.

"Why do you think that?" they ask, taking turns questioning her. There's no good cop, bad cop, they're both nice and polite.

"Because I know Frank. It's just not him. Rusty must have used Frank, loaded the dope while Frank wasn't around. It has to be that way."

That had been Frank's story, too. Whether it's true or not—they think it's bullshit but they're not 100 percent certain—they both conclude pretty soon into their questioning of Laura that she wasn't in on it. The other one, either. Dupes, both of them.

"Frank would never do something like that," Laura pleads with them. "He'd never put me in that kind of jeopardy."

Which, although the hard evidence points inescapably to the fact that Frank is dirty, is what the detectives have been forced to speculate on, too. That plus the other hard fact that these are no ordinary citizens they're dealing with here, this is the Sparks family. This arrest could blow up in the department's face if they get it wrong.

"Thanks for your cooperation," the detectives tell Laura, wrapping it up. "We're sorry we had to pull you away from your party."

"That's life," Calloway answers for her, his way of telling them the family won't make trouble if this doesn't go any further.

"Can I see him?" Laura asks. "Frank. I want to see him. Is he all right?"

"He's fine. You can't see him. He's in the men's section of the county lockup, women aren't allowed except family."

"When will he be arraigned?" Calloway asks. He'll have to handle that. He won't be Frank's lawyer, since that would be a conflict of interest, but he'll have to find one for him, a crackerjack.

"Probably tomorrow morning. Check the court's calendar."

"We'll see you then."

They escort Laura and Calloway to the lobby. Miranda and Frederick are waiting, Miranda wearing a hole in the floor with her pacing. They weren't allowed into the interrogation even though Miranda and the sheriff, Ralph Walker, are good friends, since she's helped raise money for police projects through all kinds of charitable activities, has gone on several drive-arounds at night with both city police and county sheriffs, and has toured the county jail on numerous occasions; she's even walked the cellblocks, where she got plenty of appreciative whistles and obscene catcalls.

She'd managed to contact Ralph Walker on the phone. He was up in north county and hadn't been able to help her: procedures have to be followed strictly, this was no small-potatoes deal here, her foreman is in jail and could be in serious trouble; if she wants to help she should be looking for a good lawyer for him (which had brought a snort of derision from Miranda); he dug his hole, Frank, he can figure his own way out.

Laura says nothing, too numb to talk. God, this is bizarre. Frank's in a cell somewhere, with other men, real criminals. Poor baby. She'll take extra-good care of him when he gets out.

Her parents flank her as they walk outside to the car. It's nice to have them standing by her at a time like this. She's glad to be who she is, instead of someone like that poor cow Morgan, who's going to be thrown out onto the street on her ass, not knowing a soul in town. If for no other reason than common charity she should take Morgan in for the night, until Morgan can figure a way to go home. Her grandmother would do it in a heartbeat. But she won't; she does not want any part of Morgan or any of this, not now, it's too heavy to handle.

Frank Bascomb sits hunched up in a corner of the common cell he's sharing with a dozen or so other new arrestees, his back pressed up against the wall. They're being housed temporarily in what is normally a day area, because all the regular cells are occupied. This condition is an emergency one, because there are strict limits, by law, as to how many prisoners the jail can hold; right now it's over the limit. So, bright and early tomorrow morning the six superior court judges who are currently sitting will start ordering releases, to get the number of inmates down to where it's legal. This means some very bad men who shouldn't get out will, and others who pose no threat to society will stay locked up. It's an imperfect system; no one pretends otherwise. That kind of self-denying bullshit is for the politicians.

These other men in here with Frank had been booked and dumped in as one group, a few minutes before Frank's arrival. When the police brought Frank in, they went at him in an extended interrogation, plus fingerprinting and mandatory strip-search—including the humiliation of some guard's latex-gloved finger shoved up his ass ("normal procedure, pal, nothing personal"). Then, over an hour later, they initially placed him in a one-man medium-security cell, a level 3 (level 1 being the easiest, honor farm and trustees, and level 5 the hardest, hard-core evil fuckers), because although the crime he was arrested for is major, a man like Frank Bascomb isn't considered dangerous to the guards or other inmates.

This is a good sign, Frank hopes, trying to look on the bright side. Like most first-timers, he mistakenly thinks you are assigned to a particular level by the severity of your crime, as opposed to your profile. So he's starting off on the wrong foot, assuming the sheriffs who run the jail don't put someone they think is a hardened criminal in a group tank with a bunch of common drunks. Maybe this means they believe his story, which he had started chanting like a mantra from the moment the cops came down on them near the beach: that he didn't know anything, that Rusty did it all on his own.

And maybe the tooth fairy will fly down tonight and leave a dollar under his pillow.

Fuck it. At least Rusty's dead. He can't say otherwise to Frank's song-and-dance. The other guy, Rusty's helper, he's a good soldier, he'll keep his mouth shut, because he knows what'll happen if he doesn't. The other guy is in another part of the jail somewhere—the cops segregated the two of them. Just keep your cool until tomorrow, my friend, until you can make bail and go live in Brazil for the rest of your life, an option Frank may have to reserve for himself if nothing else works.

At least they'd have that—the bail, no matter how high it was set, and it would be high, that he knew. As soon as he was booked Frank had called his backer, the deep-pockets financial angel for this scam.

You'll be out by tomorrow morning, his backer had promised him. You'll have the best lawyer, the best everything. Until then, don't say anything to anybody.

He knew all that was true, if for no other reason than to ensure that he kept his mouth shut. A lot of heavy people could come crashing down if Frank Bascomb started telling tales to the DA.

"Hey, man," a voice sings out from across the space. A lilting voice, mocking. The rhythms are Chicano.

Frank glances up for a second, looks away quickly. Don't acknowledge these assholes.

"You got a smoke on you, man?"

Just fucking ignore them. As if these clowns didn't know smoking isn't permitted in here, they take your cigarettes away along with everything else you had on you.

"Hey, man, what're you, deaf or something?"

Frank turns away.

"Get the wax out of your ears, shithead. I ask you a question, man."

"I don't smoke." Like it fucking matters.

"Not even grass?"

They all laugh. They know how come he's in here, the word seeps through like a virus.

He turns to them. A pathetic-looking lot—clothes in shambles, hair matted, body stink their only aura.

"Who wants to know?"

Confront the fuckers head-on, let them know you have no fear.

"Maybe you're the one has the wax in his ears, whoever asked," Frank says. "I don't smoke, *comprende?*"

"Sure, man. Whatever you say."

He's a tall man, reed-thin. Impossible to tell how old; could be twenty-five, could be forty-five. The dark, sallow skin of the addict/alcoholic/headcase; unshaved face, hollow burning eyes. A long scar from one eyebrow up to the hairline, a permanent reminder of a past encounter with somebody's straight razor.

The others are of the same tribe, more or less. Men who sleep in one set of clothes a month at a time, who scrounge for dinner in dumpsters and sleep in the weeds down by the railroad tracks.

"That's what I say. Got a problem with it?"

"You got the problem, man, not me. You're the number-one guest in this hotel." He laughs, a raspy, phlegmy croak.

Frank glares at the man, daring him with his look to make a move. The man tries to hold the look but can't; he turns away, as do the others, leaving Frank a healthy space: at heart they're all cowards.

He won't sleep tonight, that's for sure, not with all these freaks in here giving him the eye.

He pushes up against the wall, feeling his back on the hard concrete. He can do without one night of sleep and still be sharp for tomorrow's arraignment. That's when the shit will really start hitting the fan.

"Were you crazy? Were you out of your stupid mind? Are you really this stupid, or is this something you picked up in college?"

The party's over at Frederick and Miranda's. Everyone's gone home, Frederick's in bed, the servants have retired, no one's around. Just Miranda and Laura, mother and daughter.

They're in the same study where earlier they'd talked to the police; an episode Miranda never, *ever,* wants to repeat. She paces the floor, a tiger in a cage, while Laura, curled up into herself, cowers on the couch, trembling uncontrollably, trying to become invisible, to escape this monumental wrath.

"Why do you think we sent you clear across the country to the most expensive schools in the world?" Miranda thunders, building up a full head of steam. "So you could build a snowman in the winter? We didn't want you at Santa Barbara High, hanging around all those baggy-pants eastside hoods. I keep hoping some of my toughness will rub off on you, but it doesn't look like it's ever going to. You're a spoiled child of privilege—it's your blessing and your curse."

"But I didn't do anything!" Laura wails.

"You didn't do anything? What do you call what happened tonight?" she yells, her arm shooting out in the vague direction of town, of the jail.

"It wasn't my fault!"

"I don't give a damn about *fault!*" her mother thunders. "I'm talking about *responsibility!* You were there. On that boat. With a ton of marijuana on it. You were smoking marijuana on that boat, don't lie to me, Laura, you were smoking on the boat along with all of the rest of them, what else were you doing, cocaine probably . . ."

"I wasn't doing coke . . ."

"Because there wasn't any, that's got to be the only reason. You were on that boat, with Frank Bascomb, who I've warned you against a million times, I told you he'd use you. You think you're so damn grown up but this proves you're still a kid."

Laura doesn't answer. She's crying, wiping her nose with her forearm.

"And you let these slimy bastards, these sons of bitches, you let them use *our* property to unload their goddamn drugs!"

"I was trying to help them out. They took me on their cruise with them, I was just trying to be helpful."

"Well, you were that. You were definitely helpful. You almost helped yourself right into jail."

Her feet hurt. She kicks her shoes across the floor. That helps. Her head is pounding like a kettle drum.

"Which could still happen," Miranda adds, "I hope you realize that. I hope you realize the gravity of the situation you might find yourself in."

"What do you mean?" Laura asks, frightened by the statement.

"What happens when they haul Frank up in front of a judge tomorrow, he's going to be arraigned tomorrow, or the next day at the latest, and he says 'Laura Sparks was my partner in this, she knew everything about it'?"

"He won't do that!"

"Why not?"

"He's already said I wasn't involved!"

"That's today. Tomorrow he's going to get hit with the fact that he's facing years and years in jail; but if he turns on you, if he says it was your idea, your money even, he can cut a deal. What do you think he'll do then?"

"But that's not true!" Laura cries.

"You may get a chance to tell the judge that," her mother warns her. She collapses into a chair. "Jesus, what a mess." She stares at her daughter, who is sitting across from her, shaking uncontrollably. "Between you and me—and I want the truth, Laura, no bullshitting—were you involved?"

"I swear to God, no!"

"You didn't put up the money?"

"God, no!"

"And you didn't know anything about it?"

"I didn't, Mommy, I swear to God!"

"God, you're stupid. You sure didn't get that from me."

"Daddy isn't stupid," Laura says in a small, babyish voice.

"No, he isn't. You didn't get it from him either, I know that for sure."

Miranda's on her feet again. Sitting's too passive, she needs to be up, she can think better on her feet.

"As long as you're clean we'll get by this," she declares.

"Mom, I am, how can I convince you?" She's retreated into herself, almost into a fetal position.

Miranda stops, looks down at her daughter.

"Okay, I believe you. I do believe you, I have to. Otherwise we have no future, not just you, all of us, the entire family. And that's not a possibility."

"Thank you," Laura whines. She stares up at her mother. "But I wish it was because you love me, not because of the family's future."

"I do love you. That's why I worry about our future. You're our only child, you *are* our future."

"I know that."

"And you'll never see Frank again." A statement, not a question.

"I'll never see Frank again," Laura vows.

"Drive carefully," Kate tells Cecil. "The streets are full of crazies tonight."

They're standing in the potholed driveway, by his old Cadillac. Her own car, a '74 low-rider 327 Camaro hardtop, pearl on purple with rolled velour upholstery, which she bought at a police auction years ago, is parked next to it. She calls it the Rooster, because it's a tough and feisty little bird. She keeps a sleeping bag in the trunk, which she'll roll out on the deck for herself.

That they both drive big old American cars is a good sign, she thinks.

If they're compatible in this area, maybe they'll be compatible in lots of ways.

"Nice wheels," Cecil tells her. "Don't see many of these old muscle cars around anymore."

"I don't have the heart to dump it," she confesses. "It gets about four miles to the gallon if you're coasting downhill, it would wind up in a junkyard. Be like putting an old pet to sleep. I'll just keep it till it flat-out dies on me."

He glances east, towards the horizon. "Besides, it's almost dawn. Fiesta's officially over."

"I've kept you up way past your bedtime and you don't have one damn thing to show for it." Sexually, she means. The emotional stuff, she doesn't know where that's been going.

"I've got no complaints."

He opens the car door.

"One more for the road," she says, spinning him back towards her.

The kiss feels good. Better than good.

"Now go." She pushed him into the driver's seat.

"I don't have your phone number."

"I don't have yours, either."

He reaches into the glove box, rummages through what appears to be ten years' worth of gum wrappers, auto registrations, grocery-store coupons, plus a shitload of other forgettable stuff, extracting in the midst of all that a dog-eared checkbook, from which he tears out a check and hands it to her.

"Don't spend it all in one place," he drawls.

"I need a pen."

He hands her one from off his visor. She tears the check in half, keeps the part with his vitals on it, writes her name and phone number on the back of the remaining half, hands it to him.

"I'll call you soon," he promises. "Or you call me."

"You," she says. She doesn't want to push it; it was nice, but it's only the one night. These things have a way of losing their glow when the morning light hits them.

"Sleep well," he tells her, with one last kiss of benediction on the forehead.

She watches his taillights fade off down the driveway. You be careful, she warns herself. Just because you've had no "relationships," to use the term in its broadest sense, since leaving Eric, that doesn't mean you should shut yourself off from a better man.

"You're okay, as men go," she says after him. "Hope you call."

Both the city police chief, Bert Jenkins, and the county sheriff, Ralph Walker, had taken the same vow: the violence that had erupted in town during the past few Fiesta celebrations wasn't going to be repeated.

Last year had been particularly gnarly. Two rival gangs up from Ventura had gotten into a dust-off right in the heart of State St., and when the shit had settled one teenage kid had been knifed to death, several people were seriously wounded, and the entire Fiesta *raison d'être* had been called into question. What had always been a celebration of the old Spanish heritage, bringing all the different ethnic and economic elements together more or less harmoniously, had evolved over the past decade into an excuse for roving gangs of kids who didn't know what Fiesta was all about to band together, get drunk and high, and go looking for trouble, mainly along ethnic lines, with the major Hispanic gangs in particular visibly flaunting their colors.

The police covered the town like a blanket, especially the downtown shopping and restaurant areas that are the tourist centers. The bike patrol was especially visible—teams of uniformed cops wearing bicycle shorts and safety helmets, .44 automatics prominently strapped to their sides, rode their mountain bikes along the streets all day and night the entire weekend.

The extra vigilance had paid off. The gangbangers laid low, people had fun. To ensure the public tranquility, more arrests than normal had been made. You looked drunk—in the slam. Tell it to the judge tomorrow. And the same mind-set applied to the overaggressive panhandling from the homeless population.

Which means that the jail is jammed to overflowing, which is why Frank Bascomb, instead of being sequestered all night in his one-man lockdown cell, where a suspect in a big dope deal normally would be held, found himself unexpectedly transferred to a common tank, occupying the same space with drunks, derelicts, and scumbags of every description. It wasn't what his jailers wanted, but there had been a highly publicized kidnapping and murder in the county a few months ago, and the case had gone to trial on the eve of Fiesta. All those defendants had to be quarantined, which took up most of the individual cells. Some of them had been doubled up in a single cell, which technically is illegal, but in a pinch you do what you have to. The rest of the individual cells were already occupied with level 5 inmates who had a history of violence and couldn't be allowed into the general population. Frank Bascomb is a known quantity, the foreman of the Sparks properties, until tonight a respected member of the community. He isn't going to cause any trouble. So when some really bad guys were brought in late, men who have to be kept in isolation, Frank was kicked out into the general population.

In the county jail, as in all modern jails, there are television cameras everywhere, high up on the walls, that monitor what's going on. This doesn't mean that they see every inch of territory—there are plenty of blind spots. But they give a sweep that allows a good general overview, so if anything is happening out of the ordinary, the jailers manning the observation areas, which are centrally located islands in each wing of the jail with banks of monitors receiving the TV camera feeds, know right away and can take the proper steps to fix it.

In addition, visual counts are made hourly, cell by cell. The guards look in each cell, making sure it's full, that the inmate who's supposed to be in it is, in fact, there. It's a good system, but like all human systems it isn't foolproof.

Tonight is a good example. Because the jail is over the legal limit there are areas, like the one in which Frank's being kept, that aren't properly monitored, since they normally aren't used at night. Not that that should matter—they're all drunks and derelicts, they're sleeping it off, it's one big den of bums.

So when one of the homeless winos sharing the tank with Frank starts yelling early in the morning, even before wakeup, the jailer running section duty in this wing doesn't think it's any big deal—another drunk fighting off a hangover. He drains his coffee before leaving the protection of the observation room to go inside and see what all the commotion is about, because by now it isn't one voice screaming bloody murder, it's all of them.

"Motherfucker!"

Some asshole's lost control of himself, the stench from his diarrhea shit drifts halfway down the hallway, no wonder all the prisoners in there are yelling like banshees. Nothing worse than a drunk shitting all over himself.

"Oh, Jesus Christ! Jesus fucking Christ!"

Where the rope had come from, a length of clothesline like what you hang your wash from, they had no idea: the sheriff repeated that statement later on to the hordes of media vultures who jammed into his conference room, while glossing over why Frank had been sequestered in a drunk tank in the first place; he'll have to do some fancy dancing later with Sacramento and the attorney general's office about that little fuckup.

Bottom line, there shouldn't have been any rope in there, it was an inexcusable fuckup, but so many men had been forced in here during the night there hadn't been enough time to search everyone properly, that's the only logical explanation.

Frank's neck hadn't snapped. He'd died from suffocation, which is no picnic—it could've taken up to fifteen minutes. His face was purple-black from the concentration of blood and his eyes had bulged out of their sockets like Roger Rabbit's. There were claw marks around his neck where he had tried to loosen the rope.

What happens when a man hangs himself is that all the extremities open. Snot comes out of your nostrils, drool from your mouth, piss from your dick. And your sphincter relaxes as well, so if you have anything in your bowels out it comes, usually pretty watery. This is the reason the stench in the cellblock that morning was especially vile.

3

VERY DRY BONES

Frank Bascomb is dumped uncere- moniously into the ground in a small, private funeral at a tiny rural cemetery next to an evangelical church near Lake Piru, in Ventura County, where most of the markers have Hispanic surnames and no one's ever heard of the Sparks family, none of whom attend except Laura, who comes out of a sense of guilt, fear, and anger, and confusion, standing near the scrubby grave site in the heat, listening to the funeral home preacher mumble the usual homilies about a man he'd never met, glancing up sharply as he suddenly snaps the dog-eared Bible shut, her eyes for a moment meeting those of the half-dozen other mourners, cowboys from the ranch who had worked under Frank and came because it was their duty to, plus two common-looking women she's never laid eyes on before, not relatives of Frank's, he'd had no family they'd been able to contact, his past had been strangely ambiguous, now it would be forever sealed under this hard-baked clay, who are these women, she thinks, her curiosity piqued, other girlfriends, people who wander into funerals, what?

There had been no public announcement. The family had wanted to get this over fast, without fanfare. Miranda had arranged everything, she pushed the coroner (another family acquaintance) to waive an autopsy, which is SOP in such deaths, so that the corpse didn't lie around in the morgue for a week or more, which is the common practice in most over-burdened county labs. She even supervised the purchasing of the casket, by phone: a plain pine box, the cheapest one. Frank was to be buried as cheaply and quickly as possible, the book to be closed and sealed shut.

The others drift away from the grave site. The cowboys glance at Laura, heads down, mouthing homilies of condolence. They get into ranch pickups and drive off; the boss might be dead, but they've got work to do, a 20,000-acre ranch doesn't wait on anything.

Who are these women? Laura thinks, watching them from a distance as they linger a moment at a respectful distance from the grave, moving to the side as the backhoe starts pushing the dirt over the casket into the hole. They are both in their mid-thirties, she guesses, wearing bought-for-the-occasion cheap summer dresses that look like they came off the same rack at the Broadway, pantyhose (even in this heat; Laura is bare-legged), cheap rickety heels. They aren't the type of women who are comfortable wearing heels, Laura observes.

Could they be women Frank kept on the side? They're not particularly attractive.

She can feel a wave of jealousy and insecurity washing over her. God knows how many women Frank had stashed all over creation.

The two unfamiliar women approach Laura, hands in vague salute on their foreheads to shield their eyes from the piercing sun. Laura is wearing sunglasses and a wide-brimmed hat. The light is fierce, and the kick from the hard clay ground compounds the glare.

"You are Laura Sparks, aren't you?" one of them asks.

"Yes," she answers, tight-lipped.

· "We work on your ranch," the woman informs Laura by way of introduction. She nods to her companion. "She cooks, I clean."

"Oh." Laura is taken aback. "Nice to meet you." She extends her hand. And she had thought Frank was fucking them. That's a relief, at least.

The women shake hands with her. Their hands are rough like men's.

"Appreciate somebody from the family coming."

Laura half-nods, half-shrugs. She's uncomfortable and dazed.

"Must have been a shock."

"Yes," Laura says.

"That's Frank," the second woman offers. "Always scheming."

"I . . . wouldn't know."

"Lot about that man you wouldn't know." The woman looks at her frankly, her eyes slits in the white sunlight.

"Obviously," Laura replies firmly. These are employees of the family, they should be addressing her with a certain civility.

"Live hard, die young," the woman tosses off.

They turned away abruptly, walking towards the road where the cars are parked.

"Hung himself," one says caustically to the other, not realizing Laura's still in earshot. "You think anybody's stupid enough to believe that shit?" Her voice is flat second-generation dust belt, from Coalinga or one of those ugly Central Valley towns, Laura thinks.

"Newspapers bought it."

"You believe anything you read in the dumb newspapers? Or TV? You got more sense than that, girl."

"Nobody seems to be making much of a fuss over it."

"People are stupid. Anyway, nobody gives a shit about a dead dope dealer."

"The stories the walls could tell about that family."

"And everything they touch."

Their laughter is bitter.

What is going on? Laura wonders. And what are those references to her family? Is the whole world in on some sick joke and I'm the only one that doesn't know about it?

Kate rides her body board, taking a long wave all the way into shore. She's been out in the ocean—Butterfly Beach, near the Biltmore—for over an hour. It's not mid-morning yet and the sun is already blazing, it's going to be another scorcher, especially by Santa Barbara standards. But not as humid as it's been, thankfully; the weather's coming back to central coast normal.

The waves have been breaking good. She's ridden several of them, enough to give her arms, shoulders, and legs a good healthy soreness.

———

The first thing she'd done the week she hit Santa Barbara was find an apartment, a furnished studio she survived in for six months before moving to her present digs. The second thing was to walk into a local surf shop down by East Beach and start asking questions about boards. That afternoon she took her first lesson.

She loves water, particularly the ocean; the sensuousness of it, the salt taste, cold temperature, the danger in the undertow, and the fatigue when you've been out for hours but won't come in until you've ridden one more set.

J . F . F R E E D M A N

That she had never surfed before didn't matter. That many times she's the oldest person out there, definitely the oldest woman, doesn't matter, either. What mattered was that she was going to do all the things she'd wanted to do and hadn't, including things, like surfing and swimming, she hadn't even thought of. She was California born and bred, she should know how to surf. She doesn't look like a surfer girl—her eyes are gray, her skin closer to olive than ivory, it matches up well with her luxurious hair, which she streaks occasionally, depending on her mood.

"You look like a rich Sausalito Jew-broad with that hair," Eric had sneered once when she'd come home from Cut 'N Curl with tastefully feathered platinum streaks.

"In your dreams."

He had probably smacked her for that crack. She doesn't remember. If not for that, for something else equally trivial. Any excuse would do.

She windsurfs, too. Once, after she erroneously thought she knew it all (a big part of her stubborn nature), she went out way past the safe point, halfway to the islands almost, like she'd seen the hotshots do, and when it had been time to turn back the wind was against her and the tacking back and forth was tiring, too tiring to keep at, and finally, completely exhausted, she had dropped her sail and laid on the board and watched the sun fading in the horizon behind her and realized this was a way people died.

She wasn't ready for that. It had scared the shit out of her, sitting out there all alone, no one around to help. She'd been more scared that afternoon than she'd ever been during any of her titanic battles with Eric, even more than she'd been during any of the terrifying incidents she'd encountered in all her years on the police force (including the Losario family disaster, the incident that had changed her entire life).

A fishing boat had spotted her, a tiny speck on the flat twilight horizon. That was a lucky fluke, because the boats don't normally fish in that area, but on this day one was. They pulled her on board and took her in with the halibut and abalone.

After that she cut down on the windsurfing and put her energy into board surfing, where she's more in control, closer to the water and the shore.

———————

She grabs her board, towel, lotion, slips into her sandy thongs, and walks up the path to her car, which is parked along Channel Drive. A quick run back to her apartment, shower and change—then she has to go to work.

"How did you hear about me?"

Kate and Laura are sitting in a back booth at Esau's Coffee Shop, eating a late breakfast; rather, Kate's eating. Laura, too nervous to eat, is drinking herb tea and picking nervously at a bran muffin, the crumbs scattered on her side of the table.

"From Mildred Willard. She's a friend of my mother's. She once told me she'd met this woman detective who'd moved here recently. She thought that was pretty neat, 'a real lady gumshoe,' she called you, 'not a character out of a novel.' "

Mildred; from her group. That's a first—a job referral from someone in the group. Almost all her cases come through lawyers, which she prefers, civilians coming in off the street aren't always trustworthy.

"Do you have an attorney?" she asks.

"Tom Calloway's our family lawyer."

Kate knows Tom Calloway. Tom Calloway is no friend of hers. When she first started out on her own Tom Calloway hired her to do a background check for him, since the agency he normally used was too busy. Calloway's one of the big guns in town; this was a chance to improve her clientele and her standing in the field, so she worked extra hard at it. She did a good job, quick and professional. Calloway told her he was very pleased with her work, and she never heard word one from him again. He went right back to his regular way of doing business, working solely with PIs who pee standing up.

Most of the lawyers she works with have gotten past that antiwoman nonsense, thank God. After all the feminist rhetoric, it's still a man's world sometimes. Taking a case from a Calloway client will taste extra sweet: if you can't join 'em, kick their ass.

"He doesn't know I'm seeing you," Laura informs her. "I'd prefer he didn't know," she adds.

"That's fine." She knew that already.

She'll have to remember to thank Mildred Willard, while at the same time tactfully making sure the woman keeps her mouth shut about how they really know each other.

She cuts into her order of ham, a slab large enough to cover a butter plate. With it she's having eggs over easy, home fries smothered in salsa, sourdough toast, and coffee laced with half-and-half. She doesn't worry about cholesterol or calories, the surfing works it off.

Laura watches Kate chow down. She takes a sip from her tea, to have something to do with her hands.

Kate looks at the girl sitting across from her. She's having a hard time with this. If she wasn't, Kate would be concerned.

"You didn't see it, I hope? Or afterwards?"

"Oh God, no." Laura places her cup in the saucer. "I never saw him again, once I left the boat." She brushes strands of fine blonde hair back off her face, a nervous tic. "I tried to see him when he was in jail," she adds, wanting Kate to know that, "but they wouldn't let me."

"I'm really sorry," Kate says, instinctively reaching across the table to touch the girl's pale hand. "Was he—"; she hesitates, wanting to get this right—"close to you?"

"He worked for us. Our ranch foreman. For several years." There is an awkward pause, which Kate doesn't attempt to fill.

"We were dating," Laura admits, after some hesitation.

"Uh-huh." Kate mops up the last of the yolk with a piece of toast, drinks some coffee, holds up the cup to the passing waitress for a refill.

"Actually, we were . . ."

"I understand." He was the girl's lover, Frank the foreman. She'd assumed that as soon as Laura had started in about it. The girl shouldn't have to speak of something so personal with a woman she doesn't even know, not this early in the game.

The subject needs changing. "So what is it you would like me to do for you? About your friend's suicide?"

Laura looks up at her. It's the first time she's looked directly at Kate since they sat down.

"I don't think it was a suicide," she says.

The statement hangs heavy in the air between them, like a sudden sopping humidity.

The words reverberate inside Kate's head. "You think your boyfriend was murdered? Inside the county jail?"

"Yes," Laura says, "that's exactly what I think."

They stand in the late-morning sun next to Laura's BMW convertible, in the parking lot on Gutierrez next to the freeway. The reflection off the asphalt burns Kate's eyes.

"My fee is sixty-five dollars an hour, plus any out-of-pocket expenses I incur."

"Okay," Laura says without batting an eye. She takes her checkbook out of her purse. "How much do you want now? Will three thousand dollars be enough?"

"Half that amount will be fine for now." It'll be refreshing to have a client who doesn't nickel-and-dime you to death. "I'll provide you with summaries of my progress and itemized vouchers. If there's any money left over after I'm finished, I'll reimburse you the difference."

"After you find out what happened to Frank."

"Not necessarily," Kate cautions her. "If it looks like it really was a suicide, or I run into a brick wall, I'll terminate my work. I don't like to take a client's money for no good reason."

Laura shakes her head. "I don't want you to stop until you find out what happened," she tells Kate with determination.

"Open-ended investigations can be expensive," Kate cautions her. "It adds up fast."

"I can afford it." She signs the check, tears it out, and hands it to Kate.

"I'll be in touch as soon as I find anything out. I won't call you until I do," Kate warns her, "so don't bug me, okay?"

"Okay."

They shake hands. Kate starts across the lot towards her own car.

"One more thing," Laura calls. She runs back to Kate. "I don't want my parents to know about this." She touches her tongue to her upper lip, a nervous tic that expresses her embarrassment. "I don't mean just my parents, I don't want anyone to know. It's not like I'm doing anything wrong or anything, it's . . ."

"You're free, female, and twenty-one," Kate says, shortcutting Laura's nervousness. "And you're my client. I only report to my client."

"I just wanted to make sure," the girl says. She's jumpy as hell about all of this.

"We'll be talking," Kate says, signing off.

"No matter what you find out?"

"You'll know everything I know."

Laura's parting shot is a raw plea. "I have to know."

The heavyset nurse, a young woman with the soft twilight skin of *café con leche,* her white uniform stretched tight against her body like Saran Wrap, ankles spilling over her Reebok high-tops, wheels Carl X. Flaherty out onto the veranda, where there is a view of the beach and the sea air blows in from the islands onto his face.

Carl can wheel himself around fine, which he does when she's off duty. He isn't an invalid, he just can't walk anymore. His forearms are sinewy like a carpenter's, he could wheel himself to Carpinteria if he felt like it. He lets her do it without grumbling too much because it's her job, it's how she pays her rent.

"Your visitor is here," nurse Luisa Maria Montoya tells him in a lilting Salvadorian accent. "Such a pretty lady."

She positions the umbrella attached to the wheelchair so it shields his face from the sun, puts a large Styrofoam cup of Diet Pepsi into the cup holder on the chair arm, adjusts the purple Lakers baseball hat on his head.

"You all set now," she sings to him. "I'll check back later."

The veranda overlooks Hendry's Beach, where a volleyball game on the sand is in progress below his perch. The players are bikini-wearing UCSB coeds. The nurse put him here deliberately, so he could see the pretty girls.

"So how's life treating you these days?" Carl asks Kate, who sits in a beach chair facing him, her back pointedly turned away from the volleyball game. "You holding your own?"

"I met a man," she abruptly informs him. She's wearing a tank top and shorts against the heat, is drinking a Pepsi out of a paper cup, crunching the ice cubes with her teeth.

"I didn't know that was a problem for you."

"A nice one. A keeper. Maybe."

"How's he feel?"

"I just met him. We haven't had a proper date yet."

"You'll blow it," he says succinctly, taking a pull from his straw.

"Thanks for the confidence." She knows it's repartee, his way of maintaining, but it stings.

"He won't be good enough for you," he explains, smoothing her feathers.

"I've lowered my expectations."

"Not you. Not in a million years. And you shouldn't—you've got to hold out for quality. In a man or a bottle of wine or anything under the sun." He smiles at her, both of his rheumy pale-blue eyes half-clouded with cataracts, which he's resisted having removed. "I can see plenty good enough for government work" is his standard rejoinder when his few living friends, Kate foremost among them (although she's known him the shortest amount of time), implore him to have surgery.

"Is he as good as me?" Carl teases her, glancing down at the volleyball players.

"If I wait for a man as good as you, Carl," she says, "I'll die an old maid."

"An old maid is a virgin," he corrects her.

"An old nonmaid, then."

Carl X. is Kate's mentor. The man has been a legend among West Coast private investigators for over half a century, as famous in real life as Lew Archer or Sam Spade are in fiction. Eighty-two years old now, he has been wheelchair-bound for the past twenty months, when he took a bullet in the spine down in Hermosa Beach from a Los Angeles County sheriff in what many think was a payback for all the times he had made that department look like dolts, although it has officially been classified as a mistaken identification on a dark street.

Case closed.

The shooting did what hundreds of criminals and dozens of police agencies couldn't—it stopped Carl X. Flaherty from being able to work. Never married, no kids, no hobbies; work was his religion, the only passion in his life. The inoperable bullet pressing against the nerve bundles in his spine brings frequent, wracking pain. It makes him double over and scream, and sometimes he pisses his pants, which mortifies him.

Kate came into Carl's life a few weeks after he'd been released from the hospital. She was new in town, needed to make some money (a week of waitressing at Frimple's convinced her that was not the way to go), and she'd heard about this old PI, now laid up, who had a bunch of cases on his docket and needed assistance.

They'd stuck him in a low-rent convalescent home on Olive St. Eucalyptus Manor was the name of the place, a bunch of clapboard cottages connected by walkways, the floors cheap linoleum that was easy to mop up, the food starchy and utilitarian like a school cafeteria's, all they could afford, the stench of stroke and Alzheimer's clouding the air like cigarette smoke in a saloon.

He didn't want to talk to her. He didn't want to talk to anybody, he was angry and he hurt like hell and he flat-out did not give a shit.

"I'll come back tomorrow, when you're feeling better," she told him that first day, when he'd given her the cold shoulder.

"You can come back any damn day you feel like it, I don't have anything to talk to you about," he groused.

"You need help. You have cases outstanding."

"I'll take care of my own work, thank you," he stated belligerently.

"Not·in the condition you're in," she rejoined bluntly. "I need to make a living. I'll be back tomorrow."

She did come back the following day, and Carl X. was ready for her, and pretty soon he'd taught her everything she knows about detective work in the private sector. She thought she knew a lot, having been a police officer for ten years. She found out she didn't know anything about being a PI.

"The worst PIs in the world are ex-cops," he told her. "You know why?"

"No."

"Your average cop is heavy-handed, has no finesse. Brings an institutional disdain towards the very people they're working for. They don't know how to listen. That's what being a good PI is all about. Knowing how to listen. You listening to me?"

"Yes," she said. "I'm all ears."

He looked her up and down, lingering on her breasts.

"You're a wise-ass, aren't you?"

"Sometimes, I guess."

"A good-looking one."

"Thanks." Often from a man she was offended by a remark like that. She wasn't this time. It meant they could be friends.

Kate picked up his pending cases, operating under his license until she took the test to get her own. When the convalescent facility had done what they could for him, she helped him find his current digs, a decent nursing home in a nice area of Goleta near the beach.

She would have stayed partners with him, sharing her fees, but he would have no part of that.

"I don't take charity."

By then she knew him well enough not to argue.

Out on her own, she's doing all right. Carl lives on his pension and his memories. She comes to see him when she can, once a week usually. They talk about her cases, he listens, gives her advice. But he doesn't tell her how to do it; he steers her towards finding the right answers herself.

"So if this foreman character was murdered, so what?" he asks, after she's filled him in.

"So what? What do you mean, so what?"

"If a bunch of drunken bums killed the guy, what difference would that make in the great cosmic scheme of things?"

"It makes a difference to my client. I'm not working for the cosmos."

"But that's not what your client's looking for, is it?" He stares at her, like a schoolteacher awaiting an answer.

"You mean, what's the reason," she says. "Assuming there is one."

He glances down at the volleyball game. What he wouldn't give.

"I'm sitting here," she commands, grabbing his chin and jerking his head towards her. "You can drool over the babes on your own time."

"I am on my own time," he reminds her.

She crunches ice cubes.

"Whether this turd-bird killed himself or a bunch of rummies did it is not what matters," he repeats. "It's barely relevant."

"If somebody ordered it up, though, that would sure as hell make it relevant," she offers, her mind in lockstep with his. "That's what this is all about—if the men who killed him had been put up to it by someone else, because let's face it, where would a ranch foreman come up with the money to make a dope buy of that magnitude, unless he had a partner? A partner who would be scared that Bascomb would talk once he realized he was looking at ten to twenty-five."

"Now you're thinking like a detective," he says, unable to hide the grin.

"But the men in the tank with him were derelicts, falling-down drunks," she continues, following her train of thought. "If someone wanted Bascomb permanently shut up he wouldn't trust a bunch of drunks to do the job. It could be botched too easily, and then Bascomb would really have incentive to spill his guts. Anyway, it all happened in less than twelve hours. It's impossible to put something that heavy together in that short a time."

"If you've got enough money, you can do anything. And as far as the *who* of it, beggars can't be choosers," Carl lectures her. "If that's the only hand you're dealt, you play it and hope for the best."

"Do you really think this is a plausible scenario, Carl?"

"It's something," he shrugs noncommittally.

"Then why doesn't it smell better?"

"Finally!" he waxes sarcastic.

"Finally what?"

"Finally you're thinking like a detective, not just going by the numbers."

"Thanks a bunch."

"Some people never get to that place, Kate. Look," he continues, building up a good head of steam, "any time you find a bird's nest on the ground you'd better be suspicious as hell. It could be booby-trapped, blow up right in your face."

She thinks about that for a moment.

"What else could it be, then?"

"I'm thinking out loud here, that's all I'm doing, thinking out loud, okay? What if this client of yours wasn't innocent after all? What if she was part of it? The boyfriend, who's also a hired hand, is sitting in jail, cooling his heels, she's going to make his bail in the morning and get him a fancy lawyer who gets him off somehow. That's what they've cooked up, okay?"

"Maybe," she concedes dubiously.

He laughs at her skepticism. "I'm just thinking out loud, I didn't say that's what happened. If you're not asking *what if* all the time, you're not doing the job. Am I right?"

"Yes," she admits, "you're right. When you're right, Carl, you're right."

"Which is most of the time. Practically always. So—she's going to hire the fancy lawyer and the foreman walks and everybody is happy. Except she goes on down to the jail and realizes that's not the way it's going to be. The hired hand is going to bring her down with him. Might, anyway; so she thinks."

"But if she arranged to have him killed why would she hire me? If I find out she did it, she's screwed herself. The police have already closed this case. She's home free."

"Maybe she's afraid it isn't. Look, Kate. You haven't lived here too long. The Sparks family is wired in this town like you can't imagine. Maybe the DA told them something off the record that scared the bejesus out of them."

She shakes her head, stubbornly. "No. It doesn't total up. I don't understand why anyone would hire a private detective who could blow it up in their face."

"Fear. Panic. Guilt. Stupidity. Any or all of those. The girl has an agenda," Carl says, schooling her. "She tells you she thinks maybe he didn't kill himself. And maybe that's all it is. What you see could be exactly what you're going to get. Maybe it's no more than guilt. She probably feels guilty, like she should have saved him somehow. Rich people can get that way, they get that socially conscious hair up their ass. Her grandmother's the prime bleeding heart in this town, she's the patron saint to every homeless bum living along the tracks down there." He slurps some of his drink. "What the hell, it's her life. She's actually a fine woman, old Mrs. Sparks. She just doesn't know the real world, not thing one."

He turns pensive for a moment, glancing at the volleyball game, then to Kate before she can rank on him again.

"The mother, though. That's a different story. She could make a decision like that in a heartbeat."

"Laura's mother?" Kate asks, reeling from all this information.

He nods. "A tough customer. When she has to be."

"Maybe I should find out a little about this family," she says. "Some research on this client of mine."

"Yes, I think you're going to have to," he confirms for her.

She sighs. "So my client could be setting me up, to throw me off the real trail, or her mother could have been a player, which really seems off the wall, since I can't see what she could have had to do with anything. Or it could be a plain old suicide, just like the police say it was."

"Or none of them," he adds. "Give you yet another option. Maybe he pissed one of his cellmates off, and they jumped him. Maybe he was gay and hit on the wrong hombre, or they were and he wouldn't play catch, or some other combination. You pays your money, you takes your choice."

"What do you think?" she asks him. "That vaunted intuition of yours—what's it telling you?"

He drains the last of his drink, turns his attention to the volleyball game.

"There's one rule that's inviolable," he tells her.

"What's that?" she bites.

"There was a lot of money at stake here," Carl reminds her. "Some of it's lost now, a hell of a lot more than lunch money. Somebody might want to make sure more of it doesn't float away."

"When in doubt, follow the money," she states. Another of Carl's maxims.

"You're the detective, detective."

There are many beautiful buildings in Santa Barbara. The County Courthouse is the most famous, an enormous Spanish colonial design built in 1875 that occupies a full square block of downtown space, featuring an immense sunken garden and the famous Mural Courtroom. Directly a stone's throw to the south you come upon the arresting purple-tinted whitewashed adobe buildings of Meridian Studios, while a scant block to their west, forming the borders of De La Guerra Plaza, sits City Hall and the Santa Barbara News-Press Building, the oldest daily newspaper in Southern California. You find such buildings all over town, blocks of them—lovely structures, many with important historical significance.

And smack-dab in the middle of all this tectonic beauty sits one eyesore: the County Administration building, a gigantic aggravating bunker situated directly across Anapamu St. from the courthouse.

The way this sad state of affairs came about is a classic example of why bureaucracies are intrinsically fucked. Back in the early 1960s the geniuses in Sacramento contracted out the construction of a raft of county buildings to be erected up and down the state, and in one of those strokes of inspiration that can only come from the minds of entrenched civil-service mediocrities, they (whoever *they* are) made it a one-style-fits-all deal, the style being poured concrete, about as appealing as a wart. *They* did it to save money; and of course, by the time all the cost overruns were accounted for, it came out more expensive than if each locality had done its own plan. So right across the street from one of the prettiest courthouses in the U.S. sits this four-story slab which would be marginally acceptable in some bombed-out place like Chernobyl, but in lovely Santa Barbara is flat-out pitiful.

Dorothy and Miranda Sparks are seated together in the back of the Board of Supervisors' hearing room on the fourth floor of the county building, listening to county staff drone on about some triviality they, the bureaucrats, hold sacred.

The staffer falters to an end of his presentation. Miranda sits up, immediately alert. She taps Dorothy on the shoulder.

"They're about to call our item number," she notes. Smoothing her dress, she escorts her mother-in-law to the front of the chamber.

———

"Mr. Chairman, members of the Board of Supervisors. Thank you for allowing me to speak. For the record, my name is Miranda Tayman Sparks." She speaks in a clear, distinct, and forceful voice, establishing eye contact with each supervisor sitting on the rostrum above her.

"I am appearing here today as chief executive officer of Pacific Land and Trust," she continues, "and also as the board chairman of the Sparks Foundation, which is a charitable organization known not only in this county, but statewide and nationally, as a contributor to women's causes, children's-rights causes, and environmental causes."

Miranda is dressed demurely and professionally in a business outfit by Jil Sander, sheer hose, black pumps with a modest heel. Her makeup is subdued and her hair is conservatively styled, falling naturally around her high-cheekboned face.

As she squares her notes preparatory to starting her formal presentation, the man she had fucked out on the ranch slips unobtrusively into the room through a door at the rear, taking a seat in the last row. No one pays him any attention.

Miranda takes a sip of water, begins her formal presentation.

"As you know, we own coastal property north of town. It's a fairly large piece, a few thousand acres, and it's all undeveloped. From time to time we've run some cattle on it, and raised a few crops, grains mostly, which haven't worked out particularly well, due to a million problems, none of which I want to bore you with, so we've basically left it fallow. Except for a few small farm-type buildings, this land is pretty much like it was two, three, four hundred years ago, before anybody except Native Americans had set foot on it, and even then it wasn't habitated, because it didn't produce, not even on a subsistence level. That's the sad truth. It's a beautiful piece of property. It would be a great location for multi-million-dollar homesites or a big resort, none of which we've ever contemplated, even though there have been resorts and golf courses and developments approved all around it. We've never asked for that, and I'm not here today to ask for that, so if you've been getting jittery just now listening to me you can relax. I'm not going to ask you to approve five hundred homesites or a thousand-room hotel or anything like that."

There are a few smiles and nervous chuckles around the room, including up on the podium where the supervisors are sitting, looking down into the chamber. No one's quite sure what Miranda wants from them, so this disclaimer is a relief.

She pauses, slips on a pair of half-frame tortoiseshell reading glasses. Opening a folder in front of her, she flips a few pages.

"I should mention that this particular piece of property is very important to my husband and my mother-in-law, because it was the first piece of land their family acquired, well over a hundred years ago. The leases they arranged with the railroads and the state over the years enabled them to buy other ranches and properties, to grow and prosper."

She looks behind her to Dorothy, then turns back to the supervisors.

"Because the Sparks family did well, which was the result of hard, hard work, perseverance, and guts, they wanted to help others do well also. So they established the Sparks Foundation, which, as I mentioned, is a benefactor to many charitable causes, particularly environmental ones. I don't think there's any question that Dorothy Sparks is the main mover and shaker in this county as far as donating her time, her energy, and her money to worthy causes."

Dorothy sits ramrod-straight behind Miranda. She doesn't like having attention called to herself, but she endures it.

"Dorothy Sparks is modest and self-effacing," Miranda continues, laying it on nice and thick, "but she is energetic and demanding. And she and all of her family back up their demands with cold, hard cash."

Again, she looks at the documents in front of her, gracefully slipping her glasses on and off.

"Last year," she states, reading from her notes, "the Sparks Foundation donated one point eight million dollars to charitable causes, seventy percent of that locally."

Sean Redbuck, the supervisor who had been at the Sparks family's Fiesta party, leans into his microphone. "That's extraordinarily generous," he says. "On behalf of the county I'd like to commend you."

Other supervisors join in, voicing their appreciation.

"Thank you," Miranda tells them. "We were happy to do it." She pauses for another sip of water. "Actually," she continues, "that sum, as generous as it sounds, was down six percent from the previous year."

She shuts her folder. Another quick look back to Dorothy: "Which brings us to the reason I'm appearing before you today."

"Last year, while we were donating almost two million dollars to charity, our coastal property took a one-point-six-million-dollar tax hit. We lost one and two-thirds million dollars doing nothing but watch the grass grow. And this year it will be worse, because the economy in general is worse."

She pauses, looking at each supervisor in turn. "We can't afford to maintain this level of generosity anymore. That's the bald truth of it."

Another pause. Miranda turns, her glance shifting to the man in the last row of seats. Their eyes meet for a moment, but there is no acknowledgment.

She turns back. "Would you please put up the transparency?" she requests.

The room is darkened as a county staffer places the requested slide in the overhead projector and shines it onto a screen at the side of the supervisors' rostrum.

The slide is an official county topographic map of a large parcel of property, bordered on one side by the ocean: the parcel of Sparks property that housed the dock on which Frank Bascomb and his confederates were caught in their aborted dope-smuggling attempt.

Miranda walks over to the screen, picking up a pointer from the table.

"This is a portion of the property I'm talking about," she informs them. "There are several unimproved roads that criss-cross it"—pointing to various lines that run through—"and a dock, which is rarely used anymore, since no one in our family sails."

She waits for everybody to get a good look.

"As charitable as we are—and I'm not shy about stating the obvious, that we are very charitable—we can't keep running at a loss. Especially since it affects our giving.

"Every dollar that we lost maintaining this piece of land is a dollar that could be used to protect our environment, or support an AIDS hospice, or provide needed funds to worthy artists. Those dollars could be doing good, instead of doing nothing."

She looks around the darkened room, from the supervisors to the audience. "We are requesting that this very small section of property—a mere one-tenth of the total acreage," she states, to emphasize the puniness of its relative size to the whole—"be changed in its designation from Ag Preserve to agriculture-rural-commercial, so that in the future we can make something of this land, instead of its being an albatross around our necks. Because if we can't get some kind of use from this—profit or nonprofit—we're in danger of the Sparks Foundation drying up. And that would be a catastrophe."

The room vibrates with voice. Redbuck, the chairman, gavels for silence.

"Quiet, please," he implores the twenty or thirty people who have heard this plea.

This request has come from out of the blue; the agenda had merely stated "consideration of Ag Preserve Parcel #1217," which normally would have meant some petty detail involving paperwork; no one except a few county drones expected anything this radical, and for once, out of respect to the family, they hadn't leaked the proposal. Had the specifics been publicized in advance, the room would have been packed with members of the environmental movement. As it stands, there is no one who has asked to speak to this project, pro or con. Only Miranda.

Redbuck leans forward, peering down to Miranda.

"What kind of enterprise were you thinking of, Mrs. Sparks?" he inquires. "Mini-estates, fifty-acre ranchettes, anything like that?" he probes.

Redbuck, from an old valley ranching family, can't completely lose the sarcasm from his voice; in the last thirty years hundreds of wealthy people from Los Angeles and Orange counties have moved into fifty-acre parcels, especially in the Santa Ynez Valley, termed themselves instant ranchers—although they wouldn't know a Holstein from a quarter-horse—and immediately called for tighter controls on county development. A classic example of "I've got mine, fuck you, Jack."

"No, absolutely not, I already said that, it's on your record," she replies emphatically.

"Can you give us a hint?" he asks.

"We have a few concepts in mind, Mr. Chairman, but I'm not at liberty to disclose them yet," she answers candidly. "We want to make sure we can pull them off, from a financial point of view."

"Then why are you here at this time?" he asks quizzically

"Because we need to know if we are going to be able to put this piece of our property to good use, a use that could be beneficial to everyone, for our own long-range planning for the foundation. Look," she continues, "it's real simple. We give a lot, but we're not a bottomless pit. Nobody is anymore. The new tax laws and the changes in the economy in California have ended that kind of philanthropy forever, sad to say. Everything has to pay its way now, even charity. Or else," she warns, her voice tinged with sadness, "there won't be any charity, when it's really needed."

She pauses once more, making that last important eye contact with the five powers that be. Then she turns and takes her seat in the first row, next to Dorothy.

"Well done," Dorothy whispers. "A good presentation."

Redbuck leans forward.

"Does county staff have a recommendation on this item?"

"Yes, Mr. Chairman, we do." Rebecca Soderheim, the resource manager on this project, a nondescript woman in her thirties, shuffles some papers.

"And . . . ?"

"We recommend that a change be approved, as requested."

"What could they do with that designation?" he asks.

"Lots of things. They could expand their harbor, for example. For pleasure boats or commercial fishing or both. There's a real need for expanded dock space in the county, as you're aware of."

"That's a good idea." He glances over at Miranda. She cocks her head—"maybe."

Redbuck looks to his colleagues. "Any questions?"

They all look at each other. There are no questions.

"Well then, if there are no questions of the applicant, I suggest we put this in the form of a motion."

"I have some questions, Mr. Chairman," rings out a male voice from the rear of the room.

Everyone turns.

A man stands. He's somewhat disheveled in appearance, wearing a beat-up corduroy sports jacket with leather patches on the elbows, the kind you used to see on graduate students who never finished their degrees, faded khakis, a plaid work shirt, hiking boots. Long uncombed hair.

Redbuck sighs. "What is your question, Mr. Pachinko?" he asks with exasperation.

The man works his way to the front of the room, stands at the speaker's rostrum.

"For openers," he begins, "what's the rush?"

"No one's rushing this. There is no rush."

"Seems to me like there is. A quick presentation, a quicker positive response from county, and wham-bam, we've got a major change in county land-use designation. That looks like a rush to me."

He rocks on the balls of his feet, a welterweight ready for the opening bell.

"Do you have a question?" Redbuck asks again, icily.

"As a matter of fact, Mr. Chairman, I do. I've got a couple."

He walks over to county staff's table, snatches up their copy of the agenda, walks back to the speaker's rostrum, leafs through it, shaking his head in sorrow every few pages. Then, holding it as if it were a dog turd wrapped in yesterday's newspaper, he flips it back. It falls to the floor. Rebecca quickly picks it up, holds on to it proprietarily.

"The Environmental Citizens' Association views with alarm any change in land designation from agriculture to other use," Pachinko states. "Little good ever comes from these changes, but extraordinary harm often does. Witness the recent oil-tankering controversy, where after decades of being promised no tankering, now we have it within the Channel Islands day and night. Someday one of those tankers is going to spill its guts all over our beaches and this community is going to be living with the consequences of that disaster for decades. 1969 again, quadrupled."

A few loud whistles and claps come from the back of the room. Redbuck forcefully gavels them down.

"We're not discussing oil here, Mr. Pachinko."

"Okay, you're right. But the best intentions in the world—and I am here to testify that Mrs. Sparks, Dorothy Sparks that is, does have the best intentions—the best intentions in the world are for nothing if you can't control everything, and I mean every single thing, about your own system. And to give anybody, even the Sparks family, who are without question the most generous people around when it comes to helping preserve our precious environmental treasures, a blank check without knowing on what account it's being written, is dangerous."

He turns and faces Dorothy.

"You'll have to forgive me, Mrs. Sparks. I respect you, you know that. Probably a hell of a lot more than anyone else in these chambers, especially these five . . ." before the word "clowns" can escape his lips, he turns and looks at the supervisors, who are intently staring down at him . . . "these five distinguished, intelligent, all-knowing founts of human knowledge and foresight . . ."

Bam! The gavel comes down.

"You're out of line!" Redbuck thunders.

"No!" Pachinko yells back, even louder, so loud that everyone, even the few of his own people who are scattered about the room, are shocked at the vehemence. "I'm not the one out of line here today! You are! For not being extra skeptical, extra cautious. Okay. So the Sparks family are environmental heroes. I agree, they are. My organization can attest to that directly, because Mrs. Sparks and I have worked shoulder to shoulder many a time. But what happens fifteen, or twenty, or fifty years down the line, when they're not around anymore, but this decision is? How do we know how their children or grandchildren will act? The blunt truth is, we don't. And that's why we don't write a blank check against the future."

Once again he turns and faces Dorothy Sparks.

"Can't this wait," he pleads to her, "until you have a real in-the-flesh plan? I'd be the first to support anything reasonable, you know that. But to say yes to any down-the-line idea is wrong, Mrs. Sparks. If this wasn't your own action item you'd be standing right up here next to me, arguing my case."

He glares at the supervisors. "This is too important a change to rush through willy-nilly," he cautions them. "I suggest you table this for a couple of weeks, so that the general public can be made aware, and can participate in helping you make the right decision."

With one more look to Miranda and Dorothy he turns and marches up the aisle and out of the room.

"Duly noted," Redbuck says dryly to Pachinko's retreating back. He looks up and down the row at the other four supervisors.

"Lest we forget," he states, "we have a mechanism for control. Ourselves. Changing a land-use designation does not, Mr. Pachinko's gloomy forecast to the contrary, give anyone a blank check. It may give them a check, that's true, but we're the only ones who can sign it. When, whether it's tomorrow or ten years from now, this family decides on a specific course of action, they'll have to come before us again and make their case, and if we don't like it, we can say no. That's what we're here for, isn't it?"

"Yes." "Yes." "Yes." "Yes." They are in agreement.

"Do I hear a motion?"

As the motion on the application from the Sparks family is made, seconded, and approved, the man sitting in the last row gets up and walks out. By the time Miranda senses his movement and turns to look for him, he's no longer there.

J . F . F R E E D M A N

4

WITHIN AN INCH OF YOUR LIFE

T he women park in the cracked-
asphalt lot behind the church,
walk down a flight of shallow concrete steps that are easy to slip on
whenever it rains, especially if you're coming from work and are wearing
heels, enter through the back door, and pass into the low-ceilinged,
dimly lit basement. The church is AME, the largest black church in town,
located on the east side, off Milpas. No one presently in the group is
African-American, but the price is right: it's free, because when the group
first started as an offshoot of the county shelter program, this church volunteered the space.

It's evening, coming on eight-thirty. The light is fading in the sky. As
they get out of their cars the women greet each other with muted hellos.
A few hug. The cars are Mercedeses and Jaguars, twenty-year-old
Datsuns and Pintos, pickup trucks, the full gamut in between. Those who
don't have cars take the bus or come on foot.

Inside, the women set up metal folding chairs, arranging them in a
loose circle on the yellowing, lumpy linoleum floor: twelve clients and
the therapist, Maxine, an MFCC who's working on her doctorate at
Fielding.

In age they range from twenty-three to sixty-one. As in all free-
floating recovery-type therapy groups this one is in flux, women move in
and out depending on how they're doing and what they're doing; right
now in the mix there are five Anglos, four Latinos (three Mexican-
American, one illegal from Guatemala), two Asian-Americans (Filipino
and Vietnamese), and one Native American (Zuni-Navajo). Some have
college degrees, some never graduated high school. Two of them, including Mildred Willard—who had told Laura about Kate—are rich women

who live in big houses in Montecito and have servants, gardeners, pool men, swim at the Coral Casino and play golf with their husbands at Valley Club and Birnam Wood. A few others are working professionals—a paralegal, two schoolteachers; while others are working-class, at the level of checkers at Vons; and at the bottom of the economic rung are the welfare wives and mothers, the ones you'd expect. As different as twelve women can be.

They only have one similarity in their lives, one fragmented piece that binds them tight. Half of that piece either took place in their past, as is the case with Kate (who was the last one to arrive tonight and then dawdled over fixing her coffee, classic procrastination), or is happening now, present-day, like the young woman sitting across the room whose left cheekbone looks like somebody took a sledgehammer to it last night. The other half of the piece is that the past can, without warning, become the present, and that the future holds no secure promises.

"So, Kate," Maxine states in a clear, sympathetic, but no-nonsense professional voice, "tonight's the night, right?"

"Right," Kate answers reluctantly. She doesn't like to talk about this shit; she doesn't mind hearing it from others, but doing it herself, opening up her own wounds, she has a hard time with that. Being a cop for so long has something to do with it—if you show your vulnerable side you can get wasted.

But she has to, she has no choice, unless she wants her life to stay fucked up and incomplete. So four months ago she decided to give up her armor. On a clear full-moon night she walked down the slippery flight of stairs into this basement and joined up.

Joined up, but not opened up. Last week, after the others in the group had challenged her to put up or get out, she had declared that tonight was going to be the night, the night she came clean.

"Okay, Kate," Maxine states emphatically. "The meter's running."

Kate surveys the group. They're waiting, everyone's attention focused on her.

She plunges in.

"My name is Katherine Theresa Blanchard. Most of you know that already," she adds, feeling lame and scared.

She realizes she's looking at the floor. She forces her eyes up, making eye contact with some of the group members, who smile encouragingly at her.

"I've been married twice," she continues. "The first time when I was nineteen, young and dumb, your basic classic move. That sorry state of affairs lasted six years, don't ask me how or why, we had zero in common. I divorced him when I was twenty-five, but I'm a slow learner, two years later I up and got married all over again. We had things in common, Eric—my second husband, that is his name—and I, several things, one was we were in the same profession, we were both police officers, as most of you know about me, I don't know how many of you know he was, too, which can make for extreme closeness because of the suspicion and isolation a police officer is constantly being subjected to, it's easy to become paranoid, having an understanding partner can be a real asset. Plus we both liked the same sports, the same kinds of music."

She takes a sip of her coffee. It's gone cold.

She's gotten through the easy part. When she speaks again her voice unconsciously lowers to a monotone, as if she's telling someone else's story, someone far removed from her.

"I was married to Eric for almost ten years, until twenty months ago when I finally got up the courage to leave; during that time, almost from our wedding night when I think back on it, I lived in fear, the fear that someday his rage would go so out of control that he would kill me."

She exhales, a deep sigh from the spirit.

"I am a battered woman. Who is trying to redeem her life."

The Losario murders-suicide had been so devastating, so guilt-provoking, that she had wanted to quit outright; but Captain Albright would have none of that, he'd torn her "Request For Retirement" into confetti and thrown the pieces in his trash can. "You are a good officer," he told her, "you don't end a solid career because some uncontrollable schizo goes on a rampage."

The local newspaper and TV coverage was brutal. For three days there were reporters everywhere, they camped out on her front porch, followed her to the supermarket, tried to interview her at the precinct house.

Lurid headlines shrieked at her from newsstands: COPS STAND BY WHILE WACKO HUSBAND MURDERS WIFE, DAUGHTER, TURNS GUN ON SELF. *Local TV stations roasted the entire police force.*

"They know nothing," the captain told her when she went to him in tears.

It was so unfair, what else could she have done?

He was a veteran of these dustups. "Just let it blow over," he counseled her. "In a couple of days nobody will remember your name."

In the meantime, she had to move to a motel to get away from the mob pursuing her.

Eric railed at her for making his life such a mess, for fucking things up so royally. The first night they moved to the motel he punched her out in the ribs, almost breaking some. She barricaded herself in the bathroom until he left to go drinking with his buddies; then she locked him out of the room altogether and instructed the manager not to give him a key.

They didn't speak for a few days after that, until the clamor died down and she was able to go home. He acted, as he always did, like nothing had happened, just another day in the life.

Despite Captain Albright's rock-steady support, however, she was put on a four-week administrative leave of absence while awaiting her hearing. With full pay; she had not been found guilty of any dereliction of duty or other conduct unbecoming a peace officer.

"I have no questions about your performance, Kate, and I will personally testify to that effect," Captain Albright told her at that time. "I'm sure I would've handled it exactly the same way, but the department has to do this by the numbers, there was too much publicity not to; and besides," he'd added, assessing the major bags under her eyes, the pallid complexion of the face sitting across from him, "you need some time off. You don't walk away from an experience like what you went through without weird stuff going on in your head. You need time to process it. And remember, a leave of absence is SOP in cases like this, so don't take it as a reprimand. The hearing will determine if any action is necessary, which I strongly doubt. Use this free time wisely," he counseled.

In those two weeks she saw a department psychologist five times. He assured her she wasn't crazy, and she began unburdening herself of a lot of old garbage. The process itself blew her mind, because she'd always thought all shrinks were quacks; that therapy could actually help her was both exciting and frightening.

The hearing, which came three and a half weeks after what had been the worst day of her life, was anticlimactic. It took less than half a day and proceeded without incident. She was absolved of any wrongdoing, misconduct, or lack of professional judgment, and was formally instructed to report back to work the following Monday, at which time she would be assigned a new partner, Ray having resigned less than twenty-four hours after the debacle.

Eric had talked his way into the hearing, shmoozing the hearing officers while simultaneously pulling rank—a veteran of the force, a former instructor in the Academy, a concerned husband. To Kate he was a vulture, a dark presence slouching in his seat in the back of the room. She hadn't wanted him to come, but he'd insisted—they needed to show they supported each other, he'd told her, it was important to their careers. She knew that was bullshit, her career meant nothing to him, he wouldn't shed one tear if she was kicked off the force; and she also knew it was futile to try and stop him, it would only make matters worse.

"You're damn lucky you're a woman," he said to her on their way out of the hearing room. "If that had been me in that house and I'd botched it up the way you did it, I'd have been suspended for a month, if they didn't shitcan me outright."

Always supportive, Eric.

She stayed out of his way the rest of the week. They were alone in the house, just the two of them, she'd sent the girls to her sister's until all this blew over.

Late Sunday afternoon she drove across the bridge into the city to pick up her daughters. Teenagers, Wanda fifteen and a half, Sophia just turned thirteen. Good girls, the lights of her life. All this shit with Eric had taken its toll on them—in the past six months Wanda, who'd always had a model's complexion, had broken out with acne, and Sophia had gotten into the habit of biting her nails to the quick, to the point where they would bleed.

Worst of all, they were doing poorly at school. They had always been good students, honor roll from first grade. Last semester it was C's and D's for both of them. She didn't blame them—she blamed herself. How can you study when you're scared your stepfather is going to kill your mother?

Julie and Walt, Julie's husband, coaxed her into staying for dinner. They had a large apartment in the Haight, close to the UCSF Hospital, where they both worked as lab technicians. They'd never had any children—hers were the closest they would ever come, which made *them extra-special. They loved Kate too, they were on her case constantly to leave Eric, they didn't know the whole story between her and Eric but they knew enough to know he was a ticking time bomb.*

She was never able to explain why she couldn't leave what everyone who loved her knew was a dismal marriage. The girls had something to do with it, even though Eric wasn't their real father (their real father, that pathetic loser, had vanished without a trace, they hadn't had a word from him in three years, not that she gave a shit, not having to deal with him was one less problem in her overloaded life).

She sure knew how to pick the losers, she sometimes thought, during those times when she would be overwhelmed with self-pity, guilt, and remorse; always feeling, somehow, that this condition was her fault, that she deserved it.

She was Eric's prisoner, that was her bottom line, as real a prisoner as if he had her chained to a wall.

Julie and Walt couldn't understand that. No one could, no one in the entire history of the world had ever walked in her shoes.

Dinner was so easy, it was a relief, no stress. What would it be like to live like this? she'd often thought. She'd have to leave Eric and quit the force to even start trying to achieve it; and those two things, marriage and career (along with her children), were the defining elements in her life, she would be lost without them. She firmly believed that.

She decided to let the girls stay with her sister for a few more days. They had moved their stuff over to their aunt's, it would be a hassle to load the car up tonight and unload it again when they got home. The girls could take the BART to school, which they'd been doing anyway. They wanted to stay, it was mellow compared to their home life, who could blame them? They hardly had to beg her at all. She would have stayed herself if she could have.

The hugs, when she had to leave, were long and clinging. They didn't want her to go. She wasn't crazy about the idea, either, but no way was she going to let Eric drive her out of her home. She could handle it, like she'd done every time before.

"Will you call tomorrow morning before we go to school?" Wanda implored her.

"Of course." One last group hug, the three of them. "I love you."

"We love you, too."

She could see them in the rearview mirror, watching her as she drove away.

All the lights were out when she drove up. Maybe Eric was gone, as usual, out drinking with his cronies, other cops who viewed the world through equally jaundiced eyes, with any luck he'd come in late, after she had fallen asleep (or feigned it, which she often did), mellow enough from an evening out with the boys that he'd leave her alone.

No such luck. He was home, and waiting.

"You have dinner with Julie and Walt?" he asked. He was sitting in the dark watching an NBA playoff game on the tube, Portland–Golden State, a half-empty Loco Pollo box dumped on the coffee table.

"I called you but there was no answer," she told him. "I figured you'd gone out," she said. "The girls stayed overnight," she added, "they weren't packed, it was getting late, I'll pick them up tomorrow after school."

His calling her sister and brother-in-law by their real names was a hopeful sign—she wished. When Eric was more pissed off than usual he would refer to them as "those bloodsuckers in the white coats," because one of their duties at the hospital involved taking blood samples, or, even more cruelly, "the sterile duo."

"We'll talk about it later," he said.

She didn't know what that meant but it didn't sound good. His voice was dark in tone, ominous in feeling.

"I'm tired," she said. "I'm going to bed."

"Peaceful dreams." He was locked into the game, it was like she wasn't even there.

She put on a fresh nightgown, even though it was warm out and she preferred to sleep nude. Tomorrow was her first day back on the job, she wanted a good night's sleep, which meant she didn't want Eric staggering in at midnight and demanding that they make love. A cumbersome-to-take-off nightgown might be enough to discourage him.

No such luck. He stumbled into the bedroom, knocking against the bed, the night table, the bureau, making sure he woke her up. For good measure he left the bathroom door open when he turned the light on, ran the water loudly, and dropped the lid with a slam after he flushed.

"What're you wearing this for?" he whined after he climbed into bed and felt cotton instead of skin when he put his hand on her ass.

"I'm chilly," she answered. She rolled onto her side away from his touch. "I'm tired, Eric, I want to go to sleep."

"I'm not," he rebutted, his hand reaching under the bottom of her gown, working his way up the backs of her legs.

She turned away, pushing his hand off her.

"Not tonight. I'm not in the mood, I want to sleep, tomorrow's a big day for me."

"This won't take long." He reached one hand over her back, inside her gown at the top, touching a breast.

"You just don't know how to take no for an answer, do you, goddamnit!" she yelled at him, pushing the covers down on her side and jumping out of the bed.

"Where the hell are you going?"

"I'm sleeping in the girls' room tonight." She started walking around the bed, towards the door.

"The fuck you are," he told her, jumping out of his side. He was between her and the door, blocking her escape.

She stood in the middle of the room, arms folded across her chest, glaring at him.

"Eric, get out of my way."

"Get back in bed, Kate."

"Get out of my way, goddamn you."

"Not till we make love."

"We're not making love tonight."

"Fine, then we'll just have a quick fuck."

"No. Nothing."

"So now I'm not even good enough to fuck, is that it?"

"I don't want to tonight, that's all." Her voice started rising in concert with her anger. "I'm not some dog that has to lie down for you any time you order me to, okay?" She was glad the girls hadn't come home with her, she didn't want them hearing this, not that they hadn't, many times.

"You're a cunt, you know that, Kate? A world-class, A-number-one cunt."

"Fine. I'm a cunt. Now get out of my way."

He stood with his back against the door, naked, hands on hips like a gunslinger, glaring at her, daring her.

She could feel tears coming. Don't, she commanded herself, don't let him do this to you.

"Why do you have to do this, Eric?" she asked, trying to keep her voice from shaking.

"Because you're my wife, and I'm sick and tired of you not being a wife. I AM SICK AND FUCKING TIRED OF IT, ALL RIGHT?!" he screamed.

She felt dizzy, lightheaded. She put a hand on the dresser to keep from falling.

"Can't you appreciate what I've been through?" she asked, trying to reason with him. "My life has been hell for a month, Eric, you more than anyone should be understanding about that."

"My life hasn't been hell?" he countered. "You think this has been some fucking bed of roses for me?"

"It's been rough on both of us, I know that, but I'm the one that had to go through it all. If it happened to you, Eric, I wouldn't be taking this attitude. I'd be trying to support you, not tear you down, for godsakes."

The tears were coming, dribbling out the corners of her eyes. She scrunched her lids up to try and stop them before he could see. Thank God it was dark.

"The problem with that, dear wife," he sneered, "is that it would not have happened to me. That's the goddamn problem in a nutshell, Kate"—now it was pouring out of him, an avalanche of anger and emotion, "you fucked up because you're not good enough, that's the fucking problem, that's why three people are dead, the fact is that you're a shitty cop and shouldn't ever have been let on the goddamn force in the first place, that is the fucking problem!"

"You bastard. You fucking bastard!" she screamed.

"You talked that guy into doing it, you cunt, didn't you?" he screamed back. "You're not just a shitty cop," he continued, his voice at fever pitch, "another shitty woman who got on the force because of the bullshit quota—it's you, lady, your own specific personality, your own poison. That's what pushed that poor bastard over the edge!"

"Eat shit and die!" she came back at him.

"I understand," he snapped. "I understand like no one understands. Because you do the same fucking thing to me."

Her eyes dried up immediately. She felt a cold chill passing through her body like a cleansing shower.

"I'm done listening to you," she told him. "I'm leaving. Now get out of my way."

"Over my dead body."

"Have it your way."

"That's my intention," he told her, and in one step he moved to his bureau, with a second he took his service automatic out of the underwear drawer where he kept it, and with a third he drew on her.

Pee dribbled down her leg. It felt cold. She didn't try to stop the flow.

"Put it down," she said.

"The wrong woman was killed back there!" he ranted. "That's the problem. He killed the wrong woman. But I can fix that now."

The gun was in his hand, dangling, his finger light on the trigger.

She was going to die; he was going to kill her, gun her down in her own house, and she realized with that terrible clarity people have when they're facing their own mortality that she was that woman back there in that house, that her fate was that woman's fate.

"My children," she chanted to herself, as if saying a final act of contrition, "my girls." Because she was never going to see them again; of all the worst things death would bring, it would be that she would not see her children again.

And then he was on her, two steps forward and his hand was going up and coming down, the side of his pistol smashing against the side of her head, she actually saw stars, it was like her head was exploding, and then he was beating her, beating her to a bloody pulp, smashing his fists against her face, her body, his arms working like jackhammers, beating her within an inch of her life.

She was curled up on the floor in the fetal position, unable to move. She felt the pistol barrel pressed against her temple.

"The next time," he threatened her, "the next time, I will pull the damn trigger. Consider yourself lucky this time."

She knew that was true. It was a matter of time.

She lay on the floor, semiconscious, listening as he got dressed, went out, drove off in his car.

Somehow she managed to drag herself onto her bed, to peel off her nightgown, stained with blood, her blood, to stagger into the bathroom; seeing herself so wasted and so beaten was as frightening as when he had been beating on her, she wanted to cry now, to wash this horror away, but she couldn't, she was far beyond tears, bone dry, somehow she managed to wash off the worst of it and pull on some sweats and get her feet into flops and stagger out of the house with nothing but her purse and her gun. Somehow she managed to get down the sidewalk to her car, start it up, and drive away. To the Oakland Women's Shelter, the only place she knew she would be safe.

"Jesus!" one of the women in the group exclaimed, shaking her head.

"That's bad," mutters another. They've all heard these stories, but they never, thankfully, get inured to them. "That's brutal."

While she was telling this story Kate had maintained her composure; now her hands are shaking, her entire body shivers involuntarily.

"Can I have one of your cigarettes?" she asks the woman sitting next to her. She doesn't know why she wants a smoke, since her lips are dry, she has cotton mouth to the max, but she needs a crutch, an immediate fix.

"I didn't know you smoked," Maxine says.

"I don't, but I want one now."

The woman sitting next to Kate holds Kate's hand steady while she lights the cigarette and takes a deep drag. Another woman puts a fresh cup of coffee into Kate's free hand.

"Thanks," she mutters. She feels completely wiped out.

"Did you go back?" a woman ventures to ask. They have to ask these questions, even if they seem insensitive, it's the way the group works.

"No. I never went back," she tells them.

"Good," several say, cheering, encouraging her. "Way to go."

"Piece of *shit!*" This expletive comes from Conchita, who is sitting two seats away, vaporizing her own Marlboro Light 100. First-generation Mexican-American, thirtyish, strong and proud. On the edge of her chair as she listens, she is always the most empathetic woman in the room. Kate feels closer to her than to anyone else in the group, and has from her first time here, there's a similarity in backgrounds and attitudes—neither suffers anything easily. Conchita is blind in one eye, the pupil fixed, opaque. A gift from a customer when she was, as she insists on bluntly putting it, peddling her unliberated ass on Haley St. several years ago.

"I've never laid this out to anyone before," Kate tells her group. "Not even the shrinks. Not this way."

"You did great, wonderful," Maxine assures her. She comes over and gives Kate a hug. Several of the other women do also. She can feel the evil shit pouring out of her body in a rush.

"All those years I'd been feeling this incredible guilt," Kate tells them. "I was convinced that whatever punishment Eric dished out to me, I deserved it. That's how I felt."

"You were *not* guilty," Conchita says, getting in Kate's face. "You *thought* you were guilty," she amplifies. "*Thought*, not were. You were not guilty of any fucking thing!"

The women laugh at the double entendre, much-needed relief.

"Of anything, period," Conchita continues, laughing herself. "Fucking or not fucking."

"I know that now," Kate says. "I know that. Hey," she adds, "don't forget—I won."

"What did you win?" Maxine asks.

"I got out," Kate answers. "And I never did let him have sex with me, he couldn't make me screw him."

"Screw him!" Conchita crows.

"All of them!" cries another woman.

"Not all of them," Kate says, disagreeing. "Just Eric."

"God Almighty, girl, aren't you down on all men, after living in hell like that?" yet another member of the group throws out.

Kate shakes her head emphatically.

"No," she answers. "I liked men before Eric, I liked men during Eric, and I like men now, after Eric. He was a prick, but that doesn't mean they all are." She smiles, almost sheepishly. "I like men, what can I tell you?"

"You've got guts, lady," Maxine tells her, admiringly. "It's a great thing, too, after you've been through what you have."

"I'm not going to curl up and die because one asshole wants me to," Kate answers.

"That took incredible courage," Mildred Willard tells Kate.

"Thank you, but I didn't have much choice. It was either that or let him kill me."

"Telling your story, that's what I meant," Mildred clarifies. "You told it so cleanly, so directly."

The two of them are standing in the near-empty parking lot, next to Mildred's Range Rover. The others have left, they're the last stragglers.

Kate admires Mildred. Mildred is a substantial woman in her own right. Just coming here, week after week, a woman of her age and stature. Most women in her position would say the hell with it, they wouldn't have the guts to come out of the closet.

"Thanks. And thanks for the recommendation," she adds.

"Laura Sparks?"

Kate nods.

"She's my client, which, by the way, is privileged, but since you sent her to me, I guess I can tell you that much."

"I wouldn't say a word to anyone, believe me," Mildred swears.

"She doesn't know about . . . how we met, how we know each other?"

"Oh no," Mildred vows. "No one knows about this except the people in our group. And I would never want that information divulged."

"Don't worry," Kate assures her. "Me, either."

"She's a nice girl," Mildred comments. "I hope you can help her."

"I don't know yet."

"With her life," Mildred clarifies. "She comes from a powerful female lineage. She needs to find her own space."

"That's not what people hire me to do," Kate states. "Out of my range."

"You can help," Mildred rejoins, touching Kate's hand. "You have your own brand of power. Let some of it rub off on Laura."

Kate shakes her head. "No," she repeats adamantly. "No way, that's just . . . The answer is no, I'm sorry, Mildred. I'm not a social worker and I'm not a psychologist. They get involved in people's lives in ways I don't ever want to. I'll do as good a job for her as I do for all my clients, but I'm not a nursemaid." She's talking more rapidly than usual, there's a nervousness in her voice, the cause of which she doesn't quite understand. "I do not want that kind of personal involvement with a client," she insists. "With anyone," she adds in a sudden but not completely unexpected flash of clarity.

"That's not me."

5

SLEEPING DOGS

The third man on the boat—Rusty's helper—is named Wes Gillroy. Laura had been introduced to him when she'd first come on board. After that they had barely exchanged a dozen words; anything that had to be communicated to him from Morgan or her had gone through Rusty or Frank, like Wes was someone who didn't exist for the women as a person in his own right.

That's all Laura remembers about him, his name. And what he looks like, in a vague, general way. She wasn't paying him any attention, she had tunnel vision for Frank.

Kate hands her visitor's slip to the duty officer at the county jail. He looks at her. She's wearing a professional suit, low heels, not much makeup.

"Are you a relative, or the attorney?"

She hands him her identification. "I'm a private investigator assigned to this case."

"Does the prisoner know you? Know you're coming?"

"No."

"He doesn't have to see you if he doesn't want to." He hands her back her ID.

"That's up to him."

"Hang on a minute." He punches some data into the computer on his desk.

Jesus, these guys, she thinks. If you're a civilian who they don't know they'll give you the runaround from here until Tuesday. She recalls a line of dialogue from *The French Connection*—"Never trust nobody."

The duty officer looks from his screen to her. "No can do," he tells her.

"Why not?"

"He's not in custody here."

What the hell? "Where is he?"

"He made bail. He's gone."

Well, fuck. She's just starting out on this case and already she's on the wrong foot.

She goes back to her office, thinking about her next move. She'll have to find out who wrote Gillroy's bond, where he lives, all that drudge stuff she was hoping to avoid.

The phone rings.

"Hello," she answers curtly. She hates getting phone calls when she's thinking unpleasant thoughts.

"Is this Blanchard Investigations?" the voice on the other end of the line asks; a man's voice, one she knows. "The famous Blanchard Investigations?" he adds.

She laughs. "That's debatable—the 'famous' part."

"I heard you were at my shop earlier," he says.

"How'd you know that?" she asks, astonished. "I just left there."

"The walls have ears," he tells her. "Especially when it concerns you."

"Well, I'm impressed. I do need to pick your brain, though."

"I'll meet you at the cafe at Hendry's Beach in an hour," he tells her. "It's a nice day. We can take a walk."

Talking on the phone with this man is okay because it's anonymous; her going down in person would be another matter, she isn't welcomed where he works. His colleagues view private detectives with strong skepticism. But this man talking to her on the phone from his desk likes Kate, he knows she's good people, he'll help her out when he can if he thinks it's the right thing to do, but they shouldn't be seen together.

————

Kate and Juan Herrera stroll down the beach in a westerly direction, away from the restaurant and parking area. It's midweek—except for mothers and kids there are few people about; a good place to not be seen while taking a walk.

Kate had gone home and changed. Now she's wearing last year's Big Dog Fiesta T-shirt over a pair of cutoffs, and a big floppy straw hat on her head for protection against the sun. She's barefoot, she left her sandals in the car. Herrera, by contrast, has on a short-sleeve dress shirt, tie, seersucker sports coat, slacks. It's his lunch hour, he came straight from the office. He doesn't even bother to take his well-worn Dexter dress shoes off; as they walk the hard-packed sand along the water's edge he takes care not to get them wet, salt ruins the leather. His pistol rides his hip, hidden under his jacket, which is why he's kept the jacket on.

He's a tall, rangy man, a few years older than she is, good-looking. He appeals to her—but he's married with kids. She doesn't know if he fools around or not; being married and a cop automatically puts him off limits, a double whammy. She has to keep vigilant in her stand against dating cops; it's like quitting smoking, you don't tempt fate by trying it even one time. Her relationship with Herrera is clean; better that way.

"You're not exactly inconspicuous, dressed like this," she teases him. "What if someone see us?"

He shrugs, loosens his tie. "What I do on my lunchtime, that's my business," he says dismissively. "Meeting you at work, that would be waving a red flag."

She knows a fair amount about him, from the several conversations over coffee they've had during the past year. A detective in the Santa Barbara County Sheriff's Department for over twenty years, Herrera is an eastside homeboy who joined the force after his tour of Vietnam. A lieutenant for a long time, he's advanced as high as he'll go.

After she started taking on Carl's caseload her natural instinct had been to go for information to the people she knew, the police; but she found out very quickly—as soon as they learned she was working as a PI—that door wasn't open to her anymore. Oh, they were nice enough, they weren't rude or nasty, nothing like that. They just didn't tell her one thing she couldn't have learned from the papers, the library, or her computer network. There are two kinds of people in this world: cops and everyone else. She isn't a cop anymore.

Herrera, Kate learned, was the exception. He's going to night school, getting his master's degree in sociology at UCSB; working with kids and gangs is where he wants to go at some point in his life, he's told her with strong conviction. He knows she's been shut out and that hasn't sat well with him. He doesn't believe the police have a mission to protect society from itself, and he doesn't go along with the attitude of secrecy and benign deceit that too many cops practice.

"It's bullshit," he'd said when they'd first gotten to know each other and were swapping war stories. "We don't have the answers any more than anyone else. Just because I've got a badge and a gun doesn't make me omniscient."

She'd never known a cop who used words like "omniscient." It was little things like that that made her feel she could trust him, that he wasn't using her. That and the fact he didn't hit on her.

"So what is it you need my expert advice on today?" he asks.

"The suicide in your jail."

A wave washes up in front of them. The wet cold brine splashes on her feet, a tangy, stinging feeling. Herrera sidesteps the water, attempting to keep his wingtips dry.

"You serious?" he asks, looking at her sideways.

"Is that a problem?" she asks, searching his face.

"Not for us," he tells her. Without breaking stride he bends down to pick up a shell, a small mussel shell, perfectly ridged. "Unless somebody decides to make it one."

"What can you tell me?" she asks.

"It's cut and dried. The man was staring at life without parole, he took the lesser of two evils."

"But he hadn't even been arraigned. Why so soon?"

He shrugs.

She hesitates a moment before continuing, she doesn't want to turn him off, but she has to say what she's thinking. "You don't sound like you're being completely open about this, Juan."

"This one's different," he admits.

"Like how?"

He polishes the shell on his tie, sticks it in his jacket pocket.

"It was a screwup."

He picks up another shell, a flat one, skims it out across the water. It skips three times before it sinks.

"It was a fiasco for the department. Somebody dies in your jail, it's lousy public relations."

"Frank Bascomb's friends must not be very happy, either," Kate says.

"Frank Bascomb? Hey, fuck him, the guy was a dope dealer. That's the bottom of the food chain, down there with child molesters."

"You knew him as a dealer?" Kate asks. "Before this incident?" she adds. That surprises her; she doesn't know anything about Frank

Bascomb, except Laura would have, and why would Laura hire a detective if Frank really had been dirty? Of course, Laura had been duped by Frank, so maybe there had been others.

"No, I didn't," he says quickly, covering. "That was a libel, I shouldn't be talking like that." He pauses. "You hear things. In this job hearing things is a part of it. You were a cop, you know that."

"What kind of things did you hear?" she presses.

Instead of answering her, he asks his own question: "Who hired you? Who wants to know about this?"

"Laura Sparks. That's confidential, of course," she adds. She has no good reason to hide this from him, he won't tell anyone, and she wants to keep him on her side.

"Figures," he says, "since she was there. Lucky for her she wasn't there then. She probably feels guilty, don't you think?"

"I don't know."

"She seems like she's a nice girl, even if she does rake the department over the coals in that horseshit newspaper of hers. She was his sweetie," he adds, half-question, half-accusation. "That's what I hear."

"That I wouldn't know either," Kate lies. Laura is her client. Kate will be straight with Herrera whenever she can, but the client's privacy and protection comes first.

"That's the story out there," he says, vaguely waving his arm towards a cloud.

"Anyway, how did a prime suspect in a major drug bust wind up in a common tank with a bunch of drunks and crazies?" Kate asks, trying to focus the conversation.

This is the first sixty-four-thousand-dollar question; if she can find out what really happened—not only in that tank but why he was in there at all—she might get several steps closer to the truth.

"How?" Herrera says. "We made a mistake. People make mistakes, even the police, or don't you remember?" He grimaces. "The officer in charge that night has been put on administrative leave."

"That's all? Just a plain old mistake?"

"What else could it be?"

"I don't know. Maybe he got somebody angry and he was being taught a lesson," she ventures cautiously.

"Somebody?" His voice takes on an immediate edge. "Like one of our people?"

She shrugs her shoulders.

"Maybe that's how they do things in the big city, Kate, but that's not Santa Barbara style. We're clean—as clean as we can get, which is pretty good most of the time. We're too square not to be. Like the T-shirt says, shit happens."

"Did you guys interview the men who were in the tank with Bascomb?"

"Of course."

"What can you tell me about them? Any of them."

"Your garden-variety bunch of drunks and crazies."

"Did any of them have records?"

"They all have records. What kind of people do you think go to jail?"

"For a violent crime. Assault, rape, B&E, attempted murder. Stuff like that."

"These pieces of shit? They're a bunch of sad cases, they can't get out of the way of their own vomit. I heard secondhand a couple of them might have been petty drug dealers or low-rent pimps, but that's conjecture." He shakes his head, sadly. "These poor bastards. You think they should've been in there in the first place? Man gets drunk, he goes to jail? What kind of society is that? Most of those people are so screwed up they can barely remember their own names. They ought to be in an institution where they can get treatment, which is where they used to be until they let all the inmates out of the asylum." He picks up a handful of sand, sifts it through his fingers. "This is my favorite subject. Don't let me get started. The cops and the schools, we're supposed to cure all society's ills. It's a crock," he spits out.

"Were they interrogated about the suicide?"

"Of course."

"And?"

"The same story, more or less. Everything was filtered through a haze of booze, so there's holes, but the general theme held up. They went to sleep and when they woke up—hello, swinging from the rafters. Enough to cure a man of drinking, at least for a day or two."

"Are their names and addresses on file?"

"For what it's worth, yes. For what it's worth, it's worthless. You think people like these have a real address, or real ID? Like they have valid California driver's licenses and Visa cards? They sleep on the street and they use whatever name pops into their head at the time. They're poor, pathetic bastards."

"So what?" Kate counters. "Why couldn't one of them, some, all of them be a suspect? Frank Bascomb died in the same cell they were occupying."

"One of *them* killed Bascomb? You think that's possible?"

"It's possible. Not likely, but why isn't it possible?"

Herrera laughs. "Go back to Oakland, Kate. You've obviously got a more capable breed of criminal there. Here's why it's not logical," he tells her. "If these sad morons are going to commit great bodily harm they aren't going to go to the trouble of stringing a man up. That's hard work. They're going to stomp him to death is what they're going to do. Kick his ribs in, his eyes, kick in his teeth, kick him in the balls, wherever."

He looks at her to see if he's getting through.

"You were a cop. You know this is a futile exercise. Now look—I have no intention of telling you how to conduct your business, but you could raise some hopes that shouldn't be raised, and you could piss off some people who you don't want to be unfriendly to you."

"Are you one of them?" she asks, beginning to get pissed.

"I'm a police officer, not a politician," he answers without answering. "Can I give you a piece of free advice?" he continues. It's a rhetorical question. "Do a pro forma investigation for your client, and then bail out. For your own good."

"Why?"

"Do I have to spell it out for you? The Sparks family was highly embarrassed by Frank Bascomb, that's why. They are not at all unhappy that he met his accidental demise, except for Laura, who's too young to know better."

"That's pretty cold."

"It's a fact of life."

"A cold fact."

"Doesn't matter. They want the lid kept on, so that's how it'll be. Nothing illegal, mind you, no sandbagging, but nothing out of the ordinary, either."

"I've got to respect my client's wishes," she insists.

"If you truly want to do good by your client," he advises her, "you'll wrap this up neatly and move on. Look, Kate, if her parents and grandmother find out she's hired a PI behind their backs, it won't sit well with them."

"What could they be afraid of?" she asks him.

"Something unpleasant. There are circles within circles, it's not always clear-cut, these investigations."

"I don't know that?" she bridles.

"And hey, make sure everything's by the book." He pauses. "If by some miracle something floats to the surface—nothing should, but if it does? And it looks like it could be a law-enforcement situation? You keep me informed, hear?"

"Yeah," she agrees reluctantly, "okay."

She takes out notebook and pencil, a reporter's notebook, the style that can fit into your back pocket.

"How do I get in touch with these men?" she asks.

"You'd have to go into their files for that."

"Will you?"

He turns to her. "You're really looking to put my ass in a sling, aren't you?"

"I thought you were above that petty stuff, that you couldn't be intimidated," she taunts Herrera. "That's okay, Juan," she says, "I'll get hold of that information, with or without your help."

"Fuck." He throws up his hands. "Me and my big mouth. I'll do it, this one time. But then drop it, okay? For your own good."

That's what she loves about men, about cops, especially men cops: hit 'em in their macho and they'll rise to the bait every time.

"No promises," she tells him. "And I'll be the judge of my own good."

He sighs. "As long as I'm not implicated."

"I said."

"I'll drop copies of their booking slips in the mail to you."

"You couldn't fax them this afternoon?" she asks, hoping. She's double antsy now, she wants to get it on, see what's hidden under these rocks that everybody's trying not to show her.

He hesitates. "I'll get them to you as quick as I can."

"Thank you," she says. She means it—he really is a nice guy. "Meanwhile, while I'm waiting, can you give me an address for any of them off the top of your head, even if it's the Rescue Mission?"

"That's as good a place to start as any, but I don't think you'll have any luck."

"Why not?"

"Because they don't exist," he explains. "They're like illegal aliens—they're here, but they really aren't. It's like trying to catch smoke."

"They exist," she insists. "They were there."

"They were there all right," Herrera agrees with her. "But they aren't anymore."

It's a beautiful day at the beach. Eleven in the morning, the sky is blazing blue without a hint of haze, wisps of cirrus clouds float high above, the temperature is unseasonably mild, there's a slight breeze coming in off the ocean. In the near distance, so close you feel you can almost touch them, the Channel Islands rise up out of the water, jagged ridges of rock and vegetation, the only land between this coastline and Hawaii, four thousand miles to the west. In the channel, clusters of oil rigs reach their deceptively spindly frames to the sky. They've been there so long—going on thirty years now—that nobody much notices them anymore. Closer, to the south, the high-rise buildings of the university tower above the waterline, the windows glittering as they catch and reflect the mid-day rays.

A familiar dock protrudes out into the water. Frank and Rusty sailed into this dock. Rusty was killed and Frank was arrested. The Sparks family's dock is no longer the private sanctuary they want it to be.

Several dozen people are here. Some by invitation; the rest, mostly members of various local environmental groups who devote much of their time and energy towards preserving the local oceanic ecology, have crashed the party. No attempt was made to stop them from coming, even though this is private property. The order to let them in came directly from Miranda Sparks.

At the center of this crush Miranda and Dorothy stand with their backs to the sea, facing their guests, chatting with friends. They're both dressed ranch-style, although Miranda's jeans have been tailored to flatter her ass.

The principal guest of honor (whom Miranda has situated next to her) is John Wilkerson, a patrician gentleman who bears a pretty good resemblance to the late Eric Sevareid, the famous CBS correspondent. Wilkerson is president of The Friends Of The Sea, which makes him the most important figure in oceanography in the world after Jacques Cousteau. He flew here from his home in New York solely for this presentation, that's how important it is. Other notables are Dr. George Woolrich, chancellor of UCSB, and Dr. Jan Lovellette, a world-famous oceanographer and marine biologist who is a senior professor at the Scripps Institute in La Jolla.

Among the local environmentalists on hand, standing near the back, is Marty Pachinko. As he looks at Miranda, she turns to him and smiles. Caught by surprise, he smiles back, then averts his gaze.

Miranda waits until everyone is in place, especially the television crews. Satisfied that all is in order, she steps forward to the portable podium, which is adorned with the crest of the University of California.

"On behalf of all the members of the Sparks family, I want to thank you for coming out here today," Miranda tells her guests, who include over a dozen TV crews, anchorpeople, and news reporters. This is a carefully staged media event.

"We have an announcement to make," she continues, making eye contact with her guests, each in turn; as her gaze falls upon Wilkerson she smiles seductively.

He returns her smile with an almost imperceptible nod, checking out of the corners of his eyes to make sure it was for him alone. Wilkerson is in his early sixties, an attractive man, a powerhouse, CEO of a large Wall St. brokerage firm as well as a renowned conservationist. Women find him attractive, which he makes good use of.

But this woman: very special. Maybe, if he's reading the signals correctly, he should plan on staying over; he'll call his office in New York, rebook his flight to leave tomorrow instead of tonight, as it's now planned. His secretary can reserve a suite at the San Ysidro Ranch. The suite the Kennedys honeymooned in; he's found use for it before. First he'll want to check her intentions out, to make sure it isn't mere flirting.

"This piece of property has been held in preserve for several years," Miranda says to her audience, breaking Wilkerson's reverie. "It's never been used for any commercial purposes. The Sparks family has always wanted it to be that way, going back decades."

She looks at Dorothy, who nods as if on cue.

"However," Miranda continues, "we have recently come to believe that if a proper use of this part of our property could be found that would be beneficial, without violating its integrity, we would be selfish and shortsighted not to grant such a usage."

She pauses for a moment. She's been speaking without notes, standing in front of everyone, completely at ease, hands in jeans pockets like a regular person.

"We're happy to say that we've found a good use. We have

decided—" here she pauses for a moment, glances at Dorothy, who again smiles and nods, ". . . to set aside fifty acres of our property to establish a comprehensive school of oceanography under the aegis of the University of California, for research into marine life and for the use and education of the public. This project will be jointly controlled by The Friends Of The Sea, whose president, Mr. John Wilkerson, has graciously consented to be with us today, and by what will be the newly established oceanography school of UCSB, to be headed by Dr. Jan Lovellette, one of the world's leading authorities on marine life, who will be coming to Santa Barbara to assume the chairmanship of this department. To ensure that Dr. Lovellette would leave her present position at Scripps to come up and take over this new department, we are also pledging five hundred thousand dollars to endow a permanent chair of oceanography."

Everyone breaks into applause, accompanied by whoops and shouting. TV cameraman rush towards Miranda, trying to get a good closeup.

Miranda looks over at Marty Pachinko. He's looking at her with a stunned expression on his face, like she had pole-axed him with a two-by-four.

She turns away from him. "John Wilkerson, president of The Friends Of The Sea, would like to say a few words." She steps aside for Wilkerson.

"On behalf of The Friends Of The Sea," Wilkerson begins—he has one of those Boston Brahmin accents that comes only after generations of schooling at Choate and Harvard—"we wish to thank you. This is indeed a wonderful donation, one of the largest and most important ever received anywhere in the United States. We are thrilled to be a part of it, along with the university."

He smiles at Miranda, checking out her ass at the same time, casually but so that there's no mistaking his look.

Miranda doesn't miss the look. Men have been checking her out like that since she was twelve.

"The Sparks Foundation is happy to do this," Miranda says, taking charge again. "It's the right thing to do, the right time to do it, and, most importantly, the right place. This is the only place," she informs the gathered group, "that would work for this project." She turns to the oceanographer. "Dr. Lovellette will say a few words about the project specifics."

Jan Lovellette, as plain and unadorned as Miranda is beautiful and put-together, and clearly uncomfortable in the limelight, smiles tentatively. "This will be a world-class research and teaching facility," she says. "Upon its completion we'll be able to study, observe, and protect all the sea life of this part of the coast, which has certain unique characteristics found nowhere else in the world, and also this will make possible a wonderful educational experience, not only for the people of Santa Barbara County but for everyone."

"How much will the total cost be?" a reporter calls out from the crowd.

"That's a good question," Miranda answers. "We don't have all the specifics yet, but we estimate the total cost will be about one hundred and fifty million dollars."

"Where is that money going to come from?" another reporter asks.

"Another good question. Did you bring your checkbook?" Miranda asks with a smile. "Seriously, that is *the* multi-million-dollar question. I can give you an answer, but only in part. The Sparks Foundation, as I have announced, will donate all the land, which is worth several million dollars, as well as endowing the chair—" she pauses—"providing that private groups and citizens raise the money to build the physical facility."

"Are there groups out there that you know of that will do that?" comes yet another question.

Wilkerson steps forward again. "Our organization will make a contribution, as will many other environmental groups from all over the world. It's going to be a huge task, but this is too good an opportunity to waste. If we don't pull this off we'll never get another chance like it. We have been in close contact with a major corporation that has indicated they might cover the entire cost of the project, but it would be premature at this point to identify them."

Miranda smiles again for the cameras. "Thank you all for attending. We'll be keeping you posted as to our progress."

The party's over. The newspeople rush to file and air their stories. The attendees cluster in groups, talking excitedly.

Marty Pachinko approaches Miranda.

"Congratulations," he offers with chagrin.

"Thank you," Miranda answers with a smile.

"I feel like a jerk, after the way I carried on back at the county. But you blindsided me, when you didn't have to."

"Well, Marty, you are a jerk," she states, still smiling. "You should have known better. The truth is, you blindsided yourself, you didn't need any help from me. Anyway, I like to tweak you," she adds teasingly. "It's so easy."

He flinches. "You could have said something then," he replies doggedly.

"I wasn't sure we could pull this off. I'm still not; we have a lot of money to raise, and I'm sure you and your friends will find something in this to oppose. You always do."

Wilkerson holds back until the others have moved ahead of Miranda and him.

"Your generosity is extraordinary," he tells her.

"That's very nice of you to say that."

He pauses a moment, diplomatically. "I would like to thank you . . . a bit more formally," he says.

"Diamonds are a girl's best friend," she laughs. Quickly, she puts a hand on his forearm, lets it linger a brief moment, then withdraws it. "Being of assistance in an undertaking so important and so compelling is plenty of reward for me—for all of us." Again, a light touch, this time on the back of his hand.

"Perhaps . . ." He hesitates. Is he going to look foolish? The hell with it; he has to go with it.

"Yes?"

"I'm staying in town tonight. The San Ysidro Ranch." Betty Sue, his secretary for over twenty years, will get him in there tonight. She's done this countless times. "If you're not busy, perhaps you . . . you and your husband . . . could join me in a celebratory dinner."

She smiles; a thousand-watter. "Unfortunately, my husband is in San Francisco, on other family business. But I'm free, and I'd love to join you."

He walks her to her car as they make arrangements for the evening. She'll meet him at his hotel, it's easier than making him drive to her house.

"Seven o'clock, then," he says. His heart is beating like a tom-tom, he feels like an adolescent, for chrissake.

"I can hardly wait," she says as they part.

The Sparks family owns several buildings in the old section of Santa Barbara, where the first adobes were built by the initial wave of Spanish settlers: the Ortegas, the De La Guerras, and others, dating back to 1810. Their two-story building, at 188 East De La Guerra, which houses the family foundation and their business offices, is considered one of the most historically important structures in the county.

Native American blankets, baskets, bows and arrows adorn the walls of the family's inner offices; an accompanying motif is carried out in the rest of the complex, which is decorated in 19th-century western style— old rifles and shotguns, saddles inlaid with silver, sombreros, all the trappings.

Miranda enters, briskly striding across the reception area to her office.

"Your five o'clock appointment is here, Mrs. Sparks," her personal secretary informs her. "Mr. Hopkins, from San Francisco."

Miranda, whose mind has been going in a million different directions, looks over, momentarily startled.

Blake Hopkins—the man waiting for her—is the man who fucked her standing up on her own porch out at her ranch, the same man who watched from the back of the Board of Supervisors' chamber when she made her request to have her beachfront property rezoned.

He smiles at her pleasantly, puts down the copy of *The New Yorker* he was glancing through.

Miranda recovers in a flash. As she passes into her private office: "Put the telephones on hold, Celeste, and then you can leave. I'll close up when I go."

"Yes, Mrs. Sparks." Celeste has been with Miranda for six years. She knows how to do what she's told.

Miranda ushers Hopkins into her office, closes the door, locks it.

"Busy day," Hopkins comments.

"No rest for the weary," she tells him. She doesn't look weary—she looks sharp, preternaturally bright, almost.

"How did your meeting with the dolphin lovers go?" he asks.

"They're happy campers."

"And you?"

"We get a ton of great publicity and a humongous tax writeoff on a piece of property that we aren't doing anything with, and we still own it. And most importantly, we've gotten the most extreme faction of our local environmentalists off our back."

"You're cynical," he understates admiringly.

"I'm realistic," she corrects him.

"All in all, not a bad day's work," he remarks.

"The day isn't over yet," she says, crossing to him and kissing him full on the mouth. He responds by kissing the back of her neck, lightly nibbling his way up to her ear. She shudders as he bites the lobe.

"We have to be careful in here," she cautions. "Someone might walk in."

"You locked the door," he says. "And since when do you care?"

"Because if anyone sees you . . ."

"No one in this town knows me."

"But they will."

"But they don't."

With intense, sudden ardor she's on him, she's taking off his clothes and hers at the same time, he yanks her boots off her, her jeans are down around her ankles, he's tearing off his own shoes, socks, pants, all the while she's kissing him, his chest, his back, their shirts come off, she's braless, her breasts stand straight out, the nipples tipped up, goosebumps popping, he lifts her hard tight ass off the floor and goes down on her while he's on his knees, eating her through her cotton panties, they get into sixty-nine position on the floor, his cock in her mouth, his mouth on her vagina, middle finger inside, they turn to each other, embracing, she takes him in her, slowly, inch by inch, they fuck intensely, savoring each other.

When she comes it's with her whole body, scalp to soles and all in between, one massive contraction of muscle, pulling his ass to her so tight he'll be black and blue later.

"Shit, lady," he says, panting, lying on his back, his torso wet with her sweat.

She wipes herself in the adjacent private bathroom, pees, comes back into the office, puts her clothes back on. He's already dressed, sans tie.

Sex was good, it's over, it's time for business. He takes a sheaf of papers from his briefcase, hands them to her.

"Where do we stand?" she asks, leafing through them.

"We're a few months away from finishing up our geology studies," he tells her, "and it's all looking good."

"How good?" She's impatient, and she doesn't want him to see her being nervous, she never shows a lack of control.

"As good as we hoped for. Better."

"I feel like Faust," she says. Her hand is shaking—from holding the papers, not the sex. She never loses control from sex.

"Don't ever look back," he advises her firmly. "The people of Santa Barbara County are going to have a world-class oceanography school."

"I'm going to be vilified. My family's going to be smeared."

"Not if you present it the right way. We'll be the heavies, that's our job. You go along with the program, you and your family will be fine."

She runs her fingers through her hair, a nervous habit. "It isn't a good idea for you to come here anymore, not until this is all settled." She hands him back the documents.

"Whatever you say." He puts the papers in his briefcase. "It's an imperfect world, Miranda. Don't beat yourself up over it."

"I never beat myself up," she says.

He starts out. "I'll be in touch."

"Go out the back way," she says, leading him to a private exit at the rear of her office.

"Don't get paranoid," he cautions her. "It'll show."

"I'm in control," she assures him. "Don't worry."

The doorbell is ringing. Kate jumps out of the shower, hurriedly wrapping herself in a bath towel.

"Who is it?" she calls through the front door as she stands in the hallway, dripping all over the floor.

"Juan Herrera," comes through the door. "I brought those files that you wanted. I was in the neighborhood, and you said you wanted them pronto."

"Shit," she curses to herself. She'd thought he'd drop them in the mail, she wasn't expecting a personal delivery at her apartment. This guy's faster than Federal Express.

"Just a sec."

She grabs a pair of shorts and a T-shirt off a chair, pulls them on. Despite her hurried toweling-off she's still damp from the shower; her nipples are outlined against the white cotton.

He rings again.

"Okay, okay." They're only breasts, the man's a cop, in the line of duty he's seen hundreds of breasts, plenty of them better than these.

She throws the door open. "Sorry," she starts to explain, "I was running at the beach and I wanted to wash the sand off . . ." She stops talking. He's gaping at her, not able to hide his look.

Her hands go quickly to her breasts, cross-armed. She feels her face flushing.

"Sorry," he fumbles. "I didn't . . . here." He thrusts a manila envelope at her.

She reaches to take it, again exposing a wet breast. What's going on here, she doesn't mind guys checking her, it's retro and antifeminist as hell but so what, it doesn't hurt anyone, it's a compliment, so why is she feeling shy with him? Because he's a married cop, the big no-no?

"Don't stand outside," she says, "come in, my neighbors don't need to see you standing on my doorstep. A cop," she adds, having to make some kind of justification.

He comes in, a couple of steps. "How would they know?"

"A blind man could tell."

He tries to look away from her, but he can't.

"I'll be right back. Make yourself at home, such as it is." She goes into the bedroom, closing the door for modesty.

The apartment has all the personality of a motel room. It's clean, that's the best compliment you can give it. Totally sterile, not a woman's touch in it, not even some personal photos. She sleeps, eats, showers, and shits here, but she doesn't live here.

She comes out of the bedroom wearing a summer dress that hangs on her loosely. Her bra straps stick out under the shoulders.

"Thanks for the personal service." Trying to undercut the awkwardness, she asks, "since you made such a special effort, can I get you a beer? I'm having one."

"No, I don't . . . all right, one quick one."

"Quick isn't my style," she joshes him.

They sit catty-corner from each other, couch and armchair, drinking Coors out of the bottle.

"How long have you lived here?" he asks. Now that she's decent he's more comfortable, his coat is open, revealing the gun snug against his hip.

"Chez Kate? Six months, eight. I don't know, it's home." She takes a hit from her brew. "Not!" Another swallow; this beer's disappearing fast.

"You're too busy," he offers politely.

"Too lazy. I keep meaning to find a decent place, but something always comes up, if it isn't one thing, it's another." She's about to joke "I need a wife," but catches herself. A remark like that would not be appropriate at this particular moment.

He is a handsome fellow, which nobody can deny. She certainly can't.

She drains her beer. "Can I get you another one, since I'm getting myself one anyway?"

"Sure." He tosses her his empty bottle.

She takes two more out of the refrigerator, church-keys the tops, and as she turns to take them back into the living room he's standing there, right behind her, so close she almost bangs into him.

The thought that flashes through her mind is, This is the wrong thing to do, and the right man to do it with.

"Cheers," she says, and as she leans forward to hand him his bottle her arms go around his neck instead and she's kissing him, a full kiss, their tongues massaging each other's, his arms around her, one on her back, the other moving down to her ass, stroking it, oh Jesus, fuck me right here, standing up, on the counter, in the sink, on the floor, anywhere, anyhow, quick or slow, he's a cop, you jerk, a *cop* for chrissakes!, *and* he's a married man, where is your self-respect, where is your sense of worth? Do you have any, any at all?

She wants him; badly.

So it turns out there are no rules, no rules you can't break.

The phone rings.

They both jump. Some beer sloshes out of the bottles.

"Sorry about that," she says, handing him a wet bottle while shaking the foam off her hand. She's breathing like she just ran a ten-K.

She takes the phone off the wall, facing him, smiling. He'd been hard, she could feel him through her dress. "Kate Blanchard," she says into the receiver.

"Hello, Kate. It's Cecil Shugrue," the voice on the other end announces. "From Fiesta. Do you remember?"

"Sure," she says back. She's been waiting all week for him to call, checking her messages every day, hoping he'd be on the machine. So of course he calls now.

"How's it going?" he asks.

She can feel all the air seeping out of the balloon.

"Oh fine, fine."

Juan has drifted back into the living room.

"I'm in town. I thought maybe we could get together, have dinner. If you're not busy, that is, I realize I'm calling late, but I thought in case . . . I'd like to see you," he tells her.

She can tell from the way he said it that he really does.

"Kate?"

"Yeah, I'm here." Something has to give. "Hang on a minute."

She lays the receiver on top of the phone and walks into the living room, where Juan is sucking at his bottle, trying to act nonchalant and not doing a very good job at it.

"It's a client," she lies. Usually she lies easily, it's a part of the job that doesn't cause her any sweat. This one does. "Who needs to see me, right away."

It's simple—one's married, the other isn't. If Juan has to have her, he'll come back. Otherwise, it's better they don't get started. She needs to keep him as a useful source, on the inside. That could be a problem if they became lovers.

"I've got to be going anyway," he says, his voice flat.

She walks him to the door. "Thanks for bringing me that stuff. I really appreciate your doing it."

"*De nada.* Remember, you didn't get it from me."

"I'll call you." That sounds weird, what with them all tangled up thirty seconds ago, and the phone off the hook right now. "To let you know what's going on—with my case."

"If you want."

"I mean if anything comes up you should know about."

"That would be good." He turns and walks away, straightening his tie and buttoning up his jacket.

That was close, she thinks. About ten seconds; or less.

She goes back into the kitchen, picks up the phone.

"Sorry for the delay," she says to Cecil. "As it so happens, I just had a cancellation in my incredibly busy schedule, so I'm completely free."

Sixty-plus-year-olds don't have a sixteen-year-old's on-call hardness, it's an immutable fact of life; but for his age, John Wilkerson is more than satisfactory in the sack.

They're in his five-hundred-dollar-a-night suite at the San Ysidro.

"You're marvelous," he tells her. "You've got a body like a twenty-five-year-old," he adds.

"It was good for me, too," she says, warmly. "Thanks for the compliment," she adds. As if she doesn't know that most twenty-five-year-old women would kill to have her body.

Now she can enjoy dinner without the specter of sex and conquest hanging over their heads. She's going to need strong support from big shots in the environmental movement when Hopkins goes public with his plan; the locals will have ten thousand cows. Wilkerson will be an important ally.

They have dinner at the Wine Cask. She makes him pay for their roll in the hay by ordering an '85 Romanée-Conti La Tache, which runs $450 a bottle.

"I spoke to Dick Hartstein earlier this afternoon," he tells her over dessert. "He's the editor for the Environment section of *The New York Times*, very important man. They're going to do a feature on this project. Everybody and his brother will want to, but they're the ones you have to take into account. And the Friends Of The Sea magazine, of course, but our lead time is three to six months. The *Times* will be a matter of weeks. They'll be sending one of their top photographers out, and they'll require a picture of you as well."

"I'm not doing this for publicity," she says abruptly. "The foundation operates behind the lines. The less that people know about us, the better."

"I understand completely," he tells her. "But it can't be avoided," he states. "This is a very big deal."

"If you say so. I defer to your judgment. But as low-key as possible, please."

"I'll let them know. I'll come along, of course, to insure that everything is done in the best of taste. Nothing sensational—nothing except you," he can't refrain from stating.

"You're sweet." She smiles at him, a dazzler, a smile that could light up a ballpark.

She needed to be with him tonight, to set things up. He made it easy by coming at her up on the ranch, but she would have found a way. "We could still come off looking bad," she says, her smile turning into a frown.

"How in the world could anybody knock what you're doing?" he asks incredulously. "You're establishing a world-class research and teaching facility."

HOUSE OF SMOKE

"What do you think the hard-core environmentalists will do when the big corporations start donating money to this? Because that's where it's going to come from, it always does. What are people going to say when RJ Reynolds or Chevron write big checks for this?"

He shrugs. "It's the nature of the beast."

"Not in these parts."

She sips her dessert wine. "You should have seen what went on when we applied for the rezoning on this," she continues. "This man from one of the local environmental watchdog groups was up there ranting and raving like this was the greatest rape of the land since they strip-mined West Virginia. We don't even mention a specific project, but he was absolutely against us. And the worst part is, my mother-in-law sits on the board of his organization and is their biggest contributor."

In anger she knocks back the rest of her drink, which she immediately regrets; you don't drink a great Sauternes like it's a bottle of Pellegrino.

"The environmental movement can lose sight of the big picture sometimes," he agrees, "and I say that as a committed, vigilant environmentalist. You have to know what's intrinsically wrong and what is benign. There are extremists in every facet of society," he explains, "including ours.

"Listen, Miranda," he continues. "No one in the world can doubt your environmental credentials. Not after today."

"I wish."

"This is a promise," he tells her, "from me to you. If you ever have a problem with an environmental organization, any group, for any reason, I'll defend you. I will stand shoulder to shoulder with you and tell whoever it might be where the hell to get off."

"Thank you." She doesn't bat her eyes at him but she does slip her foot from her shoe and give his ankle a quick toe job under the table.

"You have my solemn word," he vows. God, what a woman. He's becoming aroused again, just from the touch of one stockinged foot.

———

Three tables over, so close you could almost pass a bottle of wine back and forth but just far enough away so that you can't hear the other table's conversation, Kate is having dinner with Cecil. He's dressed like a regular person this time, he left the cowboy stuff back at the ranch. More comforting is the fact that there's no ring on his left hand.

She did the right thing. She told herself that as she watched Juan walking away from her apartment, when she was drying her hair and arranging it, when she was selecting a suitable dress to wear to dinner.

Juan had gotten her hot. It was glands, no question. At least she hopes that's all it was. Maybe she'll find out with Cecil here, later. Maybe he'll light a fire under her. She'll supply the matches, she's primed.

She checks out the various customers, force of habit, narrowing her focus on the man and woman seated three tables away. The woman looks familiar but Kate can't place her. Someone rich, whoever she is. Her dress cost a couple thousand dollars, easy, and she has a big diamond ring on her finger, which this man didn't give her, they're not married. She's flirting with him too much to be married to him.

As the maître d' passes he pours some wine into Kate's glass, the house chardonnay, eighteen dollars a bottle, a nice wine.

"How's everything tonight, Mr. Shugrue?" he asks. "It's nice to see you."

"Everything's great, Wayne, thanks."

"Enjoy your dinner," the maître d' says, moving away.

"You're a regular," Kate observes, forking up some eggplant puree.

He nods yes. "It's a nice room, and they have the best wine list in town. So what're you working on these days?" he asks, deflecting the conversation back to her.

"This and that," she answers. Working hours are over for the day, she doesn't want to talk shop. She takes a sip of wine. "Umm, good."

"Locally grown grapes. The county is one of the best wine regions in the world, which people are beginning to recognize."

"Do you know about that stuff?" she asks. "About everybody in this town seems to. Me, I just drink it."

He cocks his head, looking at her kind of funny.

"What?" she asks.

"I didn't tell you? When we met?"

"Tell me what?"

He laughs. He's got a nice, genuine laugh. "I grow grapes for a living," he tells her.

"You're a winemaker?" She's astounded.

"I make some wine. I sell grapes more than I make wine."

"I'm impressed."

"It's farming," he says modestly, "like growing artichokes or cantaloupes. We used to run cattle, now it's grapes."

A sudden thought comes to her. "This wine—" she holds up her glass—"the grapes from this wine, did you grow them?"

A big grin: "Yes."

"I'll be damned." She takes another sip. "You've been holding out on me, Cecil. You're a man of many talents."

She was turned on before and now she's more turned on, this guy is cool.

"I don't know about that," he responds. "Anyway, we were talking about you, what you're up to these days. Are you working on a case, do you do a bunch at the same time, what I know about detectives comes from novels and movies."

"Can't we talk about something other than business?" she asks.

"If you sold insurance, I'd say yes, but what you do is interesting."

"I guess to an outsider it is," she agrees. "When you're doing it, though, it can be pretty boring. As a matter of fact, though," she allows, "I am working on something kind of interesting."

It's the wine, it's his being close, it's wanting to make a connection. "I shouldn't talk about these things, a client wants to know his PI isn't blabbing his story all over town."

"I'm not much for gossip," he says. "If you tell me not to say something, I won't."

"I'm working on a murder case," she confides.

"That sounds pretty important."

"It could be."

"Is it something local?" he asks. "I haven't heard about any murders around these parts recently."

"It's local," she tells him. "The reason you haven't heard about it as a murder is because it hasn't been called that."

He shoots her a quizzical look.

"Officially, on the books, it's a suicide. My client knew the deceased. She—" That was a slip, she can't give away names or otherwise identify Laura. "My client thinks it might not have been. Suicide. That this person was killed and it was made to look like a suicide."

Now he really is staring at her.

"You're talking about Frank Bascomb," he says.

"I knew I shouldn't have started up with this."

"That's high-profile, Frank dying in the county jail, everyone in town knows about it."

"Keep it to yourself, okay?"

"Like I said, I don't gossip." He hesitates before asking her the next question. "Who hired you?"

She shakes her head. "I can't tell you. My client doesn't want anyone to know. I have to respect that."

"Of course, I understand." He looks away for a moment, in the direction of the couple nearby who are finishing their coffee.

"You see that woman?" Cecil asks Kate.

"How could I not? Everyone in this room has noticed her. She's a stunning woman."

"That's Miranda Sparks," Cecil says. "She was Bascomb's boss."

So *that's* Laura's mother. "I've heard about her," Kate says.

"She's famous around town." He cocks a finger at her. "One thing I do know—whoever hired you to look into this suicide of Bascomb's, it wasn't Miranda."

"You're right, it wasn't, but why would you say that?"

"Because Bascomb, her longtime faithful employee, was caught smuggling a million dollars of contraband onto her family's private property," he says. "It made the Sparks family look terrible, and Miranda was furious, especially since she was going into the county the next week to have it rezoned. Frank's getting caught like that could've screwed things up. You don't screw things up for the Sparks family without paying a big-time price—although not that big, I'm not implying anything. But if old Frank had ever wound up beating the case Miranda would've fired him, run him out of the county on a rail, the Sparks family is very protective of their image. Plus it's common knowledge the foreman was sleeping with the owner's daughter, which is a strict no-no. I'll tell you one thing—if you're making a list of people who wanted to see Bascomb out of the way, you put Miranda at the top."

"It sounds like you and Mrs. Sparks aren't exactly bosom buddies," Kate says. No wonder Laura didn't want her mother to know she had hired a private eye to investigate the mysterious circumstances surrounding Bascomb's death.

"I personally don't have any complaints about Miranda. We get along okay . . . considering."

Considering what? she thinks; but doesn't ask.

"Different points of view. About life," he says, reading her mind.

Their dinner completed, Wilkerson pays the bill and pulls Miranda's chair out for her. As she rises she leans in and says something to him in his ear; he turns and looks in Kate and Cecil's direction.

Miranda links arms with him, leads him over to Cecil's table.

"Please don't stand up, Cecil," Miranda says, but he already has. She touches her cheek to his, which Cecil endures self-consciously. A look passes between them, which Kate, who's watching, picks up on with curiosity.

"Cecil Shugrue, I'd like you to meet John Wilkerson, from The Friends Of The Sea. John and I are working together on an important project." To Wilkerson she says, "this is my friend and fellow-rancher Cecil Shugrue, who makes lovely wines, among other nice things."

Cecil extends his hand. Wilkerson takes it reluctantly, wondering if Miranda and this guy ever had a relationship of any kind.

"Nice meeting you," Cecil says. "And this is my friend Kate Blanchard. Kate, Miranda Sparks."

Kate looks good tonight—better than good, she put some thought and time into this outfit she's wearing, but next to Miranda Sparks she's wallpaper, invisible. Poor Laura, she thinks, to have a mother this powerful.

"Hello," Kate says.

"Hello," Miranda says back, checking Kate out cursorily. "It's good to see you," Miranda says heartily to Cecil, for one brief moment focusing all her attention on him. Turning it off as quickly: "And you, too, nice meeting you . . . Kate? We've got to run. I'll see you soon, Cecil?"

"I'm sure." He's pretty dry.

"Watch this one," Miranda says to Kate, half-winking at her, woman to woman.

"Nice meeting you, too," Kate says to Miranda, who doesn't hear her, she's already taken Wilkerson's arm and is leading him out, greeting a few other parties as they make their exit.

"Close personal friend of yours?" Kate asks Cecil, as she watches Miranda make her regal retreat.

He shrugs his hands: *comme ci, comme ça.* "We've known each other a long time. I wouldn't call it close or personal. I run across her husband once in a while, he's an okay guy. Like I said, we come at life from different angles."

"Butter wouldn't melt in her mouth," Kate states, chewing the bone raw. She doesn't want to be catty but Miranda Sparks rubbed her the wrong way. She hopes Cecil's being honest, that he and Miranda aren't friends; but if they are, tough shit. She goes where her gut leads her.

"Deep down she's ice," Cecil says, mollifying her.

"But she covers it with a lot of heat."

"She covers it with a lot of heat," he agrees with her. "And I don't feel like wasting my time talking any more about her, if that's okay with you."

Dorothy Sparks sits in a weathered Adirondack chair on the back lawn of her waterfront estate, looking out to sea. All the lights are out; she's in darkness. On the eastern edge of the horizon the low-hanging moon, a few days past full, casts lantern ripples that make the ocean look like it's lit by pale-yellow fluorescent globes from underneath the surface. Far down the beach, near the Miramar Hotel, a lone nocturnal fisherman is casting his line, standing at the water's edge, the foam breaking over his high green-rubber boots, the anchovy on his hook shimmering silver against the sky, against the blackness and the clouds and stars.

It's a warm night, not very humid, and clear. The air is still. Dorothy wears an old summer dress, of the style that was fashionable when Rita Hayworth was a movie star; she was never one to spend money on clothes, she wears the same dresses for decades. On the table next to her is a vodka collins in a highball glass.

Dorothy's house, which she's lived in for forty years, is an old rambling mansion that was built in the craftsman style at the turn of the century. It's two stories, redwood construction, too many windows and french doors, the kind of inefficient house that isn't built anymore and is great to live in, especially for large families with lots of kids. She and her late husband didn't have lots of kids, they only had Frederick, but they had dogs and horses and servants and they filled the place up.

Frederick would have benefited from having brothers and sisters, but after his birth, which was difficult, Dorothy couldn't have any more children. All the energy went into their son, all the love and concern and fear and pampering.

Besides the main house, which overlooks the ocean from a bluff about forty feet high, there is a guesthouse, a studio (which used to be a house for the gardener and his wife, who was the laundress, when they had a live-in gardener and laundress), a large garage with chauffeur's quarters, a stable for horses, a tennis court. In the old days, up until the 1970s, Dorothy and her husband maintained a large staff, more servants than family. You needed a lot of help to run a house, with all the entertaining and so forth. Now she's down to two live-ins, a maid and a cook. A gardener comes three times a week, but doesn't live on the property.

After her husband died, Dorothy cut all the dead wood away. It's easier, you can spend too much of your life worrying about what's going on in your house, consumed with the minutiae of routine. Now she has time to think, to do what is important, which to her means protecting the environment and helping those less fortunate. Miranda oversees all the family business, but the foundation is Dorothy's child, her passion. She is someone who believes that one person can make a difference in the world.

As she ponders the events of the day she reflects on Miranda. Miranda always wanted more. That was the reason Dorothy turned over the company's reins to her instead of to Frederick, her own flesh. He already had enough, he wasn't hungry. Dorothy is a good businesswoman in her own right, and one thing she knows, you have to want it. If you don't you'll lose what you have.

The ceremony this morning was a good example of Miranda's mind at work. The family lost nothing, really, they don't do anything with that land up there, and they gained a great amount of goodwill and support, which down the line will pay a dividend. For every motion there is a corresponding countermotion, in moral deeds as well as physical ones.

Dorothy also believes (or she's convinced herself she believes, which by now has become one and the same) that deep down Miranda is a good person, that her pushiness and bravado and toughness is a shield against her humble beginnings, a need to prove herself. It's pop psychology, Dorothy knows that, but that doesn't mean there isn't truth to it, she knows her daughter-in-law, after twenty-eight years you can't not know somebody you're that intimate with. She's seen Miranda in unguarded moments, when the vulnerability shows through.

Most importantly, what she has forced herself to find peace with, is that Miranda is the wife of her only child, and she has always been blind when it comes to Frederick. His artistic needs and dreams, his lack of toughness in the business world, his etherealness—she has cherished those qualities in him for all of his life, delighting in those attributes that have made him the sweet man he is—have been the cause of her pain and of letting him go alone into the world.

Dorothy knows that Miranda has always believed that she manipulated Frederick Sparks, the scion to one of the largest fortunes in California, into falling for her, and then marrying her, which despite her looks and brains and drive was a major coup to pull off. But the wise old lady is no fool; she was the one who did the manipulating, it was the protective mother who warded off all the logical candidates of their set and maneuvered her shy, endearing son into union with this powerhouse of a woman.

Miranda married Frederick for his money. Dorothy knew that. But she felt that over time Frederick would come to love Miranda (if he hadn't already by the time they got married) and depend on her. What she hadn't anticipated was that Miranda would love Frederick back, in ways more fierce and unfathomable than Dorothy can imagine. There's a lot that's imperfect about their life together, but somehow it works.

As a mother, she takes satisfaction in that.

A pair of headlights cuts through the darkness. A car pulls into the compound, a door opens and shuts.

"Dorothy," Laura calls out, "is that you sitting there?"

"Yes, it's me," Dorothy answers.

Laura walks barefoot across the broad expanse of lawn, her sandals in one hand, canvas briefcase in the other. She flops into a chair next to her grandmother's. "I'm beat," she tells Dorothy. "I should go to bed."

Laura lives here with her grandmother, in the guesthouse, which is situated on the far side of the compound from Dorothy's. It's a good arrangement—neither bothers the other, but both are there to be a sympathetic and understanding ear when needed. Laura can tell Dorothy things—secrets, fears, and dreams—that she can't say to her mother. Her grandmother knew she and Frank were lovers long before anyone else did, and never said a word.

"Where have you been?" Dorothy asks solicitously. "Out with some friends?" She likes Laura's friends, the wilder ones, not the spoiled rich kids. She wishes Laura was wilder more often.

"I had dinner with some friends. Then I took a walk, by myself."

"You've been spending a lot of time by yourself recently. Which isn't like you."

"I've been thinking about Frank. I can't get him out of my mind."

"In what way?"

"His suicide."

Dorothy shifts uncomfortably in her chair. "I don't know if dwelling on what happened to Frank is the best thing for you to be doing, Laura," she says, choosing her words carefully. "I know you want to remember him, but you have to go on with your life, too."

"I know that, Gram, but there are too many things about the way Frank died, and what happened after, that seem weird to me."

"I don't understand."

"Everyone jumping to such a quick conclusion that it was a suicide, for one thing."

"I see." Dorothy picks up her drink. "You don't think it could be anything else, do you?"

"Couldn't it be? Is Frank taking his own life the only possible answer?"

"Unless someone else did, which the police have said didn't happen."

"Maybe they're wrong."

"You think the police are wrong?" Dorothy asks, the worry coming through in her voice.

"I think it's possible, and that maybe they should be looking at it harder—at other possibilities."

"Have you talked to anyone about this? Besides me? Your mother?"

Laura hesitates. Should she tell her grandmother she's hired Kate? She needs to share this secret with somebody, it's hard being alone with something like this.

"I hired a private detective."

"Do you think that was a good idea?" Dorothy asks calmly.

"Why not?" Laura asks.

"Have you ever heard the expression 'Let sleeping dogs lie'?"

"What's that supposed to mean?"

"Frank Bascomb disgraced our family," Dorothy tells her. "*Your* family. He could have hurt us, he could have caused us an awful damage."

"Like what?"

"Like casting doubts on our good name, which is the most important thing anyone can have. Our money is less important than our reputation, Laura. And Frank sullied that."

"How can finding out how he really died, if it wasn't suicide, sully our good name?"

"I don't know. But merely keeping this episode alive, the notoriety of it, can cause damage, can't you see that?"

"Covering it up could cause worse damage."

"But what good is hiring a detective going to do? Especially *you* hiring him. You were there, Laura, and Frank worked for us. People will think you know something, that maybe you were involved and that you're holding information back. This could be very serious and harmful, don't you see that?"

"I don't think anyone will think that," Laura answers. "I'm *not* covering anything up, that's the point."

"At the risk of sounding like a pedantic old lady, maybe you should rethink this." Dorothy shakes her head. "Your mother's going to go through the roof."

"I can't help that," Laura responds, stubbornly.

"That's another thing to rethink."

"I don't need her permission."

"That's a thoughtless remark, Laura. It's not about asking anyone's permission, it's about common decency towards your parents."

"But that's exactly the point, Grandma, don't you see? If I have to check with Mom before doing something that might be controversial, then I *do* need her permission. I'm sick of that. I'm twenty-five years old. I'm sick of having to ask my parents' permission to live my life."

Dorothy steeples her fingers. "Sleep on this," she counsels Laura. "Let us both think about this action, a day or so. If you still want to keep your detective on hire after that, I'll go along with it. But don't do something rash you could regret later."

Laura bites her lip. "All right. I'll sleep on it."

"Thank you."

"But I don't think it's going to change my mind. And Grandma," she adds hastily, "you have to promise me something in return."

"What?" Dorothy asks warily.

"Don't tell Mom. Not till I do."

Dorothy finishes her drink. She'll need another to help her fall asleep tonight.

"All right. I won't tell your mother," Dorothy promises her. "That would be betraying a confidence, which I would never do. But if you continue along this line of action she'll find out, sooner or later, and when she does—well, you know your mother."

"That's why I don't want her to know." Laura stands up, stretches. "I'm beat. I'm going to bed." She gathers up her stuff, kisses Dorothy on the forehead. "Good night."

"Once you let the genie out of the bottle it's not so easy to get him back in," Dorothy counsels her. "Think about that."

"I want to know what it is everyone's so afraid of," Laura responds. "That's what I've been thinking about."

"Is this where you make the wine?" Kate asks Cecil.

They're in the large wine-holding room at his ranch, surrounded by dozens of sixty-gallon oak wine barrels. Even now, in the middle of summer, the room is cool and dark, the concrete floor exuding a musty moistness.

"Where you make the wine is in the field, working the soil and the grapevines," he says. "What happens in here is refinement."

"Come on, there must be more to it than that. Otherwise anyone could do it. I know I couldn't do it."

"You have to have the feel," he tells her. "Like hitting a curveball or blowing jazz tenor."

"I can't do those, either." Looking around some more, she asks, "What kind of wines do you make?"

"Sauvignon blanc, chardonnay, pinot noir. What grows well here. What kind of wine do you like?"

"I like chardonnay."

"Want to try some?"

"Sure."

He leads her down a row, stopping at a barrel that has a silicone bung in it. He takes a tasting-room wineglass off a wooden overhead shelf, picks up a glass wine thief, siphons some wine from the barrel into the wineglass, hands it to her.

"We'll bottle this in the fall."

She sips. "Um, good." She takes a deeper drink. "This is *really* good. This is better than the wine we drank at dinner."

"This'll be a reserve bottling. It's our best stuff." She can hear the pride in his voice. "I'm glad you like it."

"How much will it cost?" she asks.

"About twenty-five a bottle in the store," he says.

"Oh." She looks at the glass. "I shouldn't be drinking this so fast. My speed's the six-dollar category at Long's."

"I'll give you some."

What he just said to her, that was a commitment. She's a woman who doesn't believe in commitments anymore.

"Thank you." She feels shy, suddenly.

———————

They stand on the floor, kissing. He leans her back against a barrel. It's cool to the touch.

"I don't have protection on me," he says. "I didn't last time, either," he admits.

"How come last time you didn't say anything?"

"It was our first time. I didn't think anything would happen."

That figures. He's the kind of man who thinks nice women don't fuck on the first date. That wasn't even a date, it was a pickup. She almost let him, anyway. What he's saying is, he wouldn't have even if it had been okay with her.

Old-fashioned. That's new and different.

"I'm on the pill." Which is a lie, but she doesn't want them to stop this time. "From when I was married, I never quit. It gets to be a habit, like brushing your teeth," she rambles like it's no big deal, wanting him not to read too much into it. "Are you clean?"

"Yes."

"You know for sure?"

"I've only been with one woman for the last three years, and we tested, so I guess I am." Leaving the decision to her, an out if she wants one.

She's been with more than one man, and she's always made them use a rubber. Usually she has one with her; tonight she doesn't, but she wouldn't pull it out anyway. She doesn't want this man to know she's the kind of woman who carries a contraceptive in her purse.

"We'll be all right," she assures him.

They make love in his bedroom. Nice, gentle, unhurried. As he begins to enter her, his blocky muscular body poised on top of hers, the hair on his chest tantalizing her nipples, her hand guides his erection as it finds the fit between her legs and she flashes for a moment on a memory of an image she recalls having seen, of whales copulating in the ocean, roiling the water as they plunge and dive, the male whale's penis gliding in and out of the female like an underwater muscle-sword finding the soft sensual scabbard.

If she could will it he wouldn't come until dawn, they would fuck all night long. She wants him in her, the orgasm is almost irrelevant.

Without warning, Juan Herrera flashes into her mind, staring at her breasts through her wet shirt, her arms around him, her mouth eating his.

She can feel her body tightening. Keep the rhythm going, don't lose this, people's minds wander during sex, it's natural, this *is* where she wants to be, she opens her eyes and looks up at Cecil, whose eyes are closed, the way she wishes hers were, he's not thinking of any other woman, *this* is where she wants to be, trying to bring herself back to being with him again.

She would have fucked Juan Herrera—a married man, a policeman—if the phone hadn't rung at that precise moment. What kind of woman are you? she thinks. How easy are you, anyway? What was Cecil really thinking as he entered this woman he barely knows, who gives herself to him so eagerly, so willingly?

Shame courses through her body like a river of mercury, she feels on fire, burning to ash, all that will be left of her will be a thin plume of smoke that will drift out the window, into nothingness.

She wants this man. And all her instincts tell her she shouldn't have him, because it's too clean.

Let it be, she pleads with herself. Give yourself permission, to believe that you deserve it.

He must feel what she's thinking, that connection she wants so bad, because he is in her a long time.

She wills herself to be back with Cecil, in the present; her orgasms begin, wave after wave, each stronger than the one before.

"How are you doing?" he asks her.

Where does this sweetness come from, she wonders, in such a rough package? "I've come a million times," she breathes into his ear. "I'm going to pass out."

"Good," he says, and then he explodes, and she feels yet another orgasm building, coming on top of his.

———————

They doze for a couple of hours, waking up at the same time, about one in the morning.

"Are you tired?" he asks her.

"I should be, but I'm not."

"Me neither." He sits up out of bed, pulls her up. "Come on, I'll show you something."

They stand at the top of his property in the middle of rows of gravevines, his old ranch pickup truck parked off in the dirt. She is in her light dress, nothing on underneath, and he's wearing a beat-up pair of shorts. Both are barefoot, they threw on whatever was handy. It's hot and the wind is beginning to pick up, foreshadowing a Santa Ana.

He kneels down and plucks a handful of ripe rose-colored grapes off a vine, holds them out to her. "These are Pinot grapes we'll be picking next month."

She takes a couple from his palm, pops them into her mouth.

"Delicious," she tells him, juice running out the corner of her mouth.

Far down below them a set of headlights comes bouncing along a gravel road, heading for a small, dark house that's set back under a grove of eucalyptus trees. The car parks in front of the small house. A man gets out, the moon casting his shadow like a spotlight.

"Hmmm." Cecil grunts.

"Do you know him?"

"I don't think so," he answers cautiously.

The front door of the house opens. A woman comes out onto the porch. The eaves shadow her face.

"I know her, though," Cecil says.

The man walks up to the porch. He and the woman exchange a hurried kiss, say a few words to each other, go inside.

"You didn't recognize her?" Cecil asks Kate, his eyes fixed on the dark house.

"Should I?"

"You just met her." A moment's pause. "That was Miranda Sparks."

"It is?" Talk about weird coincidences. "People tell me this county is one small town. Now I know what they mean."

He nods. "My property line ends there," he says, pointing to a low two-strand barbwire fence about forty yards off. "On the other side is the Sparks ranch, one of the biggest in the county. You stand up here in daytime, you couldn't see to the end of it."

"You're neighbors," Kate says, starting to get the picture.

"I'm just a little old winemaker, Kate. Our property line is the only thing we have in common."

"I wonder who that man was?" she says. "It wasn't the man she was having dinner with, I could tell that from here. Could that be her husband?" she queries, casting a line. Cecil should certainly know Miranda Sparks's husband.

"No. Even without seeing his face I could see that man is younger than Frederick."

So now I've met the daughter and the mother, Kate thinks to herself. I wonder what the husband is like—Laura's father.

And who's this midnight caller? her mind continues on. From the way Miranda Sparks greeted him his visit wasn't unexpected. It's none of her business, as far as her business goes, but the detective in her is intrigued.

They walk back along the row of grapevines to his truck.

"That lady gets around," she comments, the dry earth puffing up around her bare feet.

"That is for sure," is Cecil's terse reply.

The ranch house is dark. There's enough moonlight coming through the windows so the lights don't need to be turned on.

Miranda likes it in the dark. She's always known that illusion is more exciting than reality, more compelling. She feels strong when she's in darkness, sensing her surroundings rather than seeing them. One of the reasons she loves sex so much is that senses more imaginative than sight—touch, smell, taste—are the most important. It is of second nature to her that she uses her sexual power: why was she given it if not to use it? But no matter how calculating she can be, some amount of pleasure is always there, some touch, some taste, some smell. Years ago, more than half a lifetime, she had slept with a man who was unremarkable in bed, in most ways he was a turnoff (she was very young and he was an older man, as old or older than her father, the sexual encounter they were having was strictly to help her out—he was a professor at her college and she needed a B or better in his class to keep her scholarship and the course was utterly baffling to her, so she fucked him, once, to get the grade she needed), but at one point during the grunting and groping she had smelled his hair, his stiff, white-yellow shock of old Swedish ancestral hair, and it had brought a memory of a haystack that she had jumped and played in at a farm once, a memory that she loved. Her orgasm with this man she otherwise had no attraction for at all was so intense she has always remembered it.

Her father always said you can find some good in everyone, one of many stupid homilies her father lived by. Her father was a jerk and a loser, a total failure, but he was right about that. But only, she had to qualify, when it came to sex. The rest was all bullshit, there are plenty of people you can't find anything good about. The majority of people, in fact.

Not her late-night caller, though. He has plenty of power of his own, he doesn't have to grovel at her feet. She likes powerful men, she just doesn't know many.

"I saw the shindig you threw down at the beach today," Blake Hopkins says to her, raising his Booker's-with-a-splash in toast. "It was on the Channel 3 Nightly News." He's sitting on a worn leather couch that's covered with a Chumash Indian weaving; his shoes are comfortably off.

"It was an important thing to do," she states. "I told you that." There is no cynicism in her voice.

"It was a wonderful gesture. And you're a wonderful person."

"Why are you being sarcastic?"

"Force of habit." He laughs. "If only the rest of the world knew what I know."

"They don't. And they never will, unless you tell."

"Get serious. I'd be in as much trouble as you if this ever came out."

"Then we're both safe." She takes him by the hand, pulls him up from the couch. "Come on to bed, I'm horny."

"You had dinner with that guy Wilkerson. Didn't he satisfy the inner woman?"

"He's not for me."

"How do you know that unless you try?" His shirt is off now, he's sitting on the bed taking off his socks.

"He's not for me."

They make love like a happily married couple, which she is, with another man.

———

"When's your husband getting back?" Hopkins asks. He's sitting up in bed, drinking a Coors and eating a ham sandwich she made him.

"Tomorrow night, I think. He'll call first." She takes a bite out of her own sandwich. After making love she gets hungry.

"Does he know about us?"

"No."

"Doesn't he ever get suspicious, all the nights you're not there?"

"He doesn't allow himself to be."

"How can he not be? He's married to the most erotic woman in—"

"Don't," she says, cutting him off.

"I'd be. I wouldn't be able to help myself."

"You're not him." Seemingly out of the blue: "I love my husband," Miranda says.

He thinks about that. "You know, I think you do."

"I do. I love him very much."

"I hope he never finds out about us, then."

"He won't."

The house is hot and still. They sleep naked on top of the sheets. She wakes him before dawn.

"I'll make you coffee," she offers. She's wearing a cotton nightgown, her hair is twisted back in a ponytail. She is without any makeup, which makes her look younger, but no less beautiful.

"You're being domestic this morning." He's putting on last night's clothes.

"I like pleasing men."

"You do a good job of it." He pulls his boots on. "Don't bother with the coffee, I'll grab a cup in Santa Barbara, I'm going to shower and change in my motel room."

They walk out onto the front porch. Dawn is breaking over the eastern hills, as it was when she stood out here with him before.

"Drive carefully," she says. She could be his real wife, sending him off to work in the morning.

He starts down the steps to his car, then turns back to her.

"There's a question I've been meaning to ask you."

"What's that?"

"Why do you sleep around?" he asks. "If you love your husband so much." He pauses. "I know I'm not your only lover."

"Do you have a problem with that?"

"No. I mean . . . I suppose there's a little jealousy, once in a while. Wondering who the other ones are, that kind of thing."

"Just other men. There aren't that many. Or that often."

"First among equals," he says, trying to keep it light.

"You're all first." She smiles at him. "But you're not all equal."

6

CHASING YOUR TAIL

A-1 Bail Bonds.

"So I'm the first one listed in the phone book," the proprietor had explained. "I know that's a ploy as old as the hills but you'd be surprised how many people call the number at the top. Probably adds 10, 15 percent to my gross. Besides, with a last name like mine, A-1 sounds better."

His name is Eustis Lutz—he has a point, she has to concede. The bond company he runs is not the biggest in town, or the smallest. Middle-of-the-pack. Lutz operates out of his house, normal SOP for bonding companies in cities the size of Santa Barbara. All you need are a bunch of phone lines. Kind of like being an old-time bookie, Kate imagines. Not that she's ever known any old-time bookmakers—or modern ones, for that matter. Gambling isn't one of her vices, thank God. She has enough problems without the burden of that one.

The house is a small tract on the Mesa. Lutz is a bachelor, fiftyish, with no personal style whatsoever. His decor is even more utilitarian than hers. Mostly files, and volumes on regulations.

"Wes Gillroy," he says in response to her question. He doesn't have to look that one up. "Yes, I wrote his bond."

"What was it set at?"

"A million dollars."

She raises an eyebrow.

"High," he confirms. "One of the biggest bonds I've written."

"How come?"

"Bonds for drug smuggling are always set high, even more so when the party is from out of town and unknown to the local authorities. Particularly on this one, since one of the other traffickers was shot trying to escape and the third one took his own life."

"When was bail made?" she asks, taking out her pen and notebook.

She uses a reporter's notebook, a number 800, a size that can be slipped into a jacket or back pocket. She never employs a tape recorder; it didn't take her long working as a PI to learn that people don't talk as freely when a tape machine is running. Carl could have told her that, but he reasoned she'd figure that one out for herself.

"Shortly after arraignment. As long as it took to process the paperwork."

"That was fast," she comments.

"It was set up in advance. Not uncommon. All they had to know was how big a number to write on the check."

"That's a hundred thousand cash advance?" she continues, writing this all down.

Lutz nods.

"Plus a 5 percent fee, in case he skips and I've got to go looking for him. It was paid with a cashier's check," he adds, anticipating her next question. "I called Santa Barbara Bank and Trust to make sure it was good. It was—you don't play games on this level."

Make it a hundred and a half. Real money. "What was the security? There was security, right?"

She knows that in a bond written this big, particularly with a client who isn't local, you have to, by law, put up something tangible that will cover at least one and a half times the amount of the bail, in case the person doesn't show up. In this case, probably twice the amount.

"Of course there was security. The surety company wouldn't cover me otherwise." He picks up a file that he pulled when she called and asked to come see him.

"Property," he tells her. "The security was property."

"What kind?"

"A piece of commercial real estate in San Francisco. An office building, fully tenanted. Good collateral, solid."

"What's its value?" she goes on with her questioning, writing it all down.

"Over two million."

"Can I see the title?" she asks.

He hands her the document. It's the trust-deed to a five-story building in downtown San Francisco. She doesn't know the exact building, but she knows the neighborhood. It's a desirable location, well worth the price, she assumes.

"Bay Area Holding Company," she says aloud, writing down the name that's listed under Ownership.

"Real original," Lutz remarks dryly. "As original as A-1."

"Who brought you the check?"

"A local attorney."

"Do you know who hired him? This attorney?"

"Could've been a woman," he spars.

"Okay. Or her. Who hired . . . whoever."

"I can't tell you. You got what you need?" he asks, plucking the title from her hand, quickly getting out of his chair and placing it back in the manila folder, which he sticks into a file cabinet behind him. A cabinet that has a lock on it.

His action brings her up short.

"Why can't you?"

"Because I was instructed not to."

"Isn't that unusual?" she asks, frowning.

"It's not usual, but it isn't unheard of. The party doesn't want to be known, that's their business."

Not that it was a one-party transaction, she's sure of that. This would have gone through several layers, to insulate the real source.

"Must've been someone local," she throws out, fishing, "to put it together that quickly. Or at least there was a local contact."

He doesn't rise to her bait. "Not necessarily. With computers and faxes, it could've been done from Hong Kong."

That's true. It was worth a try, though.

"Do you think Gillroy will show up for his trial?" she asks Lutz. She folds the notebook up, puts it in her purse.

"Oh, sure. He'd be crazy not to. If I didn't think so, I wouldn't have written his bond," he tells her. "His passport's been confiscated, and he has to check in with Orange County Sheriff's Department every week. He's not going anywhere."

"But you've got the title to a nice piece of property, just in case," she comments.

"You've got to be prepared for 'just in case,' " he agrees.

* * *

Kate's office is located above a tortilla factory off Ortega St., between Olive and Salsipuedes. It's not a prime location, but it has one overriding benefit: the rent is cheap.

A few law firms have from time to time offered her space, but she's turned them down because they would have a priority on her time and she doesn't want to be obligated to take work she doesn't want to do or work with people she doesn't like. Several lawyers in town fit into that category. And if a prospective client feels it's necessary to have a detective who has nice carpets and tasteful prints, there are other PIs they can go to.

It's late afternoon, the time when people who live normal lives think about what they're going to be making for dinner. Kate rarely worries about what she's going to eat, or when. Unless she's with someone, she eats on the run. One of the advantages of living alone and having a job that isn't nine to five.

There are several messages on her answering machine. She hits the playback button, scrounges a pad and pen from the pile of clutter on her desk, kicks off her shoes and puts her feet up, spreading her toes through her stockings and stretching the arches. Her legs, which she takes pride in, are sore, particularly her shins, a bad sign: too much pounding the sidewalks in heels and not enough surfing, running, keeping in shape. Since her Fiesta indulgence she hasn't gotten back into a proper routine. Starting tomorrow she'll force herself to begin her regimen anew—a promise to herself, for herself.

The playback stops rewinding. The messages start.

"Kate, Larry Wilson. It's two-twenty-five. I need you to interview prior to deposition that witness in the Glen Annie traffic accident, we're going to see the judge on Monday and I need that testimony. I've tentatively booked you to see her tomorrow before noon. Call me and confirm, please."

Click.

"This is Mark Richards's office at Watson and Stone, calling for Kate Blanchard. Mr. Richards has a personal injury case in Lompoc, and he needs to talk to you about doing the investigative work, as you did in the Moreto case last month. Please call him at 555-5557. Thank you."

Click.

There are half a dozen calls similar to those; lawyers wanting to talk to her about cases that are currently in the pipeline that she's working on for them, or new cases they want to hire her for. Some lawyers in town won't touch a female PI; others think working with a woman is a definite advantage. It isn't a gender thing—there are plenty of male lawyers who use her, and some female lawyers who won't.

She missed the last call by a few minutes.

"Hi, Kate, this is Cecil. Just wanted to tell you how great the other night was. Hoping I could catch you in. Maybe later. Give me a call if you feel like it."

She has a stack of urgent and semi-urgent calls sitting in her hand, but she calls him anyway.

He isn't in—she gets his service: "This is Cecil. I'm not here. Leave a message."

Short and sweet, no nonsense.

"This is Kate returning your call," she tells his machine. "Hope we don't play phone tag for too long. It was great for me, too. You already knew that, but I want to say it anyway. I'll be in and out, so call me."

It takes her about an hour to work her way through her calls. She has seven active cases currently, which is her average. She likes to work, it's about all she does besides exercise, but she doesn't like to spread herself so thin that she can't service each client properly. Some PIs contract out their overflow, but she prefers not to. Occasionally she'll bring in another detective, but for additional help only—usually if it's a big, complex case with a looming deadline.

The calls returned, she turns on her computer.

If there's one thing she wishes she could afford it would be a part-time secretary to keep her current on her paperwork. She's always falling behind in her billings. It's drudge work, staring at the screen, going through her worksheets, totaling up the hours. Except in the rare case, like this one with Laura Sparks, she works with attorneys and bills through them. That keeps it clean: she doesn't have to dun clients directly, something she hates with a passion. The flip side is that she has to file accurate and complete reports on a weekly basis. Lawyers spend their lives sorting out disputes, differences of fact and opinion, so whatever they can control, they will. Billings they can control.

She types in a brief synopsis of what she's done in each case, and how long it took. Her system breaks her time down into tenths of hours, each six minutes a billable fraction. As she logs in the time the machine automatically calculates the fee, depending on the pre-established daily rate. Even though her customary rate is sixty-five dollars an hour, it can fluctuate up or down depending on the circumstances.

She prints out each case as she finishes entering it, sticks it into an envelope. She'll drop them off in a mailbox on her way home tonight, and be done with it for another week.

There's a knock on her door. The skinny delivery kid from Sealy's Deli sticks his head in.

"Got a breast of chicken on a French roll, pasta salad, and a lime Koala," he announces, plunking the brown bag down on her desk.

She glances at her watch: 8:30. Is it that late already?

"Thanks, Adolfo. Am I your last stop?"

"Yes, ma'am. We're closed now. I'm on my way home."

"Well, thanks for stopping by."

The bill is $8.15. She tips him two dollars. He's a good kid.

She walks across the floor to the lone window, which faces south, and looks out. The sun is setting. She's been here for hours. In the back of her mind she was hoping Cecil was going to be in town and they'd have dinner together; the sandwich was insurance. She might as well eat it now, it's too late for him to come.

A disappointment. She likes him; it's a good feeling, and a scary one, too.

Picking through half her sandwich, she rewraps the rest and puts it in the cube fridge in the corner. Tomorrow's lunch, or next week's garbage. Getting back to business, she starts entering the information that Herrera gave her into her computer.

It's basic stuff—the names and latest official addresses (all of which she suspects are either fictitious or outdated) of the men who were present in the cell with Bascomb when he died. Eleven in all, in a cell designed for eight men. She photocopies their booking slips and mug shots. A shitload of people were arrested that night.

One thing she does notice that's a bit out of the ordinary—all the men in this cell except Bascomb were booked together. As the saying goes, they got a group rate. It reminds her of when she was still on the force up north, working the jail, and they would line the hookers up in night court and plea them, set their bail, and send them back out, all in about thirty seconds. Bang, bang, bang. Proposition a john in the courthouse corridor if they thought the cops weren't looking, which they weren't, because it isn't the act that brings the police down on them, it's where they do it, out on the streets where it's a civic embarrassment.

Next step: she cross-references the database on the statistics of Bascomb's cellmates and tries to get a line on them: current addresses other than what they put on their arrest form, driver's license, workman's comp, anything that might give her a lead.

Nothing comes up, validating Herrera's assertion that they exist but they don't, they're too far outside the system. All the names are Latino—they could be illegal aliens. Maybe there's something she can check with Immigration.

She'll have to go looking for them the hard way. Her feet start aching again, just at the thought of that.

Time to call it a day and go home; but first, one more thing, as long as she's still on the computer.

This will be a long shot, but she's here, so why not? She flips through her notes from her meeting earlier this afternoon with Lutz the bondsman, finding the name of the property that had been posted for Wes's collateral. Bay Area Holding Company. She types it in, then calls it up on her California real-estate system.

A few moments pass while the system comes on-line.

Bay Area Holding Company. The screen shows the basic data. Ownership in Delaware, Singapore, Japan. No names listed.

"Shit," she says aloud. She should have seen this one coming.

The Bay Area Holding Company is a classic dummy corporation, a front for something else that in itself is a shell company. An onion that can be peeled to the core, at which time there may be no core. The building is real enough; if Wes skips and never surfaces, the bond company and its surety partner will have clear and legal title; but who the present owners are, and what their connection to her case is, if any, she may never know. It will be a long (and in all probability) fruitless paper chase to find out who the real owners are.

Like she'd feared, she'll have to go at this one the hard way.

Bright and early the next morning she heads out into the world to earn her daily bread.

"Have you ever seen this man? How about this one?"

She's in the homeless jungle, down by the railroad tracks. Barely nine o'clock and the humidity is already going through the roof, she feels like she's exploring a Costa Rican rain forest.

"¿Alguna vez han visto este hombre . . . Y este?"

In some sections the sawgrass is up to her waist, the rough edges scraping at her arms and body. The area spans several acres in a random zigzag pattern, both sides of the railroad tracks, north of the beach and south of the freeway. Clusters of wild live oaks, their trunks ensnared in thick coils of ivy, adorn the landscape, while the old orange and lemon packing houses, faint memories now, lie rotting amidst the heavy overgrowth, a jumble of wooden ruins. Tin cans cover the ground like a grungy blanket, the hard-baked dirt festooned with Big Mac polyurethane container remnants. Beer, whiskey, and wine bottles by the hundreds are everywhere, sharing space with elephant-sized piles of dog shit, human excrement, and piles of old fouled clothing.

This is the bottom rung of the ladder, the pus of humanity. Kate knows homeless people who don't want to be where they are, who desperately want to get back into the mainstream, find a job, a roof over their heads, be part of a civilized society. Those living here have no such aspirations. They live moment to moment; they have no hope, no dreams, no dignity. They fuck, get drunk and high, shit and piss anywhere. Right now, in the oppressively heavy heat, people are sitting around in a half-aware stupor, the men bareback, the women in filthy bras or in some cases topless, their scabby withered tits hanging lank; all drinking beer, tepid water, sour hot juice. The pungent smell of marijuana hangs heavy in the air.

Kate picks her way gingerly through the muck. Despite the heat she's wearing hiking boots and jeans; protection's more important than comfort.

She hunkers down next to two people who are nesting on the ground, a badly sunburnt man and his woman companion, who are passing a quart bottle of Colt .45 between them.

They smell. The acrid odor of the unwashed.

"Do either of you know any of these men?" she says, pulling out the folder of mug shots.

The man belches in her face, a horrendous effluvium. She recoils, gasping.

"What are you, some kind of fuckin' animal?" the woman slurs at her mate. "Lemme see that," she commands, grabbing for the folder.

Kate shows her the pictures.

The woman, who is probably thirty but looks a good fifty, scans them, trying mightily to focus; it doesn't help that she's stoned out of her gourd. "You got any spare change?" she begs aggressively, getting right in Kate's face.

"Concentrate on this first," Kate orders, trying to keep her cool. These people: damn!

"How the hell should I know any of these motherfuckers?" the woman bitches. "Come on, you got money."

"Not today."

She pries the folder from the woman's grasp. Moving off, she makes sure she stays clear of the piles of dog droppings. At least half a dozen stray mutts, mangy and so skinny you can count their ribs, run in a wild pack around the grounds, biting at each other's flanks.

She works the jungle. It's hot, depressing, and tedious, but it has to be done. This is definitely worth sixty-five dollars an hour of her time. If this becomes the norm on this case she'll put in for hazard-duty pay.

"I don't know. A couple of them look familiar. I don't know, man," a young guy, his arms and torso covered with tattoos, most of them self-inflicted, tells her. "You see all kinds of weird assholes around here, you know what I mean?"

"Yeah, I know," Kate answers as she squats next to him in one of the few patches of shade. This one is truly wasted—a major drug-abuser or in a pretty advanced stage of AIDS; or both.

"Concentrate, could you?" she implores him. "It's important."

"You got a smoke on you?"

"Sorry. Not my vice."

"I got vices," he tells her.

"We all do," she reassures him. "Take another look," she asks again, showing him the pictures one by one. "Any of them, any of them at all ring a bell?"

"I got every fucking vice there is. I got vices you never done heard of."

"I doubt that. Here," pointing to another picture, "how about him?"

"Vices that ain't been invented!" He slumps down, starting to nod off.

"Maybe you do," she says, half to herself.

As she starts to get up he grabs her by the wrist, a fast, unexpected movement that catches her by surprise. She tries to pull free, but he's got her in a death grip. For someone who looks to be in as bad shape as he is, his grip is surprisingly strong.

"These fucking guys," he says.

"What fucking guys?"

"These killer fucking guys."

He's trying to tell her something.

"What fucking killer guys?"

"Ah, fuck 'em."

"What fucking killer guys?" she presses.

"They're all killers. Every fucking one of them. I'm a killer."

"Your picture isn't in here," she tells him. Shit, this one's so far gone he can't even tell himself from these pictures.

"I could have. I could have done that."

That is the point. It could have been any of these people. Any of them could have killed Frank Bascomb, and the next day they wouldn't remember a thing about it.

"Bunch of fuckin' Mexicans," he drawls.

He's referring to the men in the photos, all of whom are Hispanic. This man isn't.

It's a waste of time talking to people like him. That's what he's telling her. All the men in the cell with Bascomb were Hispanic. Maybe they were illegals, as she'd earlier thought. All back on the other side of the border. If that's the case, she can kiss this one goodbye.

With a quick, sudden movement she wrests her arms from his grasp.

"Thanks for your time," she says.

"They've been around here," he tells her, his arm sweeping the area.

Now what? Is there anything here she can hang something on? He's a fucked-up junkie; there's nothing trustworthy about him. It's a waste of her time.

"They come and go," he intones solemnly, as only a righteous drunk will do.

She talks to everyone, although she realizes it's a useless chore. No one knows any of these men, and they all want money.

One old guy, who seems to be a little more pulled-together than the others, has a hard look at two of the pictures. "This one, I think maybe was around here once," he offers, his filthy fingernail touching the picture of the man who had baited Bascomb in the cell the night before Bascomb died. "I couldn't say for certain, but he might could have. He might've been a pimp, cruising for fresh meat—he had that kind of attitude."

"How long ago?" she asks. Something in the way he says it gives the declaration a slight ring of believability.

"Wouldn't know," he tells her. "Could be a week, could be a year. My mind's gone, lady," he admits truthfully.

"You've helped. Thank you."

"You got a dollar on you? I'm dying of thirst out here."

"Sure." She digs a couple bucks out of her jeans pocket. "Go crazy."

"Thanks, lady. Sorry I couldn't help you more."

"You helped," she tells him again as she starts to walk away.

"Ventura," he calls after her.

She stops, turns back to him.

"What?"

"Ventura. I think I heard he was from Ventura. Or was it Oxnard? Fuck, I can't remember."

"But one of them, maybe?"

"I'm full of shit. Don't believe nothin' you hear from me."

She reaches into her pocket again, finds a couple more singles.

"Go take care of that thirst," she tells the hapless man. "It's hot out here."

Haley St., 4:00 P.M. Herrera had said one of the men in the cell might have been a pimp, and the man in the jungle had, too. So she has to check it out.

A handful of women line the south side (the shady side) of the street along the ten-block stretch from Garden to Milpas, miniskirted, halter-topped, their tits pushed up to the nipple out of their thin cotton uplift-padded bras.

These are not your healthy blue-eyed milk-fed Carpinteria flower growers' daughters looking to make a little extra money over summer vacation, nor are they hot, sexy, voluptuously youthful stroke-dream Latinas supplementing their income to pay for tuition to SBCC so they can get their dental technician's degrees and be fruitful members of society.

Junkies. They range in age from early teenagers to God knows how old—you age fast living this kind of life, it's measurable in weeks, literally, a girl drops off the street the odds are she's dead or on the way. Virtually all of them are HIV-positive, mostly from infected needles, many have already crossed the line to full-blown AIDS, and the rest will follow. All the other sexually transmitted germs and viruses—clap, syph, herpes, you name it—that have been pestilences of mankind for centuries are raging freely inside their systems as well.

They hang out on the corners, waiting for the lights to turn red.

"Pull over, man, do you for a dime."

Kate works the street doggedly, block by block, cornering each prostitute in turn like a bird dog flushing quail, forcing each one to look at her file pictures. Despite her disclaimers they all assume she's working undercover and hiss at her to fuck off, leave them alone, she's messing up their business.

She forces her card on them anyway. "If your memory improves, call me. There's money in this for solid goods."

That they hear; not that any of them will call. First law of the street—keep your mouth shut. Hear no evil, see no evil, speak no evil. And maybe you'll survive.

Time is passing. The street traffic begins thinning out. Most of the streetwalkers have departed; they'll reappear at dawn tomorrow for the morning rush hour.

Kate's almost to Milpas St., the eastern boundary of hooker territory.

"Can I have a minute of your time? Could I ask you to look at these pictures? It won't take but a minute."

The woman looks at her morosely. She has a strong look of Indian blood in her broad cheekbones; most likely Guatemalan or Salvadoran, probably in this country illegally—a solid reason to be suspicious of anyone who smells of authority. She is older than most of the other girls on the street, close in age to Kate, which doesn't give Kate much comfort.

Her tone is blunt. "My time costs money."

"How much have you made today?" Kate asks, knowing the answer. Even in a subterranean society like this there's a pecking order. A woman of this age and shape is at the bottom. "Take a look. There could be money in this."

The hooker nervously scrutinizes the open folder. For a brief moment her eyes narrow as they scan the photos, then quickly look away, back up the street into the sun.

Kate notices the moment of possible recognition. She looks at the pictures. One seems to be looking back at her, almost mocking her in silence.

"Do you know any of these men?" she asks, planting herself in the woman's path so she can't escape.

"Why the hell should I know any of them?" the woman asks defensively. "I don't know any one of these dipshits," she proclaims aggressively—too much so, Kate thinks.

"Okay, fine." Kate knows when to push and when not to. This is not a time to push.

She hands the hooker her card.

"If you remember anything, you call me. There's money for solid information."

The woman's eyes drift down to the pictures again.

"How much?"

"That depends on how good the information is."

"Well . . ."

Kate leans forward.

"No, I don't know anything," the woman says with forced certainty. Fingering Kate's card, she can't resist: "A lot of money?"

"Could be." Kate plays her. "For solid information."

The woman nods, as if something just came to her. "Maybe . . . I don't know . . . maybe I might know somebody that knows one of these guys. One of the girls on the street. Probably not, but maybe someone knows something."

She recognized one of the men in the photos; Kate's sure of that.

Kate has no more use for this woman, not right now. She has cast her bread upon the waters, now she'll have to wait to see if anything washes up.

"Call me if you want to strike it rich." Tapping her card, she stands face to face with the pathetic creature, giving her both a friendly warning and a nudge. "First come, first served," she cautions, making sure the woman understands her. "There's no prize for calling second."

7

WEDDING BELL BLUES

Laura drives with the top down. Her hair is blowing in the breeze, pulled together in a long braid hanging halfway down her back. Dorothy sits next to her. She's taken the wise precaution of putting on an old-fashioned sunbonnet, the kind you see in butter ads from the 1940s, which is tied securely under her chin.

Both women are decked out in light summer party dresses, fancy ones. The difference in the dresses is that Laura bought hers earlier this summer at Wendy Foster's and has worn it exactly once, while Dorothy bought the one she has on forty years ago, and has worn it countless times. And long after the dress Laura's wearing has been lost in the back of her closet, or been consigned to a secondhand dress shop, Dorothy will still be wearing this dress she has on today.

Nestled on the backseat behind them is a large, gaily wrapped package. It contains a wedding present—the attached card, which has been securely Scotch-taped onto the top, has a picture of a grinning Cupid blowing his trumpet on the front, with the cursive inscription *"On Your Wedding Day"* prominently embossed underneath.

"This is going to be weird," Laura says. "This is going to be *so weird.*"

They're driving along Coast Village Road, heading for the beach.

"It's going to be fun," Dorothy declares.

"I didn't say it wouldn't be fun," Laura answers defensively. "But don't you think it's going to be weird, too? Do you really think 'till death do us part' has any meaning for these people?"

"*These people?* What does *these people* mean?"

"You know what I mean," Laura replies peevishly. She hates it when her grandmother accuses her of expressing feelings that everyone else has.

"Yes, and I don't like it."

"Okay, I'm sorry."

"I think 'till death do us part' is an outdated phrase that has very little meaning for anyone nowadays," her grandmother says. "This is going to be a festive and lively occasion, that's what's important. How long it lasts is in the future, which is always murky, so it doesn't really matter. Especially at my age."

"I suppose," comes Laura's reply. There isn't much conviction behind it. God, but it's a pain in the ass sometimes, having a saint in the family.

"Don't be such a snob, Laura."

"I am not a snob."

"Oh, of course you are. How could you not be? It's not your fault, it's a condition of your existence."

"Well, I try not to be."

"Yes, you do try. I'll give you that. It's not my place to tell other people how to live, or to judge them because of a lifestyle that's different from mine," Dorothy informs Laura.

Because they're too fucked up on drugs and alcohol to hold a job, Laura thinks. Or crazy. They should be in mental institutions, most of them, not out on the streets. It would be the humane thing to do.

The little convertible winds around the big, expensive beachfront houses, plunging down the road as they pass by the cemetery and the bird refuge. They head west on Cabrillo Blvd., the shimmering, placid ocean spreading out to their left. It's the height of tourist season—across the wide roadway, the grassy area paralleling the beach is jammed up with bike riders, runners, skaters, sunbathers, and folks just out for a stroll. Up ahead a few blocks, the old hobo jungle, where many of the city's homeless population now live, comes into view.

Dorothy can't resist asking one more question. "Have you told your mother yet? About hiring a detective?"

"No, I have not."

"Don't take too long to tell her," Dorothy cautions. "She's going to be upset about your doing it regardless, but if she finds out about what you've done from someone else . . . you know how your mother can be."

"Thank you for caring and sharing." Laura, unable to restrain her peevishness, answers in the hip-bored-sarcastic voice of the crowd she runs with.

Dorothy tries to keep the hurt from her voice. "I'm trying to help, Laura."

"I know, I know." If there's one person in the world whose feelings Laura doesn't want to bruise, it's her grandmother, who has always been there for her; many times when her own mother wasn't. "I can't help it, I'm just tired of always being told what to do. But you're right—I'll tell her. The next time I see her."

"Good."

They turn into the jungle, down a gutted dirt road that doesn't see many cars.

"No more questions," Dorothy says, forcing the smile back on her face. "Let's have a new experience and a wonderful time."

Despite her anger at her stupid loose tongue Laura can't help smiling, too. "With you, Grandma, every day is a new experience."

––––––––––

The wine is flowing like water. Actually, there's no water to be found anywhere near here, at least no potable water, everything liquid that's drinkable is alcoholic. The beer is flowing smoothly, two full kegs are currently tapped, and they're draining at a fast, steady pace. There's no shortage of cheap vodka and blended whiskey, either.

This is a very special occasion; it's not every day any of the people down here get a paid-for party. Today is Tiny and Luther's wedding day, and Dorothy Sparks is footing the bill.

"It's nothing," she explained to Laura, who was incredulous when Dorothy told her, a few days before, about this wedding, to which she had been invited as the guest of honor; how fascinating it would be, how decent these people were underneath. And why, when she figured out the ramifications, she had insisted on paying for it.

"They're using you," Laura had protested.

"So what?" Dorothy had rejoined. "Everyone uses everyone, one way or the other. I have more money than I can ever use in ten lifetimes—why not make their sad lives happy, just for one day?"

Laura had no good argument against that. She's an advocate for the homeless herself, in an abstract way. Her newspaper takes up their causes with regularity and fervor. In the real world, though, things aren't so black-and-white.

Laura parks her car at the edge of the clearing. They start walking across the field.

"Hey, Mrs. Sparks!"

A very large woman comes running towards them. She throws her big meaty arms around Dorothy. "God damn! You came!"

"Of course I came, Tiny," Dorothy says, comfortable in the woman's embrace. "I wouldn't have missed your wedding for the world."

"That sure is a pretty dress you have on, Mrs. Sparks," Tiny says, stepping back and appraising first Dorothy's and then Laura's choice of apparel.

"Thank you. I only wear it on special occasions." She pulls Laura forward. "This is Laura, my granddaughter. Laura, allow me to introduce you to my friend Tiny."

"Hi." Laura extends a cautious hand.

"Yeah, I can see that, you look just like her," Tiny gushes, looking from Laura to Dorothy. "It sure was nice of you to come." She shakes Laura's hand vigorously.

"Thank you. I'm . . . looking forward to it," Laura says diplomatically, retrieving her hand—the woman has a grip like a lumberjack! She also notices that the bride needs a bath. And a good shampooing, manicure, and facial wouldn't hurt, either.

"Well, come on and party down!"

Tiny leads them into the middle of the gathering. She is wearing super-tight cutoffs from which her abundant cheeks protrude, and a man's T-shirt with no bra. Her breasts, almost the size of small watermelons, sway loosely to and fro.

"Hey, everyone!" she sings out. "The guest of honor's arrived."

"Hey, Mrs. Sparks! Mrs. Sparks!" Calls of greeting ring out.

There must be over a hundred brown people here, Laura calculates, getting her bearings while trying to avoid being engulfed in this unsavory sea of humanity, and at least half as many children, many of whom are running around stark naked, even though some have long passed the toddler stage. Almost all the men have tattoos, she notices, some of them covering virtually every inch of skin, and many of the women have been decorated with the needle as well. Ankle tattoos are particularly popular among the girls.

She sees these people all the time. Up and down State St., begging, hanging out, dragging their mean-looking dogs by long leashes of clothesline. But she rarely notices them, certainly not as individuals, each one different from all the others.

"Hey, have a drink." A matted-haired man, thin as a rail, his forearms a melange of primitive jailhouse ink tattoos, presses a bottle of wine into Dorothy's hand.

"What the hell's wrong with you?" Tiny cries out, immediately snatching the bottle from Dorothy's hand. "Mrs. Sparks don't drink out of the bottle!" She turns to a young girl of about six. The girl is wearing an old thrift-store dress that's filthy. "Get that special glass I put in my pouch, angel face," she says to the child.

The girl turns and disappears into the throng, returning a few seconds later with a wineglass.

It's clean, Laura notices. Spotless.

"I bought this this morning," Tiny tells Dorothy. "At Jordano's. So you would have a decent glass to drink out of."

"Well, I certainly appreciate that," Dorothy thanks her. "I wouldn't want to toast the bride without a proper glass."

Tiny pours some white wine into the glass, filling it to the brim. Dorothy brings it to her lips, careful not to spill a drop, and takes a sip.

"Very nice," she says in approval. "Here, Laura, have a taste."

Laura takes a healthy mouthful, which she instantaneously regrets. Her mouth is on fire, her eyes start watering like a four-alarm hay-fever attack. She would spit it out, it's so terrible; but she knows that would be a mistake. It could screw up the entire afternoon.

Somehow, she manages to swallow the putrid potion.

"Pretty good, huh?" Tiny crows, oblivious to Laura's intense discomfort.

"Yes," Laura manages.

"You want a glass of your own? We've got a few stashed away—for special guests."

"No, thank you," comes the rapid answer. "I can share with my grandmother."

"Your choice."

The bride-to-be doesn't bother with the amenities. She raises the bottle to her lips and chugs down a good quarter of it.

"When will the actual ceremony take place?" Dorothy asks solicitously of Tiny, as if they were two nice society ladies discussing the latest fashions.

"Shit, man, I don't know. Some time between now and midnight," the big woman sighs. "Before this crowd of crazies gets so stoned and drunk out of their stupid minds they forget what they came for in the first place." She burps modestly, wiping her mouth on the bottom of her shirt. "But seriously, Mrs. S.: by sunset. That's when I told the preacher. 'Cause he's got a night gig starting around nine, DJing at some music bar down on lower State. I think it would be pretty to have the wedding when it's sunset, don't you?" she asks delicately.

"Very pretty," Dorothy agrees.

The party is roaring like a wildfire. Everyone has a drink in their hands (some of them sporting multiple bottles or cups), and there's beaucoup grass being passed around as well.

Dorothy moves through the throng, saying hello to everyone as polite and proper as can be. She is greeted in kind. Everyone here seems to know her, and they all profess to love her. It's true she's paying for this party, but that's not the reason, Laura realizes. It's because she treats them as individual people, not as some abstract grouping in a sociology textbook.

"Want a hit?" A man holds a joint out to Laura, who finds herself momentarily separated from Dorothy.

"No, thanks," she answers.

"It's righteous shit," he tells her, grinning like a madman.

"I'm not smoking right now. Thanks anyway."

He drifts away, blending into the crowd.

A haze of weed hovers at head level, a thick sweet cloud blanketing the entire area. It's good dope, she can tell from the smell wafting off his joint. Marijuana she knows about. The primo stuff is going for four hundred dollars an ounce these days on the street, there must be a pound of it circulating here. Where do they get the money for it? Is it from petty thievery and cheap prostitution? She's seen people with shopping carts loaded up with bottles and cans, pushing them along the sidewalk. How many bottles and cans would you have to redeem to buy an ounce of grass?

"Miss?"

A woman has sidled up to her. A girl, really, not yet out of her teens. "Spare some change?" she asks aggressively.

Laura is taken by surprise. Here?

"Sure." What else can she answer?

She always carries spare change with her, for just such purposes. She reaches into her purse, pulls out a handful of coins, and drops them in the girl's hand, carefully avoiding any actual physical contact.

"Thanks."

She spots Dorothy in the center of a throng and quickly catches up to her.

"I was panhandled," she whispers incredulously into Dorothy's ear.

"What do you expect?" Dorothy, amused, asks Laura. "These people are always on the hustle, they have to be."

Dorothy moves from group to group, comfortably chatting with each in turn. Laura stays tight by her side. Her initial fear of the unknown has left her—but still, all of this, this lifestyle and these people with whom she is completely unfamiliar, makes her uncomfortable.

A makeshift band starts playing old-fashioned rock 'n' roll. The instrumentation is two ancient guitars that look like they belong in the Smithsonian, a snare drum with a puncture hole in the skin covered over with duct tape, and a bunch of kitchen-sink rhythm instruments—washboard, spoons, a steel-band-like apparatus made up of discarded pots and pans. Somebody managed to score a generator, so they've hooked themselves up electronically, and they play at an ear-splitting level. The lead singer, a man Laura has often seen on the streets downtown, a menacing figure who struts around leading his pet brindle pit bull on a leather chain, aggressively hitting on people for money and yelling curses at them when they pass him by, begins belting out an old Creedence Clearwater song at the top of his lungs, his booze-wasted voice completely off-key, improvising lyrics as he goes. What they lack in talent they make up for with energy and zeal.

Everyone jumps up and starts dancing, bopping around like crazy, arms and legs splayed wide, like a modern-day Brueghel painting on acid.

Tiny is in the eye of the storm, a wild woman, dancing simultaneously with three men who bump and grind against her.

"Hey, Mrs. Sparks, come on, join us!" she calls to Dorothy.

Dorothy turns to Laura. "Hold this." She hands Laura her wineglass.

"You're not going to dance with them?" Laura asks in disbelief.

"I'm here to have fun!"

She pushes her way into the center next to Tiny, starts shimmying like crazy. She's good. Laura watches, envious of her grandmother's easy comfort with all of this. She moves to the side, trying to fade into the scenery.

"Hey, come on, you've got to dance!"

A man grabs her by the hand, pulls her into the vortex.

"No, I don't, thank you, I don't . . ." she stammers, feeling herself dragged along, the wineglass slipping from her hand and shattering on a piece of rock, trying to dig in her heels but unable to, pulled into the center of action near Tiny and Dorothy, the man holding her now in a tight embrace, dancing a wild self-invented jitterbug, slamming his body against hers, then apart, together again, his breath against her face rank and sour, his body odor overpowering, holding her tight, forcing her legs to move in rhythm with his own, one thigh wedged tight between her two, firmly against her vagina. She can feel his erection against her leg, dry-humping her. He's going to ejaculate, she thinks, petrified at the thought, it'll seep through his pants and onto her dress.

"Having fun?" Dorothy calls out gaily.

Laura's eyes roll like a lassoed mustang's. Can't Dorothy see what this man is doing to her?

She gives Dorothy a sickly nod, summoning enough strength to push the man away from her a little, still dancing with him but at least their bodies aren't touching now, his cock isn't jammed up against her, if she closes her eyes she can almost pretend she's at a fraternity party back in college with a bunch of drunken boys who had the same hungry desires as this man. The man is young, about her age, he could have been at one of those parties.

In another lifetime.

At least he hasn't thrown up all over her, like some of them did.

The party finds its own momentum, and cruises. Dorothy and Laura find a comfortable place in the shade to sit. It *is* kind of fun, Laura thinks, if you can watch it from a safe distance. The people are enjoying themselves, she has to admit that. More than she does at the parties she goes to with her friends.

"I'm thirsty," Dorothy announces. "Are you?"

"Maybe they have some soda. Do you want a soda if I can find one?"

"I'd rather have a beer. I'll come with you."

As they walk towards the kegs they pass a group of Latino-looking men sitting off from the rest of the crowd by themselves, passing around a bottle of cheap wine and smoking cigarettes.

One of the men rises to his feet: the man who had accosted Frank Bascomb in his jail cell the night before Frank died. Some of the men with him were also in the cell that night.

"Hello, Mrs. Sparks," the man says in his accented voice, bowing slightly.

"Hello," Dorothy answers pleasantly, giving the man the kind of blank-but-warm professional smile that politicians dispense five hundred times a day when encountering someone they don't know from Adam but who thinks they do.

"Nice party here," the man observes.

"Yes, it is."

"You paid for it?"

"I made a contribution."

"Well, God bless you for that," the man tells her. He glances at Laura, who looks at him devoid of recognition, since she's never seen any of them before.

"Thank you," Dorothy says.

"Who are they?" Laura asks as she and Dorothy move away, out of hearing.

Dorothy shrugs. "Some more street people, I guess. I know many of the people here, but I can't be expected to know everyone."

They stand at the keg. One of the men who had been dancing with Tiny draws them two plastic cups. It's mostly foam by now.

"Luther, this is my granddaughter, Laura. Laura, this is Luther, Tiny's future husband."

Luther is a trim man, smaller than his future wife. In comparison with most of the others here, he's clean and neat. He's recently had a haircut, a shave, and a shower.

They shake hands. Luther's grip is firm.

They're not all the same, Laura thinks, silently chastising herself for being such a judgmental prude. She can learn things from her grandmother, if she'll allow herself to.

"This old lady is a hell of a good woman," Luther tells Laura. "A fine woman. A real fine human being."

"Oh, stop that," Dorothy protests, smiling broadly.

"Yes, I know," Laura answers Luther.

"A damn fine woman. All this today is on account of her."

"I said *stop*," Dorothy tells him. "It's your wedding day. Anyone would do what I did, it's no big deal."

"Nobody except you would do a thing like this for us," Luther insists. "You're a special person, and we all know it."

"You're embarrassing me, Luther, so no more of this talk."

"Wanted you to know how I feel."

"Well, that's fine. I'll see you later, at the ceremony."

She and Laura walk away.

"A damn fine woman," Luther calls after her.

The day slides by. The sun starts to drop.

Everyone is pretty drunk by now. The band has stopped playing, but a few women still dance to the music inside their heads. Laura watches, feeling like an anthropologist observing a primitive, less-advanced culture. The women, especially, are incomprehensible to her. Some wear nipple rings, she can see them, most of these women don't wear bras and their tits bounce in and out of their shirts. Some, she knows, even have their *vagina* folds pierced!

"I think it's about time for a wedding," Dorothy comments as a man, not someone homeless, a regular person, approaches them. "There's Wally Jackson. He's performing the service. Hello, Wally!" she sings out.

"Hello, Mrs. Sparks. Hi, Laura. I didn't know you frequented functions such as these." He squats next to them, a garment bag draped over his arm.

"I'm keeping my grandmother company."

"Stick with her, kid," Wally winks. "She'll teach you a thing or three. You been listening to my show lately? KYTT, Saturday mornings at nine."

"I'm not usually up Saturday mornings at nine," Laura tells him.

"It's a struggle for me, too," he admits.

Wally's the best-known radio jock in Santa Barbara. His signature show, *The Rock 'n' Roll Classic Review*, has been a local fixture for years. He stands up. "Time to put on my preacher face."

"I didn't know you were a minister," Laura says. "What church?"

"Universal Life, honey," he winks. "Ordained me mail-order, twenty-five years ago. Sent in the form and a check for thirty dollars. Best thirty dollars I ever spent—kept me out of Vietnam."

He drifts off.

Dorothy points excitedly towards Cabrillo Blvd., where a Channel 3 truck has pulled up. "The television people are here, right on schedule like they promised."

A woman newscaster and her crew get out and begin setting up.

"Is *The Grapevine* going to have an article?" Dorothy asks Laura.

Laura nods. "I'm writing it myself." She reaches into her purse, takes out a miniature Olympus. "I'm even going to take pictures."

Wally Jackson, now flamboyantly attired in a full-length rainbow-hued robe, topped by a clergyman's traditional vestment-shawl over his shoulders, has set up on a small grassy knoll at the edge of the clearing. There's a clear view to the beach across the street, facing west towards the sunset.

"I love weddings," Dorothy says, as she and Laura walk towards the ceremonial area with everyone else. "There's one in particular I'm looking forward to before I die," she adds with a gleam in her eye.

Marriage is not on Laura's agenda, especially after recent events. She bites her tongue so as not to say something she'll regret.

Everyone forms a rough semicircle around Wally.

"Here she comes!" a child calls out.

People turn to look. Tiny comes marching across the field, head held high, the full late-afternoon sun shining on her face like a beacon. She's wearing a wedding dress, a real one, all white satin and lace. Pastel-colored ribbons and pink baby roses have been woven into her hair. Her large bare feet have been washed clean, and her fingernails have been polished.

"She's beautiful!" Dorothy pronounces in a whisper that seems to express satisfaction and justification.

"Yes, she's beautiful," Laura echoes, astonished at Tiny's transformation.

Luther is wearing squeaky-clean clothes, a mismatched ensemble from the Salvation Army Thrift Store. He takes his place in front of Wally, next to Tiny.

They clasp hands, holding on tightly, as if to ground each other to this spot.

The assemblage is completely still. A spell is in the air; what's happening here, right now, is so different from everything that takes place in their lives that it seems almost dreamlike, suspended in time.

The Reverend Wally Jackson of the Universal Life Church makes note of this special moment.

"If there's anyone who doesn't believe that love can change the world, they should be here today, in this spot, with us," he notes. "Because every one of us, right now, is in personal change, and it's deep. Real deep."

Laura flashes on what he's saying. It penetrates right to her core—why Dorothy makes her pilgrimages to places like this, to be with people who are so different from her. This is a righteous learning experience, one she hopes will stick.

"Dearly beloved . . . we are gathered here today . . ." Wally begins.

The television camera is poised, focusing on them, on all of those assembled here, to record this wonderful moment for posterity. And as the video camera begins to roll, the men who were in the jail cell with Frank Bascomb turn their backs so they're not spotted by the lens; unnoticed, they casually drift away, crossing the busy street against the traffic and disappearing from sight.

8

KNOW WHEN TO FOLD 'EM

Night, nine o'clock. Kate sits in her office going over some notes, a half-eaten order of kung pao chicken coagulating in a cardboard container on the corner of her desk. This afternoon she spent three grueling hours interviewing a client for Paul Larson, a lawyer she works with who specializes in personal injury cases. It was hard, tedious work that left her drained.

She finishes typing her notes into the computer, backs it up, turns the machine off. She'll print the report out in the morning, walk it over to Paul's office. Dumping the remains of her dinner in the trash basket under her desk, she starts turning off the lights.

The telephone rings. Once, twice, three times. She debates with herself whether or not she should pick it up; she's done with work for today, all she wants now is to pick up a cold bottle of wine, drive up to her hiding place above the city, and soak the grime away in the pool.

The call could be Cecil. She snatches the phone from the cradle a second before the machine would pick up. Hopefully: "Hello?"

"Is this Detective Blanchard?" It's a man's voice, unknown to her; slightly Latino-accented, soft, breathy.

"Who's calling?" she asks cautiously.

"I heard you're looking for some men."

She holds the receiver away from her mouth for a moment, so he won't hear the sharp exhale.

"What men are you talking about?" she parries.

"You know."

"I do?"

"You been out on the street looking for them, ain't you?"

"I've been talking to people, yes."

"Well . . ."

She waits. Nothing more. "Yes?"

"The men that were in the jail. With that dope dealer that killed himself. You're looking for those men . . . aren't you?"

She closes her eyes, nods silently. "Yes," she says into the phone. "I'm looking for them."

She stands on the corner of Soledad and Indio Muerto, the heart of the barrio. It's dark out, quiet. Her car is parked down the block.

The street is quiet, empty. She's dressed for fast, easy movement—jeans, running shoes, a comfortable light jacket over a T-shirt. She carries her wallet in the jacket pocket. She didn't bring her purse, or anything else. She was instructed not to.

"You'll be picked up in an hour," the voice on the telephone had told her. "Be alone, and unarmed."

She glances at her watch. It's been an hour, a little more. Where are they? She crosses her arms, uncrosses them, jams her hands into her back pants pockets. She doesn't like standing out here alone: this is not a good area for a single woman to be at night, especially—she doesn't like thinking this, but it's a reality—a single Anglo woman. She's a sitting target standing out here. A lot of bad shit happens in this neighborhood.

A black Infiniti Q45 comes cruising down the street, heading her way. The car pulls up to the curb in front of her.

She tenses.

The driver is a young Chicano, dressed in the standard uniform—white T-shirt, baggy khakis. Slicked-back hair. Big, muscular. He looks at her through the window, his face impassive. A second man, about the first one's age, similarly dressed, is riding shotgun. Smaller than the driver, bone-lean. Much meaner-looking.

In the backseat, alone, sits the older hooker Kate had talked to on the street. She's nervous, hyper, a bundle of twitches. Probably overdue for a fix, Kate guesses.

"This her?" shotgun asks the hooker.

"Yes." Her voice is low. Her face is drained of color, the smell of fear is on her. Kate sees that at first glance.

He steps out of the car, looking her up and down, a quick, brutal appraisal.

"Let me have your jacket," he says.

She takes off her jacket, hands it to him. He removes the wallet, rifles through it, checks out there's nothing in the other pockets, puts the wallet back in the pocket he took it from, drapes the jacket on the roof of the car. The first man sits behind the wheel, watching stolidly.

"Turn around. Legs spread, arms out."

"I'm not armed. As you requested." She doesn't want him touching her.

"Wire."

"No recorder, either. I'm clean."

The choice is not hers. "Do as I tell you," he persists politely.

She turns her back to him, spreading her legs shoulder-width, arms ninety degrees from her body, stiffening involuntarily as he squats and begins patting her down, starting with her legs, moving up her body, sides, back, front. He knows how to do it—the way it's been done many times, she's sure, to him.

He hands her jacket over. She puts it on.

"Get in," the man commands.

She stands on the curb, hesitating a moment. Anything could happen; no one knows she's doing this. She's a single woman, she comes and goes, answering to no one.

She opens the back door and gets in. The hooker slides against the opposite door, as far from Kate as she can get. The car pulls away in a smooth surge of power. Three blocks down it turns left on Milpas, heading towards the freeway.

———————

They driver south on 101, a careful five miles over the speed limit. The traffic is sparse. The radio is turned on low to a Spanish-music station. Out of Santa Barbara they travel, past Montecito, Summerland, Carpinteria, crossing the county line at Rincon. The moon, three-quarters full, illuminates the low-breaking ocean waves, the lapping whitecaps etched with a phosphorescent glow, spreading out from the shoreline for several hundred yards.

No one talks. Kate stares out the windows as they glide past Rincon to her right and the small town of La Conchita to her left, then past the funky Cliff House motel, the highway a black winding ribbon paralleling the train tracks.

Where are they taking me? she wonders. More importantly—what have I gotten myself into?

They turn off onto California 1 at Oxnard, cruise down Oxnard Blvd.

As they pass 5th St., 6th St., 7th St., the signage on the stores becomes increasingly, then completely, Spanish. Kate has only been in this area once. She and a Chicana friend who grew up around here, who now works in Goleta as a social worker, drove down for Mexican food. "The best Mexican food in the state," the friend had boasted, and it was true: great, great food. You have to be from the area to know about it, or be introduced by someone who is. She had been the only non-Latino in the place.

The driver hangs a right onto a residential street. Small stucco houses, closely spaced on both sides, well-groomed vest-pocket front yards, many of them fenced with chain link. Rottweilers stare out through the links at anything passing close.

They park in front of a house in the middle of the block, a bungalow like the others around it. The grass has been recently cut, the edges trimmed. A large weeping willow overhangs the house, the branches brushing the roof. Inside, a few lights are on.

The two men get out. The driver walks around the car to Kate's side, opens her door.

"Come with us," the shotgun passenger tells her, getting out on his side. He looks over at the woman crouched low in the backseat. "Stay put," he orders her.

Kate follows them up the path to the front door. The man who rode shotgun unlocks it with a key, ushers Kate in with a nod, then closes the door behind the three of them, double-bolting it.

The small living room is empty, but the television in the corner is on to an informational, the sound muted. The furniture, ordinary pieces, looks familiar to her. Her home in Oakland was furnished very much like this.

"Follow me." Again the order comes from the man who's done all the talking—it's obvious to her that he's more important than the driver. The driver is muscle. This one is more than that.

The driver guards the front door as the other man leads Kate through the house.

The kitchen is all the way in the back. A big room, larger than the living room, with the family room adjoining it—a built-on, garage conversion; a good, professional job.

Two men are seated at a table in the breakfast nook. They stand as she enters, a polite gesture. They're older than the two that brought her; she guesses one of them to be in his mid-thirties, the other in his late twenties, although it's hard to tell. They've led a hard life, that's clear to see—much of it behind the bars of state prisons, she'd bet. They have the look of the con. She saw that look a lot when she was in law enforcement.

"Have a seat," the older of them says to her, in a voice that, while polite enough, is used to being obeyed without question. To the man who led her in: "Wait in the other room."

Shotgun-seat turns on his heel and leaves. He's not important enough to remain for their conversation; this she understands immediately. There is a hierarchy here—the two men in this room are at the top.

She sits down as she was instructed. The two men sit opposite her, chairs turned backwards, their heavily muscled forearms resting on the seat backs. Both fix her with a strong, unwavering gaze.

"Coffee?" the man who told her to sit down asks. He gestures to a Mr. Coffee machine sitting on the kitchen counter, the "on" light glowing.

"No, thanks." She doesn't know how long this will take, she doesn't want to have to use their bathroom.

No offer of anything stronger.

"You've a private detective." Again, the same man asking the question. He's going to do all the talking, she assumes.

"That's right."

"You got a state license?"

"Yes."

He nods. "Interesting job for a woman."

"Beats waitressing."

"Not too many of you, are there?"

A little bit of cat-and-mouse going on here. Establishing territories, boundaries.

"No," she answers. She's going to give him what's necessary, nothing more.

"You work out of Santa Barbara, then?"

"Yes."

"You live there?"

He can find out where she lives simply by looking in the phone book.

"Yes."

"Most of your work . . . is it in Santa Barbara?"

"Almost all of it," she answers. "I'm a one-person firm, I don't have the resources to spread out."

He nods, letting that settle in.

The second man hasn't blinked. His look is right into her eyes.

"You good at what you do?" her questioner continues.

"I get the job done. My clients don't have any complaints."

"That's good to hear."

Why? she wonders.

"I appreciate professionalism," he explains, as if reading her mind.

"I do too," she says.

"It's good we got that established." He leans forward slightly, locking into eye contact with her. His partner maintains his posture. His eyes have not left her face the entire time she's been in the kitchen.

She makes an assessment from her gut: he's the one to worry about, the one you don't ever want to turn your back to. He's the one who will have no compassion, about anything.

"One thing about a professional," the one doing the talking continues. "They know when to walk away from a losing hand."

"I don't play cards."

"This thing you're doing . . . looking for these men? That were in the same jail cell with that dope freak that killed himself?"

"I'm looking for someone who knows what happened to him, that's right." Don't back down, you can't back down from this.

"Don't."

She's glad she didn't take them up on the offer of coffee. Her leg begins to twitch under the table, involuntarily. She pushes down on her thigh with her palm to still it.

"I'd like to leave now," she says, amazed at the audacity in her voice.

"You can leave any time you want. We'll take you right back to where we picked you up, no *problema*. But hear me out first."

She looks from one man to the other. "I'm listening."

"You're a smart woman. I can tell that just by being here with you for five minutes. I got good instincts for that."

She breathes slowly, deeply, concentrating on her breathing. "I'll take that as a compliment," she allows.

"It is. One thing a smart woman knows, a smart woman detective especially, is when she's in over her head. And right now, lady, you are in over your head."

"How do you know that?"

His eyes flash.

Be careful, she warns herself, don't push him too far. Listen to him, let him do the talking.

"I know shit you'll never know," he says, his voice low, barely audible. "This little investigation of yours, it's much bigger than you realize, lady. You are out of your league. A lot."

They said she could leave whenever she wanted to. If she asked to leave now, she doesn't know if they'd let her. Either way, she's afraid to try—that she hates herself for having that fear is of small consolation in the moment.

The man gets up from the table, walks to the end of the kitchen counter. He opens a black leather briefcase and takes out a manila envelope.

"Take this," he tells her as he sits back down, sliding the envelope across the table to her.

She opens the clasp, looks inside. The envelope is full of money, crisp bills in bank wrappings.

"That's twenty thousand dollars," he says. "Count it if you don't want to take my word. I won't be offended."

Her hands are shaking. She doesn't try to hide it from them.

"I can't take this." She pushes the envelope back to their side of the table.

"You earned this. It's yours."

She shakes her head. "I can't do this. I wish you had never shown this to me."

"These men you're looking for," he says. "They can never be found. Never. Do you understand that?"

She doesn't answer.

"Do you?"

"I don't know."

"Whatever happened . . . the jail, whatever . . . that is over and buried. It should stay that way."

"You mean somebody wants it to stay that way. Enough to offer me twenty thousand dollars." And scare the shit out of me, she thinks.

"It should stay that way," he says again.

She nods. "You asked me to listen to you. I did. Now I want to go."

She gets up. Her legs feel like bags of water; for a moment she's afraid she's going to collapse, but she manages to steady herself.

The man's eyes narrow. "You're not taking this money?" he asks in surprise. "It's untraceable," he adds, in case she mistook the content of the offer.

"That doesn't matter. I can't do it." She forces herself to stare back at him with as much force as he's using on her.

He stands up. "Then go."

The other man, the one who said nothing but stared holes into her soul, stands also.

"Something you should remember," the speaker tells her. "You have revealed yourself. We know who you are, and where you live."

"Are you threatening me?"

"No, lady. That's not our way. We're telling you facts."

"Thank you." She turns away from them, ready to leave.

The sound of a different voice stops her: "One more thing."

She turns back. The other man, the one who all this time had said nothing, has spoken.

"What?" She feels her throat constricting, she's immediately dry, unable to breathe.

"You have two daughters," he says to her. "And where they live, that we know also."

The world is turning black, utterly dark. "If you lay a hand on my kids . . ."

"That's not our style," the first man says quickly, reading her fear, taking pains to try to obviate it in that regard. "But you should know what we know about you. Which is everything."

There is an ominous finality to his last sentence.

"This is not your fight," the second man cautions her. "Walk away from it."

On the ride home time exists in a vacuum. No one says a word. The men who brought her stare straight ahead, their eyes glued to the road. Kate doesn't know if they know what happened in the kitchen. She figures they think whatever their leaders wanted, that's what happened.

The hooker hasn't said anything, either. She casts a glance at Kate now and again, but she, too, keeps still.

The car pulls off the freeway at the Milpas off ramp. They drive up to Mason St. The man riding shotgun turns to the backseat.

"Get out," he orders the hooker.

As she opens the door the woman stares at Kate. "Where's that fancy reward you promised me?" she finds the courage to ask.

"Get the fuck out of here!" the man yells at her.

"She said . . ." A whimper, like a beaten dog.

"Don't piss me off," he warns her.

"It's all right," Kate cuts the man off. "I'll take care of it. The men you brought me to see would want me to," she adds.

She takes out her wallet, pulls out three twenties. Except for a couple of singles, it's all she has on her.

"Here, take this," she says, thrusting the money into the woman's hand.

The woman looks at the bills like Kate has handed her a bag of wet dog shit. "You said big money," she sneers, too stupid to know to quit when she's ahead.

Kate snaps: a five-dollar junkie whore jerking her chain is the last straw. Reaching across the seat, she grabs the door handle and yanks it shut, almost crushing the woman's hand in the process.

"Go!" she orders the driver.

He stomps on the gas, fishtailing up the street.

"I have had enough shit for one night," Kate says to no one in particular. "Take me to where you picked me up," she demands of the men in the front seat.

The streets are deserted as she drives home. She feels like she'll sleep until noon.

The *Santa Barbara News-Press* hits the doorstep outside her apartment. Kate rolls over, looks at the clock by her bedside: 5:45. With a groan she forces herself from her bed, pulls up the window shade, peers out. The sky is lightening to a shade of pale white, with not a hint of morning fog.

The street outside her apartment is quiet, empty. No ominous-looking cars are parked anywhere. Her paranoia, which she had thought she had washed away in the dark water of her secret place, is strong enough in the clear, harsh light of day that she is afraid there might be something out there, waiting for her.

She hasn't slept—not for one moment, all night long, since she returned. The reference to her kids: that's what got her, more than anything. She couldn't have gotten that out of her mind if she'd swum to Catalina.

It was a bluff, she knows that: a scare tactic, a means to an end, the end being that she should pay attention to them. In her mind she knows that. Her mind must take control, over her emotions.

It *would* never happen, but it *could*. She has to deal with that distinction, make sure the two stay separate.

She throws on her robe, goes into the kitchen to brew a fresh pot. Her hands are doing their own private dance, independent of the rest of her. She puts the unfilled pot down, jams the uncooperative appendages into the pockets of her robe.

This is too much—she has to do something, right this minute.

She dials the number on the card, gets his answering machine, which gives his pager number. She calls it.

In less than five minutes her telephone rings. She snatches it up, realizing that she's been pacing the floor the entire time.

"Hello?" she says. Her hand is shaking, holding the phone.

"Do you know what time it is?" the man on the other end of the line asks her.

"I have to talk to you. Right away." She doesn't try to hide the panic in her voice—she wants him to hear it, to motivate him to get his ass over to her place, pronto.

He gets her intention, clearly. "Are you all right?"

"Yes, but I need to see you."

"I can be there in half an hour," he promises.

She hasn't fired her weapon in six months. She needs to clean it, go out to the range, fire off a box of shells. Otherwise it could jam up when she needs it. She gets it out of the closet anyway, checks to see that it's loaded, sits waiting on the couch, the heavy automatic clutched tightly in both hands in her lap.

She knows he's coming but she jumps anyway when the doorbell rings. On tiptoes she crosses to the door.

"Is that you?" she asks, not opening the door, even on the chain.

"Yes," he answers reassuringly.

She stashes the gun in a drawer, takes the chain off the latch, unlocks the door. She doesn't want him to see her holding a gun; she doesn't want him to know she's scared that badly.

Juan Herrera stands on the threshold, wearing sweats. He hasn't shaved or showered, but he looks good, she can't help but notice. Strong, supportive. What you look for in a man in these circumstances. He has a McDonald's take-out bag in his hand.

"I assume you can use this," he says, handing her a cardboard cup of coffee.

"Thanks." She closes the door behind him, locks it.

Now that he's arrived, the tension, which has been what's holding her together, sags from her body like air slowly leaking from a balloon.

They sit on her couch, drinking coffee. In a voice that becomes calmer as the telling unwinds she recounts what happened to her the night before. He listens attentively, carefully, sipping his coffee, not inter-rupting or asking questions. Only when she tells him about their refer-ences to knowing how to get to her at any time, and about her daughters and the covert threat against them, does she start to lose it again.

He moves close to her, a reassuring arm going around her shoulders. She sags against him, feeling his warmth, his solid musculature.

"They're not going to get at you from that direction," he assures her. "They want you to leave things alone, not get more involved."

"I know that, but I can't help being scared about it."

"I understand. And I want you to understand that that's an emo-tional reaction, not a logical one."

"Yes, I know that, too."

"People like this don't work out of emotion, unless it's something personal, which I don't think this is."

"Okay, good. I knew that, but it's good to hear it from somebody else."

She had been a cop. She knows what he says is true. But it's happen-ing to her right now, and thinking straight isn't as easy when it's this up-close and personal.

"It's scary, I mean they were talking about my kids," she continues, and she starts to shake again, it's the last thing she wants, but she can't help it.

She begins to cry. She's been holding it in all night.

His hand is on the back of her neck, gently caressing her, she moves to him, her mouth finds his.

Kissing him. That's all she's doing. Kissing him, and being held. It feels so good.

His hand is on her thigh under the robe. She parts her legs so he can find her. She's wet, even before he touches her there.

He's more direct than Cecil, more forceful. They don't say a word: he leads her into her bedroom, takes off her clothes, sheds his own—he has nothing on under the sweats—lays her on the bed, enters her.

She's all nerves and emotion. He is in control, bringing her off several times before spending himself.

Her fear sloughs like an old unneeded skin. She can make a pot of coffee now, standing in her kitchen with her robe wrapped around her, pouring two cups, taking his into the bedroom where he sits up in her bed, his hirsute pelt glistening with her perspiration.

She hands him his cup. "Would you mind getting dressed?" she asks him.

———————

"For what it's worth, I don't step out on my marriage," he tells her. "You're the only one."

They're both dressed, back on the living-room couch, a safe, discreet space between them.

"Don't be hard on yourself," he says.

"You're married, I need to work with you, I can think of lots of other reasons we should not sleep together."

He states the obvious: "It was hanging over our heads like a rain cloud. This way . . ." he shrugs. "It was an excuse to not feel as guilty as we would have otherwise. I'm human, I wanted you."

She shakes her head. "I can't sleep with you again and ask you for help."

"I don't equate the two."

"But I do."

He nods slowly. "I came here to help you. I still will."

"Whether or not we sleep together. Because . . ." She hesitates.

"What?"

"It's not about your being married. I just said that, for an excuse."

He looks at her with a puzzled expression.

"I'm seeing another man," she explains. "I don't know if anything's going to come of it, but I don't want anything getting in the way. I want to give it a chance," she adds.

He nods, drinks some coffee. "Why didn't you call *him*?" he asks.

"He can't help me with this," she admits candidly.

Herrera has commandeered a small conference room at the station. Mug-shot books are stacked on the table. Kate leafs through the books page by page, carefully looking at each picture.

"Here," she says, pointing excitedly to a stark black-and-white photo. "This was one of them. One of the two I talked to in the house."

He looks over her shoulder; frowns, but doesn't comment. "Go on. See if you can find any of the others." He inserts a Post-It to mark the place.

She pages through, more quickly.

"This is the other one," she declares, pointing to a picture of the other man who was inside, the one who had been silent until he spoke up about her daughters. "This one sent chills down my spine."

"Well." He looks at the mug shot. He flips to the first picture, then back to the second.

"Was I right?" she asks. "To be scared?"

He sits on the edge of the table. "Being scared was the healthy thing to be. This is major bad news here," he says, staring hard at her, to make sure she's hearing him good. "They're in the Mexican Mafia, both of them, big time. Hard-core offenders, nothing sissy about any of their convictions." He points to the second man's picture. "Rafael here, he's a major offender. He just got out of Lompoc about six months ago. Assault with intent. He's killed three men we're sure of, but we could never stick him with those. The Feds have been trying to RICO him for years so they can bury him in a federal pen, although now, with the three-strikes law, anything the state can pin on him will put him down forever. Believe me, we're hoping and praying."

"That's comforting," she says, beginning to shiver again.

"The other man, Orestes Marrano, he's no Sunday walk in the park, either."

"Shit."

"Yep, that's right, shit. You're in a pile of it. Jesus," he wonders aloud, "what are these guys doing in this?"

"Maybe it was their deal," she says.

"That's an obvious possibility. One the department is going to have to look into."

"I don't want to get involved in any of that," she interjects immediately, her kids' faces flashing before her eyes. "If there's repercussions it could make things even worse for me."

"I'll see to it you're completely covered," he assures her.

"How can you do that?" she asks, not assured at all.

"If I can't, I'll let it slide."

She knows how hard that is, for a cop not to pursue something he knows is dirty. "I appreciate that. I really do."

"I don't have a choice," he answers. "Not after earlier."

"I wish things were different for us, too."

"They're not. It's okay."

"What should I do in the meantime?" she asks. "What would you do?"

"I can't tell you what to do with your life," he says, "much as I'd like to. But if it were me, I'd be watching my ass. Day and night."

"What about my client? I've got her to think about, too."

"I don't know about her. I don't much care, either." He takes her hand, a protective gesture. "You're important to me, Kate. So when I tell you these men are not to be fucked with, at any cost, I mean exactly that."

"That's good advice," Carl tells her. "Your friend the cop sounds like he's got a brain in his head."

They're sitting outside again, in the same spot. This time she has his undivided attention, at least for the moment.

"What would you do?" she asks him. "If this was your case?"

"Are you going to ask the same questions to everyone you know until you get the answer you want to hear?"

"Sorry I bothered you," she flares, standing up.

"Sit down, goddamnit!" He grabs her wrist, hard. "Don't treat me like this."

She drops back into her chair. "Sorry."

He lets go. She rubs the wrist. It's sore, he's got a grip like iron on him.

"If this was my case . . ." He peters out, his mind drifting. He's getting old, she realizes with a shudder. Wearing out.

"What?" she asks impatiently. It's the game he plays, to keep her staying longer; normally she doesn't mind, but her nerves are frayed down to the last strand, she needs an answer.

". . . I'd follow it to the bitter end," he finishes, snapping to.

"I knew you'd say that."

"But it isn't what you want to hear."

She doesn't answer.

"You aren't doing this to please me," he reminds her. "You do the job for yourself. Only yourself."

"I can't help trying to please you."

"That's nice. I've always wanted to be somebody's mentor. But that's not the point, is it?"

"I guess not."

"I'm not forty years old and I'm not a woman. And I don't have children."

"But you are a professional. Which I am, too. It says so, on my card."

"If you got killed over this, you'd be a dead professional."

She rubs her eyes with her knuckles. She's bone-tired, she hasn't had any sleep for a day and a half, and the fear has fatigued her even more.

"Bag it," he advises her—forcefully, almost vehemently.

She jumps, startled by the power in his voice.

"Look," he tells her, ticking the numbers off on his fingers. "One, you can't locate any witnesses. Two, heavy people want you off this case. Three, putting your life on the line is not what you enlisted for."

"I hate quitting."

"This isn't quitting. You're not a quitter, I'll go into court and swear to that if I have to."

"I hate quitting more than anything."

"You were hired to find out if some joker committed suicide, or if somebody did him. Okay, you've found out. You've done your job. Anything beyond that is *not* your job. Finding *who* killed him is *not* your job, can you understand that?"

"It feels like quitting to me."

"Your life is not worth this. Listen to me," he presses, "it isn't. Certainly your children's lives are not worth this." He grips her hand again. "Resolving what happened to this scumbag is not worth your life. Or anyone else's."

Kate takes her gun out of the drawer where she's kept it locked up since she moved to Santa Barbara. The S&W automatic sits in an expensive leather gun box (a birthday gift from Eric, in lieu of earrings or flowers), a full box of ammunition beside it. She hasn't fired one round since the day she left the police force. She doesn't carry it. She has never used it in a real-life situation.

She holds the lethal weapon in her hand, turning it over. It's hefty—she feels the weight of it. A fine layer of dust has settled on the stock and barrel, which she wipes off with a piece of rag.

She should oil it before she fires it. Give it a good cleaning, make sure all the parts are in proper working order. Your weapon is one of your most valuable allies. Treat it with the respect it deserves. It says so, in the training manual.

Right now, she doesn't have the time for that. The patience—that's what she doesn't have. She just wants to pull the trigger, feel the explosion in her hand.

She pops the clip: empty. She won't keep a loaded gun in her house.

She puts the gun, the box of ammo, a pair of thin leather gloves, and a set of earplugs into a duffel bag, carefully lays the bag on the seat of her car next to her, and drives out of town up Highway 154, turning off onto one of the camp trails past Lake Cachuma.

The shooting range is in an arroyo. You fire at your targets against a limestone bluff. There are millions of bullet holes in the side of the bluff.

Kate pays her fee and walks down to the far end. Only a few people are out here, all men. Two are pistol shooters like her. The other has a target rifle, a .22-long. None of them pay her any attention; they're here for a purpose.

She takes her gloves out of the duffel bag and puts them on, snugging the leather on the fingers against the webs. Then she takes her weapon out of its case and loads it, a bullet at a time. Eleven in the clip, one in the chamber. The plastic cups of the earplugs cover her ears. As soon as she puts them on the sounds from the other shooters diminish to almost inaudible pops.

Firm grip. Eyes on your target. Squeeze, don't jerk.

The gun explodes in her hand with a kick much stronger than she'd remembered. She feels the action of the recoil in her wrist, especially the tendons. The bullet hits high above her target, several feet above where she was aiming.

She should have worn a wrist guard. She'll have to ice the wrist down when she gets back to town, or she'll be sore tomorrow. She grasps her right wrist with her left to steady it and give it support.

She fires fifty rounds, half a box. By the time she's finished she's doing well, the bullet holes grouped together on the target in a nice tight cluster. She was in the middle of her class during training. Good enough to get the job done.

She's never had to shoot at a real person in earnest. She hopes never to have to. If she doesn't carry, she won't have to; she won't be able to. People do kill people, this is true, but they use guns to do it. Killing is not her style.

When she's finished she removes the clip, making sure there isn't one left in the chamber. She puts everything carefully away, walks back to her car, and drives off.

Instead of locking the gun up where she had before, in a safe place but not easily accessible, she puts it along with a box of ammunition in a drawer in her bedroom, where she can reach it without even having to put her feet on the floor.

"What have you found?" Laura can't keep the anticipation from her voice. Dread mixed with excitement mixed with hope. "Have you found anything out?"

"Yes," Kate informs her. "I found something. Several things, in fact." Her voice is calm, her manner understated—she is the professional private detective that Laura Sparks, her client, hired.

"Was I right? About Frank?"

"Yes," Kate says slowly in answer.

She's been dreading this, since calling Laura on the phone earlier, several hours ago, and telling her they had to meet ASAP. She has information for Laura, things to tell her; but they aren't going to be what Laura wants to hear.

It's not about Frank Bascomb, how he died, why he died. She doesn't know those things, and she isn't going to. And not because the trail is dead, that there are no leads. That's not the truth. *She* can't go on, she has gone as far as she can go. As far as her sense and guts will let her.

She's never quit on a client before; the thought of it is repulsive to her. More than anything else she hates quitting, because that is her deepest fear, that at the core she is a quitter. It's what Eric always told her, over and over, until she believed it, for a long time.

She managed to get past that, to put it in the shitcan where it belongs. He was wrong, she came to understand that. The therapy and the groups taught her that.

If you quit on one client, what's to stop you from quitting on others? More importantly, on yourself?

They are in Kate's office, seated opposite each other in the only two chairs in the room. Kate had asked Laura to meet her here, so that this final rendezvous would have the semblance of a formal meeting. A professional meeting. That, as she clearly sees now, was a shuck. But the client doesn't know that—not yet.

"He *didn't* kill himself." It isn't a question Laura poses, but a vindication, a triumph. She was right and everyone else, the elders who knew better, were wrong. "I *knew* it!"

"I'm pulling off this case," Kate tells her in a low, flat, emotionless voice.

If she had thrown a bucket of ice-cold water square into the girl's face she couldn't have stopped her faster in her tracks.

"What? What did you say?"

"Yes, he didn't kill himself," Kate says. "That's what you hired me to find out. I don't know how he died, but I am convinced, beyond a shadow of a doubt, that Frank Bascomb did not do himself in."

"I don't understand."

Kate looks at her. "You asked me to try and find out if Frank Bascomb took his own life in the county jail. I don't have any proof, but I know he didn't."

"Then how do you know?" Laura asks, suspiciously.

"Trust me. If I know one thing, it's that."

"I'd like to know how you know. You must know something to say what you've just said. I'm entitled to know what you know, I've paid you for it."

Kate shakes her head. "You paid me to find out. Now . . ." She takes a long breath to compose herself. ". . . as I said, there is no proof, no tangible piece of evidence. Maybe there is, somewhere, but I don't have it, and I can't get it. Look," she implores Laura, "listen to me. This is bigger and deeper than I could have imagined. I can't get to it, not without putting myself in personal jeopardy, and I'm not willing to put my life on the line for this case—or any case, for that matter. And I'm not willing to tell you what I do know because then *you* would be in jeopardy, and that would be even worse."

"That should be my decision, shouldn't it?"

"He was murdered. That's off the record, I didn't say that, but he was. By people you do not want to mess with."

"Who says?"

If Kate could strangle some sense into Laura, she would. If she could hug some sense into her, she would do that, also.

"Let it go," she begs Laura, suddenly feeling old. Not *old* old, but grown-up, not young and blissfully unknowing. "It's not your life, it's not your world, it has nothing to do with you."

"It has *everything* to do with me! I was there, with him!"

"Don't you understand that that was a setup? That he used you for that very purpose?"

"He didn't use me. He didn't even know there was dope on that boat. He was the one who was used."

Joan of Arc was the only martyr Kate would have been willing to throw her hand in with. Certainly not with Laura Sparks, a young woman who doesn't know shit from shinola about the real world.

Carl was right. Herrera was right. If this spoiled innocent wants to be the first lemming off a cliff, why should Kate follow her?

"Did you spend all the money I gave you?" Laura asks coldly.

"You got your money's worth," Kate answers bluntly. Last night was the price of admission by itself. "And then some."

"When will I have your written report, like you promised me?"

"Tomorrow."

"Good. Maybe there will be something in it the next detective I hire can use."

No one else will touch this with a ninety-foot pole. Not in this world; not with that family. That's why Kate was hired in the first place, or has Laura already forgotten that?

"Please," she beseeches Laura, one last time. "This is not your fight. It never was. Let it go."

Laura stands. Three strides takes her to the door.

"Thank you for your . . . 'help.' "

"Thank you for shitting all over me" would have had less of a bitter ring to it, Kate thinks, as she inwardly winces.

Laura closes the door behind her. Even in anger she's too much the product of her breeding to slam it in Kate's face.

Kate slumps back in her chair. She did the right thing, she tells herself. An irrational client is impossible, particularly one who has never been told "no."

Still, it eats at her, and will for a while, until she's able to look at it rationally, not emotionally. She did the right thing. She is a professional, and a professional acts from her head, not her heart.

9

THE PEN IS MIGHTY

"**S**hit. That sucks."

Laura Sparks sits in her coroner office, staring intently at the writing on her computer screen.

Chastising herself for not getting it right. The story of her life.

Laura started up *The Grapevine*—Santa Barbara's left-slanted, ecology-oriented alternative weekly newspaper—two years ago, when she moved back home after graduating from Wellesley and living in New York. She had worked in the Museum of Modern Art's documentary film department (two members of the museum board are friends of her family) for a while until it got to be boring, and followed that with a briefer stint as a production assistant in public television. That was even more boring, a lot of drudge work—getting coffee for directors and mundane shit like that—and hardly any flash, nothing like what she had envisioned. She had never been introduced to Jonathan Demme or Meryl Streep, for example.

Being a newspaper publisher suits her. It's hip, cutting-edge, relevant. She especially loves the perks of her position, the social parts: the art gallery openings, the literary cocktail parties, the UCSB fund-raisers, rubbing elbows with writers and artists, all that stuff. And it's a real job, her own legitimate entry, not her parents' or grandmother's, it makes her feel grown-up and self-sufficient.

The offices of *The Grapevine* are located on the second floor of an old commercial building off Gutierrez St., a stone's throw from the freeway, which provides a constant teeth-jarring din throughout the building even when the windows are closed, like an urban crash of waves against rock.

This raucous ambiance suits Lester Wolchynski, a transplanted Chicagoan who is the paper's editor-in-chief and driving force, just fine. Lester is in his late middle age, a wire-haired dynamo who cut his teeth on Mike Royko and Studs Terkel; the paper reflects his progressive, in-your-face brand of political involvement.

Laura funds the paper with her own money (actually a loan from her grandmother; she doesn't come into the bulk of her inheritance until she's thirty, but her allowance is generous, she can do most anything she wants, within reason). Once in a blue moon she'll get her back up and contest some editorial policy or specific article that unfairly, by her lights, blasts a part of Santa Barbara that's important to her. She's progressive herself—at one time she was Dianne Feinstein's deputy county campaign chairman, for example—but this town and what it stands for is dear to her, you don't put it down for no good reason, throw a bomb for the sake of doing it.

Lester likes to break plates to hear the noise. Laura doesn't like uncomfortable sounds, anarchy is not her metier.

It's late in the evening; everyone's gone home. The heat hangs heavy in the air. She's wearing shorts and a tank top. Sweat moistens her upper lip. She wipes it off with a tanned forearm, scrolls up a page, makes a correction in her text.

This is important, what she's writing, the most important editorial she's written. The *only* editorial; she's never written one before.

"What are you doing here, Laura?" The sudden voice is harsh, nasal, vintage South Side Chicago.

"Ahh!" She screams, jumping half out of her skin. A row of rrrrrrrr's, the last letter she was typing, skips across her computer screen. "Jesus, Lester, you scared the shit out of me!"

He stands in the doorway. "You're the last person I'd expect to find in here this late."

"I needed to write something and I didn't want it to wait until tomorrow," she explains, disregarding the cut, "I want it to be fresh."

"Want what to be fresh?"

"I'm writing an editorial," she tells him, trying to sound firm, assertive. It's her newspaper, goddamnit, her money.

"The editorial staff writes the editorials," he firmly reminds her. "*I* write the editorials," he adds, to make his point clear.

"This one needs to come from me," she says to him, her stomach churning.

He glances over her shoulder, trying to sneak a look. She turns her body to face him so that she blocks his view. It's a work-in-progress, not ready to be critiqued, especially by him. Even if it was good, which it isn't yet, he'd tear it to shreds.

"So what's it about?" he asks.

He's mocking her, she can hear the mocking tone in his voice.

"Drugs. In our society. What they're doing to us."

"What *are* they doing to us?" he asks, pushing her.

"You know what I'm talking about," she answers.

"The bust on your property, I assume. And the fallout from it."

"Partly."

"What else?"

"Look, I'll finish it, I'll print up a copy and leave it on your desk, we can talk about it later."

"We send the paper out tomorrow morning," he informs her, as if she's a child who doesn't know how the operation works.

The paper is printed in Camarillo in a big industrial shop which does several small papers in the Tri-Counties. When the printing bill comes in, it's her signature on the check, that she knows.

"That's why I want to finish this now," she says.

"It's too late," he argues. "There's no room for any last-minute changes in this issue."

"We'll make room. I'll make room."

"You don't do that," he says forcefully.

"This time I'm going to," she says with equal force, surprised at hearing the defiance come out of her mouth. "Why are *you* here so late?" she asks, trying to change the subject, "are you spying on me?"

"Do I need to? Maybe I do, if you're going to start doing my job for me."

"I'm not trying to do your job, Lester, for godsakes. I'm writing something I think needs saying. I've never stepped on your toes, you should be happy I'm involved."

Bluntly: "I'm not."

"Are you telling me we're not going to print anything I write?" she asks, directly challenging him.

"The paper's closed and I haven't read it" is his answer.

"Come back in an hour," she instructs him.

He stares at her for a moment before turning on his heel and stalking away.

Goddamn him, she thinks, he doesn't have to treat me this way. I give him plenty of space.

She turns back to her processor and stares at the words on the screen. This has to be right.

————————

Lester marches into her office one hour later (virtually to the second) from when he had been asked to leave it, and demands to see her work.

She's been waiting for him. The editorial had been written, rewritten, buffed and polished as best she could make it. Then she had closed her eyes and gone inward, looking for the strength to stand up to him.

She hands him the two double-spaced pages and sits back, waiting. It is her paper, her money. She is going to take a stand.

He skims the first paragraph; then he rereads it, and the rest, more slowly and carefully. Finally he hands it back to her.

"You're short on proof," he says flatly, the seasoned newspaperman's antennae immediately aroused.

"I know," she agrees. "That's why it's an editorial instead of an article."

"Where did you get this information?" he probes.

"I have a source."

"Someone inside the sheriff's office?"

"No." A beat. "Not precisely."

Keep him hanging, wondering. Mystery can be the great equalizer. Blanchard probably did have sources in the department; don't all detectives? Blanchard had been a police officer once, Laura remembered, she had to know the police down here.

More importantly: Lester thinks she, Laura, knows something, or someone, that he doesn't know. That gives her power over him, real power for the first time. Signing his check doesn't give any real power; knowledge does.

"This is inflammatory," he tells her. "If I were you I'd be nervous about publishing this."

Nervous? Yes, but it's a delicious feeling, like forbidden sex.

She hasn't used Kate's name in the editorial, nor did she use the words "private detective" or "independent investigator." Her terms were "reliable sources" and "on the condition of anonymity." Like they use in the *Washington Post*.

"Well," he says finally, "it is intriguing. Your phone will be ringing tomorrow, that's for sure."

She's surprised. "You like it?"

"Good old muckraking journalism—the smell of blood. Of course I like it. I'm not the one who has to pay the insurance premiums, though."

"Do you really think I might be sued?" she asks him. Her ardor has been so great, her concentration on getting it right so demanding, she hasn't even thought of that possibility. As a publisher, she would demand more proof from a reporter than she has from herself. Maybe that's why newspapers have separate publishers and editors.

"If you don't have backup you could be in trouble. Because Woodward and Bernstein got away with it doesn't mean you can."

Woodward and Bernstein: the Holy Grail. They give Pulitzers for local papers, don't they?

"If I were you I'd sleep on this," he cautions her.

"What about if *you* were you?" she asks.

"That's a different story. Different situation."

"Because you're a real newspaperman and I'm just a girl with a fat checkbook?"

"Because I have nothing to lose, and you do. This is your hometown," he reminds her.

"That's why it's so important," she answers. "Because it is my town."

"Are you sure you don't want to think about this?" he asks, testing her nerve. "There's always next week's issue."

"If I think about it I might chicken out." She gets up, stretching her back. The tension is physically painful. "Send it out for me, would you?" she requests of him. "I don't know how to work the modem."

He takes it from her. For one second he lets a smile out, then his face reverts to its habitual curmudgeonly frown.

"You've got more guts than brains, Laura."

It's after midnight when Laura parks in front of her little guesthouse and turns off the car lights. Across the lawn she sees the light still burning in Dorothy's bedroom. Reading in bed, Laura knows. Dorothy hardly sleeps. She's getting older, she doesn't have that much time left, she doesn't want to miss anything.

Getting out of the car, Laura takes the manila envelope from the passenger seat and walks across the grass to Dorothy's house.

The side door is unlocked. Dorothy never locks up until she's ready to go to sleep.

"Is that you, Laura?" she calls.

"Yes," Laura calls back.

"What are you doing up so late?"

"I was at the paper."

There's a corked half-full bottle of Sanford sauvignon blanc in Dorothy's refrigerator. Laura gets a wineglass from the cupboard, pours herself a generous amount. She's earned it.

"Bring a glass for me, too," Dorothy calls out.

The woman is telepathic sometimes. It's scary.

Laura walks through the house to her grandmother's bedroom. Dorothy is sitting up in bed, bolstered by several pillows, reading glasses perched on the end of her nose. She lays the book facedown on the covers next to her.

"I didn't know you worked late," Dorothy remarks, taking a sip of wine. "I thought that was for the peons," she adds, smiling so Laura will know she's kidding.

"Tonight was special."

She reaches into the envelope, takes out some 8 × 10 glossies, hands them to Dorothy. Pictures of the wedding at the homeless encampment.

"These are wonderful!" Dorothy exclaims. "These people will be very grateful."

Laura swallows a bracing mouthful of wine. She can't avoid this any longer. She takes a copy of her editorial from the envelope, hands it to Dorothy.

"What's this?"

"Read it. You'll see."

Dorothy begins reading, her brow immediately furrowing upon seeing the headline.

The furrow deepens as the gist of the piece comes clear.

WHAT IS EVERYONE AFRAID OF?

Less than three weeks ago one of the largest drug busts in the history of Santa Barbara County took place on a private dock. Over a ton of high-grade marijuana was seized, and two men were arrested. A third man, who apparently was the ringleader, was shot and killed while trying to escape by a member of the county sheriff's department, which made the arrests.

This drug bust was highly publicized. The sheriff's department, acting on a tip from a county employee, moved quickly and decisively. They did a thorough and professional job, and they are to be commended.

Subsequent events, however, have clouded these initial positive actions.

One of the men arrested was the partner of the ringleader. Although he did not have a substantial criminal record, it seems obvious from his background that he and the man who was killed were experienced players in the drug trade.

The third man, however, is a different story. His name was Frank Bascomb, and he had been the foreman of Rancho San Miguel de Torres in the Santa Ynez Valley for over ten years. He was an esteemed member of the community, and had no criminal record whatsoever.

Frank Bascomb swore upon his arrest that he had no knowledge of the cargo of the ship he was on. There is compelling evidence that Frank Bascomb was duped by the other two men, whom he had known casually for many years. Bascomb claimed he thought he was on a pleasure cruise and was doing his friends a favor by allowing them to anchor their boat on his employer's private dock because the harbor, in town, was overcrowded with boats celebrating Fiesta. The dock is owned by the Sparks family, who also owns Rancho San Miguel de Torres.

The morning following his arrest, Frank Bascomb was found dead in a jail cell in the county lockup. A piece of cord was around his neck, the other end tied to a bunk.

Although there were over a dozen men in that cell and those adjoining it, apparently not one of them saw this happen. They claimed they were all asleep.

In less than 24 hours, the county coroner certified that Frank Bascomb's cause of death was suicide. The body was buried a day later. No autopsy was performed.

Since then, a veil of silence has fallen over this case. The third man was granted bail and has left the county for parts unknown. Whether he will show up for his trial is questionable. More importantly, there has been no inquiry into whether or not Frank Bascomb, a man with no criminal record, who had sworn his innocence, actually did take his life, or was killed in that cell by someone else.

(A personal note, for the record: Another woman and I were on that boat with Frank Bascomb. The dock is, in fact, owned by my family. The other woman and I were also told it was a pleasure cruise, nothing more. The police believed our stories, and did not charge or book us. Why, then, did they not believe Frank Bascomb?)

Questions:

1. Why did the sheriff's department and the county coroner make the immediate and unconditional conclusion that the cause of Frank Bascomb's death was suicide?

2. The cause of death is officially "suicide, caused by suffocation by self-strangulation." Why was no autopsy performed to make sure this was, in fact, the method by which Frank Bascomb died?

3. Why weren't the other men in the jail cell with Frank Bascomb detained and questioned? Every one of them was let out of jail less than twelve hours after Frank Bascomb's body was discovered. They were all homeless transients. Their whereabouts are unknown.

4. Why won't the sheriff's office talk about this case? Neither this reporter nor anyone else has been able to get any straight answers from the department. Their attitude is, "This case is closed, there's nothing to talk about." Unnamed sources close to this situation tell us that this case may involve organized crime figures, which stands to reason, given the quantity of drugs that were seized.

The point of this editorial is not to accuse anyone of anything. It is to ask questions, and to try to shed light. The death of Frank Bascomb may be officially over, but it is not finished, not with so many important questions unanswered.

Is there a cover-up going on? If not, why isn't anyone in a position to know talking about this?

WHAT IS EVERYONE AFRAID OF?

Laura Sparks,
Publisher, *The Grapevine*

Dorothy finishes the editorial. The pages drop from her trembling fingers. Her heart rate has gone sky-high—she can feel it. She is an old woman, and at this moment she feels every one of her years.

"Your unnamed sources. It's that detective you hired, isn't it?"

Laura lies: "One of them."

"This is awful. You're accusing the sheriff's office of covering up a murder."

"I am not!"

"That is what I read."

Laura grabs the pages from Dorothy's lap, skims them. Did she actually say that? Covering up a murder? She couldn't have been that blunt.

She wasn't. She was forceful, but she wasn't accusatory. Not directly. "I did not say the sheriff's office covered up Frank's murder," Laura says. "What I said was, and I was very clear about it, was that Frank's death was not a clear-cut suicide, foul play might have been involved, that anyone looking at the evidence could see that, and that the investigation should have been more thorough."

"This is a disaster," Dorothy tells her. She's angry, as angry as Laura's ever seen her.

"Well, if it is, it's *my* disaster," Laura shoots back defensively, "and I'll live with it."

"You do not exist in a vacuum, Laura. We will *all* have to live with it. You should have thought of that before you did something so stupid as this. So reckless."

"Why is getting at the truth reckless?"

"There's no truth in this, only accusations."

"Well, maybe this'll be the catalyst to blow this thing up, and the truth will come out."

"Or maybe it'll blow up in your face. In all our faces."

They glare at each other.

"Have you shown this to your mother?" Dorothy asks. "Have you had the courage to do that?"

"She'll see it tomorrow," Laura states.

"Tomorrow?" The old woman's voice rings with alarm.

"The paper comes out tomorrow."

"No. You cannot do that to her. Or your dad. You have to tell them first."

"Okay," Laura capitulates. It's the last thing she wanted to do, but Dorothy's right. Her mother has to know about this before she sees it in the newspaper or, worse, hears about it from someone else. "I'll call her first thing tomorrow morning. I'll go see her, show it to her."

Dorothy nods. "What you really should do," she counsels Laura, "is sleep on this. When you wake up you might have a fresh perspective."

"That's what Lester Wolchynski told me to do," Laura admits.

"Well, that makes two of us," Dorothy says, relieved that Lester had put the brakes to this rash, precipitous impulse. "Lester's a bright man, he certainly knows the newspaper business."

Laura hesitates. "Anyway, I can't stop the run now, even if I wanted to," she confesses.

"Of course you can," Dorothy tells her. Her voice sounds a bit shrill to her ear; she takes a break and brings down the volume. "You're the publisher, you can do whatever you want, darling."

Laura shakes her head.

"I told Lester that I had to publish my editorial, that it was my decision and I'd take the heat for it, if there is any. It's gone over the modem to the printer," she explains. "We publish every Friday," she states matter-of-factly, "and tomorrow is Friday. We'll be on the stands by noon tomorrow."

"Tomorrow?" Dorothy echoes in disbelief.

"Twenty-five thousand copies. Our normal run. All over the county."

Call it avoidance. Call it willfulness. Or fear. Whatever the reason, Laura does not tell her mother or father about her front-page editorial before *The Grapevine* hits the streets of Santa Barbara County a little before noon.

Miranda is sitting down to lunch on the veranda of the Locust Club with two of her oldest and best friends, has just ordered an iced tea, and is about to exchange some juicy gossip, when the headwaiter approaches her table and quietly hands her a copy of the paper, cover page up. She always peruses *The Grapevine*, because her daughter is the publisher and she's a proud mother, even though there's seldom anything in it that's of interest to her. Lucky Jenkins's society column can be cute and quirky, and sometimes the political coverage, especially concerning malfeasance in county government, is better than the daily. Her favorite section is the personals: Men Seeking Women, Women Seeking Men, Men Seeking Men, Couples Seeking Bi Women. She's entertained the idea of responding to an ad, to have the experience. It would be a kick to meet someone who took out that kind of ad.

It doesn't register on her that being handed a counterculture newspaper by a waiter at the Locust Club, even if her daughter is the publisher, is unusual. In fact, it has never happened before. Locust, like most private clubs, is conservative in its membership and posture; *The Grapevine* is inappropriate in such a location. It is consistently against everything that places like the Locust Club stand for, even though the publisher's parents and grandparents have been members for decades.

"Is that your daughter's paper?" one of her friends inquires.

"Hers and hers alone," Miranda responds dryly, as she glances at the headlines and then casually flips through a few pages. She's more liberal in attitude and lifestyle than any of her friends, but there's the proper time and place for everything. She'll read it more thoroughly later, when she's not here.

"I didn't know that was part of the reading material here," the other woman says, as they all have a chuckle. Her name is Estelle. The third woman's name is Patricia. They have, at least in their own minds, rich and interesting lives, but here they are addressed as Mrs. Steven Arch and Mrs. Holcomb Smith, as Miranda is addressed as Mrs. Frederick Sparks.

"I'm sure it . . ."

The laughter dies in Miranda's throat, almost choking her, as in a delayed reaction her mind processes what it had subliminally perceived. Slowly, she turns back to the front page.

Laura's editorial, positioned in a box in the lower part of the page, leaps out at her.

"Jesus Christ!"

"What is it?" Estelle asks, alarmed by Miranda's violent outburst.

"Nothing. Everything. Never mind." She springs up from her chair, knocking it backwards onto the stonework. Folding the paper over so that the offending article is hidden, she rushes to the telephone.

The switchboard at *The Grapevine* is in a state of gridlock. Miranda gets four busy signals before she gets through. Although Laura is on another line, trying to fend off a reporter from the *Los Angeles Times*, she quickly disposes of that call.

"I should have warned you," she says immediately, before her mother can go into the tirade she knows is coming. "I didn't realize this was going to be such a big deal."

"That is quite an understatement!" her mother screams at her over the phone. She's in the women's locker room at the club, which thankfully is empty except for her and a couple of attendants, who are trained to hear nothing. "What did we talk about?" she continues, "the night you were arrested? Do you remember?"

"About whether I was involved or not," Laura answers.

"Bullshit." She hates having a telephone line between her and her daughter, she wants to be doing this face-to-face, to be *in* Laura's face, inside her very skin. "That was the tip of the iceberg," Miranda continues. "We talked about responsibility, Laura. About the family. About how ruinous this affair could be for us, for our future."

"How is asking questions about Frank's suicide—which I know it wasn't—going to affect our future?" Laura asks.

"Don't play games with me, you stupid little twit. We were his employers, and you were his bedmate, and it was our property. There are people out there who are sure we were behind that narcotics deal. People who hate us and would love nothing more than to see us go down. We fought like hell to put the fire out, and just when the flames are dying down and people are forgetting about it you go and throw gasoline on it. Now it's a bonfire, damn it!"

"It wasn't a suicide!" Laura wails over the phone. God, she's glad they're not in the same room right now. She'd be dead. "Doesn't that matter to you?"

"Not in the slightest," is Miranda's retort. "And it shouldn't to you, either. The family is what should matter, nothing else."

"Well, it does matter. The truth matters, Mom."

Miranda pauses, thinking. "How many calls have you gotten on this today? Who have you spoken to?"

"A lot. But I haven't really spoken to anyone. I mean, people have called me, people from in town and people from L.A. and stuff, but I haven't said anything to them."

"Listen to me," Miranda commands, "and listen good. You are to talk to no one. Nobody at all. I want you to get out of there, right now. Don't tell anyone where you're going, so they can't track you down."

"But they need me here!" Laura counters.

"DO AS I TELL YOU!" Miranda screams. "You leave that office this instant and you drive up to my house. I will meet you there in ten minutes."

She slams the phone down before her suddenly headstrong daughter can offer any resistance.

Laura is waiting for her in the solarium.

"Sit down," Miranda commands her.

Laura does as she's told. This is not the time to proclaim her independence, she's smart enough to know that.

Miranda sits in an overstuffed chair across from Laura. "Where did this come from?" she demands, brandishing the newspaper.

Laura doesn't answer.

"Don't play games with me, Laura. Somebody whispered in your ear and you responded. Now who was it? Who's using you?"

"Nobody's using me!" Laura flares.

"Bullshit. You didn't come up with this on your own. Who is it, that slimy editor of yours?"

"Lester had nothing to do with this. In fact, he tried to stop me from printing it."

"Yes, and the Pope's Catholic."

Laura glares at her mother. "Why is it that nobody gives me any credit for having a mind of my own?" she cries out, finding a reservoir of courage she didn't know she had in dealing with Miranda. "Why couldn't I have researched this myself? I'm capable, whether or not you're willing to believe it."

"You researched this? Somebody told you information that's in this editorial?"

Again, Laura doesn't answer.

"Somebody in the sheriff's department talked to you?"

Silence.

"I don't believe it." She throws down a gauntlet. "I don't think you'd know enough to even know who to approach, let alone have the guts to do it."

"You don't think I can do anything, do you?" Laura answers quietly. "You don't give me credit for anything. No brains, no curiosity, no backbone. Well, in this case, Mom, you're wrong."

Miranda regards her daughter. This is not the superficial, compliant, wanting-to-please daughter she's always known, the wannabe rebel who might put a toe in the water if everyone else would first.

"Maybe I have underestimated you," she concedes.

"Only all my life."

Miranda shakes her head. "Obviously." She pauses a moment to collect her thoughts. "Okay, so you did some homework. Who did you talk to, to get this stuff? Somebody in the sheriff's office? From the jail? You have to tell me, I want to be your ally in this, but I have to know what you know."

"Why?"

"So I can protect you."

"Who do I need protection from?"

"Anyone who feels they might be threatened by this."

"Like who?"

"Like the sheriff of this county. Like the district attorney. Like people you don't want to be upset with you."

"You're being melodramatic, Mom."

"Am I? If any of this editorial, even one piece, has some truth to it, don't you think somebody might want to stop it from going any further? If somebody really did kill Frank to shut him up, why wouldn't they come after you, too?"

"You're trying to scare me."

"You're damn right I'm trying to scare you!"

Laura bites at her lip.

"If you know something, Laura," Miranda goes on, "tell me."

"I can't, Mom."

"Why not?"

"Because I'd be betraying a source," she says. "You can't betray a source in the newspaper business."

"So there is somebody in the sheriff's department who talked to you about this."

"Why does it have to be somebody in the sheriff's office?" Laura asks her.

"Who else would have this kind of information?"

"Someone who was there. In the jail."

Miranda catches her breath. "A prisoner?"

"Maybe," Laura answers, trying to be cagy.

"Then I have to tell Ralph Walker. He has to reopen this." She moves to the telephone, picks it up, begins to dial.

"No!"

Miranda hesitates.

"Don't do that."

"Why not?"

"Put the telephone down, and I'll tell you."

Miranda hangs up. She crosses back to where she was sitting.

"You have to swear you won't tell anyone this," Laura says.

This time it's Miranda's turn to stay quiet.

"Swear," Laura begs her.

"All right," Miranda says. "I swear."

Laura chews at her lip. It's practically raw.

"I hired a private detective."

Miranda slumps. This is getting worse and worse. "Oh, no. You didn't."

Laura nods yes.

"Who was it?"

"I can't tell you."

"What did this detective . . . ? What information . . . ?" She's stammering. Composing herself: "What did he tell you? Is there any hard evidence?"

"Hard enough so—" She almost says "she," like she gave herself away to Dorothy, but she catches herself.

"Laura, you have to tell me this detective's name."

"I can't, Mother, please don't make me."

"You have to. I can't stand up for you if you don't. I'll keep it to myself, I promise you that, but you have to tell me."

Laura's lip is bitten raw. She knows her mother: sooner or later Miranda is going to find out, whether she tells her or not.

"The detective's name is Blanchard."

"Who? I've never heard of him."

A beat. "*Her,* not him."

"A woman?" Miranda asks. Now that is a surprise. "I didn't know there were any women detectives in Santa Barbara. Where is she from? L.A.?"

Laura shakes her head. "She's from here. She's kind of new." Quickly: "You can't tell anybody. And you can't talk to her, she can't know I told you any of this," she pleads.

"Don't worry," Miranda assures her daughter. "I promised you I wouldn't, didn't I? And I never break a promise." She pauses. "Not to a member of my family."

"Your client has a big mouth on her," Herrera tells Kate.

"What are you talking about?"

He called her at her office. She was in—preparing Laura Sparks's final billing, in fact. She had just licked the envelope and attached a stamp. In a few minutes she was going to walk down to the corner and drop it in the mailbox, along with some other mail.

"You haven't seen this week's *Grapevine?*"

"No." As soon as he says the word *Grapevine,* her stomach starts churning.

"Well, you're one of the few people in this town who hasn't," he says. "I'm heading in your direction. I'll drop a copy off on the way," he says before he hangs up.

He shows up a few minutes later, walking in without knocking, closing the door behind him quickly.

"Feast your eyes on this." He shows her the front-page editorial.

She skims over it. " 'Unnamed sources.' That's me." She lays the paper on her desk. "Just what I always wanted—notoriety."

"Who knows about this?" he asks her. "About you working for her?"

"Nobody except her," she answers. "Wait a minute," she says, amending that in her head, remembering Mildred Willard and their conversation in the church parking lot. "There is one other person, but she doesn't know anything, just that I'm working for Laura."

"What about your friends from Ventura?"

"They don't know I'm working for her."

"You don't think they can put two and two together?"

"Maybe." Nervously: "I guess they can."

" 'Unnamed sources.' That's you, all right. They're gonna know that."

"I didn't tell her anything," Kate protests. "I didn't tell her who they were or anything. I just told her I was leaving the case and that she should drop it."

"That's enough, if somebody wants it to be."

She glances down at the newspaper again. "Well, I know I'm clean. I don't know what else I can do."

"Hope there's no more articles like this, for one thing."

"Maybe I should call her," Kate says. "Make sure she leaves me out of this."

"That's a good idea," he agrees. He thinks a moment. "There's nothing on the record between you two, is there? Paperwork, billings, that sort of thing?"

Her eyes go to the envelope on her desk, addressed to Laura Sparks, with Laura's address on it, and her own return address. "I was about to send her my report, with my findings and a list of expenses," she admits. She picks it up gingerly, like it could explode.

He slits the envelope open with a thumbnail, looks over the three-page report. "Shitcan this," he instructs her.

"She gave me an advance," Kate tells him, disturbed. "I owe her an accounting."

"Hey, fuck her!" he answers in anger. "She used you as a source without your permission, without even the courtesy of an advance warning. She might well have put you in serious jeopardy. You don't owe her squat."

"She didn't do this deliberately," Kate says in defense of Laura, although she can't think of a reason why she should be defending her—Laura's put her in a terribly dangerous situation. What the hell could she have been thinking?

"So what? The results could still be the same."

That's true. Very true.

"You've probably got this on your computer, don't you?" he asks, fingering the report.

She nods.

"Erase it. Erase the backup, too. If you feel you've got to have something, put it on a safety disk and hide that thing away someplace safe, really safe, not in a drawer around here."

"Don't you think you're overdoing this a bit?" she asks him, feeling a bit testy. "It's one article."

"Let me tell you about the impact this thing has had already, this 'one article,'" he says in reply. "I just came from a meeting with Sheriff Walker, my boss, who is an important figure in this county and no one to be trifled with. He asked me point-blank, like he asked every other ranking officer in the department, if I had had any communication whatsoever with Laura Sparks. Fortunately, I was able to look him in the eye and tell him the truth, that I hadn't. But it was a close call, Kate. Careers have been ruined for less. Anybody finds out I talked to you about this, I'm done."

"I've never told anybody about your helping me," she says. "I never would, you know that."

He comes close to her. Leaning down, he smells her hair, the nape of her neck. His breath stirs the light hairs, giving her goosebumps. Then he backs away. "We can't be in contact for a while," he tells her with some sadness. "Which is good for both of us, in more ways than one, unfortunately." He turns away for a moment, looks her in the face. "I never talked to you. About this or anything else. That's the way it's got to be."

"People have seen us together," she reminds him, knowing that what he says is true; nevertheless, she doesn't like hearing it.

He stares at her. "We were hot for each other. But we didn't take it anywhere."

"No," she answers him. "I guess we didn't." He's a cop, a married man. She doesn't mess with married men who are cops. If you do that, you can get hurt.

"Let's get rid of this," he says, flapping her report. He tears it up, until it's confetti.

"Get it off your computer," he orders her as he empties the shreds into his jacket pocket.

The sharpness in his voice causes her lips to set in a hard tight line. Damn it, she thinks: he has no right to talk to her this way, even if what he's saying is necessary.

"I stuck my neck out for you," he reminds her, reading her mind. "And it wasn't to get you to sleep with me, although I'm glad we did, no regrets there."

She feels color rising up her neck, to her face. Whether from anger or embarrassment or both, she's not sure.

"I stuck my neck out for you, Kate—now it's your turn."

Dumbly, she nods in agreement. On that he is right. She did her job, she earned her pay. What's a couple pieces of paper?

She sits down at her computer, brings up Laura's file, starts erasing it. Behind her, she hears the office door opening, then closing with a solid finality.

"I'm a strong believer in the First Amendment," the district attorney, Wally Loomis, says, "but there are limits. And frankly, you're getting close to them with this."

He holds a copy of *The Grapevine* in his hand. He's seated behind the big oak desk in his office. Standing near him, his back resting against a credenza, is Sheriff Walker. The person Loomis is talking to, Laura Sparks, is sitting opposite him in a hard, straight-backed chair. She's flanked by her mother on one side and Tom Calloway on the other.

Laura would like to answer him, but she's been instructed not to. Tom Calloway will carry the water here.

Laura doesn't want to be here at all. Her mother set this meeting up. And having Calloway represent her, that's a load of crap. He might be an alright lawyer on land-use issues, but he doesn't know anything about publishing. The paper has a lawyer, Moira Bates, who happens to be a specialist on the First Amendment. But Miranda nixed having Moira here.

"This is a family affair," she'd said firmly, aborting any dissent. "Tom is the family lawyer."

"It's about the newspaper," Laura had answered back anyway. "We have a lawyer, a good one."

"If the sheriff or the county decides to sue your paper, you can use whoever you want. Right now I want to smooth things over. Tom is right for that."

Calloway and Loomis play poker every Thursday night. That's what this is all about.

"Close how?" Calloway says in reply to Loomis's statement. His tone is mild, but there's an undercurrent of pugnaciousness behind it. "You bring up First Amendment limitations, you'd better make sure you're on pretty substantial ground."

Laura glances at him. Is he actually going to act like a real lawyer, an advocate?

"Making knowingly false and defamatory statements is not protected," Loomis answers.

Calloway actually laughs. "You've got about as much chance of going to court with that as I do of pole-vaulting over the moon," he says. "To begin with, that falls in the civil realm, not the criminal, which you damn well know, and more importantly, there's nothing on the face of this editorial, and let me remind you, this is an editorial, not an article, editorials are by definition statements of opinion, there's nothing in this that is knowingly false, let alone defamatory, and most importantly, how do you know for a fact that this is false?" He picks up the offending article. "What's knowingly false in this?" he asks.

"Frank Bascomb was caught red-handed transporting a ton of marijuana," Sheriff Walker interjects, clearly pissed off. "So by saying he was an 'unwitting dupe,' you lose all your credibility."

"Not necessarily," Calloway answers smoothly. "The marijuana was in containers. For all Bascomb knew, it could have been trombones or baseball gloves."

"That's bullshit and you know it," Walker retorts.

"I don't know it and no one's ever going to, because the guy's dead, Ralph," Calloway shoots back, "and he died in your jail. At the least, there's negligence here. Even you have to admit that."

"I don't admit that," Walker answers, not giving an inch. "The man killed himself. And no one can prove otherwise." His frustration erupting, he foolishly adds, "What's going on with you, Tom? Whose side are you on, anyway?"

"My client's," Calloway shoots back. "You have a problem with that?"

"Back off, Ralph," Loomis cautions the sheriff. This isn't going the way he expected it would.

"I'm here to help you people," Calloway tells Walker and Loomis, "and so are Miranda and Laura." He's successfully called their bluff, now he's going to rub it in a little, so they'll remember. "We came down here as a favor to you, but if you're going to give us grief we can leave."

"Let's everyone calm down," Loomis says. "Maybe I did come down a little hard on this newspaper-rights thing."

Miranda speaks up. "I think you did, Wally." She reaches over and takes Laura's hand. "You're upset. We understand."

"Can I say something?" Laura asks. She feels like a schoolgirl pleading permission from the adults.

"Go ahead," Loomis tells her.

"Why are you so sure that what I'm saying is wrong?"

"You're attacking my department without any foundation. That's my concern," Walker answers.

"How do you know that?" Calloway asks, following Laura's lead.

"Because I talked to every deputy sheriff and warden who might have known anything about this. And none of them spoke with her," he says, indicating Laura. "There are no 'unnamed sources.' She made all this up."

Laura steals a glance at her mother. Is Miranda going to give her away?

Miranda feels Laura looking at her. Still holding her hand, she gives her daughter the briefest of smiles, then turns her attention back to Walker, presenting a blank face to him.

Laura breathes a silent sigh of relief.

"Isn't there a chance one of your people *didn't* tell you the truth?" Calloway throws out. "If you'd asked me that question and I had been the source, I sure as hell would've lied to save my ass."

"My officers don't lie to me."

"I won't touch that one," Calloway says with a smile.

Loomis pushes the focus back to the center. "Let's get friendly, folks, since we're all friends here." He turns to Laura. "I don't tell newspapers what to publish. And I apologize if I intimidated you. That wasn't my intent." He leans forward. "You don't have to answer this question, but it would help all of us if you did: do you really have any evidence that there was foul play around Frank Bascomb's death? That it wasn't a suicide? Because if you do, you are being irresponsible by not coming forth with it. And that could constitute criminal action, serious action."

Laura bites her lip. "No," she admits. "I don't."

"But someone did tell you it was possible."

"Yes."

"Could you tell us who that is?"

Again, Laura looks covertly at her mother. And again, Miranda's face is blank.

Calloway answers for her. "Laura can't betray a source, Wally. That goes against the foundations of a free press."

Loomis nods. "I thought . . . in the interest of clarity, of getting at justice, she might want to," he says disingenuously.

"Wally . . ." Calloway chides him.

"I don't," Laura tells Loomis, very serious. "And I won't."

Loomis nods again. "Can we go off the record?" he asks.

Calloway looks at Laura and Miranda. "What's your question, Wally?"

"Is there going to be follow-up to this?" he asks, brandishing the newspaper. "Should we be bracing ourselves for another bombshell?"

Everyone turns to Laura. She feels her mother's hand on her own, increasing the pressure.

"I've had my say," she tells them after some hesitation.

There is a stillness in the room.

Laura has to pee something fierce.

Miranda releases her grip on Laura's hand.

The telephone call awakens Kate out of a troubled, dark, dream-filled sleep. Completion dreams, having to get somewhere, not being able to, losing your way, swimming against the tide, caught in quicksand, in locked-up subway turnstiles, traffic jams, train wrecks.

She sits bolt upright, lost for a second, not knowing she's in her own bed, her own place.

"Shit!"

Late-night calls always frighten her—the fear of the chilling message, the hopelessness of separation—but this time she's glad to be woken up.

"Hello?" Her voice is Lauren Bacall–thick with sleep. She grabs for her bedside glass of water, takes a sip.

"Detective Blanchard?" A man's voice, slightly Latino-accented.

With trepidation: "Yes?"

"You got a bad memory on you, lady."

"Who is this?" Illogically her eyes dart around the darkened room, as if the voice were coming from some hiding place within the walls.

"We warned you to keep quiet."

Without thinking she replies, "I did." And wants to bite her tongue.

Shit—what did she say that for? She doesn't know who the voice on the other end belongs to, but now she's admitted to something, even if it was nothing. "I don't know what you're talking about, whoever you are," she says, trying to change course. "Now who is this?" she asks again.

"You know who."

"Don't call me anymore."

"We don't want to. You ain't offering us no choice."

"I heard you loud and clear the first time," she says, hearing her voice ringing out in her ears. Calm down, don't let him hear the panic.

"Listen. Lady detective . . . You still there?"

She should hang up on him. Slam the phone down, call Herrera—fuck, she can't do that anymore—call somebody. Get this fear out of her life.

"Yes," she answers. "I'm still here."

"Good." She can hear his breathing: low, slow, steady. "This is not your fight, remember? Leave it alone." He pauses. Again, the slow, steady breathing. "We told you once, now we've told you twice. You don't get a third warning."

The phone clicks in her ear.

Her heart is pounding like it is going to break through her chest. Bastards. Sons of bitches. They can't intimidate her like this: they can't.

At least she didn't tell them she had resigned the case. It would have been the smart thing to do, since she has; but she doesn't want them to have the satisfaction of knowing they blew her down.

A small satisfaction, but her own.

Miranda flies United Express into the Oakland airport. It's closer to the city than SFO, and it's less likely she'll see anyone that she knows in the Oakland terminal. Normally she would take one of the family planes, but she doesn't want anyone to know she's coming up this time, not even her own pilot.

She could have conducted her business over the telephone, but a personal meeting will better convey the gravity of her concern. Also, the family has some business interests in the Bay Area, and she likes to shop here as well.

She hails a taxi, gives her destination. The cabbie is a blackened-tooth Russian who drives his beat-up Mercury like a kamikaze pilot. They drive across the Bay Bridge into the city. He pulls up in front of a restored Victorian mansion near the Presidio that's been converted into offices.

She's wearing a business suit with a slit skirt that rides two-thirds up her thighs as she gets out. She tips generously. The driver takes a long, appreciative look at her legs and backside before peeling off into traffic.

The secretary, a woman about Miranda's age who looks a generation older, ushers her into Terwilliger's office. He owns the building, it's his firm. His personal office is large, octagonal-shaped, filled with mementos Terwilliger has picked up while working on cases around the world. The sun refracts through the beveled-glass windows.

Terwilliger Investigations is not a large agency; at any given time no more than a dozen operatives. But they're the best in the world at what they do, and they charge a fee commensurate with the quality of their work: two hundred dollars an hour and up, plus expenses. And they turn away five times as many cases as they take.

"Mrs. Sparks." He comes to her from behind his desk, shakes her hand. He's a big man in his late forties, power forward–size. "A pleasure to see you again."

"Thank you." She sits across his massive desk from him, her legs crossed. Her relationship with this man is strictly business. She's never given him the signal that he should make a play for her.

"This is a bit unusual," he tells her. She had called the day before and outlined the problem. "We don't normally do surveillance on people in our own line of work."

"I understand. But this is an emergency."

"I see." Even for an agency as much in demand as his, the Sparks family is special. Aside from their wealth and position in the state, they have been steady clients from the beginning of his practice. Some years he's billed them over a quarter of a million dollars: serious money. The Sparkses are clients to whom being loyal is good policy.

"Someone has hired her to check up on my family. I need to know what she knows, if anything."

"Is there something in particular you think she's looking at?"

"The incident regarding the dope trafficking on our property, of course. And the aftermath. That's my main concern."

"Do you want background on this investigator as well? What's her name"—he opens a manila folder on his desk—"Blanchard?" he says, reading the name. "Where she comes from, her credentials, family life, that sort of thing?"

"I want whatever you can dig up on her," Miranda says forcefully.

"You don't want her finding out things that could be harmful."

"That is precisely what I don't want."

He pulls a legal pad and ballpoint towards him.

"Okay," he tells her. "We'll get to it right away."

"How long will it be before you can give me what I'm looking for?" Miranda asks.

"I'll have a detailed report to you within a week."

———————

Another taxi drops Miranda off at the St. Francis. The family maintains an apartment in Pacific Heights, but she'll stay in a hotel tonight to maintain the secrecy of her mission. No one she knows would stay at the St. Francis, it's too large and commercial. To play it extra-safe she even takes her suite under an alias, "Mrs. Torres," after the original owner of the family ranch. She'll pay the bill in cash.

Room service brings up a bottle of champagne in an ice bucket, with two glasses: Veuve Clicquot '85, the best the house offers. She draws a bath, and while she's waiting for it to fill she places a phone call.

"I'm in town," she tells the party at the other end of the line, "the St. Francis. Suite 2312." She listens to the other end of the line. "I'll be waiting."

Hanging up, she disrobes where she stands, pours herself a glass of champagne. At the vanity in the bedroom she puts her hair up, then goes into the bathroom and steps into the tub, sinking to her neck in the oil-scented hot bathwater.

She's toweling off when there's a knock on the door. Throwing on the courtesy robe, she walks across the living room and opens the door, tendrils of hair at her neck still wet from her bath.

"What took you so long?" she asks Blake Hopkins.

He smiles as he looks at her. "I left the office as soon as you called. This is the big city—we have a problem called traffic."

Taking his face in her hands, she pulls him to her in a kiss, the robe coming open, her moist body dampening his shirt and tie. Then she leads him in, closing and locking the door behind them, the Do Not Disturb sign on the outside handle. As they head for the bedroom her robe drops to the floor next to her dress, undergarments, and shoes.

10

SLOUGHING THE PAST

The women sit in their circle. Almost all of them sit in the same chair every week, consciously. It gives them the security of being grounded, at least in this one part of their lives. Being grounded, if only for a few hours a week, is important to them, because most of the time they aren't.

As soon as check-in is over Kate claims the floor. Her last time here she had to be dragged into opening up her soul. This time she's eager to, almost impatient.

"When I was in the shelter," she begins, "I got into therapy—it was mandatory. I resisted like crazy, partly because of the fact that it *was* mandatory—that's my MO, if someone tells me I have to do something I'll do everything in my power not to. I'm a champ at cutting off my nose to spite my face. Even though the police psychologist had been helpful when all the shit came down, I was still suspicious, paranoid. But anyway, even someone as obstinate as me has to figure out that finding out why you're fucked up might have some benefit. So then I started working things out a little.

"One psychologist there got to me to the point where I decided I could trust him, and from then on things went better. I didn't live there very long but I went back twice a week for therapy. One time he said something that was really important to me. I wrote it down, so I'd never forget it."

She fishes a four-by-six card out of her purse, reads from it:

Most of us come from the past, and we re-create the present. Those who excel come from the future, their vision, their mission, and it pulls them forward.

She puts the card back into her wallet. "I'm still bogged down in my past," she explains. "It becomes my present, so I don't have a future, I can't. And that's what I've got to get to: my future, my vision. It's why I'm here. And to do that I've got to get the past out of the way."

She thinks of the events of the past weeks: sleeping with Juan, a married man and a cop to boot; the frightening and humiliating encounter with the men from the Mexican Mafia; leaving a case without having it come to a conclusion—all which she knows she's responsible for, there are no accidents in life.

"Otherwise," she goes on, "I'll always be a prisoner. I'll always be held captive. It'll be like living with Eric all over again, except I'll be my own warden."

"Don't be so hard on yourself," Maxine interjects. "You're doing great. These are big changes you're going through, they take time, they don't want to be rushed."

Kate shakes her head.

"If I don't push myself through this," Kate tells her, tells all of them, looking them all in the eye, "I won't get through it. I've got to be hard on myself, much harder than I have been up to now."

The first thing the people at the Women's Shelter did was take her to the hospital. They wanted to call the police—her own force—and press charges against Eric. He'd beaten her up bad, she looked a mess, although her training had saved her from being hurt much worse.

She wouldn't let them make the call—she didn't have the strength to go through another departmental ordeal so soon after the previous one. Besides, even though she had been cleared, she knew there was residual resentment towards her from some members of the force, and this would be like throwing gasoline on a dying fire.

Miraculously, she looked worse than she was. Two ribs were broken, some teeth were knocked out, swollen eyes, a fair amount of internal bleeding. About as much damage as a boxer might endure in a tough fight, except she didn't get to do any punching back: her biggest regret.

No one knew where she was except Julie and Captain Albright. She didn't want the kids to know because she was afraid Eric might wheedle it out of them, and she didn't want them to see her until the initial swelling and bruises had gone down. She'd had to tell Captain Albright that she couldn't come back to work like she was supposed to, and why. He took it okay, but she could tell he was pretty worried and maybe suspicious, too. Like none of it was her fault but was she one of those cops who somehow drew problems? A jinx?

She stayed in the shelter two weeks, until she was presentable enough to go out into the world. Then she went back to work. Captain Albright put her right back into the swim, assigned her a new partner and a car, and she was back on the job. She moved in with Julie and Walt. They were happy to have her.

Her daughters' attitudes were more ambivalent. Their lives were totally screwed up and she was part of the reason, even though it hadn't been her fault. Except that she'd brought Eric into their lives, so some of it really was her fault, in their minds. Wanda's acne flared up fiercely, and Sophia turned inward, barely communicating even the simplest requests. She tried to be there for them, but her own problems were so overwhelming she didn't do very well at it; they were young, she rationalized to herself, they could bounce back. That part of her life would have to wait—it would be over pretty soon, and then they'd have her full attention. It was selfish, thinking that way, she knew that; but she couldn't do anything about it, not right in the moment.

The girls withdrew from her and turned to her sister for affection and attention.

She got a restraining order against Eric. He couldn't come within a hundred yards of her, and he couldn't see the kids at all. She felt better after that was handed down, safer, not only for herself but for Julie and Walt and the girls, too.

So on the outside things were getting better; but on the inside they were turning to shit. She was under a lot of stress. The therapy sessions were helping, but it was all too much. People were talking about her at work behind her back. Not only Eric's buddies, of which in this situation there were plenty, but other male officers, too. Like if there was this much smoke around her, there must be something burning somewhere.

With every passing day her anger built. She started talking it out on the people who were closest to her: her kids. Everything they did was wrong. Their schoolwork, their friends, the way they put on their socks, whatever. Yelling at them like crazy, really ragging on them. She was crazy, impossible. Wild mood swings. And she could see herself doing this shit while she was doing it and she knew it was fucked and crazy and she couldn't stop herself. Which had to be some kind of definition of some kind of insanity.

The girls started going to therapy with her. That helped. Not them, but her. She started seeing what demons were driving her. When the truth about you comes out of your daughters' mouths and the truth is ugly . . . you don't want to hear it, but you'd better. She was in total denial most of the time around it, but she heard it.

After a while the girls started resisting therapy. She had the problems, not them. They stopped going with her. She didn't push it. They were right—it was her problem, not theirs.

It got claustrophobic living with her sister, who couldn't help but disapprove of her behavior, so she gave them all a break, she moved out and got her own place nearby, a small efficiency. Technically she was supposed to reside in Oakland, but no one ever checked. The little place was all she needed, because the girls stayed with Julie and Walt. She saw them almost every day. It was better for them there, more stable. Until things worked out. Not for long.

After three months she hired a lawyer and filed for divorce. Eric had been expecting the papers.

"What took you so long?" he sneered at the marshal when he was formally served, right in the middle of the squad room, one morning after the daily briefing.

He laughed about it—big fucking joke. Some of the other cops laughed about it, too. Not the women, just some of the men.

———

"Looking good, Kate," Eric taunted her. Checking her out: "Your ass is getting kind of big, though, isn't it?"

She ignored him.

They were in the corridor outside the courtroom, waiting to go in. Her with her lawyer, him with his. The first time they'd laid eyes on each other since that night. Normally, before a divorce can proceed, the participants have to go to meditation, to try to work things out by themselves. She and Eric had filed waivers for that, because of their special circumstances.

Most divorces are basically settled by the time the participants get to the courtroom. Not in this case. A third party, a judge who didn't know them, would have to decide. There was no middle ground between them, no way they could work anything out. They were both in it for blood, especially her—Eric had had his ration, she wanted retribution.

The proceedings started off badly. The judge wasn't on her side. It was subtle but unmistakable, at least to her. Eric's lawyer was better than hers. She was the cop with the negative publicity, and now she was the one filing for divorce.

"He is not the father of the girls—my children," she told the judge when she took the stand. They were in the custody phase, the most important part to her. She didn't want Eric to be able to ever see them again. She wanted him washed from their lives, as if he never had existed in it. "He only adopted them because I bugged him until he agreed. He's been a stepfather in name only. He means nothing to them, and they mean less to him."

"And you're capable of raising them in a proper manner," the judge asked her, leaning over from the bench.

"Of course I am. I'm their mother. I have a job that pays well, and I love them. I already have raised them, all their lives. What more would you expect from me?"

He made some notes on his legal pad. There might be more testimony on this subject later.

The emergency-room doctor who had fixed her up testified for her. He was young, in his first year of residency, and he looked even younger.

"She was beaten severely. Some ribs were broken, teeth knocked out. She was fortunate her jaw wasn't permanently damaged, or her liver, spleen, kidneys."

"Why wasn't this reported to the police?" Eric's lawyer, an oily prick in a good suit, asked the ER doc. Her own lawyer's suit was blue, two shades too bright. And he wore brown shoes instead of black ones. He had been recommended by the people at the shelter, who only knew good price, not good quality. She had been too discombobulated to notice his shortcomings; by the time she did, they were too far along in the process for her to get a better one.

"She didn't want to," the young doctor answered. He looked like Huck Finn up there.

"Isn't it obligatory? By law?"

"She was a cop herself, man. She said she'd handle it. We figured she knew what she was doing."

"So it was only on her say-so." Eric's lawyer was examining the head of the shelter now, who had taken Kate to the hospital.

"I'm not blind," the woman responded, as if insulted. "She was beaten to a pulp."

"I've seen the pictures," he said. "That it was her husband, I'm asking. No one else."

"There was no reason for her to lie," the woman countered. "I've seen lots of these cases. It's always the husband or boyfriend."

"But you didn't check to verify that. And you didn't call the police to verify it, either. Not then or later."

"I was worried about keeping her alive. She didn't want to get into that right then, and I didn't press her. It's common not to want to sic the cops on your husband. You're scared he'll come back and do you worse. All you want is to get away from him, and keep away from him."

Eric took the stand. He looked sharp. A poster boy for the police recruiters.

He'd been on the stand a hundred times in a hundred trials. He knew how to talk the right way.

"Yes, I hit her," he admitted. His lawyer was eliciting his testimony. "I had to do something. She was pointing her gun at me."

Kate got halfway out of her chair before her lawyer managed to restrain her.

"That's a goddamn lie!" she hissed.

"Calm down," her lawyer warned her. "This judge won't tolerate a ruckus. We'll nail him on cross, don't worry."

She was worried. This wasn't the way she had been told it would go.

"Why was she pointing her gun at you?"

"She wanted to leave the house. Leave me. I didn't want her to leave, especially then, the stress she was under. I wanted to talk to her. She didn't want to. She pulled her gun and told me to get out of her way. So I took the gun away, and I had to fight her to do it. What else could I do?"

"Had she been under a lot of stress?" Eric's lawyer asked, leaning heavily on the word "stress."

"Tremendous stress. She was going back to work the next day after being on administrative leave for a month. She'd been this close to getting kicked off the force." He held up thumb and forefinger, an inch apart. "If I hadn't gone to the board beforehand and pleaded for her she would have been."

"He's lying," Kate hissed. She wanted to scream. "If anyone almost got me kicked off it would have been him. He was totally unsupportive of me. Ask Captain Albright. Put him up on the stand."

Her lawyer had made a note about that. He seemed to be making a lot of notes, about everything.

"Why did she want to leave you?" Eric's lawyer asked him.

Eric turned in his chair, looked at her from across the room.

"She can tell you better than I can," he answered cryptically.

She did answer.

"Because he was scum. A liar, a bastard. The gun—that's a complete lie. He pulled his gun on me, on his own wife, he held it to my head, he threatened my life. He told me I should have gotten what that poor woman and girl had gotten back in that house. And he told me— promised me—that the next time he would pull the trigger. He's crazy, psychotic. Check his evaluations. Why hasn't he been promoted, all his years in service? Check that out, too."

Then she did the one thing she'd sworn she wouldn't do. She began to cry.

"I don't deserve this. No woman deserves this. I'm a peace officer, I see terrible things all the time, I was witness to the worst thing I hope ever to see, that man murdering his wife and daughter in cold blood, for no reason. No reason!"

"Would you like to take a break?" the judge asked sympathetically.

"No, thank you. I want to finish here." Maybe he wasn't against her after all, not completely. She composed herself.

"Except for killing me, when he had his gun against my head, my husband—this is the last time I will ever call that bastard 'my husband'—except for that, I was no better off than those women were. And it has to be stopped."

She could see the look in Eric's lawyer's eyes. He made a mistake, taking this client. Not taking him—everyone is entitled to a proper defense—but in attacking her character so viciously.

But witnesses had already been subpoenaed. They came forward.

"Do you know this woman?" Eric's lawyer asked Cal Collins. Collins owned a bar and grill in Berkeley that Kate used to frequent.

"Yes."

He looked miserable, sitting up there. She slouched in her chair, wanting to disappear.

"Did you have sexual relations with her while she was married?"

He looked at Kate as if to say "I'd do anything to lie, but I can't, I'm under oath." She signaled him with body language—tell the truth.

"Yes."

"How many times?"

"I don't know. I didn't keep a scorecard."

"More than once."

"Yes."

"More than a dozen times?"

"Yes."

Kate's lawyer cross-examined.

"While you and Mrs. Blanchard were seeing each other, was she estranged from her husband?"

"Yes, she was. Most definitely."

"Did she tell you they were separated?"

"Yes."

"Did you know if she was living separately from him at the time?"

"Yes. He had moved out of the house. She had kicked him out. She was living there by herself, with her daughters."

"And then she reconciled with him."

With sorrow: "Yes."

"And told you she couldn't see you anymore."

"We never saw each other after that, except if she was in my restaurant as a customer."

"So when she was living with her husband, not separated, or contemplating divorce, she was faithful to him."

"Objection! This witness does not know what else she might have been doing, or with whom."

"Sustained."

"She never slept with you again once she got back together with him?"

"Not once."

"Did she ever tell you why she went back to him, a man who was brutal to her, who she didn't love?"

"He kept at her. She felt guilty. She had one failed marriage, she said, she was willing to do almost anything to make this one work."

"Even take the chance of getting killed."

"Objection!"

"Sustained."

"Did you sleep with anyone during the various times you and your soon-to-be divorced wife were physically and emotionally separated from each other?" Kate's lawyer questioned Eric on redirect.

"I was never 'emotionally separated' from her. Whenever we split up it was her decision. I had to go along with what she wanted, but I never wanted to leave her."

He could sell ice to Eskimos, she thought, watching him up there on the stand. Lying or telling the truth, to him there was no difference.

"You just wanted to beat her senseless." Before the objection was voiced: *"I retract that, Your Honor."*

"Don't do it again," he was warned.

The judge took over the questioning when her daughters, one after the other, were on the stand.

"Do you love your mother?"

"Yes," both had answered.

"Is she a good mother?"

"Yes."

"Do you love your stepfather?"

The answer from both of them was *"No."* They both hated him and were afraid of him.

"Did your mother ever provoke him, or was it always his fault?"

"She never provoked him," the younger one said. She was fiercely loyal to Kate; she was too young to have any rebellious ideas.

"She would get in his face sometimes," the older one admitted. *"Mom doesn't back down to anyone."*

Eric's lawyer questioned her after the judge was finished.

"Was your mother ever angry at you when it wasn't your fault?"

"Sometimes."

"She was mad at your father and she took it out on you?"

"Objection, Your Honor! This is pure speculation!"

"Overruled. You may answer the question," he told her.

She fidgeted in her seat. *"Sometimes,"* she whispered. *"He's not really my father,"* she corrected, *"he's only my adoptive father."*

" 'Sometimes,' " the judge repeated to the court stenographer, in case she hadn't heard the answer. *"Disregard the rest of it."*

"Are you happier living with your aunt and uncle?" the lawyer probed.

Again, in a small, low voice: "Yes."

Julie was called as a hostile witness by Eric's lawyer.

"How would you describe your sister's current state of mind?" he asked.

"Concerned, of course. Confused."

"Angry?"

"Yes. Under the circumstances, who wouldn't be?"

"Angry at her children?"

Slowly, she answered, "Sometimes. They're teenage girls. It comes with the territory."

"Irrational anger?" he asked. "Using them as scapegoats?"

More slowly: "Yes, sometimes. I mean, rarely, the frustration level gets so high. Having to live with a man like Eric . . . who wouldn't get angry?"

"Do you feel they would be safe with her? Completely safe, all the time?" he added with emphasis.

Julie looked at Kate. Her eyes were wet.

"Not completely safe all the time. Almost all the time, but . . ." She looks at Kate, seated across the room from her. "Oh, honey. I don't know what to say, I'm sorry," crying for real, "the girls, I want them to be safe after all this. Isn't that what you want, too?"

The judge pounds his gavel.

"You are not to make that sort of outburst again, is that clear?"

"I'm sorry," Julie whimpered. "I'm so sorry."

You never had your own kids, Kate thought, staring at her sister, who wouldn't look at her after that. So you made mine yours—but they're not. You don't know what it's like for real.

You don't know what you've done to me.

The judge announced his decision. The property settlement was cut-and-dried; they split it, it wasn't much, just the house, which was already up for sale. They'd keep their own cars, their own personal things. The furniture and other tangibles that were in dispute were divvied up, not to either's satisfaction, but divorce is an unsatisfying process. Eric would pay no alimony, no child support. She didn't want either; she just wanted to get on with her life.

It came down to her daughters. Custody.

"It is the opinion of this court that the welfare of the minor children will be best served in placing them in temporary custody with

Julie and Walter Netter, their aunt and uncle. Children of this age need a stable, secure household in which to live, and at this moment in time Mrs. Blanchard is unable to provide that, given the emotional stress she has been under, which I should emphasize is through no fault of her own. She will, of course, be able to visit with her daughters as much as she wants."

Kate listened in stony silence.

"We'll appeal this," her lawyer promised. "This won't hold up."

Fuck you, she thought silently, feeling sorry for herself, wanting to lash out at the world. *You fucked this up royally.*

"This judgment will be in place for one year starting today," the judge continued, "at which time Mrs. Blanchard may apply to regain custody."

He turned and looked directly at Kate.

"I know you're upset at this," he said, "but it's for your welfare as well as theirs. Someday you may thank me."

I'll be dead before I ever thank you, she thought.

There was an up side. Eric was granted no visiting rights with the girls whatsoever. They would never have to see him again, or be subjected to his viciousness. And the restraining order prohibiting him from having any contact with her was made permanent.

She was free of him. Free at last.

But what a price she would have to pay.

Eric got the last word in. He detoured past her table on the way out of the courtroom.

"Mother of the year," he sneered. "Couldn't even keep her own kids."

"You're dead, bitch. For real this time," he hissed at her when she entered the hearing room to testify against him.

"No, you are," she rejoined, feeling confident and strong. "Your days of tyrannizing me are over, you petty little shit. And if you don't get away from me this second I'm going to make them arrest you for violating your restraining order."

She told her story, clearly and calmly. The people from the shelter testified; so did the doctor from the ER, who was more graphic this time in describing what had been done to her.

Captain Albright was her best witness. He didn't spare Eric, call-

ing him a disgrace to the department, a rogue cop who had no business wearing a badge. And he praised Kate to the skies—she was an exemplary officer, she always tried her best, he would take a battalion just like her.

The department was looking for an excuse to get rid of Eric. He had crossed the line too many times, they couldn't afford to carry someone dispensing his brand of justice anymore.

They gave him a fair trial, and then they hung him—they kicked him off the force. He had to surrender his badge and gun before he left the room. And it was made clear to him that any attempt to contact or coerce or frighten her or her family would result in extremely dire consequences.

This time he was the one who was shaking when he left the hearing room for the last time; who averted his face when he passed near her, so she wouldn't be able to see his stricken look.

———————

The room is silent.

"You took command of your life," Maxine tells Kate.

"That part," Kate concedes. "It didn't get me my kids back, but it was a start."

"What happened after that?" one of the women asks.

"I quit the force."

"Why?" Conchita asks, dumbfounded. "You had them by the *cojones.*"

"I didn't want to be in that space anymore. It was time to move on. I had to let go of everything, and that was part of it."

"What about your daughters?" Maxine questions.

"They're good where they are." She pauses, collecting her thoughts. "I go up to the Bay Area, once a month at least. Things are getting better. We feel good with each other now. I've got a court date in a couple of months. I'm going to petition for custody. If the court grants it, they'll move down here with me, and we'll start a new life together."

"That will be a big step," Maxine offers. "For all of you."

Kate nods in agreement. "I'm ready."

———————

About half of the group is going out for coffee. Kate is going to join them. She feels like she's a member now.

Mildred Willard waylays her in the parking lot.

"You're an inspiration to me," she tells Kate with admiration.

"Thank you."

"I read that article . . . Laura's editorial . . . in *The Grapevine*. Were you involved?"

"I was for a while. I'm not anymore."

"I hope I wasn't out of line, bringing you together," Mildred tells her, a bit sheepishly.

"I don't do anything I don't want to." A lie, but right now she wants to believe it. It's a goal: part of her future.

"I'm sure you were helpful to Laura," Mildred says. In an intuitive flash, she adds, "she could use a friend like you."

"Laura can take care of herself," Kate avows.

Mildred thinks about that for a moment. "Probably. But you have ballast she doesn't."

Kate states her case: "I've got to get on with my own life."

11

TWO WHITE CHICKS SITTING AROUND

Life goes on. Work goes on. Days go by.

Kate returns to her office from a working lunch to find a message from Cecil. He's been busy in his vineyards—they're picking in a few weeks, that's why he hasn't phoned. He's on his way out the door, running up to Paso Robles for a couple of days, a quick business trip, he'll call when he returns. Misses her. Hopes she's well.

She spends the afternoon on paperwork, until a few minutes before seven. A full day; satisfying, no hassles. She prints out various reports and bills, backs up her computer, turns off the lights. Her plan for the evening is to go home, have a light supper, a small glass of wine, then drive up to her own Shangri-la for a late plunge. Pretty soon, until next spring, it'll be too cold to swim.

The phone rings, as it invariably does when you're trying to leave the day's work behind.

"Blanchard Investigations," she answers.

"Kate Blanchard, please." A woman's voice—low, soft-spoken. And vaguely familiar?

"Speaking."

"Miranda Sparks here, Ms. Blanchard," the voice announces. "Laura Sparks's mother," she adds for identification.

Kate looks at the receiver in her hand as if it's alive and might bite her.

"The young woman you've been working for," Miranda says, as if further explanation were necessary. "We've met before," she adds. "At the Wine Cask. You were having dinner with my neighbor in the valley, Cecil Shugrue."

Kate finds voice. "Yes, I remember," she answers carefully. "How can I help you?"

"I hope you don't mind my cold-calling you like this," Miranda apologizes. "I don't know the protocol for directly contacting a private detective, I've never done it before. Our lawyers deal with detectives on the rare occasions when we use them."

"I mostly work through attorneys myself," Kate concurs. "But people call me direct sometimes. That's why I'm in the Yellow Pages."

"Is that how my daughter contacted you?" Miranda asks. "By looking you up in the telephone book?"

"I don't discuss clients with third parties," Kate says stiffly. "If in fact your daughter is a client of mine. Or was."

"I'd hardly call someone's mother a third party," Miranda responds with equanimity. "Don't you think that sounds a bit impersonal?"

"What gives you the impression I'm working for your daughter?" Kate asks. Maybe this is a fishing expedition. The mother read Laura's editorial, she concluded that Laura hired an investigator to do legwork for her, she's calling every PI office in town until she hits the right one.

"It's not an impression, Ms. Blanchard," Miranda states, sounding a bit bewildered. "Laura told me you have been doing some investigating for her on what happened to our former ranch foreman in the county jail." She pauses—Kate almost thinks she feels a smile over the line. "I didn't pick your name out of thin air, for goodness sakes. Certainly you don't think that's a secret, do you?"

"I like to be sure," Kate answers, defending her position.

There's a queasy feeling in the pit of her stomach. Laura had been so concerned—frightened, almost—in making certain that Kate knew she didn't want her parents to find out she had hired a PI. Now here's the mother calling and discussing it as if they were exchanging recipes.

"I can understand that," Miranda says. "Your work is confidential."

"That's right."

"I respect that. But of course, Laura is my daughter. We're very close. Whatever she's doing, I know about. We don't keep secrets from each other."

You sure could have fooled me, Kate thinks. Laura could have, anyway.

"I'd like to get together with you," Miranda says. "To discuss what's happened with your investigation."

"I don't think that would be a good idea," Kate counters.

"Why not?"

"Because your daughter hired me," Kate explains. "Any information I found and passed on to her, if there was any," she adds, maintaining her discretion, "is between her and me. If she wants to tell you what I've told her, that's her business. But I won't do it."

"You've got morals."

"I hope so."

"That's admirable. So do I."

"Then you can understand why I can't divulge anything to you."

"Without Laura's consent," Miranda adds for her.

"Precisely."

"Let me ask you this," Miranda says. "Is it unethical for two members of the same family to hire the same private investigator?"

"That would depend on the circumstances," Kate answers.

"Well, I might want to engage your services," Miranda says. "It's not like I was the subject that Laura wanted investigated, is it?" she adds pointedly.

"No," Kate admits. "She didn't hire me to find out anything about you."

"Then we can get together?"

There's something weird going on here. She can't put her finger on it, but there's a strangeness to all of this. She really wants out, is what she wants. No more late-night meetings with gang lords, no threatening midnight phone calls.

"I suppose so," Kate answers somewhat reluctantly, not entirely sure why she's agreeing to this.

That's not true. She knows precisely why—she wants to find out what's going on. She's heard too many stories about this woman. Meeting her on a more intimate basis can't hurt anything.

Curiosity killed the cat. But she's not a cat.

"Good. Let's have dinner tomorrow night, if you're free. My treat. And I'll pay you for your time, of course."

"Okay," Kate agrees. "I'm free for dinner. Where should I meet you?"

"My ranch, if you don't mind. It's not that far from where you are, and the drive at dusk is lovely."

"Dinner at your ranch?"

"Don't worry," Miranda laughs. "We may be plain old ranchers but we eat okay up here. We'll feed you good."

Plain old ranchers.

"Is six o'clock convenient?" Miranda asks.

"Six is fine."

"Let me give you directions. It's not hard to find. Dress casually, you'll be more comfortable."

I know where your ranch is, Kate says to herself. I've seen you there. With a different guest. And it wasn't for dinner.

Kate arrives about a quarter of an hour before her appointed time—she had given herself a cushion in case she had trouble finding the place. When she came this way with Cecil he was driving, it was at night, she wasn't paying attention. The destination was important, not the getting there.

She finds the entrance to the Sparks property without difficulty. A battered tin sign lettered in old-fashioned script: *Rancho San Miguel de Torres*; hangs from a wooden pole at the juncture to the highway, punctuated with a few rust-edged bullet holes. The road up to the house is almost a mile long. Indifferently paved, every so often a cattle guard bisecting it. Cattle on either side, grazing, blank stares as she drives by.

A few vehicles are parked in front of the small ranch house: a vintage Mercedes, a Ford Escort, and a commercial minivan. Kate parks next to the Mercedes, walks up the porch steps, and knocks on the door.

A bulky Eastern European–looking woman, clad in a white smock and Birkenstock sandals, her girth almost filling the frame, opens the door. "Please to come in," she says. "Madame is to be finished shortly."

Kate enters the house. Something fabulous is being cooked in the kitchen, the aromas wafting to her; lamb, maybe. That would be great, she loves lamb.

Miranda Sparks calls out to her from somewhere in the back. "I'm back here. Follow Sonia."

The large woman leads her down a long hallway into a bedroom. A massage table has been set up at the foot of the bed. Miranda is lying facedown on the table, naked. Soft New Age–style music comes from a portable tape player, scented candles burn, and bottles of massage oil have been aligned on a small table next to the bed.

Kate can't help noticing her hostess's body. It's incredible, there's no other way to describe it. It's been worked on, that's obvious, pushed and pulled and pumped up and flattened, but nonetheless it's as close to an idealization of the female form as Kate's ever seen. She forgot how beautiful Miranda is, and how youthful; she knows Miranda is at least a decade older than her, but the woman's skin is flawless.

Miranda rolls over and sits up, oblivious to her nakedness. "You're early," she says, smiling in greeting.

"I gave myself extra time in case I got lost," Kate explains, feeling ill at ease. Being greeted by a naked woman with a body like Bo Derek's isn't what she's used to. A woman she's met once, for two minutes.

"I'm just finishing my massage," Miranda says, seemingly oblivious to her condition and the effect it has. "Take a look around the place. I won't be long." She lies down again, eyes closed, body relaxed.

"Okay," Kate says, a bit nonplussed. She's been greeted casually before, but this is really laid back.

She walks back into the living room. The house is sparely decorated: western-style, comfortable. Kate admires the Navajo rugs that cover the dark oak floors, the well-worn burnished leather couches and Mission-style chairs, the western paintings on the walls. Isn't Reagan's house somewhere around here? she remembers. Probably furnished in the same style, but not as well.

Within a few minutes Miranda pads into the room, a white terry-cloth robe wrapped around her body, which is glistening like a seal's from the massage oil that's covering it.

"I think a good massage is just about better than anything, don't you?" she states.

"Who doesn't?" Kate answers. And to think she had expected burgers on the grill and talking a little business. Obviously, simplicity is not this woman's style.

"Would you like one now?" Miranda asks out of the blue. "You might as well take advantage of Sonia while she's here. Sonia is the best masseuse in the county. She'll give you a massage that leaves you feeling like melted butter. My treat," she offers.

Kate hesitates, not sure how to respond. "Do you have the time?" she asks.

"Pleasure before business," Miranda states cheerfully. "Yes, I have the time. All evening, if necessary."

"Okay, then. Sure." What the hell—the best massage in the county, why pass that up? And she's getting paid to boot.

"How's about a quick tour of the property?" Miranda asks, her face wreathed in a gracious smile.

"Sure."

"I'll get you something to drink and then we can take a jaunt around."

Miranda is wearing a simple two-hundred-dollar cotton blouse (Kate has seen the blouse at Citti) over custom-cut jeans and cowboy boots (handmade, Kate is sure). Her hair is hanging loose, framing her long, slender neck.

Kate, fresh from her massage (the best she's ever had, Miranda was right about that) and shower, is also wearing jeans. Calvin Kleins, from Nordstrom's, on sale. Nike running shoes. A man's white pocket T. Her version of a chic casual outfit.

"I like your T-shirt," Miranda compliments her as they walk through the living room.

"Ten dollars at the Gap," Kate informs her.

"I wish I could wear a shirt like that. I'm a bit too busty, I'm afraid."

We should all be so unlucky, Kate thinks.

"Is white wine all right? Or I could make you a margarita."

"White wine's fine."

Miranda leads them into the large, farm-style kitchen. Two people, a man and a woman, both young and dressed in kitchen whites, are preparing dinner.

"Ummm. Smells delicious," Miranda tells them.

"You'll like it," the man says, winking at her.

"I'll bet."

She uncorks a bottle of wine that's been chilling in the refrigerator.

"We don't want to disturb the geniuses at work," she says to Kate, leading her from the kitchen with bottle, two wineglasses, and ice bucket in hand. "See you later," she calls back.

"Ready in about an hour," the woman tells her.

Back in the living room, Miranda pours for each of them. "Cheers," she offers in toast.

"Cheers."

They touch glasses, drink.

Kate tastes the first cooling swallow, and her taste buds literally bloom. It's fantastic, the best wine she's ever had; the phrase "nectar from the gods" crosses her mind, and not in a hackneyed way. "This is delicious! Is it local?" she asks, thinking of Cecil and his wine, and also trying to sound a little bit knowledgeable.

"French," Miranda remarks casually. "Le Montrachet. I happened to find a few bottles lying around that I thought should be drunk pretty soon, and it's always fun to share. Normally we drink California wines, mostly from right here in the county. I prefer them."

They sit opposite each other in the old chairs, which sag comfortably under their weight.

"Let me be up front with you," Miranda begins.

Here it comes. "Please do."

"As I mentioned over the phone, Laura told me that you have been doing some investigative work for her, regarding our ranch foreman's untimely death in the county jail. And that you are the unnamed source she alluded to in her newspaper editorial," she adds, looking to Kate for confirmation.

Kate doesn't reply.

"I know you are; as I also told you, my daughter and I have no secrets from each other. We're each other's best friend."

She waits; Kate keeps mum.

"I'm concerned about those allegations. If Frank Bascomb, who was our ranch foreman for several years, didn't kill himself, then perhaps there are darker forces at work here than there seem to be on the surface. And if that is true—if there is any truth to that at all . . ." she hesitates. "Let me put it this way: if there are, I have to be concerned for my family's welfare, both financially and, even more importantly, physically. Very concerned."

"I can understand that," Kate gives her. "I would be, too—if there was any truth to what she wrote."

"Is there?" Miranda asks forthrightly.

"I'm not in a position to tell you yes or no," Kate answers, deliberately evasive. Let her keep guessing. "As I said, Laura was my client. It's up to her to tell you what she wants. I can't. I'm sorry."

She's off the case. She's finished with it, done. But this isn't the time to let this woman know that. Not until she finds out what Miranda Sparks knows.

Miranda regards Kate with what appears to be a look of respect. "I can understand that . . . I guess," she says. "If I hired a private detective I'd want her to respect confidentiality. Good for you." She corks the bottle, puts it on ice. "We'll finish this later," she promises. "The wine definitely, and perhaps our conversation as well. Let me give you the nickel tour now, before it gets too dark."

The ranch Jeep is an old classic: canvas top, tiltable windshield. Miranda drives expertly, the hard-sprung vehicle bouncing up rutted dirt paths where clusters of cattle are grazing along the sides of the hills, all the way to the top of the property. She points out various landscapes as they go—the ruins of an old sheepherder's hut from a century ago, the holding pens for the spring roundup, a natural pond fed by an underground spring. Groves of native oak, pine, other indigenous trees. And acreage by the thousands.

They park on a high flat plateau and get out. To the west the sun is dropping, starting to turn from bright yellow to vermilion and a deep, almost translucent purple.

"God's country," Miranda says reverentially.

"It sure is," Kate agrees.

"I count my blessings every time I come up here," Miranda goes on, confessionally.

"If it were mine I would, too."

"Particularly since I lucked into it, by marriage. I hope I never take it for granted. Sometimes I think my family doesn't truly appreciate everything they have, and how fortunate they are."

Kate nods in understanding.

"The Native Americans say the land is merely ours to borrow, never to claim ownership," Miranda continues. "And that we must protect it for those who come after us."

"That's a good way of looking at it," Kate says, taking in the landscape, the vastness of it.

"I try never to forget it."

They stand in easy silence for a few minutes.

"I hate to tear you away from this," Miranda says finally. "You can get hypnotized up here. But it's hard finding your way back in the dark."

"I appreciate your bringing me up here," Kate tells her. "Sharing this."

"You can come back again. It isn't going anywhere."

They descend by a different series of dirt paths and roads. Partway down Miranda points to a shooting range.

"My mother-in-law and daughter shoot skeet," she explains. "Laura is a terrific shot, Olympic-caliber ability. Do you shoot?" she asks.

"Pistols," Kate answers. "I try to get to the range a couple times a year. I've never tried clay pigeons. Too expensive."

"Have Laura bring you up sometime," Miranda offers.

Kate shrugs. She and Laura aren't going to be having a relationship anymore, and knowing someone as a client isn't the same as having them as a friend.

"I'd take you out myself," Miranda says, "but guns aren't my thing."

"You don't shoot?"

"I'm not talented in that direction." She guns the Jeep down the trail.

As they see the house come into view below them, close to the eye but actually at least a mile away, Kate spots a long asphalt strip off to one side, and a large Quonset-style building.

"What's that?" she asks.

"Our landing strip. We fly our own airplanes. It'll accommodate a good-sized private jet, but nothing commercial. We mainly use the planes for crop-dusting, checking the herd, ranch stuff."

You could fly a shitload of dope in here, Kate thinks, and no one would be the wiser. She remembers Carl's admonition: go to school on this family. She makes a mental note to do some heavier research than she has, maybe find out if there's ever been any involvement with drugs here. Frank Bascomb, being the foreman, would have had access to this strip; much of the time he would have been up here without any members of the family present.

"Would you excuse me for a few minutes?" Miranda asks as they re-enter the house. "I have to make a trans-Atlantic call to Barcelona, of all places. We're doing business with a Spanish company, and their president starts his day at six in the morning. You know the drill, you're a businesswoman yourself, when they want you, you jump." She explains this to Kate as if they're on equal footing, business-wise. "I have to fly over there next week," she adds, "plus Paris and Brussels. Those quick trips, they really wear you out."

You have my deepest sympathy, lady, Kate thinks. Barcelona. Spain. The stuff that dreams are made of. I'll be happy to go in your place if you're too fatigued.

"I have my office in town but I get more real work done out here," Miranda confides. "There's no distractions, and total privacy."

"Must be nice, having a hideaway," Kate mutters.

"The only way to keep your sanity. Help yourself to more wine,"

Miranda calls out as she goes into a small den off the living room. "I won't be long."

Kate pulls the cork and pours herself a healthy portion of the delicious stuff, slowly wandering around the room and checking out the art on the walls. Most of it is California impressionist, but there is also a Diebenkorn and a small Monet. She overhears bits of Miranda's end of the conversation. They're talking in Spanish. Miranda speaks with an impeccable accent. The dialogue is too fast for Kate's ear to pick up—her Spanish is rudimentary, what a cop needs to get by in California—but it sounds like it's about money.

"Eight million firm," Miranda says abruptly in English, confirming Kate's surmise. "*No más,*" she continues, switching back to Spanish again.

Eight million dollars. Kate understands that much. She and Miranda may both be businesswomen, but they operate on radically different levels.

She walks outside. Night has fallen. She sits on the porch under the stars, her feet propped up on the wood-post railing.

This is the life. A person could get used to this.

Miranda comes to the doorway. "Sorry about that," she apologizes, "couldn't be helped. Then gaily she announces: "Dinner is served."

The table is set for two. A single candle burns in the center. Caesar salads topped with tiny scallops are at each place, and another bottle of Le Montrachet is in the ice bucket. Miranda pours more wine for each of them.

"To new friends," she toasts.

"I'll drink to that," Kate agrees as they touch glasses. She's already had more wine than she's used to, but it tastes so good, and there's plenty of time for her head to clear. If she feels a bit dizzy when she's driving home, she'll pull her car to the side of the road and lie out under the stars.

She tastes the first bite of salad. Delicious.

"My compliments to your chef," she tells Miranda. "Chefs," she corrects herself.

"On loan from Citronelle. We're investors in Michel Richard's restaurants," she says casually.

Kate's never been to Citronelle, although she's certainly heard of it. Maybe Cecil will take her there someday. Or Prince Charming on his fine white horse.

And if frogs had wings they wouldn't bump their asses on the ground so much. The rich are different from you and me, she remembers. Five-star restaurants cater their dinners.

The meal proceeds leisurely. Miranda brings the plates in from the kitchen herself. "We'll drink a couple of local wines this evening, if you don't mind," she says, almost apologetically.

"I don't mind," Kate tosses off. "I don't mind at all."

"I think our local wines stand up very well to the French ones, don't you?"

"Absolutely," Kate answers.

The shellfish is delicate, flaking on her fork. "Absolutely," she repeats herself.

She helps Miranda clear the table between courses. The chefs rinse them and stack them in the dishwasher.

The next course is what Kate had smelled when she came in: a baby rack of lamb, slow-roasted. They drink a local pinot noir reserve with it—it's delicious.

Dessert is last, a killer dark-chocolate cake.

"We're taking off now," the male chef tells Miranda. "Everything okay here?"

"Everything is divine, and thank you very much," she answers.

"Our pleasure. Nice to have met you," he smiles at Kate.

"Same here. The food is great." She forks up a second bite as they leave. "I'm going on a fast starting tomorrow," she confides in Miranda, "the weight I'll put on from this meal."

Outside, the chefs load their truck and drive away.

Miranda produces the final wine of the evening. "Château d'Yquem," she says offhanded. "If you like sauternes, it's really nice." She pours off two small glasses.

Kate takes a sip and almost falls out of her chair.

"Jesus!" she exclaims, almost reverentially.

"What?"

"This is the best wine I've ever had in my life!"

"I'm glad you like it," Miranda says.

"Like it? *Like* it? Lady, you are truly understated."

Miranda smiles broadly. "I'm playing with you. It's wonderful, I know that." She leans towards Kate, touching her hand. "It's better than sex. Almost," she belatedly qualifies.

"It's better than most sex I've ever had, I'll tell you that," Kate replies.

This is so weird, she thinks. The second thing she thinks is, she is *so* high. It feels okay, though. Safe. She's met this woman once before for less than five minutes and they're talking like they've been best of friends for a lifetime. It's amazing what several bottles of outstanding wine can do for lubricating your inhibitions.

She's in over her head, she thinks through the fuzz in her brain. Way over her head. This woman didn't ask her to come up here so they could have massages, drink great wine, and eat incredible food. She wants something from her, something big.

Miranda fills Kate's glass again.

Or maybe this is normal for this woman. What the hell. She'll deal with the consequences later.

They stack the last of the dishes in the dishwasher.

"Time to relax," Miranda says. "Come with me."

If she relaxes any further she'll dissolve, Kate thinks, following her hostess outside.

The hot tub is a hundred yards up the hill, in a grove of eucalyptus trees, sheltered from view. Steam seeps from the sides of the thick redwood cover.

"I hope you like it hot," Miranda says. "I keep it at a hundred and five, so the pores can really open."

Massage. Great wine. Candlelight gourmet dinner. Hot tub. What's next, Kate wonders, Tom Cruise?

They lift the lid and lay it on the edge of the platform. A stack of towels is to one side, next to a small Igloo cooler, similar to the one Kate keeps at her secret place. Miranda, completely unself-consciously, strips down, folding her clothes neatly and laying them on the platform.

Kate sits on the warm wood, slowly taking off her shoes and socks.

"You're not embarrassed about being naked with another woman, are you?" Miranda asks, a bit of tease in her tone.

"No." Her T-shirt comes over her head. She is, with this woman.

"I hate prissy women. Some of my friends, you'd think they were raised in a convent." Miranda slips her legs into the tub, up to her knees. "Oh! Hot! Pink skin!" Slowly, she slides down until the water is up to her neck, her eyes closing in bliss.

Kate is modestly turned away from Miranda, her back to the tub. She removes her bra, lays it on top of her shirt. Unfastening her belt, she slides her jeans off, and finally her panties. Then she turns and slides across the wet surface on her butt.

One foot in. Hot; real hot. This will take getting used to.

Miranda opens her eyes, appraising Kate with a frank stare.

"You have a nice figure," she declares. "Your legs are great, athletic. You must work out."

"I walk a lot. Comes with the job." Is she going to blush? That's what it feels like. If a man was looking at her like this she'd feel glorious. "So do you," she adds, feeling like a butterfly pinned on a board. She wants to ease in clear up to her neck, but the water is too damned hot. "Your figure is pretty fantastic," she tells Miranda. As if the woman didn't know.

"I work at it. You have to as you age."

Kate slides in to her knees, to her thighs. Acclimating faster, she keeps descending, her vagina contracting as the steaming water engulfs it, feeling the rush of blood, like the feeling that comes with arousal; then only her head is showing, her breasts are floating upward as almost immediately she feels her nipples starting to prune up.

"Too hot?" Miranda inquires solicitously, her voice slightly slurred in pleasure.

"Just right," Kate answers. She feels like a soupbone slowly softening in a simmering pot. "Couldn't be better."

They sit in silence, hair drifting behind them, bodies floating in the hot watery embrace.

"I know about you," Miranda says after a while. Her voice is low, almost a whisper.

"You do?" Kate's voice, too, is low and slow. What does she mean by that?

"You and I are alike."

"Oh yeah? How?"

"We both love sex. We both love men. And we take them when we want them."

Kate's eyes pop open. She stares across the tub at Miranda, who is lying serenely against the far wall, eyes cracked in slits. Cat's eyes, Kate thinks. Stalker's eyes.

"How do you know that?" This is getting too heavy. She feels her pulse in her neck. "You don't know me, we've never met before."

"I know myself. And I sense a kindred spirit in you."

This is true. Kate senses the same thing, it's undeniable.

"I have a highly developed sixth sense," Miranda says. "It rarely fails me."

Or is it the wine, the tub, the cumulative totality of the evening? If a man laid on this stylish a seduction she'd follow him to the ends of the earth.

She wonders what time it is; it must be getting late. Pretty soon her coach will turn into a pumpkin and she'll be back in her old rags again.

They subside into quietude again. Kate makes little waves with her fingertips, her eyes closing on their own. It would be so easy to fall asleep in here.

"Here."

Miranda is standing next to her, the water below her breasts. She's holding two glasses of cold water.

"Thanks." Kate drinks the entire glass down in one long gulp.

"Come with me."

Miranda climbs out of the tub and walks twenty yards along a narrow path to an outdoor shower. Kate follows. Miranda turns the tap on, the water coming out stinging cold. She turns under the showerhead, face and arms raised, the needles spraying her. Then she moves to the side, so Kate can do the same. Then they walk back to the tub and lie on their backs, on the platform.

It's a clear night. The sky is black and full of stars. A slight wind blows across their damp bodies.

Miranda reclines on her side, leaning her head in one hand. She looks at Kate. With her free hand she reaches over and takes the closer of Kate's hands, turning it over and holding it lightly, like a palm reader.

Goose bumps break out over Kate's body as if she's been touched with an electric prod. She wants to say or do something, she doesn't know what—but she feels incapable, almost paralyzed.

"You have good hands," Miranda says soothingly.

"Peasant hands."

"Strong hands. Like mine." She covers Kate's hand with hers, palm to palm. Her fingers are longer, her nails short and even. "Mine got strong here, from riding horses. Until then they were weak."

"I was born with mine," Kate says, flustered. She's always wished for beautiful hands, with long elegant fingers.

She lived in a dorm her freshman year in college. Sometimes a bunch of girls would crowd together in one room and have a late-night party. Talk about men, and their own desires. The women's gym had a sauna, and once they went to it, late at night, half a dozen young women lying on the hot dry wood seats.

She hasn't done anything like that for years; until tonight.

"Good hands," Miranda repeats. "Honest hands."

She pushes herself up onto her knees. Taking Kate's hand in both of hers, she leans down and kisses the palm, her lips barely making contact, her tongue flickering across.

Kate shudders. "I don't do this," she protests, feeling weak; emotionally more than physically. She doesn't know why exactly, but she feels compelled to be polite, not to hurt Miranda's feelings. It has something to do with class, status: top dog/bottom dog. "I'm not anti- or anything, it's not who I am, that's all."

"I'm not a lesbian." Miranda, accurately gauging Kate's fears, reassures her. "But I believe in experiencing life. How do you know what life is all about until you try it all?"

"I don't think I have to try it all. I know myself, who I am." She starts to get up.

"Lie down. Please." Miranda's voice is low, calm. "Let yourself go."

Her hands are on Kate's shoulders, pushing her down onto her back. Kate allows herself to be pushed down. It's as if she feels bad about not doing her hostess's bidding, after such a terrific dinner. Is that what this was all about, a prelude?

The wood is warm under her.

Let yourself go. Where will that lead?

Miranda is bent over her, softly kissing her right wrist, her mouth moving up Kate's forearm, the crook of her elbow, the fleshiness of the inner part of her upper arm, Miranda's hair hanging down, brushing the skin, a feather-touch titillation. Grazing the stubble of Kate's armpit, moving down along her side, the edge of her breast, then tonguing the nipple, which stiffens.

Kate moans with pleasure.

Let yourself go, her inner voice tells her.

Miranda covers Kate's body with her mouth: moving down to her belly, her abdomen, skirting the pussy, down her thigh, her calf, kissing the soles of her feet, each toe individually; then the moving mouth begins journeying up.

Kate gives herself over, abandoning her inhibitions. If sex with a woman is going to happen one time in her life, then this is that time.

Miranda's mouth caresses her nipples, which have grown almost to the size of the top joint of her little finger, the tongue licking at the edge of the areolas, then the nipples again, sucking each in turn. She inserts a finger into Kate's pussy, the digit sliding in and out, caressing the soft moist velvet inner lining.

Men have given her this pleasure. But this is a woman doing it— that's the difference. The touch of someone with your body, who knows what everything is supposed to feel like.

The pleasure-giving mouth moves to her pussy. It sucks Kate's clitoris.

Kate is humping like a machine, her hips grinding against Miranda's face, her behind pushing up against the hot wooden platform.

She comes half a dozen times, wave upon overwhelming wave. Moaning with abandon, her voice resounding in her ears, the sensations as intense as sex with a man, any man, has ever been.

"Enough." She feels like she's drowning. "Stop." She grabs Miranda's head with both hands and pushes her away, expending the last of her energy. She can't move, she's so wiped out.

Miranda straddles her. "Now you do me." She lowers herself down until her bush is on Kate's face.

Kate grabs her by the ass and buries her face in Miranda's wetness, tasting the salty fishiness she's only known from sniffing her own underpants after she's been aroused by a man.

Miranda climaxes almost immediately, her hands gripping Kate's head, fiercely pulling the hair, thrusting her pelvis into Kate's face.

Side by side they lie, completely spent.

———

"This evening's gone beyond your expectations, I suspect."

"You could say that."

"I didn't plan it. Things happen."

Don't ruin it, lady. "I guess," Kate responds noncommittally.

They're sitting in the living room, fully dressed again, drinking strong coffee. Kate, feeling about as animated as a warm pudding, is in the process of recovery.

"You're good company," Miranda says. "I appreciate that. I spend a lot of my time alone." She shifts in her chair, tucking her legs under her. "Do you like it up here? What you've seen so far?"

"What's not to like?"

"You'd be surprised."

"I guess so," Kate repeats herself, wondering, At what?

"Frederick—my husband—doesn't like the ranch," Miranda explains. "Never has. He has a circle of artistic friends he goes around with; frankly, they leave me cold. Too hip for me. Laura's an urban creature, someday she'll move to a city, San Francisco, some place like that." She pauses, sipping her coffee. "I'm different. I love the ranch life, I love to ride, to go out with the cowboys during their work. I love the space, the emptiness of it, getting lost in it." She sights Kate over the rim of her mug. "I have to confess something."

"What's that?"

"I've done some research on you," Miranda confides.

Confused: "You have?"

"You're checking up on me. I had to."

"I'm not 'checking up' on you," Kate says, concurrently feeling a sudden panic-fueled anger and a fast resurgence of energy. What the fuck is this? First the seduction, then the betrayal? "Where did you ever get that?"

"The matter you're looking into that my daughter hired you for."

"That has nothing to do with you," Kate tells her. She's hot, truly pissed off. "Where the hell do you come off? You wine me, you dine me, you—" she starts to say "fuck." She tries to rise up. The blood rushes from her head, momentarily causing her to feel dizzy, to fall back into the old leathery chair.

"Listen to me for a minute, will you?" Miranda implores. "Just hear me out."

"Let me explain something to you," Kate says, fighting to stay calm. Don't get angry, she cautions herself, don't lose control. You're in the presence of a control freak, don't let her suck you in. "People hire me to do things for them. If I can, I do. It's all legal and aboveboard. And one thing about my work is, I only answer to whoever hires me. No one else—period. Not Jesus, not Moses, not the President of the United States. I answer to my client."

"As well you should," Miranda comes back evenly. "I'm not disputing that."

"Than what *are* you saying?"

"As I told you earlier, I have to be concerned for my family's welfare. I run our businesses, which are profound and complex. It's my responsibility to see that they do well, and I take my responsibilities seriously. I have to—because no one else in my family can." She pauses. "I'm going to tell you a few things about us that aren't public knowledge. I trust you'll keep them to yourself."

"If you're paying me I'll have to," Kate answers. "Isn't that what you said over the phone?"

"Yes," Miranda confirms. "I am paying you for whatever time we spend together this evening."

"Then anything you tell me is confidential," Kate says. "Just like it was with your daughter," she adds pointedly.

Miranda pauses momentarily. "My husband is a sweet man but he's a bust at business," she confides. "When it comes to the world of commerce he couldn't find his ass with both hands and a Geiger counter. We have a lot of irons in the fire right now," she continues. "We are trying to develop some enormous projects. Much of our fortune is on the line. What happened with Frank Bascomb hurt us. We are in the spotlight because of him, and we don't like that. We don't like that one bit."

"Then Laura shouldn't have written that article, if you don't want publicity."

"I know that. So does she, now. It was a mistake. Fortunately, that won't happen again."

The poor kid, Kate thinks. She's been scared of you every day of her life, and for damn good reason.

"I don't care how Frank Bascomb died," Miranda says. "All I care about is that whatever happened, it's over. No more snooping around, no more bad publicity: *no* publicity. That's why I invited you here tonight. To ask you to lay off." She pauses. "I'm willing to compensate you for that."

The guys in Ventura offered twenty thousand. What will Miranda Sparks offer? Kate wonders; and then it hits her, like a safe falling on her head: Miranda could have been the money behind their offer. She turned them down, so now Miranda moves on to Plan B.

"How much?" she asks. "What are you prepared to pay me? Hypothetically, of course, I don't take bribes, it's unethical and illegal, too. But let's say we're two white chicks sitting around bullshitting—what kind of money are we talking here?"

"I think ten thousand dollars would be fair."

Okay—so she was wrong about connecting Miranda with the boys. Quick idea, shot down faster. They offered twice that; Miranda isn't going to come back low. Or is this the beginning of a negotiation? Ply the in-over-her-head detective with wine, seduce her, guilt-trip her, and buy her cheap? She can't shut her brain down, which would be the smart thing to do. "We're just pretending now, right?" Without waiting for Miranda to answer: "Ten wouldn't cut it."

"I'm surprised."

"Oh? Why?"

"Considering your position in your chosen line of work, ten thousand is substantial. More than you normally make on a case."

"Says who?" Kate answers, stung.

Miranda walks to a small desk in the corner. She picks up a manila envelope, opens it, and takes out some sheets of paper.

" 'Katherine Theresa Blanchard,' " she reads. " 'Private investigator, single practitioner. Less than two years experience. Assumed Carl Flaherty's business, but has lost several of his accounts. Before that a member of the Oakland police force. Forced out under pressure. Divorced, two children, both girls. Girls living with sister, by court order. Ex-husband also a former police officer, same force, also resigned under pressure. Borderline psychotic, is capable of committing great bodily harm to subject. Subject has restraining order against ex, but lives in fear of him.' " She pauses. "Shall I go on?"

"Sure," Kate says, boiling with rage. "Show me all your cards. And I'm not afraid of Eric," she adds defiantly.

" 'Currently having an affair with a married man who is a ranking officer of the Santa Barbara County Sheriff's Department.' " She looks at Kate. "That's pretty stupid. You could get him into trouble."

Kate feels a chill. This woman does not pussyfoot around. "He's a grown-up. He can make his own decisions," she manages to answer. She's drowning now, she can't let this go on.

"If a woman wants a man, he usually isn't capable of thinking clearly," Miranda corrects her. "Not a woman of your charms."

"Cut the shit."

"I mean that. I know what it is to be a desirable woman, and I know it when I see it in another woman."

"Anything else?"

"You're also sleeping with Cecil Shugrue, my neighbor next ranch over. Although I didn't need a private investigator to find that out for me," she says parenthetically, "I knew it as soon as I saw the two of you together."

For some reason, that stings more than anything else. "So what?" she says, feeling like a kid in the schoolyard.

"So I know things about you. Things you don't want people to know." She puts the papers back in the envelope. "All this is confidential, for my eyes only. No one else is ever going to see this."

"Damn decent of you," Kate manages to reply.

Miranda ignores the sarcasm. "I didn't check on you to blackmail you. I needed to know who you are. You can understand that."

Goddamnit, Kate thinks, this is bullshit. She can't sit here and passively take this without fighting back. "I know some things about you, too," she tells Miranda.

"Oh? What do you know about me?" Miranda asks nonchalantly.

"You have lovers of your own. You see them right here, on your ranch."

"And?"

"I'm sure your husband would be interested in knowing that. Not that I have any interest in blackmailing you, either," she hastily adds.

"He already does," Miranda responds in a calm voice. "I'm curious, though. How do you know?"

"That's my job."

Miranda looks at her. She smiles. "What else do you know about me that you think could be hurtful to me?"

"That's for me to know . . ."

"And me to find out?"

Kate gets to her feet. "I'm out of here. Thanks for the great dinner and the other stuff. I'll cherish the memories always."

"The pleasure was mine." Miranda smiles. "And yours, too, you can't deny it. Here," she says, handing Kate the envelope. "I don't want this in my possession anymore."

Kate doesn't take the envelope. "It's a nice gesture, but they have me on their computer—whoever 'they' are."

"I'll have them expunge you from their records."

"I don't believe you."

"Fair enough. But I promise you, no one is ever going to know about this; and I won't have you investigated any further."

"That's a relief," Kate answers sarcastically.

Miranda tears the envelope with the pages inside in half, then in half again. "This never existed," she says. "That's a promise."

And if you believe that one . . . One thing's for sure—she's going to have to watch her ass. Being the prey instead of the hunter is not to her liking. Until this moment in time she's never understood how much fear and anger that can engender.

"My daughter thinks she's sophisticated, but we both know she's naive," Miranda says as they walk outside onto the porch. "She set things in motion she shouldn't have. She could have hurt her family. She didn't, and now it's over." She pauses. "Isn't it?"

"That's Laura's decision."

"Then it's over," Miranda responds firmly.

Kate nods. This case is already over for her, but she isn't going to tell Miranda that. She won't give her that satisfaction, not after this. Let her dangle, she thinks, like she's kept me dangling all night long.

As she's about to get into her car Miranda has one last word. "Cecil was a lover of mine, too," she says from her perch on the top porch step. "He's a sweet man, isn't he? Say hello for me the next time you see him."

She goes in, closing the door behind her.

Kate sags against her car.

Miranda's last cut is a fitting end to the evening. She feels guilty and dirty about it, the whole thing, especially the seduction; not that she made love to a woman, she's glad she had that experience—but that she was used. The way, she realizes, she used Juan Herrera to help her.

She makes a vow to herself: no more sexual manipulation; and use more discrimination. She doesn't want to think of herself as being in the same space as Miranda Sparks.

What she does want—now—is to get out of here as fast as she can and be alone, until she can figure things out.

Chill out, girl, she says to herself. Chill out.

She is on the highway, heading back towards Santa Barbara. Her mind is racing. What was that all about up there? Miranda Sparks didn't need to extravagantly wine and dine and then lay her just to try and talk her out of pursuing Frank Bascomb's death. What is her agenda, and does it connect to the other events in her recent history? What is underlying all this, anyway?

Carl and Herrera had cautioned her to give it up. She had agreed to; she had severed her contract with her client. Now this.

False notes and looping trails. Miranda tells her that she and Laura keep nothing from each other. Yet Miranda doesn't know she's told Laura she's off this. So that part of it is bullshit, definitely. If that part is a lie, then is there any truth to any of it?

Give it up, goddamnit. You are an impartial observer, a gatherer of facts.

How can you give something up when they won't let you?

She's been barely aware of the road passing under her tires. Now she looks up, as something familiar jogs her eye: the entrance to Cecil's ranch, where she came and they made love—and spied on Miranda Sparks.

It's late—past midnight. Instinctively, as if the car were driving her, she yanks the steering wheel and heads up his driveway.

The door to his storage barn, where he keeps his wine barrels, is open. A light is on inside. He's back from his trip to Paso Robles—the old Caddy is parked in front.

She gets out of her car and walks across the gravel drive to the barn. Looking in, she sees a shadow playing against the far wall, cast by a single bare lightbulb hanging from the ceiling near the back.

Then she sees him. He's suctioning wine out of a barrel into a beaker. He brings the beaker to his face, examining the color of the wine inside it. His back is to her; he doesn't know she's here.

"Cecil." She's a few feet from him. She walks quietly, her running shoes silent on the concrete floor.

He turns, startled, almost dropping the glass in his hand, a look of bewilderment on his face.

"Kate! What are you doing here?" He smiles, a wide, engaging smile. "What's going on?"

She comes closer. Then she draws her right arm back and slaps him across the face as hard as she can.

The beaker smashes on the floor, wine splattering both their pants legs. His hand goes to his face, which has reddened from the blow.

"Why didn't you tell me you were screwing Miranda Sparks?" she screams at him. "Are you still humping her?"

He stares at her. "What's going on here?"

"You fucked her, didn't you, you bastard!" She's shaking. "You fucked her and you didn't tell me."

"Hey, calm down here a minute." He steps towards her.

She backs away. "Tell me about you and Miranda Sparks," she orders. "Are you still lovers?"

"Who told you this?" he asks quietly.

"Are you?"

"No."

"Were you?"

He rubs his face where she slapped it. "Yes, for a brief time, several years ago," he answers, his voice flat. "So what? I don't question you about your past."

"So why didn't you tell me?" she persists.

"Because you didn't ask, and it isn't any of your business, anyway." He moves towards her again, and this time she doesn't back away. "Let's go in the house."

———————

They're in his living room, sitting side by side on the sofa.

"Can I explain?"

"Go ahead."

"Miranda Sparks means nothing to me."

"You slept with her. That's something."

"You don't have to care about someone to have sex with them. Haven't you ever?"

"I don't know." That's a lie—she had sex with someone an hour ago she doesn't care about.

"I don't have to," he says. "Although it's better if you do care. Like with you."

Everything he's saying is logical. So why does she feel betrayed?

"It was there and I took it. That's all. She's a beautiful woman, I'm not attached. If she wanted it, why shouldn't I?" he asks.

"But what about her husband? Don't you know him? Aren't you friends?"

"Sure, I know him. Friends? No. Longtime acquaintances at best. I wouldn't sleep with a friend's wife."

"Don't you feel ugly when you encounter him?"

"No, I don't feel ugly. Sorry, maybe. Look, we both know Miranda sleeps around. We saw her with another man the last time you were up here. But that's her business, not mine or any other man's. Just like it's your decision who you sleep with."

She dumb-nods. She knows where this is coming from: her feelings of guilt about sleeping with both Miranda and Herrera. He's right—she has no reason to be angry with him. What he did with Miranda Sparks happened a long time ago, before he met her. She's the one who's been unfaithful, if that's the right word. They're not going together or anything, but she knows he wouldn't sleep with anyone else now. If anyone should be feeling ugly, it's her.

"If it's any consolation to you," he says, breaking into her thoughts, "Frederick Sparks is gay."

That's a jolt. "He is?"

"I don't have firsthand knowledge, of course," he says, "but that's the word on the street. Which is why Miranda takes lovers."

That would make sense. A woman as sensual as Miranda isn't going to go celibate because her husband isn't having sex with her.

"I've also heard that if she were to bail out of the marriage she'd lose most of her money," he continues. "Rumor is they signed a financial agreement when they got married—Frederick's desires weren't the issue then, it was a standard arrangement rich folks make, in case she turned out to be a gold digger. What's important to Miranda is if she wasn't a Sparks she'd lose her power base, which is her life's blood. She lives to hold power."

"I'm starting to discover that," she says, and suddenly she's exhausted, wasted from the effects of everything that's happened. "I'm wiped out. It's been a very long day."

"Stay the night."

Wouldn't that be wonderful, to fall asleep in his arms?

"I can't. Not tonight." He would want to make love, and she can't, not tonight.

"Are you sure?"

She nods. "Can I take a rain check?"

"Make it soon." He pauses. "Is there something going on I should know about?" Another pause. "Let me rephrase that. What's going on I should know about?"

"I can't talk to you now," she says, turning away from him. "Not about myself."

She watches him fade away in the rearview mirror as she drives down his lane. He was warm and understanding, under the circumstances. But she knows that he knows something is going on.

12

THE HILLS ARE ALIVE

Louis Pitts is a senior operative for a big PI firm in L.A. A black ex-Marine who learned his trade working for the CIA, he's one of the best in the business. Kate calls on his company occasionally to help her out when she has a case that requires backup, or when she needs the kind of specialized technical assistance they can offer.

"Your office is clean," he assures her. He's spent a couple hours checking it out for bugs and other electronic snooping devices. Before sweeping her office he checked out her car and her apartment. "Clean bill of health, the whole shebang."

"Nothing on my phone?"

"No."

"What about my computer?" she inquires fretfully.

"No taps anywhere that I can find," he says. "I'd stay off the modem for a few days as a precaution. And I've installed a warning system that should alert you if anyone's trying to access illegally."

"What do I owe you?"

"Nothing. Professional courtesy."

"Thanks, Louis. I owe you one."

He shakes his head. "Investigators tailing investigators; I don't like it. Reminds me too much of the government." He finishes packing up his gear. "If that warning I installed in your computer goes off let me know—if someone is tapping in we can track down those suckers, 'cause they won't know they've been found out unless they're at my level of expertise, which they aren't. Unless they're CIA or some organization like that, in which case you can just pack your bags and catch the first plane to Brazil."

"That's comforting."

He smiles. "Feels like a good background check is what they did. I doubt you were ever bugged."

Relieved of that anxiety, Kate spends the next two days catching up on her caseload, going out with her lawyers to interview clients, workaday things like that. She has a feeling of relief—heroics are great in the movies, but in real life she can do without that level of stress.

She returns to her office at the end of a long day in the field. It's almost nine o'clock, she realizes. She's starving—she skipped lunch, as usual; too busy.

Her phone machine is blinking—one message. Earlier she had checked the machine and cleared what was on it. This one must be recent. She punches playback, waits while it rewinds.

"This is Laura Sparks calling Kate Blanchard." Her voice sounds urgent but not frightened. "I tried your pager but didn't get a response. I have to talk to you immediately. Call me at home, 555-5538. Call no matter how late it is."

Shit—is this never going to end?

Her pager is in her briefcase. She takes it out. It's dead—the battery's down, it must have happened within the last hour. She needs to pay better attention to details like that, that's how you lose clients.

In this instance, though, she isn't upset that she was forgetful, because she's off this goddamned case. She told Laura that, clearly, firmly, and repeatedly. If she has half a brain in her head she'll shine this call on until tomorrow morning.

Reluctantly, unable not to and hating herself for it, she picks up the phone and dials.

"Thank God you called!" Laura exclaims breathlessly even before Kate identifies herself. "I was afraid you were out for the evening. Your pager doesn't work," she adds peevishly.

"Yes, I know. I'm putting in a fresh battery even as we speak," Kate answers, resisting the urge to answer Laura in kind. "What's so urgent it can't wait until tomorrow?"

"A woman called me. She has information that will help us out. She wants to talk to us about it right away. Tonight." She's jumping up and down over the phone she's so excited.

"*You*, not *us*," Kate corrects her.

Laura ignores Kate's unsubtle differentiation. "I think she really knows something. A reporter develops a sense about these things."

Yeah, right, Kate thinks. You're a real reporter. And I sing backup for Bruce Springsteen. "I'm off this case, in case you've forgotten," she firmly reminds Laura. "I don't want to be involved anymore."

Laura, at the other end of the line, is momentarily silenced by the vehemence of the response. Kate fills the space with her thoughts. She is off the case. And yet . . . she can't put that evening with Miranda out of her mind. And there *is* something heavy going on in all this, and dammit, she *is* a detective, whose job is finding things out. Playing the devil's advocate in her head, she thinks: if Miranda is involved—and there's a decent chance she is—it could be devastating to Laura. Should she be the agent to open that Pandora's box?

She tries to shake off her instincts. "I'm off this case," she says again.

"I know," Laura answers. "But can't you just do this one thing?" she pleads. "I'm afraid to meet with this woman by myself."

"That's smart thinking. You should be." You'd pee your little panties if you ever went through what I did, she thinks.

"Just this one thing," Laura begs. "She heard about you," she goes on, "from someone you talked to on the street."

"How did she wrap you into it?" Kate asks.

"From my editorial."

The conclusion is easy to draw: another leech, trolling for money.

"I promise I won't bother you anymore if you do this," Laura beseeches her. "Please."

She's off the case. She's off the case. And not only that, she's off the case.

"Okay," she hears herself saying. "I'll meet with her."

"Oh, great, thank you so much!"

"Don't thank me yet." Did she actually say she would do it? Too late now. "Do you know how to get in touch with her?"

"Yes. She's hanging around a pay phone downtown. She's been waiting a long time," Laura whines.

Kate ignores the tone of voice. That's who Laura is—you deal with her, you get that as part of the package.

"She wants to meet someplace private," Laura adds. "She's afraid of being seen with us."

"That's out of the question," Kate tells Laura forcefully. "We meet with her in a well-lit public place or we don't meet at all. I'm not setting myself up for an ambush, or you either."

"But she might not, then."

"The McDonald's in Victoria Court," Kate orders Laura. "In half an hour. There or nowhere. Call her and then call me back. I'll wait five minutes, then I'm leaving."

She hangs up before Laura can protest any further. If the woman is trying to set them up, and balks at this arrangement, she can walk away from it with her conscience clear. And if—unlikely as she thinks it is—the woman agrees, their exposure to getting hurt is low enough to be acceptable.

The phone rings. She glances at her watch. That was quick.

"She'll meet with us," Laura tells Kate. "She didn't want to do it there, but I told her it was the only way." She sounds proud of herself—that she stood up to somebody and made it stick.

"See you then."

Kate drives home and changes: dark sweater, dark sweat pants, black lightweight jacket, black running shoes. Comfortable clothes, and hard to be seen in. They're meeting in a place where they'll be surrounded by people, but she still wants to be inconspicuous.

She'll be extra-vigilant. If she gets the slightest whiff of anything wrong, she'll abort the mission. She's off the case—she has to remember that.

As she's about to leave one cautionary thought jumps into her mind. Her gun.

She takes the heavy S&W out from where she keeps it hidden on the top shelf of her bedroom closet, under a pile of old sweaters she hardly ever wears, and turns it over in her hand. A device made to kill people. Taking a handful of copper-tipped shells from the accompanying box, she loads the clip, slides the barrel to load one in the chamber, thumbs on the safety.

She's never used it in real life, and she doesn't plan on using it now; but it might provide some psychological comfort.

Lock and load. Ready. She shoves the gun into her jacket pocket.

She's halfway out the door when the phone rings. She dashes back to catch it before the machine kicks in. Maybe it's Laura, aborting the mission. Wouldn't that be nice?

"Hello?" she answers.

"I'm glad I caught you in." Cecil's voice comes on the line.

"Oh." Caught off-guard. "Hi."

"Listen. About the other night . . ."

"It's okay."

"No, it isn't. I've been worried about the way we left things. I want to talk to you about it. I like you too much to let any pettiness get in the way. I'm coming into town tonight. I can be there in less than an hour."

God, how she wants to see him. "I can't. Not right now."

She feels him tense on the other end.

"Are you with someone else?"

"No," she forces a laugh. "Absolutely not. I . . . I . . ." She can't tell him what this is about. "I'm working, a case." She laughs—it sounds tinny, phony. "Detectives are like doctors, we're always on call. I'll call you tomorrow morning, first thing. Promise."

"Yeah."

She hears the *click* as he hangs up

One more bridge burnt. How long do you live like that until you wise up?

She locks up, walks outside to her car (taking a fast precautionary glance up and down the street to make sure she isn't being watched), cranks the old engine to life, and heads towards her rendezvous with Laura; one eye on the street, the other on the rearview mirror.

She parks in the public lot behind Victoria Court. As she starts to get out she feels her automatic, hanging heavy in her jacket pocket.

She can't take it into a public place. She doesn't like carrying it anyway; a good detective doesn't need a gun—if you're in that deep, you fucked up.

She lays it in the trunk, securely wrapped in a beach towel, and double-checks that the car doors are locked.

The woman isn't one of the whores she had talked to. Kate's never seen this woman before; but she's obviously a low-rent junkie like the others.

She's young, younger than Laura, still in her teens, with a surly stance. Hispanic, with high Indian cheekbones. Her attire is vaguely punker-biker: black leather jacket with about ninety-eight zippers, baggy denims, ankle-high Doc Martens. She looks Kate up and down with a hard staring directness.

This girl is only a couple of years older than her older daughter. That jolts her.

They sit in a corner booth. Harsh, flat fluorescent lighting. A kid wearing a paper hat is mopping the floor. The girl has a cup of coffee in front of her. Kate and Laura aren't eating or drinking.

There are no introductions. "You have serious information?" Kate queries the young whore, jumping in without preamble.

The girl nods. "I don't want to talk here. It's too open." Fidgeting, staring around nervously, she turns to Laura. "I'm in deep shit anybody ever finds out I'm talking to you."

"Anybody like who?" Kate asks.

The girl doesn't answer. She blows on her coffee, scratches the side of her face, a nervous tic.

"You told me you had important information for us," Laura says, trying to push things along. "What do you know?"

"You said there was a reward," the girl comes back in reply, fixing her look at Kate. "Out there." She points with her thumb like a hitch-hiker.

"Maybe," Kate answers evenly. "It depends on what you have to tell us."

"You got the money on you?"

Laura starts to answer, but Kate puts a restraining hand on Laura's arm.

"The money will be there, if you have information that can help us. But you'll have to trust us. Tell us what you know, and then we'll decide."

"Yeah, right. Like I can really trust you."

Kate's heard a voice like this before. Two years ago, in Oakland, from the mouth of a girl whose father had a gun to her head.

The thought sends a shudder through her body. Laura and she should not be here, she thinks to herself. There's something unhealthy in the air. She can almost smell it, it's so palpable.

She turns to Laura. "We're on a snipe hunt. Let's go." Her eyes rotate to stare into the girl's.

The girl licks her lips, a dry gesture—there's no saliva coming out. She's hurting, Kate realizes. If she doesn't get well soon she's going to crash.

As if reading Kate's mind, the girl starts weaving in her seat, her eyelids slowly opening and closing, like she's fighting to stay awake.

"Shit! Don't crash here," Kate warns her.

"Don't worry about me," the girls says, her words slurring slightly. She reaches for her cup of coffee, which by now is tepid, but her hand is shaking too much to grasp it and she knocks the contents across the table, the lukewarm brown liquid spreading across the formica top.

Kate jumps up to avoid getting splashed. Laura isn't quick enough—the coffee dribbles off the edge of the table onto her jeans.

"Outside," Kate commands, grabbing the girl and jerking her to her feet. "Now." She hands Laura a fistful of napkins. "Wipe yourself off."

"These are going to stain," Laura complains, dabbing at the front of her Calvins. "And I just bought them."

"The price of doing business with scumbags," Kate informs her. "Let's go." Holding the girl tightly at the bicep, she drags her out of the restaurant, Laura hard on her heels.

They stand on the edge of the sidewalk out back. The girl has sagged against the wall, is breathing deeply.

"You okay?" Kate asks.

The girl nods. "I needed some fresh air. It was stuffy in there."

Kate waits a minute, until the girl's breathing becomes deeper, more regular. Laura watches, still trying to wipe the stain from her jeans.

"Last chance," Kate says. "What have you got?"

The girl pushes back against the wall. "I got to know you've got the money on you," she insists. "I ain't talking on the come."

Laura steps forward. "I've got the money," she tells the girl. "Trust me."

The girl snorts. "No fucking way. Show or no tell," she says defiantly.

Kate starts to shake her head no, but Laura has already reached into her purse, is pulling out her wallet.

"Don't!" Kate grabs Laura's arm before she can take out the cash.

"I'm not going to give it to her," Laura protests. "I'm just going to show her that I have it."

Kate looks at the girl, whose eyes are focused on Laura's purse. "This is getting out of hand," she states. "Let's call it a night." She takes Laura's arm. "She doesn't have anything for us. It's a shakedown, pure and simple."

"Can't we just hear what she has to say?" Laura pleads. "We're already here," she points out.

"So far she hasn't said anything," Kate reminds her. Then she sighs—this was a mistake from the get-go. Turning to the girl, her voice revealing her fatigue: "Okay. Last chance. What do you have to tell us?"

The girl stares hard at Kate. Then, suddenly, she looks away, over Kate's shoulder.

Kate jerks around, looking out into the parking lot, scanning it quickly, searching for something that looks out of place.

Normal weeknight traffic. Nothing sinister, at least nothing obvious.

She turns back to the girl. "Somebody out there watching?" she asks. She was on edge before but now it's taking over, she can feel the tingle starting to course through her body, sweat forming under her armpits.

"No," the girl says fast, eyes darting, tongue licking at the corners of her lips like they're dry to the bone. "I'm by myself. I told you I was," she says to Laura. "When I called."

Kate stares hard at the girl. There's something dirty here, she can feel it, clear and strong. "Turn around," she commands.

"What?"

"Turn around to the wall," she barks; her old cop instincts kick in, and without waiting she's grabbing the girl by her skinny upper arm and spinning her around, kicking her at the ankles, forcing her legs out in the spread-eagle position, bracing her firmly against the wall, pulling one arm behind the girl's back in a hammerlock.

"What the hell are you . . . ?"

"Shut up. Just shut up."

Making sure she has a secure grip, Kate starts to pat her down with her free hand.

"Hey!" the girl protests. "What the fuck are you doing?"

Kate pulls up on the arm she's got in the hammerlock, causing an outcry of pain.

"Hey! That hurts!"

Laura's watching, her jaw slack, stunned by Kate's rough, aggressive, and unexpected behavior.

"Why are you doing this to her?" she simpers. She looks around; a few people are watching them, but at a wary distance.

"To make sure she isn't wearing a wire or a homing device," Kate answers, letting go of the girl's arm so she can continue the frisk down the girl's cutoffs, snaking a finger inside of the top of the girl's boots.

She steps back. The girl sags against the wall again.

Kate turns to their audience, half a dozen onlookers. "Show's over, folks. I'm a cop. No big deal."

The crowd disperses slowly, casting looks back at the three women.

"That was unnecessary," the girls says to Kate, rubbing her arm where Kate had grasped it.

"It was necessary—for me," Kate counters. "So now—one last time—do you have anything that can help us? You've got about a second and a half."

The girl takes a deep breath, gathering herself. Shifting her glance from Kate to Laura.

"Okay," she begins. "There's these guys . . ."

She pauses. ". . . from Mexico," she continues. Then she pauses again.

"Some guys from Mexico," Kate repeats the girl's words, to push her along. "And . . . ?"

"And fuck you!" the girl screams, pushing off the wall with more strength than Kate could have imagined she could muster in her condition, lunging for Laura's purse and wrenching it from her grasp, starting to hightail it into the parking lot.

Kate recovers in a heartbeat. She tackles the girl from behind before the girl has taken five steps, slamming her hard to the asphalt, mashing the girl's face into the hard dirty blacktop, pulling the pocketbook from her hand. She hauls the girl to her feet and tosses the pocketbook to Laura. Then she slaps the girl in the face, hard.

"I ought to call the cops on you, you extorting little cunt," she tells the girl, right in her face, "after I kick you to half to death. But before I do that I want to know who sent you."

"Nobody."

Kate shakes her head. "You're not smart enough to set this up on your own. And how did you know about the Mexicans?"

"You showed their pictures yourself, up and down the eastside, remember?" the girl answers. "And I am smart enough. I was smart enough to get you to come meet me, wasn't I?"

Kate lets go of the girl's arm. "Get out of here," she says wearily. "If I ever see you again, or if you ever call her—" pointing to Laura—"I will make you very unhappy."

She takes a step back. The girl takes one last look from her to Laura; then she turns and runs away from them, disappearing around the corner.

Kate sags. "I knew it was going to be bullshit. I should never have let you talk me into this."

"I'm sorry," Laura whimpers, clutching her purse like a parachute.

"Yeah, me too. Well—live and learn." She holds out her hand. "Good luck. And leave this behind you, okay?"

Laura nods. Then she starts crying, crying without sound, big tears flowing down her cheeks. "I'm such a jerk," she moans.

"No, you're not. You're just . . ."

"Naive. It's the same thing."

Kate looks at her. Christ, she's young. Not only emotionally, but literally, chronologically. The age differential between them is almost enough that she could be Laura's mother, she realizes with an inner shudder.

This could be my own kid, she thinks.

She wishes she hadn't blown Cecil off for the evening, is her next thought. At this moment she doesn't want to be by herself; as importantly, she would love to be with him.

She looks at Laura, crying in the middle of a public parking lot. She knows Laura doesn't want to go off into the night by herself, either. And the man in Laura's life is dead, which is why they're in this mess.

"I need a glass of wine. Do you want to have one with me?" she offers.

Laura nods. "I don't want to be alone now," she says.

"Me neither," Kate admits.

They walk up State St. a block to Brigitte's and take a table in the corner—they want to be some place quiet, but where people can see them and they can see other people, because they're both coming off well-earned paranoia.

"Chardonnay," Kate tells the waitress. "Whatever's best." No more decisions tonight.

"I'll have the same," Laura says. As the waitress leaves to get their drinks, Laura asks, "What happened back there? Something felt wrong, more than just general weirdness."

"I'm not sure, but I agree with you about the weirdness. I'm almost certain she didn't have squat. But whether she was pulling some scam on her own or was put up to it by someone else, that I don't know."

"What would you guess?"

"I want to believe that she did it herself, because I don't want to think there's people out there trying to set you up, or me, or both of us. So I'd like to think she was acting alone, but I just don't know."

"Could someone else have been watching us? Someone with her?"

"Sure. It's possible."

Laura shudders. "What about now?"

Kate shrugs. "Maybe. Probably not. We're too public here. If someone was working this with her, they most likely would've gone after her to see what went down. Since nothing did, they'd back off—for now."

"So what should we do?" Laura asks.

"Leave it alone—permanently. After a while, if there actually is someone checking it out, they'll see we're not pursuing this and they'll give up hassling us."

"I just don't know if I can," Laura says doggedly. "Not keep pursuing it. With all this . . . stuff . . . still dangling."

Kate stares at her. "That's up to you. But I'm out. O-U-T. Which I plan to make clear to anyone who might remotely think I'm not. Including you. You have to understand that."

The waitress comes back with two glasses of white wine. They sip, not talking, each lost in her own thoughts.

"Do you know one thing I am sorry about?" Laura says, breaking the silence.

"What?"

"That I won't be seeing you anymore. I like you. You've been a friend to me."

"I like you, too."

"Because I'm not your client anymore doesn't mean we can't still be friends, does it?"

"No. It doesn't."

Laura runs her finger around the rim of her wineglass. "You know what's really weird? I barely know you, but I feel I can say things to you that I can't say to anyone else. Even my mother."

Kate shakes her head. "I don't think that's weird at all. Most kids have a hard time talking to their parents. Especially about stuff that's important to them."

Her daughters' faces flash in front of her, as clearly as if they were sitting at this table. The three of them hardly communicate at all these days. She certainly isn't making enough of an effort.

A wave of sadness passes over her. Tomorrow morning she'll call them, first thing. And this weekend she'll drive up. It's been too long. She has to fix the connection, reattach it.

"You have two daughters?" Laura asks, as if reading her thoughts.

Kate nods.

"Do they live with you? You only mentioned them once, in passing, so I didn't know."

"They live up north. San Fran. With my sister. It's temporary, a few more months, then they're moving down here. I've been looking for a larger place."

All lies, except that they're living with Julie. Shit—does she have any maternal instincts left at all? Any nesting feelings?

"That's great," Laura gushes, cutting into her dark reverie. "I'll bet they can hardly wait."

"Yeah," Kate answers flatly.

"How old are they?" Laura presses.

"They're . . . fifteen . . . almost. Next month. And the older one's seventeen."

"You're old enough to be my mom—practically," Laura laughs. "I'm only kidding—you're not nearly old enough."

Almost, Kate thinks. Biologically, she's more than old enough.

She was only seventeen when she got pregnant that first time. She had an abortion at the Free Clinic. Her mother never knew. No one did.

Seventeen. Wanda's age. Pregnant and scared to death.

"Are you close?" Laura asks. "Did you do stuff together?"

"Yes. We did . . . things." She just can't remember, right now, what they were.

"My mother and I actually do pal around," Laura says. "She's a fun woman to be with when she isn't trying to change everything in the world. We both love to ride, we have horses on the ranch. When you grow up in the ranch life you can't not ride. I'll take you out sometime. It's a beautiful place."

I know, Kate thinks.

"Actually," Laura continues, "I do more stuff with my grandmother. In most ways I'm closer to her than I am with my mom. She isn't judging me all the time, she's happy with me the way I am."

"That's important."

"She thinks I'm important."

"I'm sure your mother does, too."

Laura shakes her head. "I'll never be the woman she is," she tells Kate, "so she'll never be satisfied with me. Not really."

"You're too hard on yourself."

"I'm realistic."

Kate lets it go. It's like she told Mildred Willard, at the first therapy group when she talked about her past: she's not a social worker, a psychologist, or a nursemaid. She's a private detective, and she knows when and where to draw the line.

She finishes her drink. "I'm taking off," she announces.

"Where are you going now?" Laura asks.

Straight to Cecil's arms, that's where she'd like to go. But that's not an option now.

"I'm going for a swim." The words pop out of her mouth even before she realizes that's what she wants—needs—to do.

"Can I come with you?" Laura asks eagerly. "I've got a suit in my car. Where are you going to go?" She's almost yipping at Kate's heels, she's so eager to be with her, to not be alone.

"I've got a place."

"Where?"

"It's a secret." She makes her decision. "That I'm willing to share with you tonight. Because you are my friend."

And because I have two daughters who I should be with. But they aren't here—so you'll have to do.

———————

Leaving Laura's car in the parking lot, they cruise up Mission Canyon. It's late, there aren't many cars still on the road. Kate keeps an eye on the rearview mirror to make sure they aren't being followed. A few cars trail them, peeling off periodically onto different side streets.

As they approach the hidden entrance to her hideaway Kate sees one set of lights a couple of blocks behind them, heading in the same direction. Rounding the sharp curve a few yards before her turnoff, she cuts her lights, pulls in quickly, drives forward enough so that her car can't be seen from the road, and shuts off the engine.

"Where are we?" Laura asks, reaching for her door handle.

Kate lunges across and grabs Laura's hand before she can open the door. "Wait," she commands, feeling her pulse spiking right through the roof. If Laura opens the door the inside light will go on, revealing them.

They sit in silence. Nighttime sounds—crickets, some far-off frogs, the wind—float through the partially open windows. And the approaching sound of the car behind them.

Scrunching low in her seat, Kate turns to look out the back window. A car drives by, not slowing as it passes their entrance. It passes too quickly for her to tell what kind of vehicle it is, or how many people are in it. They can hear the sound of its engine as it continues up the hill, presumably to one of the houses further up, or else to the flat field at the top where kids go to make out.

She waits a good fifteen seconds after she can't hear the car sounds anymore before she relaxes her guard.

"Do you think they were following us?" Laura asks nervously.

Kate shakes her head no. "But better safe than sorry." She exhales—

she's been holding her breath since they pulled in. "Okay," she says, no longer worried about being tailed. "Come on."

With practiced dexterity she pulls some branches up against the back of her car so that it can't be seen by casual observation. Locking and double-checking the doors, she leads Laura up the narrow trail.

"Watch out for your face," she cautions Laura. "There's sharp branches sticking out." Normally she would light the way with a flashlight she carries in her purse, but tonight the walk will be done in darkness.

They emerge into the clearing by the swimming pool. Laura looks around in wonder. "This is incredible!" she exclaims. "Where are we?" she asks a second time.

Kate doesn't answer. She starts to peel off her clothes.

"Aren't you going to put on a suit?" Laura asks shyly.

"Not with just you here." She lays her clothes on the deck, stands naked. "We're both women. Bodies are bodies."

Laura hesitates, then follows Kate's lead, shedding her clothes and standing naked in the moonlight.

They walk to the shallow end. Laura dips a toe into the water. "It's warm!"

"In another month it'll be too cold. The sun's the only heat."

"I'll bet that doesn't matter to you."

"It doesn't," Kate admits.

Slowly, luxuriously, they walk down the chipped pool steps and push off into the water, gliding across the smooth surface. The water is dark, warm, embracing. Holding her breath, Kate navigates the full length of a lap underwater, surfacing as she touches the deep end. From the corner of her eye she sees Laura swimming backstroke, slow, easy strokes.

Kate swims a few easy laps of breaststroke to warm up, then pushes off in a hard strong crawl, legs kicking in a four-stroke beat, arms pulling down: reach, grasp, pull. Back and forth she goes, feeling her muscles work, deep strong strokes, touching the wall with a few fingers, flipping over in a tumble-turn, push off, reach, grasp, pull.

She can feel her body draining of tension.

Laura, too, has been swimming laps. She has a clean, textbook stroke, the kind they teach at country clubs. Every so often they look across at each other and smile in passing, then swim on, each lost in her own space.

She swims until she's tired but not exhausted; she doesn't want to be so depleted that she can't drive home safely. The water flows over her body, she feels like a dolphin, a seal.

She swims until she feels cleansed, expunged of everything that happened earlier.

She lies on her back in the center of the pool. Laura dog-paddles over to her. "This is heaven," Laura says.

"Close enough," Kate agrees, coming out of her float and treading water alongside Laura. "I think I've had enough for tonight."

"Okay. But I hate to leave."

"We can come back again."

"Promise?"

"Yes."

They smile at each other, start breaststroking side by side towards the edge.

The men come out of the woods. Six of them. Ragged, malevolent-looking bastards, moving towards the pool like a pack of dogs on the kill.

Kate can see their faces, illuminated by the moonlight. With a shock that almost literally stops her heart she realizes she has seen these men before; she carried copies of their mug shots around for days until she knew them cold: these are the men who were in the jail cell with Frank Bascomb.

Her bladder empties. She feels the warm water dribbling down her legs.

The ringleader points a bony finger at Laura. "Fuckin' little bitch," he singsongs in his raspy, lilting voice, walking towards the pool; the whole group of them are steadily coming closer. "You wrote about us in your chickenshit newspaper, didn't you, you little cunt."

"Don't answer him," Kate cautions Laura, keeping her voice low.

They're treading water, bodies touching each other. Her mind is racing. "Stay in the deep end, next to me."

The ringleader squats on his haunches at the edge of the pool. Kate looks at him, at the others. They stare back at her and Laura, their faces eager like dogs that have treed a bear, impatient for the bloody kill.

Out of the corner of her eye she sees her clothes lying in a heap, away from the men, twelve eyes locked onto her and Laura's nakedness. If she can figure out a way to distract them long enough to get to her gun, in her jacket pocket . . .

Her gun. She left her damn gun in the trunk of her car.

A good detective doesn't need a gun—one of Carl's dictums. This proves Carl is fallible, that there are exceptions to every rule. She and Laura are going to die here tonight proving that point.

She has to do something—but what? Two women, naked and un-armed in a swimming pool a million miles from nowhere. She could scream her lungs out—they both could—and no one would hear.

Her mind is racing but nothing comes, the absoluteness of her fear drives everything out; and then, suddenly, as in a dream, the faces of her daughters, Wanda and Sophia, float up, like nymphs emerging from the depths. This is what it must feel like when you realize your parachute isn't going to open, she thinks. Your life—what's most important in it—flashing before you, the image you carry to your death.

That she will never see them again, never have the chance to make that right, brings tears to her eyes, which she fiercely fights; she has to try to clear her head. There must be something she can do: what is it?

She hears Laura, next to her, starting to cry, a low pitiable moan.

"Try to keep yourself together," she whispers, turning to face Laura, turning her back on the ringleader—in some small ineffectual way trying to protect her client.

That's her job here, she divines with a burst of clarity. To try and get Laura out of this alive. What she would wish for someone else, in her place, to do for her daughters.

The ringleader calls out to her. "Turn around. I want to see your eyes."

She ignores him—what can he do that he isn't going to do anyway?

No time to think: go on gut instinct.

"Hey!" the ringleader calls out again. "I said turn around!"

She rotates to face him, treading water, breathing deeply, forced breaths. The man stares at her. He's beginning to run out of patience, she thinks. That could be good, if it makes him lose his cool.

Sculling the top of the water with her hands, she starts drifting to-wards the shallow end of the pool, away from Laura, her hands moving along the water's surface, gradually moving towards the shallow end, the far side from where the ringleader is standing. At the edge of her vision she sees that Laura, having realized what she's trying to pull off, is drift-ing in the opposite direction.

Kate looks at the ringleader, at the other men, who are starting to bunch up near him. They're all watching her—no one is keeping close tabs on Laura.

Her toes touch the pool bottom. Then her entire foot. She keeps moving away from Laura. Her eyes are locked onto the ringleader's eyes, who is staring back equally hard at her.

Now or never.

She drops below the surface for leverage, then pushes off against the bottom in the direction of the shallow-end steps, splashing-running in the water, it's like running in a nightmare where the ground is quicksand beneath your feet and the harder you run the deeper the hole you dig.

She reaches the steps, clambering up, but she isn't fast enough, they are on her, one grabs her by the leg, another has her around her waist, she jams an elbow hard into his nose, feeling the soft crunch, the blood spurting out onto her, across her chest, the man's grip falls away from her, but another takes his place, they're on her now, two men, now three, dragging her out of the pool, all of them wet and soaking, heavy with the water in their clothing.

At the far end, twenty meters from them, Laura has reached the edge and is pulling herself out. The ringleader, his head an emaciated skull, jerks around, seeing what's happening.

"Go get her!" he screams. "Don't let her get away!"

Two of the men take off after Laura. She's running like hell, naked, away from the pool to the path, then down the path, plunging into darkness in the closest cluster of trees, the men in pursuit, chasing her.

"Run!" Kate cries out to her. "Don't stop!"

The nearest assailant grabs at her. She stomps down hard on his shin and instep with her bare foot, at the same time driving an elbow into his windpipe, pivoting away from him, punching, kicking, biting, kneeing the men closest to her. "Run!" she screams at Laura again, throwing her body at the nearest attacker, taking the man down in a heap.

The ringleader dives for Kate, awkwardly tackling her. She kicks at him, chopping at his neck. He grabs her at the shoulders, the waist, anywhere he can get a purchase on her, his emaciated frame belying a wiry strength. She kicks at him with all her might, almost breaking free, but another one wrestles her down, then the others grab her, one on each arm and each leg, pinning her.

"Help!" she screams.

Her voice carries away into the wind.

The men who had been chasing Laura stagger back into the clearing.

"She got away," they tell the ringleader. "No way we could find her in that darkness."

The ringleader turns to Kate, held prone on the ground. "You shouldn't have been a hero, you dumb bitch!"

A fist smashes into the side of her head. Another crashes across her jaw, fists bang her ribs, she's a punching bag, a rain of blows all over her head and body, she takes a slam in her cheekbone, and she knows it's broken, she can feel the bone splintering and spreading across her face, the blood spurting out.

They intensify the assault on her, bone of fists against the bones of her eye sockets, her left eye explodes like a firecracker, against her mouth, breaking teeth, knocking them out. She's crying, screaming, she can feel her blood and her tears all mixed up flowing on her face.

Then a pair of rough, scarred, callous hands are pulling her legs apart, spread-eagling her.

The ringleader steps forward. "Stand back," he commands the others.

He towers above her, his pants fallen at his ankles. He has no under-wear on. His cock is swollen, although she can barely see him—one eye is completely closed, the other open but a slit.

She shuts it. She doesn't want to see any more. "Kill me, you bas-tard," she manages to croak from between her cracked lips.

She means it. All she wants now is release, no more pain.

He kneels between her legs. Even with her nose broken, with her face battered senseless, she can still smell his breath, his horribly putrid stench. The smell of carrion, of dead rotting meat.

Kill me, she begs to herself, kill me. That would be better than this. She can't feel a thing anymore.

The ringleader reaches inside his pants pocket and pulls out a knife, a thin fish-gutter. Bending down he grabs Kate by her hair, pulling her up and exposing her neck. "As soon as I fuck you," he says, his mouth against her ear, "I'm gonna slit you, pussy to Adam's apple."

With his free hand he reaches for his cock, to guide it in.

The first shotgun blast is deafening, the explosion lighting up the area like a Roman candle, lifting and throwing the ringleader up and back, obliterating his face. The second blast follows immediately, hitting the man nearest the suddenly dead knife-wielder between the shoulder-blades, killing him before his body hits the ground.

In the blink of an eye Cecil Shugrue has cracked the shotgun and ejected the shells, reloaded, and fires again. A third man is hit, writhing on the ground, his knee shredded like hamburger. The fourth shot goes wild, taking out a small eucalyptus tree.

The rest of the attackers are running, two of them dragging the wounded man with them, the man screaming fiercely with pain, his leg barely hanging on through the tatters of the remains of his pants leg, all of them dispersing into the night and gone.

Cecil kneels to Kate, cradling her head in his arms. "Jesus Christ," he cries.

He scoops her up in her arms and carries her, running clumsily, the branches tearing at their faces, all the way down the trail to his car, which is parked directly behind her own.

Speeding down Mission Canyon, running all the stop signs, his hand jamming on the horn all the way down, blasting through red lights, not stopping for anything, her body lying across the wide front seat, her bleeding head cradled in his lap.

"You're going to be okay," he keeps reassuring her, stroking her head with his free hand whenever he can. "We're almost there."

The old Cadillac slides to a stop in front of the emergency room doors at Cottage Hospital, laying a line of rubber halfway across the parking lot. Cecil scoops her up in his arms and carries her through the entrance, screaming for help.

Interns and nurses and staff come rushing forward, laying her on a gurney, wheeling her down the overbright antiseptic corridors to an operating bay. Cecil is right alongside, running with them, his hand clutching hers.

"I couldn't let things go with that answer you gave me," he tells her, "so I came looking for you. You weren't at your apartment, I checked your office, you weren't there, either. I took a chance and came up there. I don't take no for an answer," he says. "Not to the important stuff."

Just before they wheel her into the operating room, leaving him behind outside the double doors, the faintest shadow of a smile creases her cracked and broken mouth. Then her face goes slack with complete and blessed unconsciousness.

13

BROKEN

The hospital room is private. Kate lies on her back, motionless, eyes fluttering open occasionally, looking up at the ceiling, looking at nothing. Mostly her eyes are closed, even when she isn't sleeping. It's easier that way, if her eyes are closed she can't see anything, if she can't see anything she can shut out the world.

Her head and jaw are wrapped tightly, for stabilization. A plastic guard covers her nose. She doesn't know how badly it's been broken, but she knows it's bad. What will it be like when it heals? she thinks. A tube protrudes from a nostril to suction out the mixture of blood and mucus that is constantly draining. Other tubes are attached to other parts of her body: an ear, under her left ribs. An IV drips medicine and painkillers. Most of her face is swollen, black and blue and yellow from where their fists repeatedly slammed into her. Her left cheekbone is fractured, so severe was the pounding her assailants administered that fragments of bone broke through the skin. Four ribs are cracked, too, which makes the simple act of breathing hurt like hell.

The doctors have assured her nothing is permanently disabling. What she'll look like when she is all healed up (the process will take several months), that's another story. Right now it's too early to tell. They may have to do some plastic surgery. But one thing is certain: the face she will see in the mirror for the rest of her life will be different from the one she's been looking at all her life.

"You're lucky," the operating doctor had told her, once they had taken care of the worst of it and she was out of immediate danger. "You'll survive intact, more or less. It could have been worse, much worse."

You call this lucky? How much would she have had to endure to be *un*lucky?

She has flashbacks, to when Eric had done a similar number on her. Two of the ribs that are cracked are ones he had cracked before. She had been able to get payback for that. It had been an important step on her road to recovery. How in the world is she ever going to be able to have payback for this?

As importantly: why does she keep putting herself in situations where this can happen to her? Why didn't she learn her lesson from the Eric business? All that work with the therapists and in her group—is she bullshitting herself deep-down? Is there something in her that makes her want to be a victim?

She'll have to face that. Her life could depend on it. She escaped twice. One more time, she might not be so lucky.

After the operation. When she was wheeled into intensive care, she slept for thirty-six hours straight. When she woke up Cecil was there. He had been there the entire time.

He comes every day, early in the evening when he's finished work. They're getting the fields ready for picking, the grapes are swollen with ripeness. He sits with her, hands touching, rarely talking. He says things that don't require a verbal response. Sometimes she'll grip his hand, weakly. For the first few days that's all she can do.

———

There is a police guard at her door on the off chance someone comes looking for her to finish the job.

She calls Julie, in San Francisco, to let her know she won't be coming up this weekend to be with the girls.

"What's wrong?" Julie asks, unable to keep her voice from sounding peevish. What's keeping you from being a mother this time? is the implied, but always unasked, question.

"I was in an accident."

She hears the sharp intake of breath. "What happened?" A beat, then: "Are you all right?"

"I was protecting a client, and I got beat up some," Kate says simply, avoiding any explanation.

There's a pause from the other end. "How beat up?"

"I've got some pretty good bruises. No problem," she adds quickly, "it'll all heal fine."

"We'll drive down tomorrow."

"No!" Immediately she regrets her tone—too strong, trying to hide something. "I look worse than I am," she lies. "I don't want the girls to see me black and blue. It would only scare them."

"Well . . ." Julie hesitates.

"Trust me. I am okay, but I don't look good. In a couple weeks, when the swelling goes down . . ."

"On your face?" Julie interrupts.

More of her face is under bandages than is showing.

"Yes. A little."

"Oh, shit, baby." Julie starts to cry, over the phone.

Kate lies back deeper into her pillow. "It sounds worse than it is. Really."

She's got to get off the phone. She has more problems of her own than she can handle, she can't be worrying about her sister, too.

"Don't come down," she says again. The girls can't see her in this condition, that's the most important thing in her life at this moment—to protect them from this.

"If that's what you want," Julie says reluctantly.

She tries to force good cheer into her voice. "Just for a little while. Till I'm my old beautiful self again."

"The girls will be disappointed."

"Have them call me when they get home from school. I'll explain." She gives Julie the phone number in her room.

"There's a detective out there who wants to see you," the nurse tells her.

It's the fourth day—the first day she hasn't been completely out of it from medication. She's propped up in bed a little, enough to look at the TV if she wanted to, which she doesn't.

"I don't want to see anyone," she says. Except Cecil.

The nurse goes out and closes the door. In a moment Juan Herrera comes in, closing the door behind him. He looks down at her, shaking his head in disbelief.

"Jesus," he says quietly. "They really did a number on you."

"How bad do I look?" she manages to mumble.

"You don't know?"

"I haven't seen myself. I'm afraid to look."

"Probably a good idea, until the swelling and discoloration goes down."

She nods, her eyes slowly closing. Everything feels like slow motion, except the pain. She doesn't want him seeing her looking like this, and she doesn't want to talk to him about it.

"We need to get your statement," he tells her without preamble, pulling up a chair to the side of the bed. "It has to be done, you know that, you were on my side of the line yourself."

"I can't," she fends him off. "I can't think straight. I'm too tired, they're pumping me full of painkillers."

"Did you recognize any of them?" he presses.

"No."

"I think one or more of them might have been in that jail cell with Frank Bascomb," he continues. "One of the ones who was killed by your boyfriend. Does that sound right? We think the prints match up, but since his face was blown off we can't be certain, and besides there were so many brought in that night the procedures were kind of sloppy. Can you ID them?"

"It was too dark." She shakes her head, the gesture sending a dagger of pain up the back of her neck into her head. She cries out.

The nurse rushes in. "You can't be with her now," she admonishes Herrera. "I told you that. You have to go out."

Courteous but firm, he says, "I'll be as quick and easy as I can."

"Come back later," Kate asks, feeling the pain throughout her body. "I can't do this now."

"Get out," the nurse tells Herrera brusquely. "Police or no police. We'll call you when she's ready to be questioned."

He stands up. "Are you sure?" he asks Kate one more time.

"I can't remember anything clearly now," she says. "Come back later, when I don't feel so terrible, or look it."

"You look beat up," he corrects her, touching her hand. "Not terrible." He walks to the door, pauses, turns back. "I'm going to get the bastards who did this to you," he says in anger. More softly: "I'll check in tomorrow." The door closes behind him.

The nurse adjusts the flow of the sedative. "You'll go to sleep right away now. I'll see to it nobody comes in until the doctor feels you can, and you're willing."

"Thank you." Her eyes are closed. The pain is subsiding.

She isn't going to tell him. Not now, nor when she's feeling better and the pain is tolerable.

They were there, those men: yes. Like when they were in the same jail cell with Frank Bascomb. But she can't work with the police on this now, and she can't let them know that she knows anything.

Herrera does know—at the least he's damn suspicious. He's a good cop, he's going to push her. She'll have to keep him off her, which won't be easy. Not because he has a job to do, but because of their own personal backstory. He's taking this too personally—that implies obligation, and she doesn't want to be obligated to him.

As she's drifting off to sleep the thought that's been going through her mind once again rises: was Laura the target, as the attackers had intimated? Or was that bullshit?

The men who killed Frank Bascomb—because yes, it was a murder, she is sure of that now, beyond any shadow of a doubt—tried to kill Laura and almost did kill her. They knew who she was: they had to, she showed their pictures to every whore and bum in town, she was summoned to a meeting with leaders of the Mexican Mafia over it, that's how heavy this is. It was not a coincidence and it was not an accident. It was deliberate and premeditated. It had to be. They wanted her dead.

Her mind is too numb to think further. Within seconds the drugs take hold and she falls into a deep and dreamless sleep.

MacAllister Browne, the board chairman of Rainier Oil, the sixth-largest corporation in the world, sits in a back booth at Stars with Blake Hopkins, who works for him. Mac Browne is having his usual Stars drink, a perfect Rob Roy up. One of the reasons he likes Stars, besides the fact that it's far enough away from Montgomery St. that he doesn't feel like it's an adjunct to his office, is that they make a good drink. A man's drink like the old places make, Sam's and Jack's and Tadich's. Mac'll have two or three drinks before dinner, wine with, maybe cognac after. Won't lay a glove on him.

Hopkins is drinking a cranberry juice cocktail. He knows better than to try and keep up with the boss. Especially tonight; he wants a clear head. This project in Santa Barbara is a big step up for Hopkins: it's the largest project he's run on his own without a senior executive looking over his shoulder. When he pulls it off—he will, he has no doubts on that score—he'll be a vice-president, have his own division. That's what it's all about. This is his baby, his ticket to ride.

He looks around the spacious restaurant. Stars. An appropriate name for the place to be having this meal.

They've been making small talk, man talk: the Giants, Bill Walsh, graphite shafts versus metal. A waiter puts a plate of tiny Olympia oysters in front of Browne, a full dozen nestling on a bed of shaved ice. Hopkins, who isn't partial to raw seafood, digs into his romaine salad.

Browne forks in the first oyster, savors the small mouthful. Getting to the meat of the evening: "How is it going down south?"

"Fine," Hopkins replies. "Smooth, no problems."

"They had a clip of the ceremony on TV for that new oceanography school," Browne says.

"It was the lead story for two days—in the newspaper, too."

"John Wilkerson certainly got exposure," Browne continues. "Did you know we went to school together? College and prep school both."

"No, I didn't," Hopkins answers in surprise.

It's a funny coincidence, as Browne relates it to him: MacAllister Browne has known John Wilkerson since adolescence. Wilkerson was a class ahead at Choate and then Princeton; they even wound up joining the same prestigious eating club. But there was a fundamental difference between them: Wilkerson was born rich, from an old family. Browne, despite his highfalutin name, was working-class. He went to those places and excelled at them because he was smart as hell and because his mother, who bestowed the name "MacAllister" on him in hopes he would grow into it, had been ambitious and pushy.

They've kept in loose touch over the years, he and Wilkerson, but they're not friends; they were never more than acquaintances, bound by those old school ties. Wilkerson, although an investment banker by trade, is passionate about the environment, it's his real life's work, while MacAllister Browne wound up going in a direction that more often than not has pitted him against the environmental movement. Wilkerson's second great passion—scoring as much pussy as he can—also delineates the differences between the two old Tigers: Browne, now in his early sixties, has been married to the same woman for thirty-five years, and he's never cheated on her; as far as he knows he's the only man like him, in education and position, who has been absolutely faithful to one woman.

"Yes," Browne affirms to the younger man. "Wilkerson was the smoothest guy I ever knew. Kind of a latter-day F. Scott Fitzgerald character. Maybe we'll become reacquainted again, after all these years."

"I'd say that's inevitable."

"That will be interesting." Browne drains the last sip of his cocktail, signals the waiter for another.

"He hit on Miranda Sparks," Hopkins tells the chairman. Having just been told Wilkerson is an unbridled cunt-hound allows Hopkins the license, he feels, to dispense this piece of gossip to a man a generation older who otherwise might find it slightly distasteful, given his own marital fidelity.

"I don't doubt it," Browne says casually—being faithful doesn't make him a prude, he could give a shit about anyone else's morality. "He loved the women, and they loved him."

"Actually, she doesn't speak that well of him."

"He's getting older. How do you know all this?"

"Miranda told me."

"You've become good friends, I take it." Straightforward, no judgment. Browne keeps his own counsel.

"Pretty good. I think I know when to trust her and when not to. Make that *believe* her, not *trust* her."

"An important distinction. I'm glad you know the difference."

The waiter clears their appetizers.

"Have you finalized our deal with her?" Browne asks, that question being the crux of this meal.

Hopkins nods. "It's firm." He pauses. "It's what I told you it would have to be."

"Because of her commitment to the project?"

Hopkins shakes his head. "Because of what we're paying the family."

"I think we're paying them too much. Way too much."

"We are. But we have to."

"I'd like you to renegotiate," Browne declares.

The waiter arrives with their entrees. The chairman is having a thick veal chop, grilled with rosemary, Tuscany-style. Hopkins has opted for the sole.

"I can't do that."

He's being tested, he knows it. If you can't stand the heat, get your ass out of the kitchen.

"Because?" Brown cuts into his chop. Medium rare, on the rare side. Perfect.

The waiter uncorks the wine, pours. Browne sips, nods approval. Hopkins declines, his hand over the mouth of his own glass. Not yet.

"Because Santa Barbara County's the most environmentally sensitive and reactive county in the entire U.S."

"Tell me something I don't know," Browne responds dryly, taking a mouthful of dark, red liquid.

Hopkins begins his explanation. "It's private property. Start with that. They don't want us in there, we aren't in there. Okay? And since their property is the only workable location available to drill from, we have to come to them on their terms. I can't emphasize that enough," he says passionately. "If we don't operate there we don't do it anywhere. We're done before the first shot's ever fired."

Browne listens, his face an impassive mask.

"Now we add in the kicker: the Sparks family runs the biggest environmental trust in the county, one of the largest in the entire state. Getting in bed with a company like ours is the last thing that would ever be expected of them, which is why we're going to be able to pull this off, but we have to pay for it, and we have to protect them, which comes down to money, also."

"How much money do you see them making off this?" Browne asks.

"After the initial contribution to the oceanography school?"

"Yes."

"Two or three million a month, depending on volume."

"That's pesos, of course." He'd better cut his meat into smaller bites or he'll choke on a piece.

"Yeah, that would be nice, especially now with the peso gone to hell. But no, American dollars. That's the normal coin of the realm, last I looked," Hopkins answers.

"This is an expensive business we're in," Browne observes dryly. "And they don't even control the mineral rights, the state has those. We're paying them as much as we're going to pay the state of California, for gosh sakes."

"They have us over a barrel. No pun intended."

"No chance of a renegotiation?" Browne asks again.

Hopkins shakes his head. "I'm still surprised they went for it, being such staunch conservationists, which is not a put-on, they are true believers. Which is why we have to do it this way. Even with what we're going to be paying them I don't know if I would have done it if I was in their shoes—they sure as hell don't need the money, and they're going to catch a lot of heat."

"It's unfortunate we can't be completely straightforward in all this," Browne says. "I don't like subterfuge."

"We're not doing anything wrong," Hopkins states. "They're the ones who don't want the full extent of their active participation known."

"Still and all . . ." The older man thinks. "Down the line, once the deal is done, we'll have to be a bit more forceful with them. Bad publicity isn't in their best interest." The way he says it leaves no room for argument—nobody pushes him, he's dealt with tougher situations than this one with the Sparks family, old money or not.

Hopkins nods—a reply isn't necessary or expected.

He is over the hump—he can feel it. Without asking, he pours some wine into his own glass. So what if he's eating fish; he's not auditioning for Miss Manners. "I think I did a hell of a job," he states boldly.

"You did," his boss tells him.

Hopkins sips the wine. He can feel its heat, matching his own glow. "Thank you."

"What's our next move?" Browne asks, bringing the conversation back to basics.

"To announce our gift and the plan. They go hand in hand. The donation is our leverage, of course, so we'll announce that first, probably on site . . ."

"That's a nice touch."

"Thank you." Hopkins continues: "Then I'll drop the drilling component on them a few weeks later. It'll be pretty damn hard to say no to someone who's just handed you a check for eighty million. That's twenty-five million more than David Packard gave the Monterey Aquarium."

"Sounds like a plan," Browne comments coolly. "When do you contemplate doing this?"

"As soon as you give me the final okay, so we can move forward with our agenda. I'd like to go public at the next monthly Board of Supervisors meeting, which is in three weeks. So the grant should be made next week, if possible."

Browne nods, digesting this. "We have a board meeting this coming Tuesday. I'll get authorization for the grant then," he says, casually. "They've been briefed already."

Browne is going to tell the dozen members of his board, all big-timer players in their own rights, that they'll be spending a fortune of company money on something they won't get any direct benefit from, and he's talking about it like it's nothing more than getting permission to buy a keg of Coors for the company picnic. It must be nice to have that kind of power, Hopkins thinks. Someday, after this and a couple more successful projects like it, he'll be in that position.

"Should there be a formal news conference when we give them the money?" Browne asks.

"Sure, but not high profile. I don't think anyone from Rainier should be visible down there now except me," he cautions. "I'll work with Mrs. Sparks on the handling of it. She likes to stage-manage her affairs."

There's a double-entendre there, but his boss doesn't know it, nor is he going to. Sleeping with a business partner can be ruinous, even if the partner is as irresistible as Miranda Sparks. He'd had to, though. As if Miranda had put a gun to his head. She'd wanted it, stronger than he did. She had been the instigator, the predator. They're on a more equal footing now, but he has no delusions that the relationship is at her pleasure. Once this is all concluded, he doubts she'll continue seeing him, which will be too bad—he's never known a woman like her.

"John Wilkerson," Browne ruminates, his mind having changed course. "This Miranda Sparks—she's a very beautiful woman, isn't she? She certainly looks good on television."

"Yes, she's a stunner."

"I wonder if dear old John managed to sleep with her," Browne muses.

"I don't think she's that kind of woman," Hopkins says with a perfectly straight face.

A week and a half has gone by. Cecil's been the only visitor, at her request. She's been transferred out of ICU to a private room.

The hospital room door slowly opens. Laura Sparks's head appears like a white rag of surrender on a stick.

The television set is on, the volume set to a low drone. Kate is propped up on her pillows, watching a daytime soap; she doesn't know what it is or what it's about. Something bland and undemanding to help her get through the slow passage of the day.

"May I come in?" Laura asks, her voice tremulous with nerves.

"Sure." Kate's head swings slowly towards the door. She reaches her hand across the sheet and clicks off the TV.

Laura crosses to the foot of the bed, sits on the edge of the plastic chair. If she had a napkin in her hands she'd be shredding it, Kate observes.

"My God!" Laura exclaims as she gets a good look at Kate's face. "I didn't realize how bad it was. Oh, God." She almost breaks down.

"Believe it or not, I am getting better."

"That's good. I'm glad." She bites her lip. "Oh God, I'm so sorry!" she cries out suddenly.

Kate knew this would come, and she knew how she would respond. "Don't be. It wasn't your fault."

"I got you involved. You didn't want to come."

"I'm a big girl. I'm responsible for what I do. Nobody made me do anything I didn't want to."

"Still . . ."

It hangs in the air, like a heavy, humid smoke: Laura's need to apologize and be absolved, Kate's having to do it. So it can be over, completely and irrevocably finished.

"It wasn't your fault," Kate reassures her again.

Laura swallows. "Thank you."

Laura tells Kate she had run two miles, halfway down Mission Canyon, naked, bleeding, crying, running without stopping until she got to the Botanical Gardens and had hysterically told her story to one of the park attendants who lived there, whose cottage door she had pounded on. The attendant, a calm old pro, had wrapped her in blankets and called 911. By the time the police arrived at the site the only thing left were the bodies.

Her mother had picked her up and taken her home. She stayed at her parents' house for a week until she got the guts up to move back to her own place. She hadn't been much help to the police at all, either, except to tell them about the girl who had called her. The girl hasn't been found.

"I've decided to take your advice," she says after this recitation. "I'm going to let it go."

"Good," Kate says, lying back on her pillows, exhausted from this brief but intense exchange. She has no patience with this spoiled, protected rich girl. You can go now, she tells Laura silently. You have been blessed and forgiven. Go with God. But go.

"You're tired," Laura says, reading the signs properly. "I should go."

Kate nods yes.

Laura stands. "I'm leaving town for a few weeks. I'm going to Rome, to stay with some friends. Mother and I agreed I needed to get away for a while, until this blows over. I'm leaving tomorrow," she adds in a tone that carries self-guilt with it.

"That's a good idea," Kate agrees. Rome. Why didn't she think of that herself?

"Will you be okay?" Laura asks solicitously. She's itching to cut and run but she doesn't want to appear impolite. "Is there anything you need?"

"No."

"Well . . ." Laura lingers a moment at the door. "I'll call you as soon as I'm back."

"Fine. Great."

"You were right. It's over. I should have listened to you. You wouldn't be . . ." She turns away, unable to look Kate in the eye as the full extent of her complicity suddenly comes clear to her.

"Yes." She's tired. Really tired.

Laura blinks. "Bye," she finally manages to choke out.

The door shuts silently. Kate closes her eyes.

It's always big news when a spokesman from one of the oil companies calls a press conference in Santa Barbara. It usually means they want something to be changed, and for people in the community, particularly those in the environmental movement, it can only be change for the worse. That's a given.

This press conference has an element of intrigue, because a new player is being introduced. According to the release put out by the local office of Rainier Oil, someone named Blake Hopkins is to be introduced to the community as the new manager of the company's office here, the main office on the central coast. And along with this introduction there is going to be a surprise announcement of a new undertaking by his company.

An additional point of interest: the announcement is going to take place on the beach north of town, near the section of the Sparks property which was donated to the university and The Friends Of The Sea to establish their school of oceanography.

The beach is crowded: important environmental players, all five county supervisors, the local press. Standing slightly to the side are Miranda, Dorothy, and Frederick Sparks. Miranda looks especially fetching in a short-skirted dress that shows a lot of cleavage. Not many women around can dress like this without looking cheap; she's one of the few.

Marty Pachinko sidles up to her. "So what's going on here?" he wheedles, trying not to look at her protruding breasts.

"As me no questions, I'll tell you no lies," she answers, smiling brightly. "You'll find out, soon enough."

"Don't be so suspicious all the time, Marty," Dorothy chides him. "Everybody has their good side."

"I'll believe that about an oil company when I see it."

"Keep your eyes open, then," Miranda says, turning her back on him.

Everyone seems to be in place. Miranda steps forward to the microphone. "Something nice is going to happen here today. Something very nice. So without further ado, I'm going to let Mr. Hopkins have the floor."

She steps aside for Hopkins, smiling as he slides past her.

He nods to her, nothing more, then glances at Frederick, who's blissfully checking out the situation. Poor bastard, Hopkins thinks. She's a great lady, but I sure wouldn't want to be married to her. What the hell; what you don't know can't hurt you, he guesses.

"This is an unusual place and an unusual way to introduce myself," he begins. "My name is Blake Hopkins, and I'm the new project manager for Rainier Oil. I'll be officially moving down here next month from San Francisco, where I've been working at company headquarters, so if anyone knows of a nice rental, preferably on the beach, please let me know. I love the beach here, it's one of my favorites."

He smiles, easily.

"There are a lot of changes happening in the oil business. Hopefully, changes for the better. Ways to improve on what it is that we as a multinational corporation have to do: to keep our company profitable, to make sure this country has an adequate supply of domestic oil, and also, perhaps most importantly for you folks here today, to constantly develop new technologies so we can mitigate the impact of oil production on the environment. What we are looking to do at Rainier Oil is to continually decrease the threats to the environment from what is an essential industry, not only in this country's interest, but for the entire world."

"This joker's a better spin doctor than James Carville," Marty Pachinko stage-whispers out of the side of his mouth to the woman standing next to him, another committed environmentalist and ally.

"In the near future I hope to address some of those issues," Hopkins continues. "Today, I have something different I want to say. Something about which there will be, I would hope, no controversy."

He turns and faces the Sparks family. "We applaud your generosity in granting a portion of this property to the university to build a world-class oceanography teaching facility here. It's the type of wonderful philanthropy to one's community that civic-minded people should, but rarely, do."

"Thank you," Miranda answers.

"Oil companies can be civic-minded, too," Hopkins says. "I know that sounds strange to some of you, but it's true."

He stares out into the crowd. A majority of those here today take that exact position.

He loves it. He loves to come into a situation and turn people's perceptions upside down.

"I'm here today to make a gift on behalf of the Rainier Oil Corporation. I am speaking for our board chairman, MacAllister Browne, whose idea this is. This project is something he feels strongly about, on a personal level."

He pauses briefly. Everyone is waiting for the punch line.

"Rainier Oil is going to underwrite the construction of this facility," Hopkins announces, his voice low, even, virtually emotionless.

There is a moment before what he's said sinks in: then it hits them. The crowd is stunned, particularly the environmentalists, with Marty Pachinko, their spokesman, being the most astounded.

For a few seconds Marty is speechless; then he finds voice. "What's your agenda?" he shouts out. "The real one, not the hidden one!"

"To improve the environment, the same as yours," Hopkins answers.

"If you really want to improve the environment, pull your oil rigs out of our channel!" Pachinko fires back.

Miranda comes out of the blocks like she's been shot out of a cannon.

"For godsakes, Marty, what is wrong with you?" she cries out to him, her voice trembling with indignation. "This company wants to give us a multi-million-dollar check to do something worthwhile. What is it, if an oil company wants to give us money it's no good?"

"It's blood money," he answers hotly. "That's why." Even before the words are out he wishes he had kept his mouth shut. This could have been done a better way, less public. All of a sudden Rainier Oil is the good guy, and he's the heavy?

"It is not blood money," Miranda answers him, her voice aggrieved. "We don't like what the oil companies have done here on the coast, either, but that's history. This gift is now, and we're taking it," she states defiantly.

"Yeah, well, look how they got it," Pachinko answers lamely.

Hopkins regains control. "We don't apologize for what we do," he says calmly. "Oil makes the world go round. We donate money to good causes," he adds. "This is a good cause." He pauses. "I'm sure this gesture comes as a shock to you," Hopkins says, with the slightest touch of a smile. "You must have reacted without really hearing what I was saying; a common mistake people like you make about people like me," he adds, his smile broadening a bit.

Pachinko starts to answer; then he catches himself. This isn't a winning situation. He should shut up, for now at least.

"However," Hopkins continues, "to answer your earlier challenge: we are, in fact, developing a plan that will eventually enable us to pull our rigs out of the channel."

Pachinko can't believe his ears. "What's the catch?" he stammers.

Hopkins looks at him, still smiling enigmatically. "The catch. There's always a catch, isn't there?" Then he turns serious. "We have a *plan*. A *plan*, not a *catch*. Not some gimmick, or something dirty and underhanded. An idea, a concept, a philosophy. A plan. Which we will propose to this county when we have all the answers to the questions we're currently raising amongst ourselves." He turns to Miranda. "Please take this gift," he asks her.

"We will," she assures him.

The following day Miranda is swarmed by reporters from every newspaper, magazine, television, and radio station from Los Angeles to San Francisco. They all ask the same two questions:

Q: "Why is Rainier Oil doing this?"

A (Miranda): "I assume it is because they are a socially responsible corporation that wants to improve the quality of life in this area, especially since they're intimately involved, with their long-term oil extractions."

Q: "Are there any strings attached?"

A (Miranda): "No."

She elaborates: "For a long time, but particularly since the *Exxon Valdez* tragedy, the oil companies have been looking for ways to boost their image, especially in the area of marine life and the management of the sea in general. They've made a lot of money out of our ocean, and I emphasize the word 'our'—your ocean and mine. So this is a way of giving something back. They didn't tell me that, but that's my guess."

She's asked how long the grant negotiations have been in motion.

"Not long," she replies. "They called me after we declared our intention and asked how they could get involved. It evolved from there very quickly. They were completely open and aboveboard—a pleasure to deal with."

The broken ribs hurt like hell but Kate is up and walking, first from her bed to the toilet and back, then down the hall to the nurses' station. The nurses smile at her, and she smiles back.

"Just don't tell any jokes when I'm around," she cautions.

They laugh at that. She bites her lip so she won't.

She's been in this hospital for three weeks. Tomorrow she will be discharged. She and Cecil talked about that two nights before, during his daily visit.

"Stay at my place," he said. "You can't take care of yourself," he logically pointed out.

"I don't want to be a burden on you, especially when it's your busiest time of the year." She hates being dependent on anyone, especially when she cares about them.

"You're an ornery one," he observed.

"It's my nature."

"Think about it."

She did. She had an internal debate, and she tried to keep self-pity out of it. Part of her feels she would be weak by accepting his offer; another part thinks she's growing up, that by receiving a gift she'll be allowed to give one back.

When he returned the next night she had decided to take him up on his offer. She would stay a couple of days up there and see how it was.

There's a knock at her door.

"Come in." She's sitting in a chair in the corner of the room, thumbing through *The New Yorker,* the afternoon sunlight through the sheer cotton curtains dappling her face and shoulders. Her eyes are clearer, the color is coming back into her face. Her shattered cheek and broken nose, however, are covered with a protective mask.

Miranda Sparks enters. "Hello," she says.

"Hello." Kate is surprised. She doesn't get up.

"I apologize for not coming earlier." Miranda stands just inside the door frame.

"I didn't expect you to come at all. You certainly didn't have to. Thank you for those," she adds, looking at the bureau against the wall, upon which sits a large bouquet of fresh-cut flowers. A bouquet from Frederick and Miranda Sparks has arrived every other day.

"You saved my daughter's life."

Now Kate rises—stiffly. "Come in. Would you like some juice? There's some in the refrigerator," she says, pointing to a small cube box in the corner.

"No, thanks."

Kate thinks Miranda feels awkward; she isn't in control of the situation. It gives her some small pleasure.

"I won't stay long. I know how dreary it can be when people hang around your hospital room when all you want is to be left in peace and quiet."

"I don't mind."

"I came to tell you if there's anything I can do to help, anything at all . . ."

"I'm fine. Thank you."

The sunlight pools in the center of the room where they stand on the small throw rug like two figures in a Vermeer painting.

"Anyone would have done what I did, under the circumstances," Kate says, making her point again. "It wasn't anything heroic."

Miranda smiles. "If you insist."

They haven't come close to touching, not even to shaking hands. As Miranda turns to go, Kate says one more thing to her.

"I'm not working for Laura anymore on this," she says. "In case you didn't know. I'm done with it."

"We all are, I hope to God."

"I don't know about anyone else. I just know about me. I'm putting it behind me and moving on with my life. I'm lucky to have one, and I'm going to start taking better care of it."

"You should," Miranda says gently, "after what you've been through."

Kate shrugs. "Whatever. I'm quits with it, that's what I wanted you to know."

Miranda nods. "As I said, if there's anything I . . . we . . . can do for you, anything at all—"

Kate cuts her off with a shake of the head. "I'm doing fine. I want to stop thinking about it. Everything about it," she says with emphasis, to make her point, "and everybody."

Miranda walks to the door. "Goodbye, then. I hope to see you again."

"I don't doubt we will. It's a small town."

She waits, standing in the center of the small room until Miranda takes the three steps that get her out. Then she sits back into the chair, sagging against its worn embrace, worn out from her brief, charged encounter with this woman who has to control everything and everybody.

She can walk fine but they take her out in a wheelchair anyway, it's SOP. The nurse who is pushing her hums a tune from *Evita*, which has been running at the Lobero for a month.

"Glad to be going home?" she asks cheerfully.

"Glad to be getting out of here."

"Boy, you think I don't know what you mean? I love my work and I love the people here and the patients, too, but I am so happy to leave when my shift is over. This'll drain you," the nurse informs her. "You start thinking everybody in the world is a sick person, you start thinking you're a sick person yourself even when there isn't anything in the world wrong with you."

Kate knows exactly what she means. It's what a cop can come to feel—that everyone in the world is a bad person, a criminal, at least potentially, until you start thinking you're a criminal yourself, when you aren't. It all gets hard and certain and then you become the judge and jury and then all hell breaks loose. *Goddamn civilians.* If she heard that expression once when she was on the force she heard it a thousand times. She came to believe it herself. Deep down she still does—some of the time, anyway.

"We've got some paperwork for you to sign," the nurse says as she wheels Kate into the accounting department. "Insurance forms. Won't take long."

She parks Kate's wheelchair next to the counter. "Blanchard," she tells the clerk. "Recovery 4. Checking out."

The clerk pulls Kate's file up on the computer. "It's already been taken care of," she informs Kate. "You don't owe anything," she adds as the computer prints out the bill.

What? "Let me see that."

She stands out of her wheelchair and grabs for the document as it's coming out of the printer. "Who paid this?" she demands.

The clerk types into her computer. "Mrs. Sparks. She came in here yesterday afternoon, said she'd been visiting with you, and wanted to clear your bill. She gave us a check." She scans the machine for a moment. "It cleared this morning."

If there's anything I can do for you, anything at all . . .

Cecil is in the lobby, waiting for her. She's glad to see him. Taking him up on his offer was the right move. She needs support now, a strong shoulder to lean on. If that makes her a defenseless little woman for the moment, fuck it. He looks great to her.

14

HIGH STAKES

When Frederick Sparks plays serious poker he plays privately, be-
hind closed doors. He plays for a lot of money with other high rollers,
some of whom are professionals. He is not; he is a passionate amateur.
He has been gambling for decades, since he first caught the bug in
college.

The game is in a penthouse suite at one of the newest and most op-
ulent hotels in Las Vegas. Down below, dozens of stories, on the huge
football-field-sized floors in casinos up and down the Strip and in town,
tens of thousands of people are throwing their money at the slots, the
blackjack and craps tables, the roulette wheels. Lose five dollars here,
win ten there. Lose five hundred there, win a thousand here. The house
isn't concerned with how much someone loses as long as he (or she; half
the gamblers are women, especially at the slot machines) can cover the
bet; but if someone starts winning big, especially at the card tables, they
zero in on him or her via the surveillance cameras located in the ceiling—watching for card counters, or conspiracies between a gambler and
a dealer. Anything suspicious, the offending player is quietly but firmly
escorted from the table to a private meeting. Usually they leave the prem-
ises without further ado. Sometimes they need a little persuading; but
one way or the other they don't stay, and they don't come back—the
house keeps close watch to make sure of that, and they let all the other
places in the city know, too.

None of that applies to men in the penthouse. They don't cheat. It's
unnecessary—either they're too good to have to or they're too rich to
worry about it, or both. And second, if anyone ever got caught cheating

in one of these games, the consequences would be a hell of a lot worse than merely getting kicked out the door and told to stay out.

The living room of the penthouse is huge, at least two thousand square feet. A bank of windows lines one wall. From this perch you can see the lights of the Strip and the city glimmering far below, the suburbs beyond that, then the outskirts, and finally the endless stretches of desert.

There are six players in this game, all men in their late middle age. The deal passes clockwise around the table in turn. The dealer calls the game, draw or stud. The ante is one thousand dollars per hand, with no limits on the amounts of the bets. All the players have stacks of chips in front of them in various sizes and colors. Besides the players there are two hostesses provided by the hotel, both of them former *Penthouse* centerfolds, who are there to get the players anything they want, food or drink, compliments of the house. This is cherry duty—only the cream of the women who work for the casino pull it. Every two hours the players take a twenty-minute break, at which time they may, if they choose, ask the hostesses to provide other services as well. Nothing is denied, except drugs. All the players have smaller suites on this floor or the one directly below, also on the house.

The only other person in the room is a representative of the hotel. He's there to make sure nothing goes wrong. These are all very wealthy men playing in this game, and their comfort and security is paramount.

The house serves as the bank. It takes a small percentage for doing so, and for providing the facilities and all the amenities. These men have accounts here, they're good for whatever they need to be, that's been established over the years. Some men, these six and many others, have been playing cards and gambling other ways in this and other Vegas hotels for decades. Some of them have lost tens of millions of dollars. One man who owned a professional sports franchise lost $85 million over ten years. Another, one of the most popular singers in the world, once lost four million in one night.

The men have been playing for several hours. Two of them have large stacks of chips piled in front of them. The other four don't. Frederick is one of the latter group.

The dealer, a plump man named Easton, who is one of the biggest car dealers in the Pacific Northwest, is sitting two seats to Frederick's right. Easton is a major-league gambler who wins more than he loses. Right now he's winning big. The other winner is the man sitting to Frederick's left. His name is Simpson, and he is a corporate lawyer out of New York.

"Stud poker," Easton announces.

He deals the first card facedown in turn around the table. No one lifts to peek. Card number two follows, again facedown. Then the third card—up.

Easton surveys the table, calling the up card in front of each player. "Jack of hearts." His voice is flat, no inflection. "Four of clubs. Seven of clubs. Queen of clubs. Ten of spades. And the dealer has a six of diamonds. Queen bets."

Frederick has the four of clubs. He glances at his hole cards. One is the king of clubs. He has the makings of a club flush at this point, although there are already a lot of clubs showing. Still, worth finding out. He glances around at the others. They're all concentrating on their hands and the cards in front of the other players.

The player showing the queen is Calvin Rogers. From Dallas, real estate. A tall rangy man, from mid-distance he looks like the actor James Coburn, especially with that thick head of long white hair. Frederick's been playing in card games with Rogers for a dozen years. Win or lose, the man keeps coming back. Like all the others in this room.

"Five hundred," Rogers says, throwing a chip into the pot. He has a distinct West Texas accent.

"See you," says the man to his left, a diamond merchant from South Africa named Leewourk, who flies in once a month to play in these games. He tosses in a chip. The pile in front of him is getting low.

Easton throws in his chip without comment. The player to his left and Frederick's right is Mark Taylor, the movie star. Of all the players in the game, he is the most fidgety. He looks at his hole card, at the pot, at his hole card again. Like Leewourk's, his stack is in serious decline.

"Your play," Easton nudges him.

Taylor looks at the cards one more time. Then he turns his second card facedown and pushes them away from him, towards the middle of the table. "I'll sit this one out, thank you," he says, flashing the smile that has enabled him to command ten million dollars a picture and a piece of the gross.

It comes to Frederick. Smiling slightly, he picks up a chip and tosses it on top of the others. "I'm in," he says.

The fourth card is dealt, again faceup.

The ten of clubs to Frederick, giving him three clubs, two showing. Ace of hearts to Simpson, the player on his left. Rogers gets the king of spades. The next card is a three of diamonds, and Easton, the dealer, pulls an eight of spades.

"Still yours," Easton says to Rogers.

Without looking at his hole card, Rogers throws in ten chips of a similar color to the first one he threw. "Five thousand," he says in his flat Texas twang.

Leewourk looks at his cards. A ten of spades and a three of diamonds showing. The best he can have so far is a pair of tens—a straight or a flush is out. A hand to be folded.

"I'm probably crazy," he tells the others, smiling politely, "but I'll stay in." He throws in the necessary chips. His stack is getting perilously low.

Easton give him the subtlest of skeptical eyes, but says nothing. No one else does, either. They all know each other, having played in high-stake card games together over the years, here and in other locales, and they like each other well enough, superficially, but there is no kibitzing here, no friendly banter.

"As will the dealer," Easton says as he antes up.

Frederick glances at one of the hostesses, who is immediately bending at his side, her lightly perfumed ear an inch from his lips. He whispers something, and she nods and moves to the far end of the room, where there is a full bar. She returns with a cold glass of Pellegrino on shaved ice.

"Thank you," he says to her, giving her a hundred-dollar chip for her efforts.

"You're welcome, sir." She retreats to her position, the chip going into a small gold-lamé purse she keeps on a chair next to her. Over the course of the game, which will go all night, these women will make several thousand dollars in tips.

The final faceup card is dealt. Frederick draws the king of diamonds, giving him a secret pair. No more flush, but the possibility of two pair or three of a kind, depending on what he draws. If he stays in. To his left goes a six of spades, then a nine of spades, a nine of diamonds, and Easton deals himself a ten of hearts.

"Still yours," Easton says again, looking across the table at Rogers.

Rogers looks at his cards. At his hole cards. At the other cards on the table.

He's out of it, Frederick thinks. That was a costly try.

"Ten thousand," Rogers says, his voice still low and flat, dry as tumbleweed. If he's nervous about this hand he isn't showing it. He counts out the proper number of chips, stacks them neatly, and pushes them into the pot. They sit next to the others in the center, a tiny tower of power.

Leewourk breathes out a sigh of disgust. "That was a dumb move, sport," he says to himself as he turns all his cards over and pushes them away. He gets up from the table and walks to the bar, where he pours himself a stiff Johnnie Walker Black over ice cubes, swirls it, and downs it in one gulp. Then he looks out the window, not wanting to watch the remainder of the hand.

Easton looks at his cards for a moment. "Can't win if you don't play," he says, half-smiling. He stacks an equal number of chips to those played by Rogers, and pushes them into the pot, touching Rogers's.

It swings to Frederick. The best anyone can have so far is a pair, and he knows he has one: kings. Only Simpson to his left could have better. Playing the odds, that's what it's all about. Over twenty K in this pot already, he observes, counting the stacks of chips to himself.

He feels lucky this hand. This could be his hand, unless Simpson has that second ace.

"Truer words were never spoken," he says in response to Easton's comment, as he, too, stacks his chips and pushes them in.

To his left Simpson says nothing. He merely shakes his head and turns his cards over, at the same time cocking a finger an inch, like a bidder at Christie's. Instantly one of the hostesses is at his side, and a moment later she's handing him a Coke on ice.

Frederick breathes a sigh of relief. Simpson's out. He's the one Frederick worries about. Over the years he's lost serious money to Mr. Simpson. When Simpson is out of a hand Frederick feels a lot more secure.

Three in, three out. Last card. Facedown. He takes a peek at his card. A king: king of hearts. Three of a kind, kings. In this game, this is a winning hand.

It's Rogers's bet. He looks at the cards on the table. He peeks at his hole cards, looking at them, down at the three on the table, at the three at Frederick's spot, at the three sitting in front of Easton.

"Can't win if you don't play," he says, smiling at Easton. He pushes three stacks of thousand-dollar chips into the pot. "Thirty thousand," he tells the other two.

Easton blinks. "You are a player," he acknowledges. He looks at his own cards for a moment. Then he says: "So am I." He counts out thirty thousand-dollar chips, pushes them in.

They turn to Frederick. He looks at Rogers, at Easton. He's played hundreds of hands of cards with these men over the years. He knows them, knows their tendencies. Like they know his.

Rogers likes to bluff. This would be a time to try one. It's possible he could be sitting on a high straight, which is what he wants them to think. But that's really dicey, the odds are probably fifty to one—bad odds to be throwing forty thousand or more at. More likely he's got a pair of queens. It could even be three of a kind. That would give him confidence, forty thousand dollars' worth. Except it won't beat the three kings Frederick is holding.

Easton isn't bluffing; Frederick would take a separate side bet on that. He plays the odds. He's sitting on two pair, that's almost a sure bet. Forget the straight; you don't pull two insides on a straight. Frederick doesn't know the odds on that, but it would have to be over a thousand to one. Easton is tonight's big winner, and he's holding two pair. For him, it's a good bet.

Easton turns to Frederick. "In or out?"

"I'm in." He counts his chips, slides thirty thousand worth of them into the pot. He fingers his cards. This one is his, this one will even out the evening. Quickly, he eyeballs the rest of the chips sitting in front of him. Fifteen thousand dollars' worth of chips in five-hundred- and thousand-dollar denominations.

"And I raise fifteen thousand," he adds, pushing all but a few chips into the center. He looks up at Easton. "Your play," he says, his voice calm.

Rogers scratches hard at his nose. "You keep a tight asshole, man," he says with admiration.

"Your play," Frederick answers.

"Is it? Well . . ." He takes one more look at his cards. "In for a dime, in for a dollar, I reckon," he says finally, pushing in fifteen thousand dollars' worth of chips.

They both look at Easton. Wordlessly, he pushes the required amount of chips into the center.

"What've you got, boys?" he asks.

Rogers turns his cards up, one at a time. The queen of spades and the queen of diamonds. Just as Frederick had thought.

"Three little ladies," Rogers says. He figures he's maybe got it won, but he's not overly confident. What goes around comes around, it's happened to all of them.

They look to Frederick. It's his turn to show his hand; Easton as dealer will go last. It doesn't matter—Easton can't beat what he has.

"Three kings." He flips over his hole cards, smiles at Rogers. "You don't have to keep it tight when you're sitting pretty on it."

Rogers slumps. "Well, shit. Good hand, partner," he congratulates Frederick, with reluctant grace.

They look to Easton. He gives a sheepish little shrug. "If I had known you two sandbaggers were actually holding strong hands like these I wouldn't have stayed in."

Frederick finally permits himself a smile. A huge pot, a pot to get well on. The first one of the night. He was afraid he might go down hard.

"Lucky for me I did," Easton continues.

He turns over his cards. A seven and a nine. A straight.

Frederick sags back into his seat, a wan smile crossing his lips.

"You drew to an inside straight?" Rogers says in utter disbelief. "You were sitting on that shit and you drew to a straight?"

"Like I said, it was a dumb move. But I've been winning big, I figured it was time to let the rest of you back in the game. I tried, boys. Sorry." Almost apologetically he gathers in the mountain of chips.

Frederick looks at the few chips remaining in front of him. Less than five thousand dollars, not even enough for one more hand. He raises a finger to the house man.

Frederick gets up from the table. The man comes to meet him. They talk quietly for a moment. The man takes a pad from his inside tuxedo pocket, writes something on it, hands it to Frederick, who looks at it cursorily, then signs.

The house man walks to a cabinet on the other side of the room. He pulls a key from his pocket and unlocks it. He reaches in and withdraws a tray of poker chips, which he brings to the table and sets at Frederick's spot.

"One hundred thousand dollars, Mr. Sparks," he informs Frederick.

Frederick takes his seat again. "Thank you," he says with a smile. He turns to Taylor, seated to his right. "Your deal. Let's play cards."

It's late evening when the game, by mutual agreement, ends. They have been playing for ten hours without a break, other than the every-two-hour pit stops. No naps; eating is snacks, quick and easy—sandwiches, Mexican food, soft drinks. Virtually no alcohol.

Easton is the big winner. He gathers in a huge pile of chips, stacking them by color. Simpson has done okay, too. He's up about thirty, forty thousand. All the others are losers, in varying degrees. Frederick lost the biggest, it's no contest. He's down to fifteen hundred in chips on the table from the hundred thousand he bought midway through, which doesn't count his initial buy-in. He gives one each to the two hostesses and the last to the house man. The other players tip accordingly and generously.

Now that the game is over Frederick will have a drink—champagne. On the house, of course. A few of the other players are having drinks, also. The others have already departed, soon to be scattering to the four corners of the continent. Frederick is the only champagne drinker in the group.

"What's the damage tonight, Wes?" Frederick poses of the house man.

The house man slips Frederick a tally sheet, folded over. One deep cleansing breath, then Frederick opens it. The figure written on the sheet reads a debit of $136,500. "Not a good night," he remarks, folding the sheet and slipping it in his pocket.

"Not your lucky night, Mr. Sparks," Wes agrees with cultivated understatement. His accent is like Ben Wright's, the British golf announcer on television. "You'll do better next time."

"Let's hope so." One of the hostesses materializes at his side and refreshes his champagne glass, then discreetly moves away out of earshot. "I'll transfer the necessary funds into my account tomorrow morning," he adds quietly.

"Not a problem, sir."

Frederick takes the elevator down one floor to his suite. The elevator is private, serving the top two floors only. A bodyguard is always on board. No one can ride this elevator unless they're cleared by the hotel. The security here is top-drawer—no one has ever breached it, although some have tried.

He takes a long, refreshing bath and shower, puts on fresh clothing— linen shirt and pants, cotton lisle socks, boat shoes. He eats a fresh peach, washing it down with another glass of champagne. Two fresh bottles are nestling in the ice bucket on the coffee table.

There's a knock at the door. He opens it.

Two people stand in the hallway. A man and a woman, both with super bodies. They're dressed casually and expensively, and each carries a small overnight bag.

"Good evening, Mr. Sparks," the woman says, smiling at him fondly.

"Evening, Brittany," he greets her, giving her a peck on the cheek.

"This is Alex," she says, introducing the young stud to Frederick.

"Nice to meet you, Alex," Frederick says, shaking Alex's hand. "Are you both ready?" he asks.

"Yes, sir," Brittany answers.

They ride the elevator down in silence. At the bottom it opens onto a private garage, in which a Lincoln Town Car limousine is parked a few steps from the elevator doors. The limo driver is at the ready. "Good evening, Mr. Sparks," he sings out obsequiously, quickly opening the back door.

Frederick nods to him. The three climb into the backseat, the driver shuts the door, and they take off.

The Sparks family's Cessna Citation is parked at the edge of one of the far runways at the airport. The limousine drives across the field, directly to the plane. The three passengers get out of the limo and walk the few yards to the door of the plane and up the steps. The limousine drives away.

The pilot, Lew Briggs, is an old-timer who has flown for the Sparks family for years, on call, whenever they need him. Before that he flew for United on their international routes, and before that he was one of the ace pilots for the Flying Tigers; among his duties in that role was as a CIA courier, back in the good old days when the CIA disrupted governments at will, all around the globe. He's a great pilot and he knows how to keep his mouth shut. The copilot is a woman, who is very competent and properly invisible.

"How's everyone tonight?" Briggs inquires pleasantly. He knows the score.

"Everybody's fine," Frederick answers. It's part of their ritual, one they've been performing for years.

"We'll be there in less than an hour, folks," Briggs informs them.

Brittany's done this before. She immediately opens a small refrigerator and takes out a bottle of chilled white wine, opens it, and pours two glasses, handing one to Frederick, who is sitting opposite her, buckling himself in. The other is for herself.

"Thank you," he smiles. "You're not drinking?" he asks Alex.

"Not when I'm working," Alex replies. He's checking out the small, luxurious cabin, running his hand along the hand-tooled leather seats, the ebony serving trays. "Nice plane," he offers.

"It gets me there and back," Frederick answers nonchalantly.

Briggs revs up the engines, gets clearance from the tower. Pulling out onto the designated runway, he points the plane forward, presses down on the throttle, and in less than a minute they're airborne, heading west towards Santa Barbara.

"How do porcupines make love?" Cecil asks Kate.

She laughs, which causes her to wince. "I don't know. And don't tell me any jokes."

"Very, very carefully," he tells her, answering his own riddle. "Which is how we'll do it, when you're ready."

They are in his ranch-house bedroom. It's after midnight, but they can't sleep. Through the open windows she can see all the stars in the sky. She's wearing a long thin cotton nightgown so he can't see how bruised and beaten her body is; nobody's going to see this body until it's healed up, not even her lover—she made him wait outside the bedroom until she had changed. From below her breasts to her stomach she's tightly wrapped to protect her ribs, and her face is still bandaged along the plane of her nose and cheekbones. In a few days, after these wraps come off, she'll wear a plastic face guard for protection if she's doing anything physical, like basketball players do when they've had similar injuries. The way they're made now they don't look so bad—kind of like a big sunglass for your entire face. In beach volleyball circles they're very chic.

The thought of making love fills her with dread. Far worse than the physical pain is the emotional and psychological pain. The violation was so deep, so shattering, that she doesn't know how to handle it, she can't come to grips with it. The worst part is that ugly old belief, buried deep down for so long but now forced to the surface, that somehow she deserved what she got. That it was payback for promiscuous behavior, more—for everything she's done wrong in her life. It's the same old bullshit she's been fighting for years, and what is so fucking infuriating is that she knows it is bullshit. No way did she deserve this. She is the *victim*, not the *reason*.

"Can I get you anything? Do anything for you?" he asks.

"A pain pill. And you can rub my feet, if you're feeling particularly charitable."

"The house specialty," he tells her. His smile is almost beatific. How did this rough-looking man find such tenderness? she wonders. And how did he find me?

She swallows down the pill, leans back against the pillows. His bed is next to the window, so the view to the outside is good. In the distance she can see Miranda's ranch house. All the lights are out. Beyond the house, situated over a small crest, the asphalt runway glistens in the moonlight like a highway heat mirage.

He cradles a foot in his lap, anoints it with oil, begins to gently massage it. She buries herself in the pillows, half nodding off in bliss, the throb of her pain fading into some far distance.

The sound of an airplane is heard, approaching from the east. The lights bordering the Sparks runway blink twice, come on full.

She sits up, looks out. "What's that?"

"Someone's landing at the Sparks ranch." He lays her foot aside. "Want to see?"

He helps her to her feet and guides her onto the wooden deck that runs along the outside of his bedroom. At the far end, the end that faces the Sparks ranch, is an old telescope, pointed up to the heavens. He pulls a deck chair up to the telescope, sits her down. He points the telescope towards the runway, fiddles with the finder, then pushes her chair close.

"You'll be able to see everything with this," he informs her.

"You're a voyeur!" she exclaims, surprised and secretly delighted. "You dirty-minded man!"

"Spying is a basic human desire," he answers laconically.

How well she knows; she does it for a living, it gets her blood pumping. Sometimes it gets her into a shitload of trouble, but she knows she won't stop, she can't. Even after what happened the other night.

The small jet circles the area, then comes in from the west into the wind, touching down softly. It cruises three-quarters of the way down the runway, coming to a stop by a small garage area that houses machinery, a fuel pump, and a couple of golf carts that are used for transport between the house and the airstrip. The sounds of the plane fade away as the engines shut down.

"Can you see okay?" Cecil asks Kate, who is looking at the scene through the telescope.

"I think so, sure."

"Let me check." He puts his eye to the finder, makes a slight focus adjustment, steps back. "Go ahead."

She leans forward again, looking through the scope. At this distance the airplane, which is almost a mile away, is about full figure in the sights, its fuselage shining in the glow of the tarmac lights.

For a moment the plane sits idle. Then the door opens and the steps are lowered. The first person out is the female copilot, who walks down to the bottom of the steps and then turns back, offering up a hand of assistance.

Brittany is out next. She carries her small bag over her shoulder. Then Alex. They look like a handsome young couple in an American Express ad on TV, on their way to the Greek Islands or the Bahamas.

Kate glances up at Cecil, who's standing at her shoulder, watching the action through a pair of high-powered field glasses.

"Who are they?" she asks.

"Toys," he replies, holding the glasses steady to his eyes.

Frederick is the last one out. He skips down the steps, says something to Brittany, who smiles. Then, with one of his arms through each of theirs, he guides them to the waiting golf cart. They cram in together and drive down the path in the direction of the house. The woman copilot has gone back inside the airplane.

Kate watches intently. She's never seen Frederick Sparks, but she knows instantly who he is.

"That's Frederick Sparks, isn't it." More of a statement than a question.

"In the flesh."

Now she's seen them all: daughter, mother, father. The line is distinctly from father to daughter: the resemblance is strong.

"What do you think they're going to do?" She looks up at Cecil. He's watching the three of them tooling down the path towards the house.

"Are you kidding?"

"That's what I thought, too," she says, feeling a flush rising over her face. She can see all three of them clearly—the night is bright from the moon, and the vision through the telescope is excellent.

The golf cart pulls up in front of the house. The three alight, walk up the dark steps. A moment transpires as Frederick digs for the key, then the door swings open and they enter. In a second a single light from a lamp goes on inside, and the door closes. All the windows are curtained. You can't see inside, not from a mile away, even with a telescope.

"Show's over," Cecil announces. He easily lifts her to her feet. "Back inside."

Kate looks at the ranch house down in the valley below them. An isolated house with its own private runway that can accommodate a corporate jet, maybe even larger planes. If someone wanted to be in the dope business this would be a great location.

"Have you ever seen them fly in and out before?" she asks.

"All the time." He looks at her, reading her mind. "I've never seen any evidence that they were moving anything illegal."

"But they could. If they had been using the dock and now they can't they could make it work here."

"That's true. But you're assuming they were in business with Bascomb, which I didn't think you thought."

"I don't know what I'm thinking anymore," she answers. "But I can't get it out of my head. I'm still a detective, and that's how a good detective works."

"Listen, Kate," he states firmly, "you're not working on this anymore, isn't that what you told me? You've got to get this out of your head, babe."

He wants to take care of her. Let him; it feels good. Strange for her, but good, warm.

She thinks once again about what Carl had urged her to do: *Get to know the family.* The more she has learned about them the more devious they appear to be. "Sinister" she isn't sure about, but the circumstances are as ripe as the grapes on Cecil's vines; and she feels the vital need to follow the old pro's dictum—to know who they really are, to discover what skeletons might be rattling in their closet.

"What would you like us to do, Mr. Sparks?" Brittany asks. "Anything special?"

They're in the spacious bedroom. Brittany and Alex sit on a love seat. Frederick is ensconced in a chair. One lamp is on, in the corner; otherwise the house is dark.

Speaking low and calmly, he tells them, "I want you to fuck." He sips from his glass of champagne. "And suck. Nothing out of the ordinary."

"You?" Alex asks, surprised at the bluntness of the language coming from this somewhat effete man. "Both of us? At the same time, or serially?"

This is his first time here. Brittany had picked him out, to Frederick's specifications. She's been on this junket countless times before; she knows what Frederick expects and she does it well. That's why he brings her back.

Frederick shakes his head. "Each other. You do her, she does you. We'll try various combinations. I trust you have strong recuperative powers."

"I can go all night if that's what you're asking."

"Yes." Frederick smiles—this will salvage some of his loss at cards. "Begin by undressing each other. I'll get set up in the meantime."

Alex's body is chiseled—he spends several hours a week at the gym. His rippled muscles gleam in the low light. Brittany begins by kissing each nipple lightly. He groans softly as he lifts her light blouse off while she works her lips across his upper torso.

Her perfect breasts are braless. He bends to them.

Frederick, in the meantime, has opened a closet and taken out a 35-millimeter camera, a tripod, a couple of lights, and a photographer's parachute, for bounce. He begins setting his equipment up in a corner of the room, so that he has a clear shot to the bed.

"You didn't say anything about pictures," Alex says, stiffening self-consciously. "I don't want pictures of me floating around so some cheesy stroke mag can get hold of them."

"It's perfectly all right," Frederick assures him. "It's private, for my sole use. Nobody is going to see them. I give you my word," Frederick promises. "Trust me—I'm extremely discreet. I have to be."

"I've done this," Brittany tells Alex, soothing his anxiety. She has to calm him down so he'll get with the program—if he bails out she won't get paid. "It's completely private."

Alex eases up. "Okay." He turns his attention to her. They kiss, their lips moving over each other's bodies, stripping each other naked. Alex is large, porn-star in size. Frederick stares at Alex's penis as it rapidly becomes tumescent.

The two young people move to the bed. Their lovemaking is hot, strong, even passionate as they get into each other. Frederick shoots several shots in rapid order, moving the tripod around to get multiple angles, unloading the camera as each film load is finished and reloading quickly. He's a crack photographer, there's no wasted motion.

"Wait one moment," Frederick orders them. He takes some leather restraints from the closet where he kept his photographic equipment. He hands them to Alex.

"Tie her up."

Brittany lies back on the bed, arms and legs in the spread-eagle position. Alex fastens the restraints to her wrists and ankles, ties the other ends to the bed frame.

"Proceed," Frederick orders him.

"Anything in particular?" Alex asks. He looks down at Brittany, who is squirming slightly, her body glistening with sweat.

"Anything and everything. But no rough stuff. I'm not interested in pain. Make it last as long as you can."

Alex does her. Brittany moans and cries with passion as he fucks and sucks her.

There's a certain theatrical quality to her writhing and screaming, as if she wants to make sure that Frederick knows how incredible the entire experience is for her. She tries to maintain eye contact with him throughout the fucking, but an orgasm builds, Jesus, she can feel it happening, she usually doesn't come off like this, but Alex, in spite of his model look and sculpted narcissistic body (or because of it, she doesn't give a shit right now what the reason is), is bringing her to climax and she has to surrender to it.

She comes fiercely—waves of orgasms starting at her clit, coursing through her vagina and then all up and down her body.

Frederick shoots several rolls of film. He seems interested but dispassionate. At one point Alex glances over at him. If the guy's aroused he isn't showing any signs of it.

Then it's Brittany's turn, once she's recovered from her own pleasure. She ties Alex up, does to him as he did to her.

They take hours, breaking only to go to the bathroom and for Brittany to bring Alex up, again and again. Alex wasn't lying—he goes and goes, almost all night long.

When it's over they shower and dress. Through the curtained windows the sun is coming up. Frederick locks his camera gear away.

They stand outside on the porch. Frederick gives Brittany a kiss on the cheek, much as he would kiss his daughter. He hands her an envelope and gives a similar one to Alex. "As we agreed," he tells them.

"Thank you," she says. She stashes her envelope in her carry bag without looking inside it.

Alex, being the new boy, can't control his curiosity. He opens his envelope, glances in.

The deal was thirty-five hundred apiece. It looks to be all there. Shit, he'd fuck Brittany for free.

"See you soon," Frederick tells them.

"See you," Brittany answers. She smiles. Not a bad night's work. The money's great and Alex is a decent partner. She's had some who weren't.

The two walk to the golf cart and drive to the plane. Frederick goes back into the house.

———————

The sound of the airplane warming up awakens Kate. Quietly, so as not to disturb Cecil, who slumbers next to her, arms and legs askew, she slips out of bed, wincing in pain as her ribs twist with the effort, and goes out onto the deck.

She adjusts the telescope to bring the action up close. Three came, two are leaving—the toys. She watches as they board the jet, mentally making a note of the plane's registration number.

As soon as the doors are closed the plane taxis into position and departs, a faint plume of vapor tailing behind as it traverses the mountains and gets swallowed up in the vastness of the pale blue-gray milky sky.

15

NEED TO KNOW

Her office has a musty, overripe cantaloupy smell. She hasn't been here in three weeks; all the plants have died except for the cactus. Coming in the door felt like opening a tomb that's been shabbily preserved.

Piles of mail that the postman has been pushing through the slot are scattered about the floor; as she stands from gathering them, an awkward movement because her ribs are still taped, she accidentally catches her reflection in a pane of window glass. She's been avoiding looking at herself as much as possible, to the point of not putting on a drop of makeup since she left the hospital so as not to have to look into the mirror any more than is absolutely necessary; when she must, such as for brushing her teeth, she approaches the image sideways, after a shower, when the glass is fogged over with steam.

Seeing herself now, without preparation, she recoils, immediately turning away.

She looks like the women you see on *Oprah* or *Hard Copy*. Pathetic souls, throwaway statistics.

This is worse than anything Eric ever did to her.

She had vowed that would never happen again, and it did. The same old . . . what? Was this her fault? Does she secretly harbor a death wish, a dream of destruction?

She catches herself wallowing, snaps to. Fuck that.

Money is going to be a problem. She gets by, but there's no nest egg. Five hundred dollars a month goes up north for the kids (who she'll be seeing in a few days), the rest is daily living. She would have gone up to the Bay Area two weeks ago on her usual monthly trip—she hadn't missed once since the shit came down between Eric and her—but she can't face them seeing her looking like this. They've talked on the phone, several times. They know she's been hurt; but they don't know how badly. She doesn't want them to. When she goes up this trip she'll spend extra time there, because she wants them down here with her.

It's time to be a family again.

She isn't sure of her bank balance—she'll have to check it out. It's scraping bottom, she's sure of that.

Only one thing is really important now: to put her life back together. To do that, she's going to have to find some missing pieces of the puzzle.

———————

Surprise, surprise. Her bank account is suddenly twenty thousand dollars heavier.

"A cashier's check," the assistant manager, a young woman built along the lines of a frog, tells her, looking up the record on her computer. She seems surprised Kate didn't know about the addition to her bank account, since it is, after all, *her* account. "It was deposited a week ago."

"Is there a record of who made the deposit?"

"No, on a cashier's check there wouldn't be."

A week ago. Miranda Sparks had visited her a week ago. *If there's anything I can do for you, anything at all . . .*

"Do you have a copy of the check?"

It takes a few minutes to locate it.

"It was drawn on Santa Barbara Bank and Trust," the woman tells her, handing the copy over for Kate's perusal.

The bail check for Wes Gillroy, the sole survivor from the bust on the boat, was also a cashier's check drawn on Santa Barbara Bank and Trust. Sure, it's a coincidence, probably nothing more; SBB&T is the city's most popular bank, and whoever bought that check could have paid for it in cash, they wouldn't even have to have an account there; still, given the overstimulation her antennae have recently undergone, the congruity jolts her like a sudden injection of adrenaline.

She drives to Miranda's office, parks on the street, goes inside. Celeste, Miranda's executive secretary, flinches as she sees Kate—she knows the identity of this woman with a plastic guard covering half her face, the bandages underneath not doing much of a job hiding her swollen and misshapen parts.

"Miranda Sparks," Kate states in a firm don't-fuck-with-me tone. "I need to see her. Now."

Celeste ducks into Miranda's office, emerges almost immediately.

"Mrs. Sparks is finishing an important call. Please wait," she implores Kate. "Mrs. Sparks very much wishes to speak with you."

Kate leafs through a back issue of *Architectural Digest* that's lying on a side table. She feels hyper, she can't sit. Twenty thousand dollars. Serious money—real serious. Somebody slips you twenty K, they want something substantial in return, it's not like tipping the parking attendant a buck. Even if they don't tell you they've given it to you. You find out sooner or later, there's no way you won't, and then you're obligated. Bought and paid for. She doesn't want to be a bought woman, not under circumstances she hasn't agreed to.

Miranda opens the door to her office. "How are you?" she asks. The face guard causes her to wince in spite of herself.

"Better. I was at my office earlier today."

"Are you back to work already?" Miranda seems surprised.

"No, I'm not working. I was cleaning up old business. I won't be able to work for a while."

"Yes. You should take as much time as you need."

She takes Kate's arm and leads her into her private office, closes the door. There is a pause as she smiles at Kate, taking her measure, trying to put her at ease.

"Tea? Coffee? Something cold?"

"How about a glass of Montrachet?"

Miranda looks at her strangely. "Wine? At this time of the day?"

The woman has a short memory—conveniently. "Nothing. Thank you."

"Have a seat," Miranda offers, moving to the chair behind her desk.

"No, thanks. I'm only here for a minute."

"Are you calling on me about something specific?"

"The deposit into my account. Twenty thousand dollars. Last week. And my paid-up hospital bills."

"Yes?"

"That was you, wasn't it?"

The answer comes right away. "Yes, it was me."

"I told you I didn't need anything," Kate reminds her.

"It isn't a question of need. We are obligated to you. My family—all of us. We have to meet our obligations."

This statement angers Kate, it's so lacking in feeling, in heart. "I did not obligate you," she insists.

"We obligate ourselves. It comes with our territory."

Don't fight city hall. "I guess that makes us even," she hears herself saying.

"No," Miranda contradicts her. "You saved my daughter's life. Money can't be an equal in that equation, no amount of money."

"Then I'd better keep it," Kate tells Miranda; understanding now that she'd intended to, before she laid bare the issue. Her own woman, not someone who can be bought—a nice conceit, but this is the real world here.

"I did earn it," she stoutly avows. Okay, so there's a little self-bullshit there. More than a little—so what?

"You most certainly did."

"And I can use it."

"Then I'm glad to have been of help."

"Well . . ."

Now that it's over she isn't comfortable here. Her skin feels hyper-dry; she realizes where the expression "making my skin crawl" comes from. In the future, if there have to be further encounters with Miranda Sparks (she hopes there won't be), they'll be on neutral ground, not on Miranda's home turfs.

"I found out what I wanted to know," she declares.

"As you say, you earned it," Miranda says as she stands, a clean act of dismissal. This conversation is finished; maybe their entire relationship, as short and exciting as it was.

She walks Kate to the door, opens it. "I know you don't like my saying this, but if there's anything I can do for you . . ."

"You've done enough already," Kate tells her. In more ways than one.

"Good luck then."

"Thanks."

She leaves, feeling Miranda's eyes on her back all the way until the front door is shut behind her.

Good luck to you, too, Mrs. Sparks. I know I'm going to need my share and then some.

Maybe, down the line, so will you.

———————

Twenty big ones in the bank. That changes things. The pressure is off—for at least four months, more if she's frugal, she can do any damn thing she wants.

Twenty thousand dollars. What the Mexican Mafia guys offered her, to the dollar. Coincidence, or something more sinister? That will be one thing to find out. One thing of many.

Don't trust anybody. That's going to be her mantra, from now on.

"You're as stubborn as an ox," Carl tells her with a halfhearted feigned anger, too old and infirm to be convincingly outraged anymore. Under the crusty-shell hard-boiled persona that's evolved over more than fifty years of get-down detective work, his true colors show, and in them there is admiration for her tenacity and guts. She knows it, he knows she knows it, it's part of their ritual. She also knows that his days of being useful to her are numbered.

He's changed since she last saw him not long ago. More shrunken, more bent. It is a subject never broached by either of them, but it's there. Well, she thinks, I've changed, too. Is he looking at her any differently?

Someday, maybe pretty soon, Carl will die.

They're outside, in their usual gathering place. The day is cool, overcast. Carl wears an old-man's button cardigan to keep his fragile bones warm. He doesn't—or won't—comment on the way she looks.

"I don't have a choice." Her voice is sodden with resignation. "In my shoes, you'd do the same thing."

Any answer in the negative would be bullshit, so he doesn't give one. He looks out at the horizon, to the oil rigs reflecting what little late-afternoon sun there is, and past them to the islands, obscured by clouds.

"What do you want me to tell you?" he asks her instead.

"I don't know."

"Do you want advice?"

"I don't know."

"Well, let's just sit here a while till you figure out what it is you do want."

They sit in quiet. The sound of the breakers hitting the beach down below echoes in the wind.

She wants strength. She wants to leech some from him, but she can't tell him that. He doesn't have that much left that he can spare.

Carl is her touchstone, her family. She doesn't have a family anymore, not at the moment and not in the near future. There is pain in that which she cannot deny. That's why she keeps going back to him, over and over again—for the great relief of having someone to talk to, and to try to bottle his wisdom, his memory. He knows how it's done—he's always known.

"Don't worry about me," he pronounces out of the blue, as if reading her mind.

"What do I have to worry about you about?" His statement startled her, put her on the defensive. One of his favorite ploys.

"Nothing. That's why I'm telling you not to."

He's opened the door. She'll be insulting him if she doesn't walk through it.

"I have to find out who did this to me."

He says nothing.

"Who gave the orders to do it."

A slight nod: I hear you. Continue.

"I feel it's got to be connected to the Sparks family somehow, like you said. All my instincts tell me that. But I don't know how. I keep running down false trails."

"You're playing their game," he says.

"How do you mean?" Talk to me, you're the expert, compared to you I'm a neophyte at this. "What am I doing wrong?"

"You're reacting."

"What else can I do?"

"Someone hires you, you do their bidding, yes?" he asks rhetorically.

"Yes."

"They set the agenda. You follow it."

"I'm for hire. Isn't that how it works?"

"Yep."

"Then what?"

"Don't be for hire."

She stares at him.

"You're a person with a problem," he elucidates. "Generic you, not specific you. You need to have it solved. You hire an expert to help you, to do the work this expert is trained for. Does that compute?"

"Yeah, that sounds right."

"They tell you what they want and you get it done," he goes on, patiently. "You try to, anyway," he continues.

"Yes."

"Like this girl. She hired you to find out if her boyfriend was murdered or else killed himself. You found out he was murdered."

She nods yes.

"You did the job you were hired to do. You fulfilled your contract. You did a professional job."

"If you put it that way, I did, yes."

"She didn't come to you to find out *who* it was. Just *what* it was. And you did."

She nods. He doesn't need her to actually answer, because there is no question in these questions.

"But your problem was, you did too good a job. You got too close to *who* it was, when *what* was all that was needed."

"I didn't look at it that way," she responds. "It's not something you can separate."

"Precisely," he tells her, pouncing like a kitten on a ball of yarn. "That's the problem in a nutshell, the whole damn enchilada. You can't compartmentalize these things, because the world out there isn't neat enough. The world out there doesn't understand the difference between the *who* and the *what*. And that's why you get your tit caught in the wringer."

She winces at the metaphor.

"So how do you get around this problem?" he queries.

"You tell me." Like try to stop him. It would be like trying to stop a runaway train.

"You be the client. You hire yourself," he posits. "You set your own agenda."

"I know that," she says. That's obvious.

"Then why are you here?"

She exhales, a deep heavy breath. "Because I'm chicken. I almost got killed. I don't want to be in that position again."

He nods. "Well, you don't," he tells her.

"Well . . ."

"You don't. You can walk away from this, like I told you before. It's a different situation now, but you can still walk away."

"I'm not sure I can."

"Well, you can't."

"Then what're you talking about?" she barks out in exasperation.

"Technically you can. Emotionally you can't. So you can but you can't. Elementary, my dear Blanchard."

"I can't sleep," she confides in him. "I jump out of my skin at every sound in the night."

He leans forward so they're close, reaches out and takes her hands in his. His are liver-spotted and twisted with arthritis, but they're still strong enough to grip hers like vises.

"You need to find out who these bastards are," he instructs her vehemently. "And then you need to take whatever steps are necessary to eliminate them from your life forever."

The guest of honor at dinner at *Desierto Cielo* is Blake Hopkins. It's a small gathering, so they're eating in the informal dining room, which is adjacent to the swimming pool and has a 180-degree view of the ocean, from Ventura County all the way up the coast.

Hopkins is seated across from Dorothy. Frederick is at the head of the table, Miranda at the far end.

"Thank you for inviting me up here," Hopkins tells them.

"The least we can do is feed you a decent meal," Miranda quips. "After what your company has pledged for us."

She raises her wineglass in toast. "To a wonderful partnership."

"Hear, hear," Frederick seconds.

"To a beneficial partnership between environmentalists and business," Hopkins adds.

"Yes, that will be refreshing for a change," Dorothy notes, unable to keep the tartness from her tone. "Is your family with you, Mr. Hopkins?" she adds politely; the man is, after all, their guest, one is always civil with one's guests, even if you don't care for them and despise their policies. "Have they moved down yet from San Francisco?"

"Tiburon," he gently corrects her. "And please, call me Blake."

"That's a pretty area . . . Blake," Miranda notes pleasantly. As far as anyone in her family is concerned she has never laid eyes on this man until a few days ago, when they met to discuss his company's incredible endowment.

"It's pretty here, too," Hopkins answers, comfortably making small talk. "And I'm single," he explains to Dorothy, "so I have no family." He resists glancing at Miranda; this old dame is sharp, she'd figure them out in a second if given the slightest reason to.

The servants have been given the night off. Miranda serves. They eat a simple cold dinner: filet of salmon, asparagus vinaigrette, stuffed artichokes. The food is accompanied by a nice Santa Ynez chardonnay made from their neighbor Cecil Shugrue's grapes.

———————

Dinner is over. The sun has set. They sit outside by the pool under the heat lamps, drinking a second bottle of wine.

"What are your plans, Mr. Hopkins?" Dorothy asks. "Rather, your company's plans?" It's difficult, having a civil conversation with someone from big oil, but she was brought up that way.

"Why do you ask?" he smiles.

"Because I don't see them sending someone as capable as you down here just to hand over large checks to environmentalists," she says forthrightly. "You must have an agenda."

Hopkins turns to Frederick. "Is your mother psychic?" he asks.

"I've always thought so," Frederick answers. "She's always been able to read my mind, even when I haven't wanted her to."

"So, Mr.—Blake," Dorothy presses. "What are you really down here in Santa Barbara for?"

He blows out his breath, steeples his fingers, sits up straighter in his chair.

"I'm here for change," he says, looking directly at her.

"What kind of change?" she asks, equally directly.

"Change for the better, I hope," he parries. He's enjoying this informal colloquy.

"You weren't really serious when you said your company is planning on pulling your platforms out of our channel, were you?" she asks, smiling as she does at the absurdity of the question. He's a nice enough man and his company did give them a fortune, but he's oil, a fact not to be forgotten. "That was politics as usual, wasn't it? I don't mind," she continues airily, "developers say all kinds of outrageous things when they want to get on our good side. It's part of the game, we've been playing it for decades."

He pauses for a moment. The smile leaves his face. "As a matter of fact, that's exactly what we're planning to do."

"Are you serious?" Miranda says, acting for all the world as if this pronouncement has stunned her.

"Yes. Very."

"That's . . . remarkable," Dorothy says. Hopkins has thrown her off balance.

"Yes and no. Pulling our platforms up and giving up our oil rights are not the same thing." He leans forward, his body language all business now. "We want to replace all our offshore rigs with onshore slant-drilling ones."

"Like Mobil," Dorothy says. Now her suspicions are way up. She's a charter member of every anti-oil organization in this county.

"Same technology, different goals."

"How?" Her tone has taken on a note of belligerence. She's as blunt as she can be; impolite, almost.

"Mr. Hopkins is our dinner guest tonight," Frederick softly reminds his mother, trying to defuse an argument before it catches fire.

"No, that's okay," Hopkins says. "I don't mind talking about this. We, meaning Rainier Oil, have nothing to hide."

He exchanges the slightest of glances with Miranda as he says that.

Frederick watches, amused and detached. Big oil is the ever-looming heavy in this community, for the past three decades. Now here is this man in his house, debating with his mother, the *grande dame* of local environmentalism.

"Mobil wants to improve on what they have," Hopkins says, looking at Dorothy. She's his target—if he can sell her, the rest of the opposition will follow.

"And yours?" she asks, as if cueing him from a script.

"We don't want to rewrite the present book, patch here, modify there. We want to write a whole new book, starting from page one."

"Unfortunately, you are not the only writer of this book," Dorothy reminds him.

"That's true. But we're the biggest in this area." He pauses to gather his thoughts. "We want to take all our rigs out—not a select few—and replace them with slant drilling, every last one. We want to be the forerunner. If we're successful," he goes on, "our plan is to persuade the other oil companies to come along with us; to convince them that this is the way to go for the future. No more platforms, no more offshore spills, a cleaner environment."

Dorothy regards him skeptically. "Your gift to the oceanography project," she says. "You said there were no strings attached, but this seems to tie in awfully closely. Am I missing something? Is this all of a piece? Are you using us?"

"No," he says, "there are no strings. Our donation stands alone, as I've promised." He pauses a moment, taking a judicious sip of wine. This has to be played out exactly right. "But there is something we want from you."

"There always is," she nods, her intuition confirmed. "And what is this one?"

"We want to put our slant drills on your property."

Dorothy closes her eyes. She knew it.

"That is a definite string, despite your disclaimer to the contrary, and a very large one," she says. She turns to her daughter-in-law. "Do you know something about this?" she confronts Miranda.

Miranda looks at Hopkins, then at Frederick, finally at Dorothy. "Yes."

"For how long?" Dorothy asks her. Her lips are pressed tightly together, her hands are fists in her lap. Consorting with an oil company, the enemy, is bad enough; when it's done behind her back, that's absolutely unacceptable.

"About a month," Miranda answers easily. "Mr. Hopkins confided in me when he first approached me regarding his company's donation."

"I see." So Miranda had lied when she told the press that nothing of this nature had been discussed prior to the oil company coming forward with their "no strings attached" gift. She doesn't know if she's angrier about the deceit or about being excluded from participation.

"I run our business and the foundation," Miranda reminds Dorothy. "Who else would Mr. Hopkins approach?"

She's got Dorothy there, much as Dorothy detests it.

"When I said 'no strings,' I meant that," Hopkins interjects, reading the tension between the two. "The donation is unconditional. It's yours, no matter what happens."

Dorothy turns to Miranda. "This is diametrically opposed to every-thing we've ever stood for," she says.

"I know, Mother," Miranda answers. She calls Dorothy "Mother" only when she's being extremely deferential. "But if Rainier Oil is willing to fund our project, an incredible commitment, and if by taking their rigs out of the channel they'll lessen the chance of an oil spill, which has been a huge concern for all of us for three decades, shouldn't we at least hear what they have to say? That's why I got us all together tonight."

"A fair hearing, that's all we ask," Hopkins weighs in. He hesitates so slightly that only Miranda picks up on it.

"Technology in my industry is exploding exponentially," he tells Dor-othy. "What we can do now we couldn't even have dreamt of five years ago, and today's cutting-edge stuff will seem like museum pieces by the end of the decade. Fossil fuels are going to be a zero-based process as far as pollution is concerned. The means are available now—all that's required is the will, and Rainier Oil has the will. Our chairman wants to revolutionize the industry, and when Mac Browne wants something done, it happens."

Dorothy looks out towards the ocean. The oil rigs, their night lights twinkling like Christmas-tree ornaments, rise out of the water in the distance, like Poseidon's army on the march. In just this one quick glance over a very narrow area her eye spies over a dozen of them.

Slowly, she turns her attention back. "I've always prided myself on being a fair woman, willing to hear the other side's argument, even when I am in total opposition to them philosophically," she says to Hopkins. "So although I'm sure I'll wind up disagreeing with you, I am willing to listen."

"Thank you," Hopkins says to her. "That's more than fair."

Miranda turns away so that Dorothy won't see the expression on her face.

There's no control tower at the Santa Ynez airport. Anyone flying out of that area who wants to file a flight plan does it out of the Santa Barbara airport, on the other side of the pass.

Kate stands across the counter from a woman in the operations department as the woman looks at her identification. She can tell that the woman is curious to know about what train wreck did the damage to her face, but is too polite to ask.

"How long ago was this flight you're interested in?" the woman asks instead. "Our records go back only so long."

"Just a little while back." She gives the woman the exact date.

"We should have that, if one was filed. A lot of times planes flying in and out of there don't file flight plans."

"It was nighttime, both when it landed and took off," Kate says. "And it was a jet. A small one."

"Well, it probably did, then. Jets usually want to fly over eighteen thousand feet, and if it was at night they would have been on IFA." She pulls out a thick binder. "Do you have the N number? The registration number from the plane?"

Kate reads of the number from her notepad. She'd written it down from memory, the morning after she'd seen it.

The woman flips some pages until she gets to the one with the date Kate gave her. "Here it is. That airplane flew in from McCarran Field, Las Vegas, landed on a private strip in the Santa Ynez Valley, then flew back to McCarran." She glances up. "Do you know who that plane belongs to?"

Kate nods. "The Sparks family. I'm doing some work for them. Records verification, that sort of thing."

"They need a private detective to find this out? A phone call would do it."

"When you're in their position, you hire people like me to do things for you other people would do for themselves."

"I wouldn't know." She takes another sideways glance at Kate. "Is that all you wanted?"

"That's all."

"It must be nice to be that rich," the woman says, putting the book away. "Having others do everything for you."

"I wouldn't know," Kate says. "I just work for them."

The Sparkses fly to Las Vegas in their private jet. Kate drives. A couple hundred of the twenty thousand goes into a long-overdue tuneup of her car, particularly the air-conditioning. She isn't about to motor across the desert in a car that won't stay cool.

Don Lockridge is assistant head of security at the biggest and gaudiest hotel in town. He got the job after retiring from the Oakland PD, where he'd done his twenty-five, rising to assistant chief. He's cueball-bald, but he looks more like Yogi Berra than Kojak. He greets her warmly, his brow wrinkled in question as he sees her face.

"Line of duty?" he asks.

"Actually, it was a car accident."

"You mending okay?"

"I'll be fine."

"Glad to hear that. So when was the last time we saw each other?"

"Your retirement party."

"Six years. That long? Time isn't standing still. Although you'd think it was to look at you, busted-up face or no."

"Thank you, kind sir."

They're in his office, a small cubicle off the main security area. The walls are glass, he can look out and see everything in front of him. On her way up here she'd noticed the cameras, the computers, the elaborate security apparatus. All modern, state-of-the-art. The war rooms in the Pentagon can't be much better equipped than this, she thinks to herself. Certainly no big-city police department is.

Don's the one person working in Vegas that she both knows and feels okay to semi-confide in. He was first and last a stand-up guy, a strictly by-the-book no-bullshit cop. One of the reasons he got a cushy job like this, she figures—he can't be bought. He's probably making twice or three times his police salary, and he never has to put his life on the line.

She called yesterday and said she wanted to see him, that maybe he could help her out. He'd be happy to, he said over the phone, if he could. Explanations would come later.

"How's things going in Oakland?" he asks, making small talk. "I haven't been back in over four years."

"I don't live there anymore either, so I don't know. Not much different, I assume. I left the force two years ago myself," she explains.

"I didn't know that. What about Eric?"

"He left, too."

"Are you two still together?"

"No."

She could go into the details, but that's not the point. His not being aware of her full history is better, especially on the job. And since he knew Eric, her splitting is not unexpected news.

"Where're you living?" he asks.

"Santa Barbara."

"Ah, that's a great little city," he enthuses. "That must be a great place to live."

"Most of the time." *When you're not getting beaten within an inch of your life.* She fishes a card out, slides it across his desk.

"PI work, huh?" He turns her card over in his hand, drops it in his shirt pocket.

"It's what I know."

"Tell me about it. Old cops never die, they just . . ." He leans back in his chair, smiling at her. "How can I help you, Kate?"

"I'm looking for a woman and a man who work here. In one of the casinos, I would guess."

"Know their names?" He begins reaching for a thick book.

"I don't know either one of them."

"Do you know what they look like?"

She nods. "I've seen them. I could make either one."

He sits back. "Do you know what they do?"

"The woman's a high-priced call girl for sure. Mid-thirties, I'm guessing. The guy's the same thing for women. Probably has a day gig as a bartender, bouncer. Big man, well built. He's younger, in his twenties."

"What'd they do?"

"Maybe ripped off a client. For big money."

"Someone who comes here?"

"Can we talk?"

He nods.

"Very private," she cautions.

"I'm a good sphinx."

She smiles. It's a comfort to be with someone who talks your talk, and who you can trust.

"Here's the deal, Don. I'm doing some work for a prominent Santa Barbara family named Sparks. Ever hear of them?"

The name visibly jolts him. He takes a moment to recover. "Of course. Frederick Sparks is a regular here."

"At your hotel?" She digs in her purse for her pad and pen.

"No." He shakes his head. "He stays up the street, does his gambling there." He leans forward. "Does what you're working on have anything to do with Frederick's gambling habits?"

A bulb flickers in the back of her head. "No."

"Good, because that's off-limits."

Her intuition clicks in strong. "However much he's lost, he can afford it," she says, tossing out a line.

Don takes the bait. "It's not a secret, is it?"

"People in Santa Barbara don't go around talking about it, but . . ." She shrugs as if to say, "I know all about it."

He nods, his face a model of a man making a call. "What the hey," he says, "you're family. And you're working for them anyway, right? You're not bullshitting about that?"

"I'm in their employ. *Verdad.*" She puts her hand in the Girl Scout salute. "They just gave me a twenty-thousand-dollar retainer," she confides in him.

He whistles. "You must be doing some kind of good work for them."

"I'm earning it, believe me."

"Course, for people like that, twenty K is not serious money. Freddy Sparks'll drop that and more on a single hand of poker. What you or I think would be a fortune might be lunch money for someone else. A Michael Jordan, for example."

"Exactly."

"Anyway. What about this couple?"

"I want to talk to them. At least one. The woman, preferably. Quietly, off the books. I want to make her an offer she can't refuse."

The woman is closer to Frederick than the man. She doesn't quite know why she thinks that, but she feels it in her gut.

"Okay. Let's see what we can do."

They drive down the Strip in his car, a new Caddy Seville.

"Nice wheels," she tells him, feeling the soft leather under her ass. "The real goods."

"Twenty years bouncing your kidneys in a city Ford, I figure I deserve it."

Don's counterpart is sympathetic to her problem, especially with Don standing there next to her, rabbiing her through the process. "I'm pretty sure I know who you're talking about," he tells her, pulling a thick mug-type book off his shelf. "Mr. Sparks usually spends his time with Brittany, and I'm certain she was his companion the night in question. He was playing cards in a private party. She's a show dancer and she also works select private parties. The cream of the crop, so to speak."

"I appreciate this."

"You're doing us a favor. We can't have this kind of shit going on, pardon my French." He flips pages through the book, page after page of pictures. "Although I'm surprised at this. Brittany's never been in trouble before. I consider her good as gold."

"It might have been her partner, or maybe neither one. But I want to talk to her."

"Here it is." He points to a photo. "Is this her?"

Kate stares at the face on the sheet. It's a Polaroid, but there's no doubt that it's the woman she saw at the ranch.

"It's her."

"What about the guy?"

"Put a pin in that. If I need him we'll look. Right now it's the woman I'm interested in."

"I'll rustle her up for you. Wait here." He leaves them in his office.

Don turns to her. "You're set up now."

"Thanks, Don. I owe you a big one."

"Don't worry about it. Stop by my store before you leave town. We'll have dinner. I know a great little Italian place. You'll think you're back home."

"That sounds great."

She watches his thick cop back as he walks out the door. He's a good man, a good friend. She wishes she hadn't had to lie to him.

Don's counterpart returns a few minutes later, Brittany in tow. It's her, all right, Kate is sure of it.

The woman is dressed expensively and is heavily made up, particularly for daytime. She's no kid. Only few years younger than I am, Kate thinks. Not a life she'd like to be living, especially for a woman pushing forty.

The hotel man cocks an eye at Kate. She nods. "This woman is a friend of the hotel's," he informs Brittany, indicating Kate. "Tell her whatever she wants to know." He looks at Kate. "I'll leave you alone, but I won't be far."

"Thank you."

He closes the door behind him, locking them in from the outside— the click of his key slamming in the lock rings loudly in the silence.

"Who are you?" Brittany asks. She's putting up a strong front, like this is a major crimp in her schedule, which it is, but that's not the reason she's copping an attitude. She's scared. She doesn't know why she's here, but whatever the reason, it isn't good. She knows what happens to people who fuck up.

"That's unimportant," Kate answers brusquely, her cop training kicking in. "I have some questions to ask you, so please sit down."

"What do you want?" Brittany asks, balking at the command. She stands near the door, her back almost touching the wall.

"Sit down, please."

"Tell me what I'm here for."

"Sit down and I will."

The woman hesitates, trying to act tough, but she can't pull it off. She slides into one of the chairs in front of the security man's desk. Kate sits in the other chair, close to her. She doesn't want a desk between them— she wants to be close enough to this woman to hear her heartbeat.

It's a cruel thing, what she's about to do. But getting beaten is crueler. It's her job, her own personal stuff. The woman will be scared, but that's all. She won't lose her job. That's not the point.

"You accompanied Mr. Sparks to his ranch a short time ago," Kate begins. "You and a male companion."

Brittany stares at her. "How do you know that?"

"It's my business."

"Shit." The woman curses under her breath. Was she being watched? What the fuck was going on up there, besides the usual kinky shit Freddy has her do?

"Some valuable items subsequently turned up missing. From the ranch where you spent the night. Part of the night."

"Say what?"

"The ranch was robbed."

"Aw, come on! Are you accusing me of robbing that place?"

"You were there. You and your friend. As far as we can tell you were the only two who were, besides Mr. Sparks."

The woman turns pale underneath her makeup. "I did not take anything from that house. Not even a matchbook. I swear to God."

"For your sake I hope that's true, because whoever did is going to go to jail. And I'm not talking thirty days in the county lockup, either."

"I did not rob that house," Brittany insists.

Kate looks down to make a few notations in her pad—nothing really, but it looks scary. Then she looks up, engaging Brittany in her stare, until the woman turns away.

"I'm going to ask you some questions," she says. "If you're straight with me, this won't go any further. Do you understand what I'm saying?"

"Perfectly."

"All right." She takes a beat. "Your friend." Kate clicks her fingers like his name is on the tip of her tongue. "What was his name again?" She starts flipping through her notebook as if it's written down on the page.

"Alex."

"Right. Alex . . ." Again, the fake looking-up.

"Lee."

"Alex Lee. Right, that's the one. Tall, dark hair cut short, wearing jeans and a white pocket T-shirt."

"Oh, Jesus. Where were you watching us from?" A sudden panic comes in her voice. "You didn't see the pictures, did you? Freddy said no one ever saw those pictures."

"Well, I know about them," Kate answers vaguely.

"Oh man. If those pictures get out I'm ruined in this town. That's like a Tijuana dog-and-pony show, that stuff."

"They *are* pretty graphic," Kate says, leading her on.

"Who's seen them? Where have they been?" She slumps in her chair, her tight dress climbing to the tops of her thighs. She's wearing hose, Kate notices, real stockings. Probably silk.

"Nobody," Kate assures her. "Except me."

Brittany regards her warily.

"Yet," Kate adds.

"So is this blackmail? I don't have any money, lady, I'm a working girl like you. I've got a kid to support, and a mother in a nursing home. You want money, you come to the wrong place."

"No. It's not about money."

"Then what?"

"Mr. Sparks has some people who, shall we say, would like to hurt him," Kate begins, improvising as she goes. "I don't want to see that happen. Do you?"

"Hell, no. Freddy's a great guy. He's the nicest man I know."

"What happened that night? The night you spent with him?"

"From when we got to his ranch?"

Kate shakes her head. "From here."

Brittany takes a deep breath.

———————

Kate listens as Brittany talks, interrupting her only when she comes to the end of the card games. "How much did Mr. Sparks lose?" she asks.

"About one hundred forty thousand, I think it was."

Jesus. One night.

"How did he take it? Losing that much money?"

Brittany shrugs. "About the same as he always does. No big deal."

"He loses more than he wins," Kate continues.

Brittany nods. "Yes. It's not that he's not a good player," she explains. "He is. But he isn't quite good enough for the company he keeps. The difference is small, but over time it has a definite impact. These men he plays with are piranhas—they smell blood, they'll strip you to the bone."

Kate thinks a minute before asking her next question. "How long have you known Frederick Sparks?"

"About ten years. We're old buddies, Freddy and me. He always requests me. I've made good money taking care of him over the years." She shakes her head. "Those pictures. All those years of those pictures. He promised me they'd never be seen. That they were for him, his own private collection. And I believed him. Shit!"

Ten years. Most marriages nowadays don't last ten years.

"And he usually lost," Kate continues. "At gambling."

"He's lost more than he's won," the woman answers judiciously. "Thank God he's so rich. A mortal man would have gone bust years ago with those kind of losses."

"How much?"

Brittany shrugs. "Millions. Tens of millions. I don't know. A fortune. Several of them."

And his ranch foreman is caught smuggling a multi-million load of grass onto his dock. What an interesting coincidence.

She changes the subject. "At the ranch, that night," she begins fresh. "Describe the scene."

"Fucking. Sucking. Front and back. The usual stuff. What Freddy always goes for."

"You and him and the third party. Alex."

Brittany shakes her head, almost laughing out loud. "No way."

"How do you mean?"

"Freddy doesn't fuck."

Oh?

"What does he do?"

"He watches. And he takes pictures."

"The infamous pictures," Kate says.

"Yes."

"And watches."

"You got it."

"You and Mr. Sparks make love privately. Out of camera range."

Brittany shakes her head again. "I've never fucked Freddy."

"In ten years of knowing each other this intimately you've never made love?"

The woman nods. "He just watches. That's his whole bag. I came on to him plenty of times, too, before I got the message. I guess he's saving himself for his wife. He's a damn nice man," she says, almost ruefully. "I hope she appreciates him."

16

MIRROR, MIRROR, ON THE WALL

Every time she catches her reflection in the mirror she cringes. Is that really me? Is that who I am now? She knows she will heal, that in time the scars will fade, that no one else thinks she looks as bad as she herself does; but that doesn't help now. She tries to think of her face as a badge of honor, a testament to guts and steely resolve, but that doesn't cut it, either. If it's any kind of testament it's to laxness in keeping her guard up, in thinking she was hotter than she really is. A testament to ego, and all the stupidity that comes from that.

Macho, macho, macho woman. As tough as the guys. Yeah, right. Even if that's true, so what? Big fucking deal. What is it you have to prove, girl?

That's what the mirror is telling her, every time she catches herself in its stark honesty.

She's overreacting, this morning more than usual, because she's driving up north to see her kids. They haven't laid eyes on each other since she got busted up. They wanted to—Julie would've driven them down, she pleaded with Kate to let her, but Kate flat-out would not let them see her looking like she did in those first terrible weeks. Their relationship is already tough enough without having to absorb another emotional wallop.

This past week the girls have been on the phone with her almost every night. It's as if her pain has passed from her to them, bringing them back together. They miss her, they could feel her anguish through the wire, traveling through three hundred miles of their collective unconscious. They're her blood, they'll understand. If nothing else good comes out of this, getting tight with her daughters again might make it better, at least in that one small area.

She throws her suitcase in the backseat of the Rooster, fills the tank at the cheap gasoline station on De La Vina, kicks off her shoes, jams her bare foot down on the accelerator, and heads north, up Highway 101. Her gun, loaded, is in the locked glove box, within easy reach.

Past Lompoc the hills widen, start rolling, the classic central California look, scrub oak and eucalyptus and high grass. The air is fresh, smelling of dozens of native plants borne in the breeze. She's lost in space, drifting, like the pollen rushing by her windshield.

At San Luis Obispo she leaves 101 and starts up Highway 1, along the ocean. The prettiest highway in the world; the prettiest highway she's ever been on, anyway. If there's a prettier one somewhere else she'd love to see it. Maybe she'll go to that place someday. With Cecil, maybe.

The two-lane road winds and curves and climbs. To her left the face of the rock drops off, almost straight down, to the ocean and the sand and rocks below. She cruises, taking her time, her mind on automatic pilot, enjoying the gorgeous vistas. A few cars come up behind her, and she pulls over to let them pass. She doesn't want to be rushed—it may be a long time before she takes this drive again.

It's late in the afternoon when she reaches Big Sur. She drives past Esalen, past the gallery that contains all the Henry Miller artifacts, past Deetjen's—another place she'd like to come to with Cecil, he's on her mind more than she thought he'd be; she thinks she likes that—and then past the Nepenthe parking lot. Normally, as part of the ritual when driving along Highway 1, she stops at Nepenthe and has an Ambrosiaburger. Eat it sitting out on the deck, watching the waves, the endless ocean, and dream romantic dreams.

Today, though, she'll save her appetite for dinner with her kids.

She drives down the bumpy road to Pfeiffer State Beach, the one with the natural rock arch that Dick and Liz made famous in the movie *The Sandpiper*. No one's around; it's coming on sunset, too late in the season for tourists to walk. Stripping out of her clothes, she runs naked along the hard-packed sand and dives into the surf. The freezing water hits her like a hammer, literally taking her breath away. It feels great; a cleansing, inside and out.

The ocean rejuvenates her. It's the best way she knows of to get close to God.

She swims for about twenty minutes. Then she dries off, rough-toweling herself vigorously.

The sun is sliding into the ocean as she pulls out of the parking lot and continues on her way, heading north into the night.

Coming into the city, her battered old car cruising Interstate 280, a plume of wet-gray exhaust in its wake as it labors uphill, past City College, where she had taken courses as a young woman, two or three life-times ago it feels like now, the 280 connecting to the 101, surging up and over the last stretch of highway, until there it is: the city as seen in a million photos and postcards, revealing itself as the most beautiful and welcoming of human abodes, from this perspective especially—night, distanced—a perfect jewel, self-contained and snug in its uniqueness. Even though she had lived all her life on the east side of the bay and was in turn defensive and combative (and angry) about how San Francisco looks down at Oakland, its pull is irresistible, you can see it a million times and it still works its magic, it reaches out to her like the last long enchanting dream at the end of sleep, drawing her in with waiting arms.

Her mind is a whirl of emotions. What will her daughters' reactions be when they see her? Will she repulse them, looking like this? They've seen her looking bad before, are they going to think this is the way it is, how it's always going to be?

She peels off the freeway at Fell and heads west to Masonic, left again up the hill through the Panhandle, past Page, Haight—still in glorious hippiedom after all these years—right on Frederick, left on Cole.

All the front windows on her sister's apartment are lit. They're inside, waiting for her. She parks halfway down the block on the opposite side of the street, slowly gets out, grabs her hanging bag and backpack out of the backseat, locks the doors.

She's scared; really scared. They're going to take one look at her and run like hell. Or they'll try to fake their way through it and they'll all know it's phony.

She shouldn't have come. She isn't ready to face them, she should have been honest about that. She can check into a motel, call them from there. She's been delayed, it's getting too late, she'll come over tomorrow morning. Buy one more day, twelve more hours to find some courage.

The downstairs door flies open and both girls come running out, running right through traffic as if it isn't there, almost tackling her, both of them hugging her at the same time while being careful not to touch her face.

Her very first thought as they slam into her is: they're so *tall*. You don't see them for a few months and you forget. In her memory bank they're always younger, still kids—but these are women.

The girls back off, looking at her face. Her broken cheek still shows prominently under the face guard she wears whenever she goes outside.

"How do I look?" she asks them, nervous as hell.

"Not so hot," Wanda tells her honestly.

"But not as bad as I was afraid of," Sophia says.

"Not nearly as bad," Wanda agrees.

"I'm glad to hear that," Kate says, her voice thick with relief.

"We were worried about you, Mom," Wanda adds. Wanda is tall, thin, fair, blue-eyed. She resembles her long-forgotten father, not her olive-complexioned mother. She speaks in a voice that carries concern, exasperation, anxiety. An adult's voice with adult's fears.

She's seventeen already, Kate realizes, in another year she'll be starting college. She wants to be a doctor (the last time Kate checked—over a year ago, she realizes with another jolt). How are her grades? She hasn't seen a report card since the spring.

"How are your grades?" she asks in reply, her mind flying in random access, unable to keep up with her emotions.

The girl laughs. "My grades? They're fine, Mom. Don't worry, I'll get into Stanford. They're huge on women's soccer, I'll probably make all-city this year."

"Is that where you've decided to go?" Her firstborn is going off to college next year and Kate doesn't even know where she's applying.

"Well, Brown's my first choice. That or Wellesley. But they're too far away. I'd never see you."

You don't see me now.

"And Stanford will give me pretty good financial aid, I've already met with them."

"You have? When?"

"Couple weeks ago. Walt drove me down. They gave me the grand tour. It's bitchin', Mom, totally. You ever been there?"

"No."

"I'll show you around, next time I go you'll come with me—if you can make it," she adds with a flush.

"We can discuss that while I'm here." Her stomach's churning; she's missing everything, everything in their lives.

"That would be great, Mom."

She turns to Sophia, her younger daughter. The one who looks like her. The one who has her hair. And much more patience.

"Hello, sweetheart. I've missed you. So much."

"Oh, Mom!"

She buries her face in Kate's shoulder; she has to bend over slightly, she's a good four inches taller—taller even than her older sister. Both taller than Mom.

A woman and her two daughters.

The emotion hits her like a tsunami; how can she live without them? She pulls them to her, hard, a face buried in each shoulder.

Wanda pats her on the back. "It's okay, Mom. Really, it is." She looks into Kate's face. "You don't look all that bad," she pronounces. "You've looked much worse."

"You look great, Mom," Sophia chimes in. "Just like always."

"Your car looks gross, though," Wanda interjects, giving the Rooster a cold appraisal.

"Like always."

They all laugh. The girls have never liked her wheels, they were embarrassed to ride in it, it's too hoody.

"I'm thinking of trading it in, finally. Maybe an Accord?" she offers, wanting them to be part of the decision-making process.

"Hondas are cool. Acuras are cooler; so're Lexuses," Wanda states.

Secretly, she knows she'll never quit on her car. It would be like putting an old family pet to sleep; worse. She's slept in this car, made love in it. It will leave on its own terms, not before.

Each girl grabs a bag. As they cross the street she looks up. Julie is standing in the window, looking down at them. She smiles and waves. Kate smiles, waves back.

They're her family. They love her. It's going to be okay.

If only it could be that easy.

"Just like always." They don't know how heavy that innocent, well-meaning statement hangs on her: that their memory of her has gone so deep into denial that this is how they think she always looks; this is how they remember her.

Julie can't hide her reaction to seeing Kate's face. "God, Sis."

She says it with compassion, with concern, for what's happened to her sister.

"You should've seen the other guy," Kate jokes lamely.

They hug. Sisters, like her own two. They have to take care of each other, even when they can't or don't want to.

"Hungry?" Julie asks.

"I'm starving!" Wanda exclaims. "We expected you two hours ago, Mom!"

"It smells good," Kate tells Julie. "It's been a while since I've had a home-cooked meal," she adds, immediately wanting to bite off her tongue; she doesn't want her daughters to think about how she lives day-to-day. They've seen it, for years. That's why they're here with their aunt and uncle instead of down in Santa Barbara with her, their birth mother, the flesh of their flesh.

Dinner is roast chicken, whole new potatoes, green beans with al-monds, Caesar salad, garlic bread. Delicious to Kate's tongue; it's been a long time since she ate like this, or cooked like this. When she gets home she'll cook dinners for Cecil. He's a man who will appreciate a good meal.

She'll cook dinners like this for her daughters.

That's why she's here. She wants them to live with her, their mother. She wants her children back.

They talk at dinner; superficial, polite conversation: Walt's new re-sponsibilities on the job, local politics, the ugliness of the recent baseball strike. Walt is a die-hard Giants fan; shutting the season down was akin to an act of treason for him, he still harbors a grudge.

The girls clean up, load the dishwasher.

"Let me help." She carries a stack of dirty dishes into the kitchen.

"Sit down, Mom," Wanda commands her. "You've had a long, hard drive."

"You've always taken care of us," Sophia says. "We want to take care of you."

If only that were so.

Julie and Walt are going to the movies, over by Telegraph Hill, they have to leave now or they'll miss their show. They'll be back late, they tell the girls, do all your homework and don't stay up too late, it's a school night. No TV.

"You sound like me," Kate quips.

"Well, yeah . . ." *They need a mother, you're not here, somebody has to.*

Guilt-tripping, big-time. *Not completely safe all the time . . . the girls, I want them to be safe after all this. . . .* She remembers how it went down in court the day she lost her daughters to her sister, who'd never had any of her own.

"They'll be in bed on time, don't worry." Jesus Christ, she is their mother, she knows how to do this stuff. They're big girls, they don't have to be talked down to like they're ten years old.

She and the girls sprawl out on the living-room floor. Wanda makes tea.

"Is Julie strict on you?" Kate asks.

Sophia wrinkles her face.

"She's not so bad," Wanda answers in Julie's defense.

"We're the only kids we know who have to be in by midnight on weekends," Sophia returns. Sophia's quieter, less flamboyant in personality, but she's the one who has an earring in her nostril—a tiny diamond—and is wearing chocolate lipstick.

"Yeah, but if we're not they don't do anything about it." Wanda slurps her tea. "At least they care about us."

"I care about you," Kate responds swiftly, stung by the pain so casually provoked by the unconscious remark.

"I didn't mean you, Mom. Don't get your feelings all hurt. I was talking about all the kids we know whose parents never know where they are and care less."

They sip their tea. The traffic noise outside suddenly seems invasive.

"These guys . . . that did this to you," Wanda ventures, trying to bridge the fissure. "What happened to them?"

"A couple got killed," she says without embellishment. "The others got away."

Her firstborn's remark stung; she'll remember it for a long time. How much anger do the girls hold against her? she wonders. She's always been tied up so much in her own shit she's never thought to ask. She'll have to fix that before she leaves this time.

"Who killed them?" Sophia asks, her adolescent voice rising in excited anticipation. "Did you?"

"No. I've never killed anyone."

"Good," the girl says. "I hate guns," she adds with vehemence.

"Although I would have liked to have killed the bastards who did this to me," she tells them. "I can't lie about that."

"Who did?" Wanda persists. "The police?"

She shakes her head. "A friend of mine, who miraculously was in the right place at the right time. The police are never there when you need them, you know that."

"Good thing he came along."

"Yeah, it sure was."

Until this moment that hadn't fully sunk in: how lucky she had been.

"Is he nice, this friend of yours?"

They're not only daughters anymore. They're girlfriends as well, confidants. Which is nice; but she'd better guard about how much she lets them into her shit, they're still kids, her kids.

"Yes, he's a very nice man. Gentle."

"Where does he live?"

"On a ranch, north of town."

"Wow." Their eyes light up, even Wanda, who's a senior in high school and is obliged to be cool.

"Are you thinking of living with him?" Wanda asks.

"I've just met him."

"But eventually?"

They don't want her out there alone, she thinks. They want to be a family again. If she's with a man—a nice man—it's like it's supposed to be. Like it is with Julie and Walt.

"Maybe. I don't know. We'll have to see." She feels crowded, pushed. She can barely keep her own shit together, how can she ask a man into a life as messy as this?

"Are you working on a big case or anything now?" Sophia asks.

"No. I'm here to be with you."

"I've got a game tomorrow afternoon," Wanda says. "Can you come?"

"Of course. That's why I'm here—to be with you two."

The girls parade some of their schoolwork in front of her; different projects. Kate picks up a sheaf of papers held together by a brad, tucked under some other stuff.

"What's this?"

"Just a draft of my essay for my college applications," Wanda says, retrieving the papers from Kate's grasp. "No big deal."

"You give them all the same one?" Kate asks. It's been so long since she applied to college, she remembers nothing of the process. She's already missed the boat with Wanda—she'll have to make it up to her in other ways, and take care that the same thing doesn't happen with Sophia.

"Yeah, pretty much. I Mickey-Mouse it around a little for each application, but doing this one was tough enough, I'm not going to write five completely different original essays. It's not like they pass them around or anything."

"I'd like to read it."

"I don't know. . . ." She exchanges a look with her sister.

"What?" Kate asks.

"You won't like it. It's just a dumb essay."

"I want to read it. Please."

Reluctantly, Wanda gives her the paper. Kate turns over the cover sheet, starts to read the first paragraph.

"Read it later, Mom, after we've gone to bed." Wanda is turning red. "But don't say I didn't warn you."

It's about her.

"Okay." She sets it aside. "I'm looking forward to it."

Sophia has recently received her first quarterly report card. All A's, except for a B- in math.

"Geometry," the girl explains. "I got A's in algebra last year but I can't visualize geometry."

"You'll get it," her sister stoutly defends her. "I did, and you're much better at math than me."

This is beautiful, Kate thinks, listening to them, the way they stand up for each other, defend each other.

Wanda has a boyfriend, she informs Kate, a boy in her class, not a jock, a student. A nice boy, who treats her with respect.

"His name's Jack. Jack Schwartz. You'll meet him tomorrow, Mom, he comes to all my games."

"Classic role reversal," Sophia notes dryly.

"You don't have to have an eighteen-inch neck to be a man," Wanda says. "Right, Mom?"

"Absolutely."

She wonders if Wanda is still a virgin—probably not, but she isn't about to inquire. Wanda will tell her if she wants to. What would be worse, she thinks: that Wanda isn't a virgin anymore or that she wouldn't tell me, her mother? Does she talk with Julie about these things? She'll have to try and find out, without being clumsy.

She's never met any of Wanda's boyfriends. When they lived together as a family the girls didn't bring friends home, they wouldn't think of it. That must have been tough on them. Who could blame them, with Eric liable to go off like a Roman candle without a moment's warning?

She catches herself in the thought: that's wrong. It was *her* fault that they weren't safe. *She* was their mother, their true parent. It was *her* responsibility to keep them safe, protect them.

And she hadn't. She had failed the most important test of her life.

She looks around at her sister's apartment. Nothing fancy. Spacious, homey, comfortable. Just a home—a real home. As opposed to her own, which is a place to sleep, shower, and change.

It's later than she realized, after eleven. Julie and Walt will be back soon.

"Do you have any homework?" she asks the girls.

"Already did it," they sing out in unison.

"You should be getting to bed, shouldn't you?"

"Before the bed-check cops come home?" Wanda says with a wise-ass grin.

"What's your normal bedtime?"

"About now. I need *beaucoup* sleep, I'm in training."

"How do you get to school?" she asks. It's so weird, she's been visiting them regularly every month, except the last couple, yet she knows almost nothing about their basic routines. She's pissed at her sister for usurping her duties, yet she's done nothing to earn them.

"City bus. Right down the block."

"I could take you."

"It's no big deal, Mom," Wanda says; then, seeing the disappointment on Kate's face, adds, "but that would be special," and reaches up for a hug and a kiss, like she did when she was a little girl. "Night, Mom."

She hugs and kisses the younger one. The one who looks so much like her, except prettier.

"Goodnight, Mommy. I'm so glad you're here."

She turns off their light and floats out of the room. Her girls, whom she diapered and bathed and taught everything.

Walt drinks Samuel Adams, there's a six-pack in the frig. She purloins one—she'll replenish his stock tomorrow, she doesn't want to be beholden to them, she has enough guilt surrounding all of this already. Stretching out on the couch, she starts to read Wanda's college application essay.

"If I Could Go Back in Time, What Would I Change in My Life?"

The writing is beautiful—heartfelt and true, with great similes, metaphors, analogies. Her kids are talents, both of them. Where it comes from, she truthfully doesn't know. Certainly not from their biological father; he was out the door before Sophia was a year old and Wanda three, rarely to be heard from again, and his gene pool was mediocre at best. Eric, of course, was grotesque, he brought nothing positive, only the ugly shit of his own life. They had always hated him, and had learned nothing from him, except that there are men who are fucked up and always will be, and if you're smart (which she had not been but they will be) you stay far, far away from them.

Which leaves her: their mother. She considers herself intelligent in a native, basic, street-smart sense, but not intellectual. She doesn't read good books, she doesn't go to symphony concerts, fine-art museums. If she's passed anything on to them it's the ability to be a survivor, to keep going when everything tells you to quit.

Maybe the brains were always there, buried in her genes, for her kids to tap into.

She focuses on the paper: *"If I Could Go Back in Time, What Would I Change in My Life?"*

It's about her, and her daughters, Wanda especially, since she's writing about what she would change, but Sophia's in there too—given the theme of the essay, it would be impossible for her not to be. And although it's beautiful, its tone is elegiac (Wanda's word, not hers); sad, painfully so.

Basically, Wanda would change everything in her entire life except her relationship with her sister. Her mother never stood up to her stepfather, a complete shit (she got that part right), so the girls were always in fear of their lives. Her mother was a cop, she divided the world into cops and civilians, civilians were scumbags, assholes, an impediment to an ordered society. Everything in the world is black-and-white, there are no grays—you're for me or against me.

Worst of all, her mother doesn't have time for her. They never talked about anything important, even when Wanda was growing up and reaching towards womanhood. Men, sex, feelings, work, life—none of those subjects have ever been a topic of serious conversation between them.

She loves her mother—on that she is clear, clean. And she knows her mother loves her. But it's been a bad fit.

Her mother could have made more of her life, the writer takes a strong position about that. She was smart, pretty, funny. But she sold herself short. And she insisted on putting herself in harm's way, even though she had two children who had no backup if anything happened to her.

All that Wanda would change, and more. That's why she wants to go to college, so she can find out what lies out there in the world, not the narrow horizons of her mother, but those of someone who believes in unlimited possibility.

She loves her mother. But she wants a different life, a different world, for herself.

It's a cry of help, of pain. Intense pain for a young woman to go through. No wonder Wanda, on one level, didn't want her to read it, but on another had to make her read it.

She carefully lays the essay down. She feels numb, drained. She owes these kids so much. How will she ever be able to repay them, make it right?

The tears flow. They're long overdue; too bad the circumstances are so rotten.

By the time Julie and Walt breeze through the door she's washed her face, redone her makeup. They wouldn't notice the tears anyway; her face is too battered, you can't see past the obvious wounds to the real ones unless you're looking for them. Julie isn't looking.

"How long are you planning to stay this time?" Julie asks.

"It's open. I'm taking the girls to school tomorrow, and I'm going to Wanda's game in the afternoon. I'd like to take them out to dinner."

"Good idea. The three of you need time alone."

"Well . . ." Kate stretches. "It's been a long day for me."

"Us, too. Your room's made up for you. See you in the morning."

Walt hugs her. "We worry about you."

Julie hugs her, too. Walt's hug felt more genuine; but that's her stuff, not her sister's. Her sister took her kids in and is taking better care of them than she can—which makes her hate Julie, even though she doesn't want to. Julie's doing her best. Which right now is better than her own best.

Wanda's team wins. She doesn't score a goal, but she plays well, with assurance.

"She's like another coach on the field," Sophia observes, sitting with Kate up in the stands with other parents and siblings.

"Uh-huh," Kate says, although she doesn't see it. Soccer isn't her game. She wasn't one of those clinging mothers who went to all their kids' games in AYSO from age six. She was out in the "real world," earning a living.

They take their dinner in Fisherman's Wharf like tourists, eating off crab and pizza stands, the girls assigning outlandish appellations to where different groups of people might come from.

"Lame Duck, Wisconsin."

"Steel Balls, Kansas."

Giggling like ten-year-olds, each girl is trying to top the other in silliness.

"Pygmyshit, Montana!" shrieks Sophia.

"Cumstains, Rhode Island!" her sister rejoins, laughing uproariously.

People glance at them warily, wondering what's so funny.

"Very adult, girls," Kate gently admonishes them, feeling suddenly like an old fogey.

"Oh, grow down, Mom," Wanda admonishes her.

"I am, therefore I goof," Sophia chirps.

They pile into her car and drive up Columbus to North Beach, parking on Vallejo near Cafe Trieste, walking the streets, ducking into City Lights, where at the girls' insistence Kate buys a copy of *On the Road* ("It's like paying homage, Mom, like going to Chartres"), then crossing Columbus again and entering Spec's, where they sit off to the side and order an Irish coffee for Kate and hot cider for the girls.

She turns to Wanda. "I read your essay last night."

Wanda looks away. "I was wondering when we'd get around to that."

"It's very well-written."

"Thank you."

"From the heart."

"Uh-huh." Wanda sips her drink, looks around the room, at the floor, at her sister. Everywhere except at her mother.

"It made me sad," Kate says. "For you."

"Yeah, well . . ." She twitches involuntarily. "It's only a paper. It's not like it's my autobiography or anything."

"It isn't fiction."

"Look, Mom." Wanda turns to her. "I'm not trying to make you look bad or anything. That's not the point of it."

"I know that."

"It's just . . . I've had these feelings for a long time and I needed to get them out. This was a good way to do it. They like this confessional stuff on your essays, my guidance counselor told me. Anyone who reads this would know it's mostly made up."

"Almost anyone," Kate corrects her.

"I've got to go to the bathroom," Sophia says. She jumps up so fast she almost knocks her chair over.

"It was something I had to get out of my system," Wanda states doggedly.

"I understand." Understanding doesn't make it hurt less.

"You aren't mad at me?"

"God, no!"

"Not even a little?"

"I'm not mad at all. I was hurt, I admit that—how could I not be?—but I definitely understand the feelings."

"I didn't mean to hurt you, Mom. I had to do it, that's all."

Kate nods. She sips her Irish coffee; it's cool enough to drink now.

"Anyway, I want you to know I really love you," Wanda vows. "Sophia does, too."

"It never crossed my mind that you didn't."

Sophia returns to the table. "Pretty weird graffiti in the ladies' room. You guys ought to check it out." She looks from her sister to her mother, trying to divine the temperature of the situation.

"You two have come a long way in the last couple of years," Kate says. "You've really grown. I'm proud of you."

They smile awkwardly, mutter "Thanks."

"I mean it. Your work, your abilities, your self-knowledge—it's remarkable. I'm very impressed."

"Come on, Mom. Enough already," Wanda says.

"Okay. No more flattery." She pauses. "What surprises me is that it *is* a surprise to me. That I didn't know—that's not right, of course I knew—that I wasn't aware, consciously aware, of your intelligence and talent. And growth. That it slipped by me, your mother, who should have seen it before anyone, instead of being the last, which is the way it seems to have gone."

"You aren't here," Wanda tells her matter-of-factly. "So how could you?"

"I should've been."

"They wouldn't let you."

"Who?"

"The judge."

She shakes her head. "I can't use that as an excuse. I still should be there for you. It's what I should be doing—the most important thing."

The girls look at each other. "So are you thinking of moving back up here, Mom?" Wanda asks slowly. "Is that what you're saying?"

She places her hands flat on the table. Otherwise, they would shake. "Well . . ." she stammers, "I—I haven't thought about that," she manages to say.

"Then what?" Wanda persists.

She feels cornered suddenly, pressured. She isn't ready for this, this isn't the ideal time or place.

"We're a family," she begins. "We're the only family we have."

"Julie's your sister," Wanda points out. "That makes her family, too."

"That's true, but it's not the same. She's your aunt, not your mother." She feels like she's on the defensive, on a witness stand.

"We know that, Mom."

"I want you two to live with me. We should be living together again." There—she's said it.

The girls shuffle in their chairs.

"What?" she asks.

"How can we do that?" Wanda queries. "What about the judge? Don't you have to get his permission?"

"Well, yeah, but I mean, of course I have to do that . . . I'm planning on doing that."

"When?" Wanda presses her. "Did you make an appointment to see him this time?"

"No." She feels the air starting to leak out of the balloon. "But that's no big deal," she says gamely, "I can do that with a few days' notice."

"It *is* a big deal, Mom," Sophia says, her voice small, low.

"Okay, you're right, it is. I didn't mean it that way."

"Where would we live?" Wanda continues.

Kate sits back, upset at this line of attack. "What is this, Twenty Questions? I haven't seen you for a couple of months—"

"Four," Wanda corrects her. "You haven't seen us for four months, Mom."

"It hasn't been that long." It can't have been that long.

"Four months," the girl states forcefully.

"If you say so. I couldn't help it, you know I . . ." She can't finish. That's why they're here, with her sister, instead of in Santa Barbara, with her—because she can't help it. "I apologize. It won't happen again."

"We miss you, Mom," Wanda tells her.

"And we worry about you," Sophia adds.

They worry about her. Who's the mother here, she thinks, and who's the children?

"It's going to work out," she vows, sitting up straight. "I'm calling the judge first thing tomorrow morning, and I'm not leaving here until I see him."

She looks into their faces: that should make them happy. Their mother is going to take care of things now.

Their expressions don't show happiness. More like resignation.

"I am this time, I really mean it."

Even as the words leave her mouth she hears how tinny and hollow they sound. Like coaxing a five-year-old to bed with a promise of candy tomorrow. These are grown people, almost, they have to be dealt with honestly.

"You've said that before," Wanda reminds her.

"This time . . . I will."

"Great," Wanda says with a singular lack of enthusiasm. "So if he lets us live with you again, where will we live?"

"How will you support us?" Sophia adds.

"My apartment's okay . . ."

"It's only one bedroom," Wanda interjects.

"I can get a bigger one. That's no big deal."

The girl nods.

"And my job is my job. It's free-lance, there's no guarantees, but I've been making good money lately, I just got paid twenty thousand for one job."

Wanda stares at her intently. "Is that the going rate for almost getting killed, Mom?"

A huge wave of emotion passes over her—a drowning wave, guilt, fear, anger, emotion, pridefulness—and she has to take a deep cleansing breath to stop herself from doing something harmful, like lashing out at them, or getting up and walking out.

"That's not . . ." She exhales, sighing deeply. "Shit happens, kids. What can I tell you?"

"Mom," Wanda says. "We worry about you. A lot."

"You shouldn't."

"We can't help it."

"I'm not your responsibility. It's the other way around."

"How can we not worry about you," Sophia asks plaintively, "when you don't come up to see us for months and when you finally do you look like someone who got hit by a truck?"

"It won't happen again," she says firmly, trying to reassure them, and herself as well.

"How can you promise that?" Wanda asks her. She leans towards Kate, her face inches from her mother's. "Do you know what it was like for us, all those years? Listening to you and Eric screaming at each other, scared shitless he'd kill you, or maybe us?"

"He wouldn't . . . that wouldn't . . ." The ground under her feet is shifting, like standing on a sidewalk that's splitting from a volcano.

"He almost did. Isn't that why we're living with Julie and Walt?"

"Eric's gone. He's out of our lives."

"But you're still doing the same stuff, Mom," Sophia points out to her. "In your line of work you could get killed any day. How do you think we used to feel, wondering every night whether you were going to come home safe or not? Or even come home at all?"

"I could get a different job," she practically pleads.

"Doing what?"

"I don't know." She's flustered. "Plenty of things. I have plenty of qualifications."

"And what about school?" Wanda continues.

"They have schools in Santa Barbara. I'm sure they're as good as the ones here."

Wanda throws her hands up in exasperation. "I'm a senior in high school, Mom. I'm the captain of my team, I'm taking my SATs next month. I'm not going to move in the middle of my senior year in high school, you've got to be crazy."

Her voice feels choked in her throat. "It's just that I miss you so much!" she cries out in terrible anguish.

"And we miss you, just as much!" Wanda tells her.

"More!" chimes in Sophia.

"But we have lives, Mom," Wanda explains. "A lot of stuff. You just can't waltz in here and tell us everything's going to be fine and then just blow out."

And she'd thought Wanda's essay was heavy. This is like setting off a stick of dynamite inside your brain.

"You can't expect us to just up and quit everything just because we miss each other," Wanda continues. "That's not practical. That's not how life works."

"You're right," she admits. "You're right about everything you say. I was wrong. It was a dream, I guess, but I shouldn't have expected . . . I don't know what I expected, but I shouldn't have . . . whatever . . ." she ends lamely.

"We're just kids, Mom," Sophia tells her gently. "That's all we are. We need a place to go home to that's safe. You can understand that, can't you?"

"More than anything in the world, that's what I want for you."

"You're our mom," Wanda says. "You'll always be our mom. But it's easier with Julie and Walt, we aren't living in the combat zone anymore. We can think beyond surviving." Hesitantly: "I wasn't an honor student when we lived with Eric. I didn't play sports, I didn't think about going to college even."

"Me neither," Sophia adds.

"I didn't realize . . ." Jesus, what else didn't she know about them? Did she know anything? Were they even there?

"I could get another job," she pleads.

"Just be with us more," Wanda pleads with her. "That's what we need from you now."

They kiss goodbye outside the school gates. You can't go inside the building unless you're authorized.

"I'll be up again soon. Less than a month next time."

"Great," they respond.

They hug and kiss and then walk away from her, looking back one time to wave, then disappearing in the sea of their own kind. She stands there for a moment, leaning against her car.

She's been blindsided. She'd expected opposition from Julie, who's "come to love them like a mother," as if she could truly know. But not from the girls, *her* girls, who she raised up from birth, by herself.

All those years, listening to you and Eric screaming at each other, scared shitless he'd kill you, or maybe us . . .

That's why the girls can't get back with her, because they see how she lives, it's written in the scars and bruises she's carrying right now, it scares the living shit out of them.

And it should. It's a hard, bitter admission to face, but there's no ducking this: her daughters are better off living apart from her.

If she wants them back for real she has to get out of this work life and find a new one, something where putting yourself in the pathway of getting killed for a paycheck isn't why you get up in the morning.

Cafe Trieste was serving cappuccino back when it was something only Italians drank. She sits in a corner with her back to the wall, a latte, fresh-squeezed orange juice, and an apple bearclaw on the table. She leafs through the *Examiner*, not really reading it.

She isn't ready to drive back, even though there's nothing here for her. If the water in the bay wasn't so cold she'd go for a swim. That would be the best thing to do right now. Swim until she can't lift her arms over her shoulders, then drift back to shore on the tide, letting it take her wherever. She doesn't take notice of the people who glance at her face. She doesn't care about that anymore.

She finishes her mini-breakfast and leaves, wandering aimlessly through the streets, no destination in mind, walking. It's nice to be in a city again where you can walk. She used to walk all over Berkeley and Oakland, she only used her car to get out of town. Maybe that's why it's lasted so long.

Down Grant St., through Chinatown, in and out of shops, watching the shoppers, old Chinese ladies buying vegetables and ducks, tourists taking pictures of each other, men and women standing on the sidewalk gossiping. They're part of a community. They have a place. She doesn't have a place. The loneliness, all of a sudden, is overwhelming.

Without realizing it, she's left Chinatown and is on Montgomery St., a couple blocks east, the center of the old financial district back when San Francisco was the business hub of the West Coast. The buildings are brick: solid, imposing.

It's nice, being in the city. But it isn't nice being in the city alone. When she comes up in a couple of weeks to see the girls again she'll bring Cecil with her. The girls will like him, they'll see that there's substance to her life. And she'll show him her side of the bay, like they talked about that first night they were together.

Time to leave. She starts to walk back up towards where she left her car, on Vallejo.

The number on the building in front of her triggers something, some memory in her head. Was she ever inside it before? Did she know someone who worked here, a lawyer she might have come in contact with while she was on the force?

She doesn't think so; but there's something there, some fly buzzing in her brain. She pushes open the heavy pneumatic door and goes inside.

The entryway is small, dark, high-ceilinged. Marble floors, cherrywood-paneled walls. Rich in feel, more like the foyer of an expensive apartment building than that of an office building. Private bankers would have offices here, five-hundred-dollar-an-hour lawyers.

In the back, near the bank of elevators, there's a security desk manned by an old guard wearing a uniform that's been dry-cleaned a thousand times. He looks up from the *People* magazine he's reading and smiles pleasantly at her.

"Can I help you, miss?"

If her face registered on him he gives no sign, he didn't even flinch.

"I'm not sure. I think I've been here before, but I can't remember when or why. What sort of businesses have offices here?"

"Different kinds. Used to be lawyers almost exclusively, but now we've got some real estate folks, a direct-marketing company, whatever." He smiles like a naughty schoolboy. "Even used to be a mail-order porno business here, back in the sixties when things were wilder. But they folded, unfortunately. There were some pretty women used to come through, and back when I was young enough to do more than just appreciate them."

"How long have you worked here?" she asks him.

"Fifty years," he says proudly. "Got a job here the week I got mustered out of the Navy, right after WW II. Been here ever since. Only civilian job I've ever had as a grown man. This building supported a wife and three kids for me. I worked my way up to running the place, building manager," he rambles on, "but I'm too old now, too much responsibility. The owner keeps me on, though, not that I'm worth a day's pay anymore."

"That was decent of them." You've got to watch these old guys, you let them get started and they can talk for hours.

"Yes, I'm lucky. I'm seventy-eight years old," he informs her.

"You don't look it."

"Thank you. Some days I feel it."

"Some days I do, too," she says.

"So what is it you think you're looking for here?" he asks again.

She shakes her head. "Probably nothing. I'm not too together this morning."

He points across the hall. "There's a directory. Why don't you take a look? Might jog your memory."

The directory has about twenty listings. She scans them: law office, law office, accountancy firm, travel bureau, telemarketing firm. Some more law offices. Nothing out of the ordinary. A mutual funds company. Some kind of holding company, whatever that is. Two more law offices.

Her eyes move back up the list to the holding company. Bay Area Holding Company. The name rings a bell; but from where? She scrunches her brain, but she can't remember.

She reads the rest of the list. Nothing. No listing of the owner or manager. She crosses back to the guard desk, her heels echoing on the marble floor.

"Thanks for your help," she tells the old guard.

"Anytime," he says. "Find what you're looking for?"

"No. I think it was a case of mistaken identity." Casually she asks, "You said you used to manage the building?"

"For over twenty years," he says proudly.

"Who manages it now?"

"The Bay Area Holding Company." He points to the directory. "They're up on the third floor, but there's never anybody there. Just a small office with some phones. So they have a presence in the building."

"Do you know where their main office is located?"

He shakes his head. "No. You might look them up in the phone book."

"Thanks." She hesitates, then asks another question. "You mentioned the owners kept you on? After you retired from your position as building manager?"

He laughs. "I didn't retire. I was replaced, too old to do the job. I'm not complaining, mind you," he adds quickly. "They've treated me fair and square."

"But it's the same owners."

"Oh, sure. Same owners since before I started here."

"They must be nice people."

"The best. Let's face it," he says, "they didn't have to keep me on. This is a makeshift job so I can keep drawing a paycheck. Man draws a paycheck, he keeps his dignity."

"Yes." She smiles at him. "Well, nice talking to you."

"And to you."

She turns to go, then turns back to him. "By the way—what did you say the name of the owner was?"

"I didn't. You didn't ask."

"I thought I did."

"No—but I can tell you. Sparks is the name. A woman, actually, owns the place. The building's been in her family for a long time."

Sparks? A woman?

"This Mrs. Sparks—is she from Santa Barbara?"

He's surprised. "Yes. Do you know her?"

"I've heard of her," she covers quickly. "They're a prominent family."

Miranda Sparks owns this building. Jesus fucking Christ.

"They are," he confirms in a proud tone of voice, as if by association he, too, has prominence. Boastfully: "They used to own dozens of buildings in this city."

"They don't anymore?"

"No. Just this one and one other, over by Telegraph Hill."

"They sold the others?" she prods.

He shakes his head. "Sold some. Took some big losses. Lost some others outright. Bank foreclosures, bankruptcy filings. Building by building, over the years."

"The real estate market's been bad in California," she sympathizes.

"That's not why," he snorts.

"Oh?"

"They blew it. They're bad about managing their money. I told Mrs. Sparks that, when she relieved me of my duties. But she didn't want to hear. A tough woman, her. Kind of woman doesn't let anything get in her way." His voice takes on a bitter, angry tone.

That's Miranda, all right. "So the Sparks family definitely owns this specific building, though," she confirms.

"Yep. But not for long. You watch and see."

"Why not?"

"Same reason they lost all their other properties," he says prissily. The man is a self-righteous exemplar of the poor-but-honest school, she realizes belatedly—forever bitter. A PI's dream—you get them to open up, it's a deluge. "They squander their money."

She thinks back to the private jet, the casual meal she and Miranda had that probably cost over a thousand dollars. The perks of wealth, mindless indulgence. That role Miranda plays now—how she made it "the hard way," and appreciates things in ways her husband and his family don't—is so much bullshit.

"I tried to tell Mrs. Sparks that, but she didn't want to hear it. Hey, who am I?" he says, the bitterness in full flower now. "I'm just the ex–building manager. What the hell do I know?"

———

Back to her car, running all the way. She snatches her PowerBook out of the trunk, fidgets impatiently while it boots up, types in "Bay Area Holding Company," waits a few seconds while the computer cross-references the name.

Bay Area Holding Company. The security that had been posted for Wes Gillroy's bail.

Wes Gillroy—the third man on the boat. The sole survivor.

17

THE BIG SETUP

"This isn't kosher."

"That's okay. I'm not Jewish."

"That's funny. You don't look Jewish," Ted Saperstein tells Kate.

Kate is sitting in a booth at Jerry's Deli in Studio City in the San Fernando Valley with Saperstein and Louis Pitts, her Los Angeles–based ex-CIA detective colleague, the one who swept her office for bugs after her one-night stand with Miranda Sparks. Pitts, who definitely doesn't look Jewish, is wolfing down a four-inch-thick pastrami on rye.

"This isn't kosher, either, strictly speaking," Louis says between mouthfuls, indicating his sandwich, " 'cause they serve ham and stuff like that in here, but who's complaining?"

He's here as an intermediary for Kate, helping her out by introducing her to Saperstein as a professional courtesy, because she isn't heavy enough in the profession to be on an equal footing with a man of Saperstein's standing. "How's your fish?" Louis asks her.

"Great," she mumbles, wiping her mouth, which is full. She's eating lox and bagels, heavy on the cream cheese, with tomato and onion. Swallowing, she tells him, "there are certain basics you can't get in a place like Santa Barbara, and good deli is one of them."

They aren't talking about the food. They're discussing her problem, and how to solve it.

"I'm going to have to call in a few favors, you understand," Saperstein prefaces, spooning up some matzo ball with his chicken soup. In opening their discussion by telling her that her request wasn't "kosher," he was informing her up front that it would be difficult, perhaps costly, and potentially illegal, parts of it anyway. "And I may have to spread some goodies around, too."

"I hear you," Kate tells him.

Ted Saperstein is an "assets searcher." A former IRS official, now in private accounting practice, he's one of the best in the world at finding out an individual or a corporation's worth—net and gross—down to the dime, no matter how much they try to hide or bury it.

Revenge of the nerds, Kate thinks as she looks at Saperstein, who she's never met before. Square, baggy Brooks Brothers suit (black, natch), white socks, thin tie, Bobby Fischer haircut, the whole ensemble. A stereotypical accountant, she thinks; however an accountant is supposed to look. Which is good, because he's going to be looking into places you don't look into if you have a vanilla personality, so it's good he has a bland, almost invisible outer appearance.

"Give her whatever breaks you can," Louis tells Saperstein. "She's a working girl."

"I'm okay with money," she assures Louis and Saperstein. "I want a first-class search. Otherwise, it's a waste of my investigation. This is personal," she adds, "it's very important to me."

There's a touch of dark humor in this, but no one except her will ever know it: she's going to use a portion of Miranda Sparks's settlement (bribe?) to investigate the Sparks family's finances. It's the best use of that money she can think of—a delicious irony, especially if it pays off.

"Ballpark?" Louis asks for her.

"A civilian, it would probably be ten K, maybe more if it's really a maze, which this sounds like," Saperstein replies. "For you, I'll try to do it under five. As I said, there may be other hands in the till besides mine."

Meaning he may have to pay off some of his informants. That goes unspoken, of course.

"I appreciate that," she thanks him.

"And my shielding you," he adds.

"I appreciate that, too." Which she does, for real. Saperstein will have to go outside legal boundaries to get her some of the information she needs; but she won't know how or where, only the results. That kind of insulation is one of the biggest costs of hiring a man of Saperstein's caliber.

He nods. "I assume you've already done a lot of the preliminary work, so that'll help," he adds. "Let me see what you have."

She hands him a legal-size manila envelope filled with the data she's gathered over the past few days on the Sparks family: exact names, birthdates, and current addresses of Frederick Sparks, Miranda Sparks,

Dorothy Sparks, and Laura Sparks, for openers. He glances at the information.

"County records?" he asks.

"Voter registration," she nods. "And I did title searches on some of the properties I know they own locally, plus the building up in San Francisco."

"Good," he acknowledges her effort. "This'll jump-start the process by quite a bit. The trick," he explains self-importantly, "is to procure as many 'identifiers' as possible, meaning exact names, social security numbers, birthdates, addresses, etc. It's like cutting a key—the more specific information you put in the mold, the more complex a lock you can open."

He stuffs the information back into the envelope, sticks it in his briefcase, which he snaps shut and locks, takes a black Uniball pen from his inside jacket pocket, and opens a small notepad.

"As specifically as possible—what are we looking for?"

"Everything the Sparks family owns. Property, stocks, whatever. All their bank accounts, anywhere in the world." She pauses as he scribbles this down. "All debts, liens, judgments against them for the past twenty years. The current book value of their holdings. What their estimated worth is as of right now, and what it was five, ten, fifteen years ago." She looks up. "Have I left anything out?"

"We'll start with this," he says. "Basically, you want to know what their worth is now, what it used to be, is it going up, down, or sideways, and where it's coming from, right?"

"Yes."

"The husband's a high roller, you say," he asks, as he closes his notebook and places it in the inside breast pocket of his suit jacket.

"According to my source, he's lost millions over the years."

"Which means he had millions to begin with, which probably means he still has millions." Saperstein pushes away from the table. "Lunch is on you," he winks. "I'll be in touch."

"How much time will this take?" she asks.

"I hope I'll have some good information in a week. You can bet the farm there's going to be all kinds of paper companies, dummy corporations, any way they can think of to hide money. Not because they're crooks," he says, "but they don't want the government taking it all. All rich people are the same that way. That's how come they stay rich."

"How well can they hide it?" she asks. If Bay Area Holding Company is any indication, the Sparkses have a lot of deeply buried treasures.

"Very well. But unless they're really, really good and really, really devious, not well enough to keep it from me," he boasts. "If there's anything to be found, I'll find it," he says, smiling foxily.

He leans in to her. "This is the most important thing I'm going to tell you: you will have detailed reports of anything I can put on paper, but the delicate stuff is going to be oral, face-to-face, not on the phone. It'll be my mouth to your ear—and not even God gets to listen in."

Blake Hopkins leans against a wall near the front of the County Board of Supervisors' chamber, insouciantly checking out the scene. Hopkins has a proposal to make today; it's the only item on this morning's agenda. Oil is the eight-hundred-pound gorilla around here, so when it gets an itch, a lot of people start scratching.

The weekly board hearings are sparsely attended generally, mostly by local-government wonks; today the turnout is healthy, almost filling the room. Environmental activists are sitting on one side of the aisle, pro-oil people on the other. They never commingle—oil, for decades, has created a sacred schism. In Santa Barbara, you are pro-oil or anti-oil: there is no middle ground.

The pro-oil people are developers, businessmen and businesswomen, Chamber of Commerce representatives, and anyone who in any way profits from oil production in the county, which is a lot of people—thousands of them. Also in the pro-oil camp are ordinary citizens who simply don't see big oil as the bogeyman, who accept oil exploration in the county as necessary and inevitable.

Their opponents are a coalition that's been in existence since the sixties, when oil first became intrusive in county lives and county politics. It includes environmentally oriented legal organizations; local chapters of the Sierra Club and other national environmental groups; professors from the local universities and schools; students, from elementary schoolers to grad students at UCSB; fishermen and others in the fishing industry, which has always been one of the county's largest and most important industries, and has fought an ongoing and frequently bitter battle with oil interests for decades; and people who have no particular axe to grind but are anti-oil because they believe that oil production is the largest single danger to the quality of life in the region, which is one of the most beautiful areas in the country, and worthy of preservation.

Since his announcement of Rainier Oil's huge donation to the Sparks Foundation, which was his calling card into the community, everyone in the region who has a connection with oil—pro and con—knows who Blake Hopkins is.

Miranda and Dorothy Sparks are in attendance, of course. They've taken their seats three rows from the front, on the environmentalists' side of the aisle (right on the aisle, as if hedging their interests).

Dorothy can't control her agitation and apprehension—she sits bolt upright, spine and hips at a ninety-degree angle, lips pursed tight, hands nervously twisting a handkerchief. She knows what Hopkins is going to propose, and that knowledge, which she hasn't been able to tell any of her friends and allies in the movement, is excruciating. Once she had agreed to hear Hopkins's scheme, she was honor-bound not to divulge it. But she will most definitely speak her piece when the opportunity arises. She will not betray a lifetime's commitment, even if it's personally and familially painful.

Miranda, conversely, is relaxed and comfortable, smiling and greeting her friends on both sides of the aisle. As the time draws near for Hopkins to make his way to the lectern and begin his presentation, she fixes her attention on her lover's face, as if by sheer force of will she will be able to penetrate his brain and be as one with him, to make this all work out.

Sean Redbuck, the board chairperson, calls the meeting to order with a loud bang of his gavel.

"Mr. Hopkins. The floor is yours."

Hopkins strides to the lectern. He takes his time organizing his notes, then looks up to the five supervisors who sit above the audience like judges on the bench—which is what they are. You propose, they dispose. And they will often leave cleat marks on your hide.

"Mr. Chairman, members of the board, thank you for having me here today. To formally introduce myself for your record, my name is Blake Hopkins, and I am the incoming project manager for Rainier Oil's operations here on the central coast." He pauses for a moment, making eye contact with each supervisor in turn.

"I can understand how you folks feel about the oil industry," Hopkins begins. "Maybe if I'd lived here all my life I'd share those feelings. Feelings that I had a certain responsibility, a guardianship as it were, to make sure this area stayed as beautiful and unsullied as it always has been." A pause. "Or was, until the hordes from L.A. discovered it," he adds with a smile.

There is a rustling in the seats behind him, particularly on the environmentalist side of the aisle.

"But I haven't lived here all my life," Hopkins continues. "So my feelings are abstract. And less clouded with emotion."

Now the shuffling behind him becomes louder, less subtle: people bracing for a storm that they have vowed, for almost thirty years, to resist: to fight fiercely and to prevail against.

"The time has come," Hopkins states, "to find a way for your commitment and my company's needs, the needs of all the oil companies drilling in your channel, to strike a new path. One we're both comfortable walking on. That allows you to maintain the great quality of life that you have worked to preserve—and let me say, in the short amount of time I've spent here I can state, without exaggerating, life here really is nice, about as good as anywhere in the world that I've seen—and at the same time allows us in the oil business to do what we have to do, which is to provide quality petroleum products around the world, including here in Santa Barbara."

He pauses for a moment, taking a sip of water.

"I'm here today to make a radical proposal. Rainier Oil, the largest petroleum corporation that is currently extracting product from the Santa Barbara channel, wishes to initiate the removal of its drilling platforms from the channel. All of its platforms—every last one," he adds for emphasis.

"We plan to do this as quickly and efficiently as possible, with a timetable for complete removal in five years. It's what those of you who are anti-oil have been fighting us for for years." He pauses a moment, to let this bombshell sink in. Then he goes on: "Today, I'm here to tell you—you've won."

Everyone is frozen in the moment; hearing, but not yet comprehending the awesome scope of Hopkins's proposal.

Sean Redbuck finally leans forward in his chair. "This is a shock, to put it mildly," he says. "Why are you people making this proposal?"

"Because we have to," Hopkins answers. "The times, they are a-changing. When a conservative, pro-business governor like Pete Wilson signs a bill banning future offshore oil development up and down the entire coast, we have to adjust, because that's how we survive, even though that development has thrown off millions of dollars a year to the state, and to localities like yours."

"Please continue, Mr. Hopkins," Redbuck says. "Is there more to your proposal?" he asks. "Besides just pulling all your oil rigs in the next five years?"

"Yes."

The rancher talking: "I figured as much. You gonna tell us what it is?"

Hopkins nods.

"In exchange for abandoning all of our offshore operations, Rainier wants your permission to drill a series of extended-reach wells that will be based on a small section of property onshore. I repeat, onshore. This will allow us to increase our extraction capacity, will completely get rid of further drilling in the channel, and will create new revenues to the State of California and Santa Barbara County of more than two billion dollars over a twenty-year period. That figure is conservative, by the way—the final income could be double that amount."

The chamber is deathly quiet.

Redbuck looks at the other four supervisors. "We've heard similar proposals before."

Hopkins shakes his head emphatically. "Different technology," he answers. "Different results. Can I explain?"

"We'd like you to. Everybody in this room would very much like you to," Redbuck says dryly.

"The other companies wanted to take out one or two rigs that were on their last legs," Hopkins says. "Rigs that were economically draining for them; bleeding them in the pocketbook, where it counts. We're much bigger out in the channel—we dwarf everyone else, and our rigs have plenty of staying power, a dozen years or more, maybe a couple decades. We can stay with what we've got and still make a decent profit."

"Then what's your incentive?"

"Like I said—more production. More product. More money. Look, we're not proposing this because we're altruistic, I'm not going to insult your intelligence. Multi-billion-dollar corporations don't work out of altruism. We're doing this to make money—we're not going to beat around the bush about that. But—it's a much safer technology, which should be what's important to you. Even people who hate the petroleum industry know that slant drilling is immeasurably safer and cleaner than channel drilling. That's a given. A painful example: the *Exxon Valdez* incident has already cost Exxon billions of dollars, and there's more losses to come. Rainier doesn't want to have to pay out billions of dollars someday because one of our tankers ran aground in the channel, or a rig blew, like has happened in the North Sea.

"We get more oil with extended-reach drilling, and it is safer. That is the point: it is safer. We will make more money, yes, but your environment will be safer."

Hopkins concludes: "The world needs petroleum. It can't run without it. We want to take it anywhere we can find it, but especially in this country, because we use more oil than anyone else does, and we should supply ourselves as much as we can. It makes economic sense, it makes political sense, it takes the pressure off being held hostage by OPEC, and it's the right thing to do morally."

Jeers and catcalls come forth from the environmentalists' side of the chamber. Redbuck bangs down his gavel.

"I know talking about the morality of oil drilling isn't what you people are used to hearing," Hopkins says stoutly, defending himself, "but it happens to be true."

"What about pollution around the drilling site?" Marge Cantley, another supervisor, asks from her perch next to Redbuck's.

"Like one of our competitors' slant-drilling proposal?"

"Yes."

"Site selection is a major problem," Hopkins replies. "They had no choice but to situate their onshore operation cheek to jowl with a residential community and dangerously close by fragile wetlands. The ecology of the area might have been damaged, and it would have been unpleasant for the people who lived nearby, the university professors and so forth. Noise, oil fumes, the unfortunate but necessary by-products of what we do."

"Won't you create those same by-products?" she presses. "Which, quite frankly, this community is not willing to tolerate."

Hopkins shakes his head. "They had no choice. That was the only land they could access. But our situation is different. We're going to drill our wells on a piece of land where no one will see oil, hear oil, or smell oil. To the naked eye, ear, or nose, no one will know we exist."

Redbuck leans forward, intrigued. "That'll be the day, partner," he drawls à la John Wayne. "So where is this mystery location?" he asks. "This perfect combination, where commerce marries ecology?"

One last glance towards Miranda. Her smile is relaxed, perfectly set in her face. Dorothy's face, in contrast, is rigid as a board; but her hands are shaking in her lap.

"The Sparks ranch," Hopkins announces. "Which this board re-zoned for commercial use a few months ago, so the Sparks family could establish a world-class oceanography school. Which," he reminds the assemblage, "my company is funding."

Every face in the room turns towards Miranda, whose benign countenance is inscrutable, while all around her the chamber begins exploding in a clusterfuck of chaos.

Sitting above the melee, sensing the potential for an immediate and potentially physically threatening catastrophe, Redbuck gavels for a week's recess.

Kate drives south, listening to Tracy Chapman on her car's funky sound system, the song a metaphor for the story of her life, she's never been able to hold a man, she's forced to admit to herself; not a real man, a good one. What'll happen with Cecil, how will she fuck that up?

Anything is better. Is it?

Self-pity fills all the crannies in the car like a killer fog. What was she thinking about up north, proposing that ludicrous, pathetic pipe dream to bring her kids down to Santa Barbara? In the middle of the school year, Wanda's senior year, no less. With a court order denying her custody still in place (she's never formally requested custody, she thinks with a heavy hit of guilt), which her sister, and her girls as well, she suspects, would fight.

She can feel the pain like a vise around her heart, squeezing her bone-dry, squeezing out whatever hope she has left, which right now is precious damn little. A life of being alone, of loneliness, stretching to the horizon of her hopes.

Abruptly pulling off I-605 at Rosecrans Blvd., she drives to the nearest park, where she gets out of her car and sits down on a park bench and cries, tears flowing unchecked down her cheeks, as she had wanted to but couldn't when she watched her daughters disappear into their school and out of her life again.

Crying isn't a cure, but it helps. Cranking up the Rooster, she gets back on the 605 and continues south, into Orange County.

One person knows where she's going. She didn't want to tell anyone, but she thought somebody had better know, in case something ugly happens to her. Again.

"This isn't a good idea," he told her. "You were putting this behind you." He sounded mad—and worried.

She knew that, she responded, but she had to do it, it couldn't be helped. Something about her nature.

"Be careful," he warned her then. "Don't do anything rash."

"I won't," she promised him.

Finally: "Do you want me to come with you?"

"No," she replied. "I have to do this on my own."

So that's where she is now—on her own.

Wes Gillroy isn't living at the address listed on his bail record. There's three weeks' worth of junk mail in his box, and a cobweb woven over a corner of the door is intact.

"He moved out a month ago," the next-door neighbor in his small two-story apartment complex, a young woman sporting purple hair, five earrings in her left ear, plus a nose earring and yet another in her bared navel, tells Kate. She didn't flinch a bit, looking at the battered face protected by the sun shield.

That's interesting, Kate thinks. The court especially would find it so, since Gillroy is obliged to let them know where he's living. She knows this address is considered current by the Santa Barbara County Superior Court, because she'd looked it up in the county records before heading out this morning. If—make that "when"—she locates Gillroy, she'll pass on the advice that he'd better clean up his act in that regard, or he'll find his negligent ass back in the Santa Barbara County jail.

She *will* find him—she isn't going back to Santa Barbara until she does—unless he's skipped the state, which will open a whole other kettle of fish that's out of her league.

"Is that two-timing bastard in trouble again?" the woman asks.

"Not from me."

"You the law?" the girl asks suspiciously. It's midday and she's barely dressed; a thin kimono, open, bra and panties underneath. The smell of incense wafts out of her apartment. She's probably just smoked her first joint of the day, Kate guesses. And she was balling Wes and isn't happy that he cut out on her.

"No. I'm working for his lawyer," Kate lies. "I need to talk to him about his upcoming court date. Did he leave a forwarding address?"

The woman's expression tells Kate she isn't buying that line. "I don't know, I ain't the post office," she replies. "He's an old surfer. Old surfers never die, they only blow out their knees. Try The Wedge," she says curtly before slamming her door in Kate's face.

Gillroy's moving and not informing the court is par for the course—no big deal, really. As long as he shows up when he's supposed to, no one will give a shit. She can track him down, she's confident of that.

She wants to find Gillroy because she wants a victory, right fucking now. Locate him and put the fear of God into him, so he'll help her discover who Frank Bascomb's silent partner was: who put the money up to hire Rusty, charter the boat, buy the marijuana, and then pay Wes's bail. She knows that when she finds out who that person is she'll know who had Frank murdered, and tried to have her killed as well.

She cruises up Pacific Coast Highway, the sun burning high in her window, turning off at Newport Blvd., which segues into Balboa Blvd. Off to her right the ocean burns in the sun. She parks in West Jetty Park and walks down towards the water. The sand is hot under her bare feet and she starts picking up energy, feeling it radiating through her body, healing all her cares and woes. If it wasn't for this stupid face guard and the broken cheek, she'd plunge in, catch some good waves, be reinvigorated, ready to take on the world again.

In her dreams.

The waves funnel through the slot, crash into the jetty, rise up, and break again, thundering onto the shore. She stands on the beach, transfixed, watching. She isn't ready for this, wouldn't be even if her cheek and everything else was completely healed. This ocean is the real thing, a living beast, just huge waves, the biggest she's ever seen by far, and the ferocity of how they break is scary. She's seen movies of big waves—Sunset Beach on the north shore of Oahu, places in the South Pacific—but she's never actually laid eyes on waves this size before.

She could never go in here—she isn't strong enough. These waves would lift her up and break her like a twig, a toothpick.

She walks to about thirty feet from the water's edge and sits on the hard sand, watching the pattern of the break. A big wave crests and two surfers catch it, stretching their bodies out on their body boards and whipping along the top, riding the curl, then plunging under as it breaks against the wall, kicking and paddling furiously to keep from being picked up in the backwash and being slammed into the sandy floor.

No fucking way.

Down the beach about a hundred yards a lone surfer paddles out on his board, waiting and catching the break between waves. He obviously knows what he's doing—in a few minutes he's out past the breakers, lying on his board, waiting for a big one.

Something about him draws her attention. She stands up so she can watch him better.

The surfer doesn't have to wait long for his wave.

The curl starts way to his left, building and building, coming with a rush and a roar, bearing down on him like a fast-moving freight train. The wave crests and he catches it right at the top of the curl, pushing forward with such speed and force she can see, even from shore, that it almost tears the board right out of his hands. She watches as the force of the wave begins sucking him in. The surfer is fighting against gravity, his whole body contorting on the small board, twisted and bent, the wave is breaking fiercely against the jetty up ahead of him, he's diving down at the last minute but he's sucked under anyway—he's trapped, she realizes, he can't escape the force of the rushing water, the second, rebounding wave is going to catch him and slam him into the sand, the sand hard-packed as concrete, it's going to shred him, break him into smithereens. They'll put what body parts they can find in a small basket and there will be room left over.

She's never seen anybody die in the ocean but she's heard stories.

The surfer flushes out under the last crashing of water against shore and slides against the sand, hard, coming up for air, the water receding behind him, going back out to sea. As he picks up his board he turns and faces her.

She recognizes him from his mug shot.

————

Shaking the water from his body, Wes Gillroy picks up his board and walks across the beach to the parking lot. Kate follows him, not worrying that he might see her. He doesn't know who she is.

He jumps into a '55 Chevy Nomad, a classic surfer's car, Kate notes, and drives off. She follows. They cruise through the streets until he parks in an alley next to a surf shop. Leaving his board in the station wagon, he disappears inside. She waits a minute, until she feels cool and calm. Then she goes in.

"Wes Gillroy." She calls his name, a bit loudly for the size of the place.

He's dressed now: baggy shorts, T-shirt, flops. He looks up from behind the counter, where he's tallying some sales slips. A prototypical aging surfer, now that she can see him up close, skin like leather, washed-out blue eyes ringed with crow's feet.

"Yes?" he asks, blinking and squinting against the sun through the door behind her, silhouetting her in backlight. Women her age don't usually come into surf shops like this one. Wes would figure her to be somebody's mother come in to buy her son or daughter a cool present, to be hip with her kid.

"I'll be right with you." He turns his attention back to his paperwork, temporarily dismissing her.

She looks around. Nice place, must do good business, although at the moment she's the only customer in the place. Getting on to happy hour.

A woman emerges from the back of the store. Striking-looking: her hair bleached white, her figure almost a parody, it's so contoured—huge bust, tiny waist, hard tight behind.

It's Morgan what's-her-face, Kate realizes with a jolt—Rusty's girlfriend, the other woman on the boat along with Laura. Laura's description fits her to a T.

"How can I help you?" she asks Kate in a high-pitched voice that goes perfectly with the Dolly Parton figure.

"You're Morgan?" Kate asks in return.

"Yes." She looks at Kate. "Do I know you?"

Two birds with one stone. Not only won't this be a wasted trip, but she's won the bonus prize as well.

"No," Kate responds. "But I know you . . . rather, who you are." She takes one of her cards from her wallet, lays it on the counter so that Morgan can see it.

Morgan picks it up, reads it. "Private investigator? Santa Barbara?"

Wes snaps to, looking up at Kate with a start. He takes the card from

Morgan, looks at it, digesting the information, then at Kate again, this time paying attention to her.

"Who are you?" he asks suspiciously.

"What it says on there," she tells him, pointing to her card. "Laura Sparks is my client," she adds. "I've been looking for you, Wes."

"What for?"

"Information. I think you can help me get it. Maybe you can help, too," she says to Morgan.

Wes throws up his hands. "Sorry, lady. I'm looking at ten plus in a state pen, so I'm not talking to anyone." He hands her back her card. "Take a hike," he tells her rudely.

She puts the card back into her purse. "Fine by me," she shrugs non-chalantly, snapping the purse shut. "You don't have to talk to me. You can chat with the local sheriff instead." She pivots as if to go.

"What's that supposed to mean?" he calls out, stopping her as she knew he would.

She turns back to him, a bit dramatically for effect, for him and Morgan both. Morgan has retreated two steps behind Wes and is looking intently at Kate, her head cocked like a bird's.

"You're in violation of your bail, ace," she tells Wes. "You didn't let the court up in Santa Barbara know you'd moved. That's a major no-no. Tomorrow this time you're going to be sitting in the Santa Barbara slammer eating Spam and eggs with a spoon." She turns on her heel again. "See you in court."

"Hey, wait a minute, wait a minute!" He comes running out from behind the counter, steps in front of her, blocking her exit. "You don't have to tell on me, damn it!"

"I'm a state-licensed investigator," she says. "If I know a law's been broken, I have to report it whether I want to or not."

"Look," he says, pleading, "I was going to. It was a couple of days ago, I hadn't gotten around to it, that's all."

"According to your next-door neighbor, it was a month ago. The one you were balling," she adds quietly, so Morgan won't overhear.

He blanches, glancing over his shoulder at Morgan, who's staring at the two of them.

"All right. All right." His tone is contrite now, his demeanor subdued. "What do you want from me?"

"Somebody hired you and Rusty. Who was it?"

He blinks. "Frank Bascomb. I thought that was common knowledge."

She shakes her head impatiently. "I don't mean Bascomb. Who paid for the whole shooting match—the money man? The same person who made your bail, I'll bet."

"I can't help you with that. It was Rusty's deal—he set everything up with Bascomb. I was another set of arms."

"What about your bail? Somebody put up a million-dollar security to spring you."

"Don't know."

"That's hard to believe, Wes." She smiles. "I think we should do this by the book after all. I'll get in touch with the local authorities and you can deal with them however you have to."

He grabs her by the arm. "Don't!"

"Then stop bullshitting me."

"I'm not, I swear. I'm sitting in my cell the next morning, they come get me, take me to court, I'm told my bail's been made and I'm free to go until my trial."

"And nothing was mentioned to you about who made it?"

"No. I even asked the bondsman. He smiled at me like a Cheshire cat and said I had friends in high places, which I didn't get, since I don't know anyone up in Santa Barbara."

"Someone didn't want you around," she says, her mind spinning. "Sitting in a jail cell and thinking about talking."

"I guess." He shrugs. "Except I didn't have anything worth talking about. Still don't."

"Whoever paid for your bond doesn't know that. They think you knew who the moneyman was, like Frank and Rusty must have."

"I never thought of that," he says, thinking about it now.

"Which means they still think it," she continues.

"They're thinking wrong. I swear."

"I believe you," she tells him. "But whoever had Frank murdered in his cell doesn't."

He whistles, a low breath of air. "That was a hit?" he asks, in a tone of voice that says "Don't tell me the answer."

"I'm convinced of it," she says.

"So I might be in line," he says.

"I'd say the odds are better than even."

He looks at her as if seeing the scars for the first time. "Somebody did a number on you. Was there a connection to this?"

She nods.

"Motherfucker!"

Morgan comes up to them. "What's going on?" she asks. "Wes, you look like you just saw a ghost."

"He did," Kate tells her. "His own. Look. I think I can help you. But you've got to help me."

"What's this all about?" Morgan asks again.

"Rusty," Wes tells her. "And Frank Bascomb."

"Oh." Her mouth forms a perfect circle.

"How do you think I can help you?" Wes asks Kate.

"I need to find out who's behind all this," she says. "If I can trace the money I'll know who set it all up—the dope deal, Frank getting killed in jail, everything."

Wes shakes his head. "But I already told you . . ."

"Maybe there's some information sitting out there," she says. "Some documentation, something on paper that Rusty would have had. He was the one with experience, who would have known who to buy the grass from, where, all of that. The money person would have had to have dealt with him, I'd bet on it."

"Something at his house?" Morgan interjects.

"Maybe. Do you know where it is?"

Wes shoots Morgan a blistering look, but she ignores him.

"I live in it," Morgan says. "I was living with Rusty." She hesitates, blushing like a girl caught playing with herself. "Wes lives there, too—now."

Stands to reason, Kate thinks. Besides, who is she to pass judgment on anyone else? "Now I understand why you didn't want anyone to know where you'd moved to," she says to Wes.

"Yeah," he answers, dully.

"Rusty kept his shit all over the place," Morgan volunteers. "He was a world-class paranoid, which he was right to be, given all-what he was into. He even kept some of his records in the bathroom closet; he figured no one in their right mind would ever look for shit in a shitter." She laughs self-consciously, nervous as hell.

The shop closes in an hour. They'll meet Kate at the house at seven; they give her detailed directions.

"I'll be real angry if you're not there," Kate warns Wes.

"Don't worry," he promises her. "We'll be there—both of us."

* * *

An hour to kill.

She walks along the sidewalk, past a local bar. A beer would be nice, help her kill the time. But alcohol's the last thing she needs to indulge in, she has to be clean, sober, and alert. After it's all done, on the way home.

As she's about to get into her car and head out towards the address they gave her she thinks of one thing that could be important: she's going to the house of a man who was a principal in a huge drug bust, shot and killed by the police, his accomplice is living in the house now, and she may remove information that shouldn't be in her possession, if she finds what she's looking for. She should not be in that house; but since she's going to be, she definitely should not leave any sign that she's been there, in case it ever comes up.

She ducks into a Thrifty's Drug Store and makes a beeline for the section where they sell Ace bandages and knee braces, snatches a package of latex gloves from the shelf—the type dental technicians use when they're cleaning a patient's teeth. Whether or not she finds what she's looking for—an admitted longshot, particularly since she isn't sure what precisely it is she's looking for—no one except Wes and Morgan will ever know she was there, which is a chance she'll have to take.

She gets lost finding the place. She's three freeway exits past the proper one before she realizes she's gone too far, and has to double back through traffic.

The house is on a block of small post–World War II tracts bordering a low bluff overlooking the ocean. She cruises down the street, searching for the address Wes and Morgan gave her.

It's dark now, the moon rising low across the hills to the east.

A dim yellow mosquito bulb flickers over the front door. Inside, a few lights shine through the windows, which are covered with old-fashioned curtains. Probably belonged to the original owners, she guesses, and Rusty never bothered modernizing the place.

She hopes they're home—she's antsy already, doing this, if she has to wait for long she'll be the one who chickens out.

She could park in front, nobody here knows her, but there's a nagging itch about any kind of unnecessary visibility—she was surveilled before, by Miranda Sparks and who knows who else. If Miranda wasn't behind the attack on her and Laura—which she tends to accept, Laura being

Miranda's daughter—then there was another party tailing her; and although Louis Pitts has given her a clean bill of health, she has to play this real cautiously. A good detective doesn't trust anyone, as Carl is wont to remind her. You may not have too many friends, but you'll live longer.

She drives down the street, turns onto a narrow cross lane, and parks partway down the block facing forward, her car hidden in the gloom under a large eucalyptus tree.

Glancing at her watch. Seven-twenty. She's late.

One last precaution. She takes her loaded pistol out of the glove compartment and slips it in her purse. Quietly, she slides out of her car, locks the doors. Keeping to the shadows, she walks down the street to the corner and turns in the direction of the house.

Now that she's actually doing this she can feel her heart beating. In her chest, her throat, down to the ends of her fingertips. *Ka-boom, ka-boom,* loud and hollow like a kettle drum.

Go back to your car, she tells herself. Get in and drive home as fast as you can. This is not your life anymore. Leave it be.

Running across the street in her heels which she wishes like hell she hadn't worn, she hits the pavement, forcing herself to slow down, to walk as naturally as possible. No big deal, just a woman taking a walk along a street. Going to a friend's house, going home, just going her merry, innocent way.

The air around the house is still. Out back, down a short weed-infested concrete driveway, there's a garage, the door up. The Nomad is parked inside.

She walks up the path to the front of the house, up the two steps to the narrow wood-slat porch. She could sing out "Avon calling," but levity doesn't seem appropriate.

The door is open. A few inches, no more. "Wes?" she calls out softly.

There's no answer. Maybe they're in the back and didn't hear.

That's bullshit. Something is wrong inside—her detective's and woman's intuition both ring the same warning bell. She stands stock-still, listening, the loudest sound her own heartbeat thumping like a conch shell echoing in her ears.

If there's anyone inside they're frozen in position. Lying in wait for her, maybe? But who could it be, for that matter how could anyone know she's coming? Unless Wes or Morgan tipped someone off, which doesn't make sense.

She removes the latex gloves from her purse, slips them on, her hands shaking so badly she almost rips one with a fingernail getting it on. Then she takes her gun out, flicks the safety off, and pushes the door open with her elbow.

There's blood on the walls. There's blood everywhere. Wes lies on the floor, sprawled against the sofa. His head is matted with blood where the bullets exploded against the bone.

Her hand goes to her mouth, an involuntary reflex, but she can't stop the retching, she throws up on the floor, three fast heaves.

Don't step in it. Don't step in the blood, which is still oozing out onto the floor. The room has been trashed, torn apart. Papers strewn all about, a chair overturned, the cushions ripped open with a knife. Someone was desperately looking for something.

She steps around the corpse, towards the back hallway.

Morgan lies in the doorway to the bedroom. Shot the same as Wes, bullets to the head. Alongside her body, a bloody pillow.

She crouches down, looks at it. There are holes in the case, and what appears to be fresh powder burns. Somebody got here before she did; somebody who knew Wes and Morgan were going to meet her here.

If she had been on time would there be three bullet-riddled bodies lying on the floor?

You don't have to be a brain surgeon to know the answer to that one. The bell is tolling for her. Whoever did this has already come after her; this time they would have finished the job. Jackpot night—a three-for-one deal. But she didn't show, so the killer went on a scavenger hunt.

The big question is, did he find what he was looking for? Was there anything here worth killing for, anyway?

She looks into the bedroom. It, too, has been tossed, everything thrown about in haste, all the drawers emptied onto the floor. In the corner she sees a four-drawer legal-size file cabinet. Its contents have been ransacked, papers and files strewn all over the place. She kneels on the floor, rapidly skimming through them. Nothing relevant.

Her eye spots a small object under the bed, from this low angle catching a shard of moonlight coming in the window. She stretches her arm out, grasps it.

A bullet shell—9 mm, from an automatic. The hitman missed it in his haste. She drops it into her purse.

The bathroom. Did the killer know about the files in the bathroom?

Ever so carefully, she pushes the bathroom door open. It doesn't look like anyone's gone through it. Some dry toothpaste is caked around the drain in the sink; there hasn't been any water run through it for hours, probably since Wes and Morgan left this morning.

Across from the sink is a small vanity. Morgan's makeup covers the top. She crosses to it, squats down, and opens the louvered double doors. A small two-drawer file cabinet rests on the floor, unopened.

She slides the top drawer out. File folders are crammed into the drawer, each with an identifying label: boat rentals, rent receipts, bank transactions, telephone bills. Her hands shaking badly, she pulls the bank folder, glances at the contents. Canceled checks, monthly statements. She skims through them, finding July and August, extracts those two months' paperwork, which she jams into her purse.

The bottom drawer contains stuff from the surf shop. She randomly looks through a few pieces. None of it seems appropriate to anything having to do with Rusty's association with Frank Bascomb and the unknown backer.

From off in the distance, approaching very fast, come the sounds of police sirens.

Someone's called this in. They couldn't take the chance and wait around to kill her, so they set her up instead.

She runs into the living room and looks out the window, keeping to the side so as not to be seen. Several sets of flashing lights are coming down the streets, descending on the house. Too late to leave the way she came in, through the front door.

Blindly, she rushes into the kitchen. That door, too, leads to the front.

There is no back door. She's going to have to get out through the bedroom window.

She pries it open enough to crawl out. What the hell is out there? She thinks, looking out, trying to gauge; it's dark on this side of the house, the ocean side, she can see the moon reflecting on the ocean, but that's in the distance, what's right below her is unseen, unknown.

The sirens are almost on top of her. She braces for the screech of rubber on asphalt.

Fuck! She needs another file.

She runs back into the bedroom, pulls the top file drawer open again, grabs all of the telephone bills, and stuffs them into her purse, thank God she brought her big baggy purse, the one she can put her life's possessions in practically, jamming everything in as best she can, racing back into the bedroom, now the tires are squealing, feet out of cars, running up the pavement, up onto the porch.

Perched for a second on the windowsill, trying to see what's below her, purse tucked tightly under one arm, shoes held in the other hand. Too late to worry now; whatever's out there, here she comes.

The fall is about twenty feet down to the beach, she sees the sand rushing up at her as she's hitting it, hard-packed sand and small sharp rocks, trying to tuck but not doing it well, hitting on the flats of her feet, falling forward in an awkward sprawl, sand covering her face, down her entire front. Her right ankle immediately begins to throb—if it's broken she's fucked, she's dead. Gingerly putting her weight on it, she takes a step.

It hurts, a strong dull ache. But she can walk on it. It'll hurt a lot more tomorrow but that's okay, it can fall off then for all she cares, because right now she's going to run as fast as she can.

Lights go on in the house, above her. Men shouting at each other.

She runs along the beach, not feeling her ankle, not feeling anything, her blood is pumping like a racehorse's, running away from the house as fast as she can.

Two blocks away there's a pathway that leads up to the road. Carefully, keeping a low crouch, she climbs it.

The street is quiet. A couple of people have come out of their houses to see what's going on. None of them pay any attention to a woman who scampers across the street and down the block, veering off onto the side street where she had parked.

She sits in her old car with the lights off, deep-breathing. A couple of minutes pass. Her pulse starts to slow down, her breathing becomes more regular. Finally under enough control to function, she turns on the engine, puts the car in gear.

The car eases down the street, stops at the intersection. It turns right, away from the house and the police swarming all over it. As she heads down the main street leaving the catastrophe behind, another phalanx of police cars come flying at her from the opposite direction, lights blazing, sirens screaming.

She pulls over to let them by, then continues on, not one mile over the speed limit.

In less than a minute she can't hear the sirens anymore.

18

THE CASES FOR AND AGAINST

S ean Redbuck slams his gavel down with a bang. The weekly meeting of the Santa Barbara County Board of Supervisors is now in session.

The council chamber is packed beyond capacity. Not only is every seat filled, but people are standing against the walls at the sides and back, and others are congregating in the hallways outside, where television receivers have been set up to show the proceedings.

Blake Hopkins sits in the front row, on the pro-oil side, of course. Seated on the other side of the aisle, also in the front row, are Miranda and Dorothy Sparks. Conspicuously ensconced between them is John Wilkerson, who flew in last night to attend at Miranda's personal request.

Redbuck announces the agenda: "Rainier Oil's proposal to remove their drilling platforms in the Santa Barbara channel and replace them with an onshore extended-reach drilling operation; and to be given approval to place this operation on the Sparks family's ranch, subject to the Sparks family's willingness to be a party to this proposal, which this boards assumes has been under discussion between the two parties."

Dorothy Sparks grinds her teeth.

"I know some of you want to talk to this subject, pro and con. Anyone who wishes to speak will be heard, no one will be shut out; we'll stay all day and into the night if necessary. We do ask that unless you are a principal in this decision you keep your comments as brief as possible, that you not belabor points already made, and we urge everyone to refrain from making personal and inflammatory remarks." He peers down over the top of the podium. "Mr. Hopkins, the floor is yours."

Hopkins gets up, walks to the speaker's stand.

"Thank you, Mr. Chairman. I've already spoken my piece on this, so I'll make my remarks brief. My company, Rainier Oil, is asking that in exchange for removing our offshore rigs from state waters we be permitted, subject to an Environmental Impact Report and a review of the state Coastal Commission, which has already given us unofficial approval, to set up an onshore extended-reach drilling operation, which would be placed on a small portion of the Sparks ranch north of this city."

He returns to his seat.

Redbuck nods. Shifting his gaze, he turns to Miranda. "Mrs. Sparks. Do you wish to speak to this proposal?"

Miranda stands at her seat. "Yes, Mr. Chairman, I do."

"Please proceed."

She smooths her skirt and comes forward. She has no notes in her hand.

"To say that my family and I are between a rock and a hard place on this would be a gross understatement," she begins, her voice low and serious. "As everyone in this chamber knows, we have been in the forefront of the opposition to petroleum development in this county for almost three decades. We have put our time and energy into this fight, and we've opened our purse strings as well, many times. It has been a cornerstone of our environmental attitude that oil development is not appropriate in this county, and on balance does much more harm than good.

"That attitude is on the record. It is indisputable.

"Now this comes up. Rainier Oil is saying they want to take all their rigs out of the channel. That should be cause for rejoicing, and in great part it is. No more possibilities of oil leaks or explosions from the rigs, no more chance of tankers spilling oil into the channel. Tremendous ecological benefits. The essence of what all of us in the anti-oil camp have been campaigning for, for years and years.

"But then here comes this flip side. The dark side of the oil moon, as it were. They'll take the rigs out, but they want to drill for more oil. And to rub our noses into it, even if inadvertently, they want to place their operation on our property. My husband's, my mother-in-law's, my daughter's. Mine. And what's really painful for us, excruciatingly so, is that this same corporation is giving our foundation tens of millions of dollars to build our dream, our central coast school of oceanography, a project in which much of the research, ironically, will be centered around oil drilling in our channel and how to preserve the ecology of the ocean in the face of it."

She pauses for a moment to make sure everyone's up to speed with her. Then she continues.

"Had we known three months ago that Rainier Oil was going to make this proposal, we would not have accepted their gift to our oceanography project. It is, as they announced at the time, an unconditional grant; MacAllister Browne, chairman of the board of Rainier, has assured us in writing that regardless of what happens with their oil-drilling proposal—even if our family, in the end, opposes it—their gift will stand. And I want to thank them for that. They don't have to do that.

"Even so, a donation of that enormity cannot be put aside or removed from the equation. We are their partners now, and will be for generations to come. Oil drilling has been a lamentable part of all our lives for the past thirty years, and this proposal will extend that another twenty-five or more—over half a century of unwanted drilling. But the work, the research, the positive discoveries that will come out of this future oceanography institution will have meaningful and powerful impacts on our lives not for generations but for centuries. For our children, grandchildren, great-grandchildren."

She looked behind her—at her mother-in-law, at Wilkerson, at everyone sitting and standing on her side of the aisle. Then she turns and looks at Hopkins—a hard, penetrating look.

"We have decided not to oppose your project, Mr. Hopkins. It has been a tough, painful decision, and not taken lightly. We will, under the right conditions, allow you to place your drilling towers on a small, out-of-the-way section of our land."

She turns from him, looking again at the people on her side, her lifelong allies in the fight to get oil out of Santa Barbara.

"We all know that oil companies lie, that the only reason they perform environmental good deeds is because of public pressure, or because they need something from us; that their only real concern is profits, and that they will devastate anything in their path for profit. Look at the disasters in the Amazon, for a chilling example.

"I am making a pledge here today, to my friends here in this county: my family will hold Rainier Oil's feet to the fire. We will ensure that they make this project as clean as is humanly possible, and that if it turns out that their proposal won't improve our quality of life over what it is now, we will terminate our leases with them and kick them out, regardless of the consequences to our future."

She walks back to her seat and sits down. Wilkerson leans over, places a comforting hand on hers.

"Well stated," he whispers in her ear, inhaling her perfume at the same time.

"They hate me," she replies between clenched teeth. "I've lost every friend I have."

"Not *every* friend," he reassures her.

She turns and smiles at him for a quick moment, then looks to the front.

"Thank you," Redbuck says. He looks out into the audience and smiles. "Mr. Pachinko. You've been champing at the bit. It's your turn now; please don't make your remarks personal. This is about policy, not people."

Marty Pachinko is sitting all the way in the back. He slowly walks up the aisle to the front, glancing at Miranda as he approaches the podium. She returns his gaze with a hard stare.

Pachinko doesn't look the wild-eyed environmental radical he did before: he's under control. His hair is cut and combed, he's wearing a suit and tie. He stands square to the podium, hands grasping the sides, feet planted, looking up to the supervisors.

"I'm here today to speak against this proposal," he begins, his voice low, modulated. "Which is no big secret; but I need to correct you on one thing, Mr. Chairman."

"What is that?" Redbuck interjects testily, leaning forward.

"This debate may be about *policy* in the narrow sense," Pachinko says, "but in the true sense, *people* is precisely what it's about. The people who live in this county, who work in this county, who raise children in this county. How oil development and production affects *people*—their lives, their jobs, their happiness. Or unhappiness, as is too often the case.

"The issue before us is not whether we should have any more oil drilling in the channel or on land. The issue is whether we should have any more oil drilling at all. The point of the bill on banning future oil drilling off the California coast, a bill which Pete Wilson, a conservative, pro-business Republican governor, endorsed and signed into law, was to stop oil drilling and production on our coastline. This is not about better or worse. It's about yes or no.

"It's also about history," Pachinko says. "History, and trust. For over a decade and a half Unocal concealed their leakage up in Guadalupe, the fourth-largest spill in U.S. history—swept under the rug, in this very county. Eight and a half million gallons—double the size of the 1969 spill here; and we know the devastating effects that spill had on our lives down here on the south coast. Imagine if it had been twice as big. And that's only one case.

"Let's look back on all the promises the oil companies have made to the people of this county over the past few decades. They promised the county that they would consolidate their processing plants—yet Mobil now wants a separate onshore oil facility. Chevron promised us a pipeline—instead, we got tankering. The oil companies promised cooperation and partnership with the county—instead, we got multi-million-dollar lawsuits filed against the county by those companies. And yet, after all that, we're supposed to trust big oil. If these actions prove anything—and there is a consistent pattern here—it's that local government can't trust the oil companies to keep their word. They've gone back on it, time after time after time. And that's just here, in one county, in one state.

"Look at the global situation," he continues. "The *Exxon Valdez* disaster has permanently ruined the ecology and economy of the entire southern part of Alaska. Not for a few years, or even decades—but forever." He turns to glance at Miranda. "As Mrs. Sparks herself has just stated, we've seen damage in the Amazon basin that will permanently— *permanently*—cause widespread ruin in the largest and most important rain forest in the world. Damage that has wiped out entire Stone Age cultures, hundreds of species of birds. Not for decades, but forever. So that we, the industrialized, civilized countries of the world, can have a few weeks' supply of oil. And just this year the world at large belatedly was informed of the massive pipeline failure in Siberia, which has already decimated as much land as the entire western portion of this country."

He pauses to let the ramifications of his last statement sink in. "Think about that when you decide whether or not oil exploration is what you want in your backyard."

Everyone is quiet, listening intently.

"Right now we have the upper hand in this county. After decades of fighting big oil we're turning the tide. Their platforms are declining, they know the end is in sight. So they're trying to find a new scheme to foist on us, a new batch of poison for us to swallow, and they want to convince us it's in our best interests. Well, I don't buy it. And I don't think any reasonable man or woman who examines this in totality would buy it.

"We need oil in this country. No one is saying otherwise. The issue is where we get it from and how we get it. Oil is the tiger in the cage; a power that must be harnessed, kept under tight control. And we know from our own bitter experience that once we let the tiger out of his cage we can never get him back in—he's too strong.

"We've seen oil spills, leaks, explosions. We've seen them with our own eyes and on television, from the four corners of the world. Well, folks, let me tell you something—if there was an explosion under the sea here because of an underwater pipeline erupting, the blast would be infinitely bigger and more intense than anything any of us can imagine. We could see an occurrence right before our eyes that not even God would have the guts to try."

He glances at Miranda and Dorothy, who are both looking straight ahead, making no eye contact with anyone. Their faces are set, grim.

"There are certain parts of this world where development of this type should not be allowed," Pachinko says, turning back to the podium as he winds up his argument. "Our coastline is one of them. It's a natural treasure, not only for those of us who are lucky enough to live here, but for everyone. We are the guardians of this treasure, for ourselves and for the future.

"One thing I know—big oil looks after its own interests. That's its only job. Our job is different, and we are not their partners, and we never should be, no matter how much they want us to be, no matter what so-called treasures they bestow on us. There is a famous saying, I'm sure you've all heard it: 'Beware of Greeks bearing gifts.' The treasure inside might not be what you bargained for. Thank you for your time."

He turns and walks back to his seat. There is a moment's silence; then one side of the room bursts into applause, clapping, whistling, cheering.

Redbuck gives them a few moments, then he gavels for silence.

"Mr. Hopkins," he says, leaning over, "do you wish to answer any of these charges?"

"Thank you, Mr. Chairman," Hopkins says, rising. "I do—just a few." He comes to the podium, adjusts the microphone.

"Everything this gentlemen said—and I must say, he spoke very eloquently—boils down to one issue: safety. He wants to be assured that this won't blow up in his and everyone else's face." He leans forward, grasping the podium forcefully. "We can't do that. I could lie to you and say this process is 100 percent safe, but I won't. Nothing in this world that involves the extraction of minerals from the ground, whether it's oil or coal or gold, is 100 percent safe. But neither is driving a car, or playing football, or even jogging in the hills. There is inherent risk in life, no matter how safe or sedentary. What I said before, perhaps not as eloquently as this gentleman did in stating his opposition to our project, is that you have to judge the risks against the rewards.

"There has never been an accident of any size comparable to those he mentioned in any slant-drilling project in the world. Ever. It's much safer than offshore drilling. And the kind of accidents he mentioned— the *Exxon Valdez* and the broken pipeline in Russia—would not happen with this type of drilling. There won't be any tankering. And as far as broken pipelines go, we already are using pipelines in this country. It's what everyone wants; it's what you want, you've voted time and again in this county to require the oil companies to transport by pipeline. And let me clear up another misunderstanding. Rainier's oil rigs are healthy. They can go a long time, and will if this proposal is denied. And every day they're out there, there's a chance for an eruption. We want to lessen that possibility, not increase it.

"This proposal is safe. It will provide jobs—hundreds of local jobs for a long time. It'll provide income to the county. And it will get the oil rigs out of your channel."

He smiles a sincere smile. Then he takes his seat. There is a smattering of applause; before Redbuck can raise his gavel to quell it, it's finished.

"I'm going to call one speaker out of turn," Redbuck announces. "For two reasons—one, he's one of the most distinguished people in the environmental movement, whose word carries tremendous weight on this issue, and two, because he's flown three thousand miles to attend this meeting." He turns his attention to John Wilkerson. "Mr. Wilkerson. Welcome."

Wilkerson rises. He buttons his double-breasted navy pinstripe suit and walks to the speaker's podium with the air of a man in command of all he surveys—which he usually is, and when he isn't, he has the bearing and the experience to fake it. He smooths his hair across his forehead and smiles at Miranda Sparks.

"Thank you for allowing me to speak," Wilkerson says, his sonorous voice filling the room. "For those of you who know who I am but not what I do, I am the president of The Friends Of The Sea, the fourth-largest environmental organization in this country. I have served on the boards of the Audubon Society, the Sierra Club, and numerous other environmental organizations."

He pauses, one hand in his pants pocket à la JFK, with whom he shared a close friendship for many years, as well as a few women.

"We live in a world that is complex, shifting, and imperfect. And we have to learn to live with the imperfections; fight them when we must, bend them when we have to. In this situation, bending is preferable to fighting, because in the end, if you lose the fight, you lose everything."

He turns and faces the environmentalists, who are staring at him with anger and disbelief.

"You know who I am," he tells them. "You know I've been fighting the good fight all my life. So when I tell you, from my heart, that the benefits of this proposal outweigh the drawbacks, I hope you'll not only listen, but hear me. And remember what the man from the oil company said earlier.

"This battle has already been fought. We lost. There are oil platforms in the channel out there that defile and threaten our coastline. That's a fact and we can't change it, unless the oil companies take them out. They are going to sit there for years and years, polluting the waters—and let me remind you, as they decline in effectiveness they increase in their potential to pollute and fail, which would be a disaster beyond your comprehension, believe me. I've been in Alaska, I've been in Brazil and Ecuador, I've seen the devastation in Russia—if anything like that happened here . . . it's not possible to describe how it would ruin your lives."

He turns back to the front.

"I never thought I'd see the day when I would support an oil company's position," he tells the supervisors. "But today, that is what I'm doing. That oceanography school is going to do a world of good, and on balance, I have concluded that replacing those derricks with drills on land will be better, also. I am reluctantly—because I hate, and I do mean *hate*, endorsing anything big oil is for—asking you to approve this proposal. As I said, the world we live in today is imperfect, and there are times, regrettably, that we must choose between the lesser of two imperfections. This is one of those times."

He returns to his seat. Miranda leans in to him, her mouth to his ear. "That was wonderful," she whispers.

"I meant it," he whispers back.

Hopkins, observing this from his side of the aisle, smiles inwardly.

What a piece of work this woman is, he thinks. Thank God we're on the same team.

"How much did they pay you, Judas?" Marty Pachinko, standing on his seat, yells out from the back.

Others on his side of the aisle start yelling, too. Redbuck slams his gavel down.

"Shut up, Marty!" he bellows. "I warned you, don't make this personal!"

"It *is* personal!" Pachinko hollers back. "How much are they paying you to be their whore?" he screams at Wilkerson.

Miranda literally leaps out of her seat. She runs to the podium.

"Can I have the floor?" she demands. Even before Redbuck nods she has snatched the microphone out of its holder and is facing the audience.

"If you want to attack me, Marty, go ahead. I'm fair game. But John Wilkerson is one of the most respected and revered people in *your* movement, and mine, too, I will not allow him to be tarred by your brush because you need a scapegoat. To imply that there's anything underhanded about this man's attitude is disgusting, and you owe him an apology."

"Fine," Pachinko answers with bitterness. "I'll apologize to him. I'll pose the question to you instead: how much are they paying *you*?"

She laughs. "Are you joking?"

"I'm deadly serious," he responds.

The gavel comes down. "You don't have to answer these idiotic allegations," Redbuck tells Miranda.

"I want to," she says. "We'll get a royalty," she informs everyone. "It isn't much, because the mineral rights belong to the state, not to the property owner, which you know, Marty, better than me. And what we do receive we'll be plowing back into the school. Our family won't take a penny for ourselves, not one red cent."

"You really expect us to believe that?" he asks her derisively.

"You think we need the money? You know that's preposterous."

"You're holding back information from us," he presses on doggedly, "all of us, the supervisors as well as us regular little people. You and this guy from the oil company—you're concocting some backroom deal, and it's not as clean as you're making it out to be."

Miranda throws up her hands. "You make this all sound so Machiavellian. You know what Freud said, don't you, Marty?"

"What?" he answers, thrown off-balance.

" 'Sometimes a cigar is just a cigar.' There's nothing below the tip of the iceberg, Marty, because there is no iceberg. What you're seeing here is what you get. For God's sake," she says in exasperation, "I never even met Mr. Hopkins until the day he made Rainier's offer to fund our project."

In the back of the room, scrunched down in a seat in the last row, Kate, wearing a quickly improvised disguise of floppy hat and large sunglasses, listens to this bullshit. You're a fucking liar, lady, you've known this man Hopkins longer than that. I've seen the two of you together, with my own eyes, from your neighbor Cecil Shugrue's window. And if you'll lie about that, which you just have, you'll lie about anything.

Quitely, not attracting any attention, Kate gets up from her seat and leaves the room. Behind her, the supervisors are beginning to discuss Rainier Oil's proposal. It's obvious from the tenor of their remarks that a majority favor approving it.

The newspaper headlines were full of the double murder in Newport Beach, and it was on the tube as well. MAN AND WOMAN SLAIN IN ORANGE COUNTY. TIED INTO MARIJUANA ARREST. The police position was that it was the final payoff of a mob operation gone sour, and that the last participant, Wes Gillroy, had been taken out. Morgan had been in the wrong place at the wrong time, they concluded.

Kate's stomach churned as she watched on Channel 3's eleven o'clock news and read about it the next morning in the *News-Press*. A simple solution that cleans the books. That it was wrong was of no matter, except to the killer, or killers, whoever is behind it—and to her. Her big concern was whether the killer knew she was there or not.

She isn't sure; but if she's wrong this time she'll err on the side of caution.

She goes into hiding. She takes the essentials out of her office and apartment and rents a motel room on upper State under a false name. She leaves the Rooster parked outside her office and rents a car from Hertz, paying in cash so there won't be a paper trail. And she sleeps with her gun, loaded, under her pillow.

The most important thing she did was to call Saperstein the day after the murders were committed and give him the list of telephone numbers on Rusty's bill that had 805 prefixes. Most likely they were calls to

Bascomb; but there's the off chance some were to the secret financier as well (although Frank was the go-between and Rusty wouldn't normally have known who that person was). She also asked Saperstein to look into another specific bank account and see if there were any big deposits made around the time the dope deal had gone down. A real wild hare, but she has to check everything out. It's her life on the line now, from the moment she crossed Wes and Morgan's threshold.

Laura had called; hysterical, of course. The message had been on Kate's service, one of the few she'd returned. Had Kate heard? Laura wanted to know. Did it mean anything?

First she had to calm Laura down. That took several minutes. After Laura got herself under control—more or less—Kate answered that the cops had been right, that Frank had been in partnership with some heavy organization, maybe the Mexican Mafia, maybe some other group, they had taken him out and secured their situation by killing Wes as well.

Laura went for it—eagerly. She was sick of the whole affair, too. So what if Frank hadn't committed suicide? He had been a bastard, put her in jeopardy, almost got her killed. He's dead, it's over.

For you it's over, Kate thought as she hung up the phone.

But not for me.

"Santa Barbara County Sheriff's Department. How can I help you?"

"This is Sergeant Lane Wilcox of Orange County Sheriff's, in Santa Ana, ID number B-3386. I'm investigating that double murder down here in Newport Beach. One of the decedents was on bail from your facility on a drug-trafficking charge, awaiting trial. I need some basic information regarding his arrest and booking."

"One moment," the operator says. "I'll connect you to jail records."

Kate waits while the connection is made. She's calling from the office of a client, one of the larger law firms in town. She doubts her call will be monitored; but just in case, she doesn't want anyone to be able to directly trace it back to her.

"Jail Records, Officer Garcia. How can I help you?"

She repeats her request to him, hoping he won't ask her to give him a number at the Orange County Sheriff's Office that he can call her back on. He doesn't—her knowledge of procedure and professional tone gets her through.

"Hang on a minute," he says. "I'll punch it up."

It doesn't take long.

"Okay, I've got it," he says. "What do you need?"

"Time and date of arrest," she begins. "Officers who made the arrest. Who logged them in, the usual. The names of the officers who were in command that night, and who was responsible for assigning them to their cells—Bascomb and Gillroy. Watch commander, whatever. And if there was any unusual cell-transferring that night."

"I can do that," he answers. "Give me your fax number."

"Let me give you a number in Santa Barbara," she lies smoothly. "I'm on my way up now to interview Gillroy's lawyer. Send it to me at his office, I'll be there within an hour." She crosses her fingers.

"His lawyer." He hesitates. "Yeah, his lawyer would be entitled to this," he decides.

"Thanks. Appreciate it."

She hovers at the fax machine. The documents come out, a page at a time. She reads each as it emerges. One piece of information in particular catches her eye. She trembles as she reads it.

It's what she was hoping for—and dreading, too.

19

ANY NEWS IS BAD NEWS

S aperstein hands Kate a thickly packed manila envelope. She tears it open and takes out the contents, quickly skims through them.

"Everything you wanted?" he asks.

"And more." Jesus. "Thanks."

They've met halfway, at the Dupar's in Thousand Oaks, freeway close. He wolfs down the last bite of apple pie. She isn't eating—she was too nervous before he arrived, and now she's too upset and scared. And angry.

"On me," he says, grabbing the check for his pie and coffee. "I'll bill you," he indicates the envelope. "It won't be too bad. Louis has done favors for me." More seriously: "This is a big pile of shit you're stepping into. I hope you know what you're doing."

"Yeah. Me too."

He dumps some bills on the table, stands up. "See you around. Call if you need any clarification."

"Thanks. I will."

She spreads the papers out on the table, carefully begins digesting them. It's mid-afternoon—the restaurant is almost empty. Middle-aged waitresses in uniforms dating back to the fifties (down to the crinoline under the puffed-out skirt and the lace handkerchief pinned over the left breast) wipe tables and gossip. Kate signals to one with a raised finger.

"A pot of tea, please."

"Anything to eat? The boysenberry pie's nice and fresh."

"No, thanks. Just the tea."

Her stomach is churning. If she ate anything it would bring on nausea—reading this material is making her sick to her stomach.

It's all here—Saperstein's done a thorough job. Names, dates, places.

Transaction records, bank accounts, stock ownership, property—everything.

Now I have it, she thinks. Now what the fuck do I do?

"What're you going to do with this?" Carl looks off, his eyes clouded with cataracts.

"I don't know."

"This is incendiary material."

"Tell me about it."

They're sitting outside his unit at the convalescent home. It's late afternoon; the sun is low, it's getting chilly. Carl wraps his sweater tighter against his body, but the cold doesn't go away.

"They've come after me before," Kate says gloomily, "and that was before I had any proof." She taps the package of documents sitting on the table between them. "You don't think they'd do whatever it takes to stop this from coming out?"

Her doctor took the bandages off her face earlier in the day; she'll still wear the protective shield in physical situations. She rubs her face with both hands, being careful as she feels the fresh pink skin that's newly formed over her healing cheekbone. All the shit that's happened to her has taken a heavy toll. She's exhausted—there are large dark circles under her eyes, and the color is drained from her face. She's run out of steam, just about, she feels like it's all fumes she's going on now, adrenaline and fear.

"I have no doubts," Carl agrees. "The question is, how can you use it so they can't?"

"Go to the district attorney?"

He shakes his head vigorously. "There's no evidence of criminal activity in this stuff."

"But—"

He cuts her off impatiently. "There's stupidity, by the carload. There's venality, manipulation, lies. But there's nothing in here—" he pokes his finger at the documents—"that's against the law."

She slumps in her chair. "Maybe I should go to the *News-Press*," she thinks out loud. Laura's weekly, *The Grapevine*, would be where you'd normally go with material like this, but that's the last place she can take this stuff.

"Do you have a friend there? Someone you can trust?"

"No."

"Then it's iffy. They do love a juicy scandal—they are a newspaper, after all—but they're also part of the establishment, they're not going to print anything this explosive without corroboration, and then you're exposed again."

"They'd never come after me once I've gone to the newspaper!" she exclaims. "They couldn't."

"At this point what do they have to lose?" he counters. "Three people have already been killed, what difference would one more make?"

"You don't have much faith in our public institutions."

"No, and for many good reasons. Years of them."

She fingers the documents. This is scary.

"So what should I do?" she frets. "I've got to do something, for self-preservation if nothing else."

"You've got to find a piece of incontrovertible evidence. Do you remember the Watergate hearings?"

"Yeah. I was in high school." She would have been about Wanda's age. Full of passion and commitment, like her daughters are now.

"The smoking gun," Carl says. "That was what that one congressman kept saying—'I'm not going to vote to impeach the President of the United States without a smoking gun.' Well, they found one, and that gave them the excuse they needed to get rid of the sonofabitch. You have to find the same thing." He taps the documents again. "So far you haven't. Because that's everything. All the rest is commentary, as the wise old man said."

"You're the only wise old man I know."

"And I'm no goddamn help to anyone anymore." He bangs the arm of his wheelchair. "I'm a frigging prisoner in this thing!" he rails. "I couldn't help an old lady cross the street."

"You listen to me," she says. "You give me good counsel."

"Big deal."

"It's a lot."

"It won't do you any good out there." He points in a nebulous direction.

"If the people who did all this know someone else knows, too, it might," she counters.

"That's a flimsy hook to hang your hopes on," he tells her. "To entrust your life."

"It's better than nothing. And right now it's all I have."

"So what *are* you going to do?" Carl asks again, getting back to the root of her problem.

"Watch my ass like a hawk. The one advantage I do have is they don't know that I know what I know—yet."

"You'd better be super careful. They almost got you already, two times now."

"I will," she promises him. "Hey, fuck 'em all but six, right?" she adds in a feeble attempt to lighten the mood, which doesn't work. She stands, starts to wheel him back inside.

"Stay low to the ground," he warns her, a bony finger stabbing her ribs. "And don't show your hole card until the other side shows theirs."

Watch your ass. Yeah, right. Great fucking idea. If you want to barricade yourself in a closed room for the rest of your life. How do you watch your ass and get theirs at the same time without tipping them that you're on to them?

She has to make her move. Right now, not one day more of indecision. She has to make something happen, because she is being hunted: as of the moment she turned down the cash offer, first in Oxnard and then with Miranda, she was prey. They have her in their sights; maybe not this very minute, she's eluded them so far, but there is a plan, and she is the focus of it—and the purpose of the plan is to kill her.

20

HAVE GUN, WILL TRAVEL

Kate cleans her gun.

It sits on the center of the bed in her motel-room hideout on a spread-out sheet of newspaper, to prevent staining. She's been assembling and disassembling her weapon for years since she bought it as a cadet at the police academy, she could probably do it blindfolded like in the movies, but there's nothing to gain by doing it that way, unless you're making a bet with someone. If that were to ever come up she'd practice first, to make sure she could.

Smith & Wesson, model 411, 40-caliber eleven-shot automatic. Matte black finish, polymer plastic grip, nonglaring.

She removes the magazine.

She puts the safety on.

She pulls the slide back to the disassembly notch.

She pulls the slide-release lever out.

She removes the safety.

She removes the slide from the frame by sliding it forward.

She removes the guide rod and spring from the slide assembly.

She removes the barrel from the slide.

It's a quarter to nine in the morning. She sips from a double latte she picked up at Coffee Cat. The radio is tuned to the public radio station, KCBX-FM, the *Morning Cup of Jazz* show. They're featuring Bill Evans this morning, the *Blue in Green* album. Very mellow. It helps her chill out, stay focused.

She uses a toothbrush to apply solvent to the various parts: Hoppe's Nitro #9. The Hoppe's smells sweet, almost like a man's cologne.

She scrubs the inside of the barrel with a cleaning rod and a barrel brush.

She removes the solvent from everything with a clean cotton T-shirt from a former lover. She can't remember exactly which one.

The gun is dry.

She lubricates the slide rails with Break-Free. She lubricates the guide rod and guide spring.

She reassembles the gun:

She puts the barrel in the slide.

She returns the guide spring and rod to the barrel.

She puts the slide back on the frame.

She lines up the notch and hole, places the slide release in the hole to secure the slide to the frame.

The gun is now cleaned and reassembled.

She gets a box of bullets from her duffel bag, which had been hidden behind a pair of black spaghetti-strap three-inch high-heeled pumps in her bedroom closet. Winchester Black Talons, a bullet that has a Teflon-coated copper jacket with a nickel-plated brass case. Special bullets, to be used for special occasions, which this definitely qualifies for. This bullet, if it hits you in the arm, the arm comes off. If it hits you anywhere in the body, you die. This bullet is not for sale anymore—Winchester voluntarily took it off the market, it's too destructive. She bought two boxes years ago, in case she ever needed the extra stopping power.

She loads the empty magazine with the Black Talons, returns the magazine to the frame. She double-checks to make sure the safety's on, which it is.

She takes the gun and the cleaning implements into the bathroom, on the way in tossing the oil-stained newspaper into the trash basket in the corner.

She washes her hands, scrubbing them hard in hot water, getting off all the solvent and oil residue.

She has a long day and longer night ahead, so she lies down on the bed, forcing herself to sleep, quieting her racing mind.

Sundown.

She wakes up, showers, gets dressed: cotton underpants and bra, jeans, long-sleeved cotton sweater, sweat socks, running shoes.

She brushes her hair out and pulls it back into a ponytail. A touch of lipstick, pale red, mascara, hint of eyeliner. She wants to look good, professional.

Her face stares back at her. The left cheek still protrudes, but the swelling is going down, daily. She looks at her face objectively. The scars are receding. Not a face to hide from the world anymore. There will always be some scars, but that's okay, she can be proud of them, she'll wear them with honor. The marks of a survivor.

Night.

It's dark and the moon is clouded over, but she finds her way like a homing pigeon. She parks a hundred yards down the road, out of sight. She's getting good at that.

The bullet-punctured Rancho San Miguel de Torres sign flaps in the wind. Over her left shoulder is slung a black Nike day pack, empty now. She walks down the dark road, the trees on either side hovering like huge ominous crows over the road. Off in the fields, she sees a few beef cows, shorthorns, who look back at her with blank curiosity.

It takes almost fifteen minutes to walk the mile from the highway to the house. It's cold outside, not near freezing—it rarely gets that cold in the valley—but bracing. Her hands are in her jacket pockets.

The house is dark. There are no cars parked in front. She prepared for that; before she left town she called Miranda's office posing as a UPS dispatcher (a hoary but time-tested gimmick), to verify Miranda and/or Frederick Sparks's whereabouts for a special delivery to their house that evening. Celeste—Miranda's secretary—bless her trusting soul, had confirmed that Mr. Sparks was out of town on business and Mrs. Sparks would be dining at home that evening with Mr. Sparks's mother and Mr. Wilkerson of The Friends Of The Sea. (Kate immediately walked into the nearest flower shop and ordered an ornate floral bouquet to be sent up to the Sparks house, courtesy of "Your friends who support removing the oil platforms from the channel." Miranda could figure out who those friends might be, but in case her secretary mentioned the inquiry, she was covered. She paid in cash, of course, and declined to include a card.)

She reaches the low ranch house, standing off to one side in deep shadow. The house looms dark against the gray hills and black starless sky. The moon is shrouded by the clouds and a low fog lies on the ground, further obscuring vision.

This is risky business, but there's no other way. The proof of why Frank Bascomb was killed in his jail cell and why she was attacked and would've been killed if it wasn't for Cecil showing up and why those two people were killed last week in Orange County is in this house. It has to be.

She had thought, fleetingly, about asking Cecil to help her, but had quickly decided against it—she can't involve him in breaking the law, even though she knows he'd do it for her.

Taking one good deep cleansing breath, she walks across the open space in front of the house and up the steps.

"Miranda? Mrs. Sparks?" She knocks on the door, loudly, calling out. If anyone is at home, she's here legitimately.

No one's here, of course.

Squatting down, she examines the locks on the door. A tumbler and a dead bolt; Schlage, brass finish. The tumbler's most likely a B-460 with a one-inch dead bolt. Good quality, solid.

This is going to take some work—she hopes she can open them, she's rusty, she hasn't done this for a long time. Otherwise she'll have to try another door, which will probably also be locked, which would then necessitate breaking and entering, an altogether different situation, not one she wants to do if she can possible avoid it.

Be here and gone without anyone ever knowing is the idea. To be the hunter, not the prey.

There could be an alarm, of course. It would be a silent alarm, you wouldn't know you'd tripped it until the security people came breaking in the door. Usually, though, the security service calls to make sure you didn't trip your alarm accidentally. You give them your secret password and they caution you to be more careful next time.

If the phone rings after she's entered she'll be out of there in about one-tenth of a second, if that.

She takes her latex gloves from her jacket pocket—the same gloves she wore when she went into Wes and Morgan's house last week. Then she gets out her set of lock picks in its nice leather case. Twenty-five different picks, along with an assortment of tension wrenches. Years before, she'd busted a professional burglar—and then, as sometimes happens, she got to know him through the course of following his case through the legal chain. The friendship was helped along by allowing him to cop to a light plea in exchange for working with the force in busting a chain of big-time burglars, which he was happy to do. Part of his payback had been to acquaint her with the time-honored profession of lock picking, even giving her a good set of picks and teaching her how to use them, a piece of knowledge that has come in handy more than once.

She inserts a diamondhead pick into the dead bolt, slides the tension wrench in alongside. The lock is a five-pin tumbler. Slowly, methodically, she rakes the tumblers. It takes time, she's not a professional at this, and she doesn't practice it as much as she should.

This is the most vulnerable part of the operation—if she's caught in the act, she's dead. Literally, most likely.

It's chilly out but she starts sweating, beads forming on her forehead, in her hair, getting in her eyes, itching. She wipes her head with the sleeve of her jacket, keeps working.

She can feel the tumblers falling. She turns the tension wrench. The bolt slides open.

She checks her watch. Six minutes, not bad for an amateur.

The knob lock is easier, now that she's back in practice.

She opens the door, steps inside, and closes it behind her, turning the dead bolt and locking it as a precaution—if anyone comes up here, the few seconds it will take to unlock the dead bolt could be the difference.

It's dark inside. She doesn't want to turn any lights on—a single light can be seen for miles out here, so she stands in the blackness waiting for her eyes to acclimate.

It takes a while. She doesn't move, not one step.

Her pupils gradually dilate so that she can see where she is and what's around her. The living room is as she remembers it. She walks across the room to the den where Miranda conducted her million-dollar business.

Outside, the wind is picking up, causing pebbles and pieces of board to knock against the walls of the house. She listens carefully. Nothing. Her nerves, that's all.

Heavy curtains frame the two small windows of the den. She pulls them shut. Then she takes out a small penlight, turns it on, and points it around the room.

The den, like the rest of the house, is decorated in old-fashioned Santa Barbara County ranch style: old leather couch, sturdy wooden chairs, Native American rugs on the floor, which is peg-and-groove oak, worn from decades of being trod upon. Against the widest wall she sees the work area, which consists of an old desk made from Monterey County madrone wood, which must be an heirloom and undoubtedly worth a lot of money, a large leather chair like a lawyer from a Charles Dickens novel would sit in, a new computer and printer, fax, multiline telephone, and other contemporary instruments of commerce.

In four steps she crosses to the desk and quickly begins rifling through the papers on top. Different business and personal transactions, notes, the usual crap people who aren't particularly neat have on their desktops. She pulls open the drawers on either side, starts leafing through the contents, taking care not to mess things up, to leave everything as it is as much as possible. There is some stuff pertaining to finances; most of it she already has from Saperstein. He's done a good job, she thinks, looking the material over.

She glances at her watch. She's been in here for twenty minutes? No way. It felt like it was only a couple of minutes, five tops. You can get entranced in this stuff and lose your focus—when that happens you're likely to get your ass handed to you.

She goes to the window, peels the curtain back a nervous inch, looks out. There's nothing there—but it's so still it's scary.

Pressing on.

In the corner of the room stands an old open-top pine breakfront with photos and other family memorabilia on it. Pictures of the Sparks family, trophies from riding competitions. Nothing of Miranda, she notices.

Interesting stuff, but this isn't the time to leisurely study pictures.

She opens the first drawer. It's crammed full of photo albums, cheap souvenirs from family vacations, personal things that have value only for the people who own them. Not what she's looking for.

The middle drawer has more of the same.

Maybe she miscalculated. Maybe what she's looking for isn't here. It's back at Miranda's office in town, or in a vault somewhere, where prying eyes can't get to it.

She pulls at the bottom drawer. It doesn't come out.

Shit, she thinks, another goddamn lock to pick. This is getting on her nerves; her nerves are getting too much for her to handle is the truth of it.

She squats on her haunches, checks it out. "Sonofabitch!" she curses out loud: it's an old skeleton-key lock. The worst fucking kind.

Her picks won't work on this lock—it's too old. She'll have to open this sucker the old-fashioned way, if she can, which is iffy, even professional locksmiths have a hard time with these old skeleton-key locks.

She scrunges around on Miranda's desktop, finds a box of paper clips.

Metal, thank God, people more and more are using plastic-coated clips—if that's all there had been she'd be up shit's creek. She opens two clips so that they're more or less one straight line.

Her penlight is clenched between her teeth, shining on the burnished keyhole. She inserts the clips into the keyhole, starts trying to get a purchase on the cylindrical tumblers. Patience, girl, patience. She's starting to sweat in earnest now, major flop-sweat, she can feel water gathering in her armpits, running down her sides. She never sweats—"A lady never sweats," another of her mother's sayings, she perspires lightly at most.

She must not be a lady anymore, because she's sweating like a pig. It itches; she scratches her armpits and the sides of her ribs with one hand, keeping the tension inside the lock with the other.

"Come on, goddamnit," she whispers between clenched teeth.

Is it moving? She can't tell. She leans closer, looking at the crack between the drawer and the frame above it, turning her head so the light shines in the crack, trying to see the bolt, whether it's moving or not.

Not yet. Don't quit.

She glances at her watch. She's been working this for ten minutes. It could take another ten, or twenty. Or she might not get it at all.

Five more minutes. Then she'll jimmy the fucker, if she can find something to pry it with. The tolerances between the drawer and frame are pretty tight, it would take a thin screwdriver to force this drawer.

Five more minutes. If she can't open it by then, she'll give up.

Patiently, patiently, sweating steadily, she works the paper clip in the lock.

Outside, a gust of wind knocks a loose board against the side of the house, causing her to stiffen, her body almost jumps, if she had moved suddenly she would have lost her purchase inside the lock and would have had to start all over again, and she doesn't have the time or the guts to start over.

Somehow, her hands remain steady—they've taken on a life of their own.

She feels something starting to move. Are the tumblers turning? She turns her head crooked again, squinting through the crack, trying to see the bolt.

It's moving. She can see it.

Easy now, easy. Like talking to a fractious child. Yeah, baby, that's good, she can feel the bolt turning.

The drawer slides open. She falls back on her ass for a moment, catching her breath.

The drawer is set up as a file cabinet, legal-size, with tabs on the tops of file folders. She starts reading the labels. Land deals. Her pulse quickens.

She pulls out a thick file that is labeled "San Francisco." Flips through the pages. Deeds of trust, bills of sale, tax notices, all the paper trail of ownership.

Where is it? she thinks.

Bay Area Holding Company. It leaps out at her.

She stuffs the entire file in her day pack, continues looking through the drawer.

The last file folder in the drawer is the newest. Rainier Oil, typed in neat letters on the edge.

Carefully, as if it might be connected to a detonating device, she pulls it out.

The folder contains a bound document. Stamped on the front cover is a warning—CONFIDENTIAL—and a number under it. Like in the CIA, she thinks, and as important.

She opens it up. It's a contract between Rainier Oil Corporation of America, Inc., and Miranda Sparks et al. of Santa Barbara, California.

She flips through it, to the final page. There are places for signatures. One side for Miranda Sparks, president of the Sparks Foundation. On the other side, a name is typed in the space where the representative for Rainier Oil NA, Inc., will sign.

The name is Blake Hopkins.

Blake Hopkins. The oil honcho, Miranda's secret lover.

Pay dirt. She feels her pulse rate going up like a skyrocket.

It's time to bail out of here. Stuffing the oil company documents in her backpack, she turns off her flashlight, reopens the curtains as they were before. Then she retraces her steps through the house and lets herself out the same door she entered, locking the doorknob from the inside. Fuck the dead bolt, that'll take some time and she's already overspent her allotted time, in the karmic sense. By the time anyone finds out it isn't locked and the place has been broken into, this will all be over.

She walks back down the road to her car, still hiding in the shadows, waving to the cows, the only witnesses to her triumph, as they stare unblinkingly back at her.

She hadn't realized how much she missed him.

Cecil opens the front door as she gets out of her car. He's standing under the lintel, framed by soft light from inside.

"Hello, stranger," he says, warmly but warily.

"Hello your own self." She has to look up, she'd forgotten how tall he is.

"Out pretty late," he remarks. She had called him a few minutes ago from her car phone, just down the road.

"I'm sorry. I didn't realize," she lies. It's a white lie, it was acceptable.

"I don't mind. I'm glad you called. I've missed you, Kate."

"I've missed you, too, Cecil." She pushes up against him. Hug me, please.

He pulls her close. "Yeah," he says softly into her hair.

"Me, too."

"Been busy, huh?" He holds her at arm's length, looks at her face. "You're healing up good."

"I don't feel that," she says. "I can't hardly look at myself anymore."

"You look good to me, babe."

Babe. A term of endearment. Finally, from someone. This is a good one: she'd forgotten. You don't throw them back in, and you don't treat them casually, either. She's going to make it up to him, if he still wants her when it's all over and everything's come out in the wash.

"You're good for my ego . . . and other things, too."

"That's what I'm here for," he says.

She feels shy around him all of a sudden, leaning against him in the nighttime darkness, lit by a single bulb over the entry to his house. They haven't seen each other for weeks, she had deliberately avoided him, she didn't want anyone to see her for a long time, especially a man she's attracted to, and then there was the stuff with her kids and the stuff down south and all this shit around her life.

"Come on in." He looks past her to her car. "Do you want to stay the night? Can you?"

"Yes."

Her overnight bag, which she always carries for situations such as this, is in the trunk of her car, along with the documents from Saperstein. She's dying to show the stuff to Cecil; he'd understand, he knows these players. And she strongly wants a partner—not an ear like Carl, but a real partner, someone who will help her in a real, physical way. So she isn't all alone.

But she doesn't show him what she has or ask him to help—not yet, not until it's over. Deep down, she wants to keep this to herself. She knows that. It's her fight, she has to do it herself. That's the way she is, even if it means putting herself in jeopardy, like when she went with Laura and the whore and didn't have backup, or when she went alone to see Wes. Or just now, a mile from his doorstep.

First things first. She takes his hand and leads him into the house, to his bedroom.

"Please make love to me," she says, her voice unsteady, pulling his face down to hers and kissing him on the mouth, hard.

———

They are still asleep in each other's arms when first light comes, before sunrise. Quietly, so as not to awaken him, she slips out of bed and dresses in the living room.

Forgive me for what I'm about to do, she asks him silently. It's not because I don't care about you. It's who I am, and what I have to do. And then she promises him that once she does this one thing she'll be faithful to him for as long as. . . .

"Leaving?" he asks from the doorway. He is naked, his cock at half-mast, morning erection.

"I didn't want to wake you."

"In a hurry?" There's an edge to his voice which he doesn't bother trying to conceal.

Evasively: "I have something I have to do this morning."

He looks at her. "When are you going to let me in?"

Her first impulse is to say "What do you mean?" but they'd both know that would be bullshit. "Soon," she tells him instead. "It won't be long."

He shakes his head. "That doesn't cut it, Kate."

She doesn't want to leave. She wants to get back in bed with him and stay there all day. But she can't. "It's the best I can do right now, Cecil."

"You're using me," he tells her.

"I don't want to."

"Then don't. Be real, okay? That's all I ask."

"I want to. I . . ."

"No. You want this to be easy, without paying all the dues. At least with me."

That stings. "That's not true," she protests.

"It isn't? You don't seem to have a problem banging on my door any hour of the night and asking to be taken in when *you* need comforting. But relationships are a two-way street," he adds pointedly.

"I'm sorry if I disturbed you," she says stiffly.

"Bullshit you are," he replies. "Last night wasn't the first time, in case you've forgotten. How about when you'd been over to see Miranda and you came storming in here accusing me of being unfaithful to you because I'd slept with someone years before I even met you? You can be a little irrational, Kate. And more than a little selfish."

She feels flushed, her breathing is rapid, shallow, her pulse is racing. "I've gone through hell," she manages to say, trying as best she can to defend herself.

"I know," he answers. "And I've tried to be there for you. I've wanted to be," he goes on, his voice rising in pain and frustration. "That's all I've asked. That I can be here for you. That you stop hiding behind that damn wall of yours." He crosses to her, takes her hands in his. "Let me in, for godsakes. Whatever it is you're doing, you can't do it alone. No one can."

If it were only that simple.

"I will," she promises. "Just give me a little time. Please."

"How much?" he asks. "And when?"

"As soon as I can," she promises him again.

He nods, staring at her, his expression flat, almost a mask. "Don't take forever."

21

HOUSE OF SMOKE

Kate drives Highway 154 over the pass. It's still early morning—a few minutes before seven—so there isn't much commuter traffic into Santa Barbara yet. She calls Laura from her car phone, waking her up, which is what she wants, she wants to catch the girl unawares, when her mind is not yet functioning clearly.

Kate's own mind is racing, trying to sort out her feelings towards Cecil, and where that's going. But she can't let that affect her, not now. What she's doing with the Sparks family needs every ounce of her concentration and energy.

Laura's voice is heavy with sleep. "Hello?" she mumbles into the receiver.

"It's Kate," she tells Laura. "Are you alone?"

"Huh?" Not fully awake, she'd been up late partying, her brain right now is mush.

"Are you alone?" Kate repeats. "Can we talk?"

"Yeah, I'm alone." Her voice is becoming clearer. "Where have you been?" she asks. "I've been trying to reach you."

"Don't worry about that. I've found out who had Frank Bascomb killed," Kate says, her voice flat and calm, "and why."

"What? . . . How do you . . . ?"

"I'll get back to you later," Kate tells her. "After I finish up something I have to do." Before she hangs up, she cautions Laura: "Don't tell anybody about this. Nobody. I'll call you later." She already checked to make sure she had Laura's office and cell-phone numbers. "Stay where I can get in touch with you."

Then she hangs up.

She waits on making the next call until later in the morning, when she can be reasonably sure that Miranda Sparks has gotten to work.

Celeste, Miranda's secretary, answers the phone. She listens for a moment, then tells Kate: "I'm sorry, Mrs. Sparks is in a meeting and will be tied up the rest of the morning."

"This is Mr. Hopkins's office calling," Kate tells her, keeping her voice neutral and nondescriptive. "This call is urgent."

"One moment," Celeste answers, her voice immediately deferential.

Miranda comes on the line. "Yes?" She listens—a short time, less than thirty seconds. "Who is this?" she asks, keeping her voice calm, mindful she has people in the room with her. Her mind is racing at the information she's being given. "Who is this?" she asks again—this time to a dial tone.

She hangs up. "An emergency," she explains brusquely to the people in the room. "I have to go."

She dashes out without further explanation. Then she drives over County Highway 154 as fast as she can go, to the ranch.

Reaching the cutoff, Miranda's Mercedes 500 haul-asses down the pitted private road, throwing up dust and gravel as she stands on the brakes and fishtails to a stop in front of the ranch house. She runs up the steps of the front porch to the door.

She pauses for a moment before unlocking it: looking around, as if suspecting she's under surveillance.

There's nothing out there—nothing she can see. There's a chill in the air, the sky is clear, white-blue. No clouds.

She digs in her purse for the keys to the front door. Throwing the dead bolt, a look of surprise and fear comes over her face as she realizes it's already unlocked. Quickly she tests the doorknob—that's firm, at least. Whoever was here last forgot to lock it. She suspects it was Frederick, he's so damn careless. There's valuable stuff inside, priceless heirlooms, family mementos that can't be replaced at any price. Not that he ever seems to care—he's always had everything, so he assumes he always will. A stupid, dangerous assumption—which is why she must be on her toes at all times, forever vigilant.

She unlocks the door and rushes inside, throwing her coat onto a chair as she hurries through the living room into the den, to the old pine breakfront, which is almost as old as the house itself, glancing at the open top cluttered with the memorabilia of her husband's family's life.

Most of the pictures are of Laura as a young girl astride a horse, decked out in western tack. There are a couple of Frederick when he was his daughter's age, also on a horse. The resemblance between them is noticeable. And some older pictures (even one of Dorothy as a young girl with her father), going back almost to the turn of the century.

There are no pictures of her. She is not of this family's blood. A member by invitation only.

She hunches down in front of it, her tight skirt riding halfway up her thighs, takes out an old-fashioned skeleton key from her purse that matches the opening, turns it, pulls the drawer open, and pulls out the Rainier file.

It's empty. There's nothing inside.

"Oh, Jesus," she says softly. She can feel her stomach churning, turning to fire, taste the bile surging up into her throat and mouth. Gagging and swallowing to keep from vomiting all over herself, she starts tearing through the other files in the cabinet—maybe it was misplaced, put in the wrong file. It had to be.

"Looking for this?"

Miranda spins so violently she smashes against the open drawer, losing her balance and falling ungracefully to the floor.

Kate stands in the doorway, staring down at Miranda. She's changed her clothes. Now she is wearing an old Oakland Raiders varsity jacket over her sweater and jeans. Her day pack is slung over her shoulder. One hand holds a thick manila envelope. "The Rainier Oil file, I presume?" she asks in a clear, strong voice, holding it up for Miranda to see.

Miranda stares at her, almost as if she can't be there. She manages to rise to her knees, then to her feet.

"That was you?" she finally says. "That called me?"

Kate nods—a short, tight nod. "Yeah," she answers. "That was me." She pauses. "You had to know that."

The two women stare at each other. Miranda looks away first.

"Sit down," Kate orders her. "I don't think you should hear what I'm going to tell you standing up."

Miranda crosses the room and slumps into the seat behind her desk. Kate remains standing, the old wooden desk a protective barrier between them. So this is where ambition gets you, she thinks, when you don't have a moral base to fall back on. It's something she needs to remember, in her own life.

"You said over the phone this was a matter of life and death," Miranda says quietly. "You weren't kidding, were you?"

Kate nods. She realizes she's never felt so clear and centered in her life.

"You've been living a lie. For a long, long time."

She forces herself to stay calm, to keep her own voice on an even keel. Even though she is in control, for the first time in her dealings with this woman, her guts are churning.

"Yes," Miranda admits. "I have. We—" her arms extends towards the breakfront, towards the pictures of her husband, daughter, mother-in-law—"we all have." She sits up straighter. "What do you plan to do with this?" she asks, indicating the documents.

"That depends on the answers I get to the questions I'm going to ask you."

"What if I can't answer them?"

"You better hope to God you can, lady. Because if I leave here without getting all the answers I came for, I'm going to the DA, the *News-Press,* and every TV and radio station in town. And I'm giving them all this." She takes some more papers out of her day pack, lays them on the desk in front of Miranda. "There's more," she adds. "Lots more."

Miranda glances at the papers, looks up at Kate, then down at the papers again, as she realizes the scope of what it is that's in front of her. Slowly, her hand trembling noticeably, she picks the papers up and scrutinizes them carefully.

"Where did you get this information? This information is privileged," Miranda protests feebly. "You have no right to this."

"Big fucking deal. The thing is, I *do* have it. And by the way," she adds, "I made copies of all this stuff. They're tucked away in a nice, safe place, but if anything bad happens to me they'll immediately see the light of day. I've finally learned how to take care of myself," she informs Miranda.

Gingerly, Miranda touches the papers on her desk, as if they were alive and lethal. "Why are you here?" she manages to ask. "If you're thinking of blackmailing me—"

"Don't insult me, goddamn you!" Kate spits. "You've done that already. That fat deposit into my bank account, paying off my hospital bills—that wasn't out of the goodness of your heart. You don't have any goodness of heart."

"That money was because you saved my daughter," Miranda insists. "There was no evil motive behind it. You're wrong if that's what you think."

"Oh, cut the shit! That was a payoff, pure and simple." She glares at Miranda. "You tried to buy me off with your friends in the Mexican Mafia or whoever the fuck those men were down in Oxnard, and that didn't work. Then you did the seduction bit—that didn't stop me, either. So then you figured, might as well take the direct approach, kill the bitch off—and somehow, through some miracle, that failed, too. Now you're really getting desperate, so you tried to buy me off again, you came at it from another direction, sugar-coating it with apologies and 'Thank you for saving my poor baby's life.' " She shakes her head in wonder. "You fuck me and then you try to kill me. You are some piece of work, lady."

Throughout this recitation Miranda is shaking her head. "You're wrong," she says. "Yes, I did seduce you, and I don't recall any hesitation on your part, you liked it as much as I did, and yes, I did give you money, which one could construe as a bribe. But I did not send anyone after you, be it the Mexican Mafia or the Girl Scouts of America, and I most definitely did not try to have you killed."

"I don't believe you but have it your way," Kate responds. "That's in the past now, anyway. This is the present," she says, pointing to the papers on Miranda's desk, "and the future. Not the future you envisioned, I'm sure."

Miranda sits back in her chair. She seems smaller all of a sudden, not so impervious.

"No," she admits. "It is not."

"How long did you think you'd be able to get away with it?"

There's no hesitation. "Forever, of course."

Kate's taken aback at the forcefulness of the answer. "How?"

Miranda's mouth twists into a tight smile. "I'd find a way. Like I always have."

"The way being smuggling drugs?"

Miranda sits up bolt-straight. "I had nothing to do with that!"

Kate can't help smiling at the woman's brazenness. "Cut the shit, Miranda, would you? It's way too late for that now."

"It's the truth! I've done a lot of stupid and ugly things, I'll admit it, you've got me dead to rights so there's no point in conning you, but I was not involved in that. You have to believe me."

"I don't have to believe shit," Kate snorts. "Everything about you is a lie. What do you tell people you're worth, the mighty Sparks empire? Two, three hundred million, isn't that the figure you've been throwing around? You haven't been worth close to that for twenty years, and it keeps draining away. Your former empire is nothing more than a mirage now—a house of smoke. The fire that fueled it has burnt itself out."

She gets up, walks around to Miranda's side of the desk. Miranda's almost slumped over, limp. Her face has gone pale, all the life, that great vitality, draining out of it—Kate can see it happening before her eyes.

"Let's go through it together, shall we?" Kate states, savoring the moment.

She picks the pages up, starts rifling through them. "Here's a good one to start with," she declares, pulling a document from the stack. "Three office buildings in San Francisco. Your family—your husband's family—bought them as a block in 1936." She looks at the figures. "Boy, they really stole them, no pun intended." She flips some pages. "Great moneymakers for decades, steady growth. But then you sold them— 1986, it says here. Below market value, too." She shows the papers to Miranda. "Let me refresh your memory."

Miranda waves the papers off with an aggravated air. "We had to. California real estate went into a depression in the eighties," she explains.

"Not in '86. Things were still booming then. I don't know that much about real estate, but this doesn't look like very smart business to me."

"We had other expenses."

"I see." She picks up another document. "More real estate. This one's in San Jose. Commercial storage space, almost a million square feet. Whoa, you really took a bath on this puppy."

Miranda doesn't respond.

"More expenses, I take it?"

Again, silence.

Rifling through more documents: "Now these I can understand. Los Angeles. You owned an entire city block, almost. You got killed."

"Everybody got killed in L.A. real estate."

"You more than most, I'd bet." As Miranda looks up inquiringly: "I've researched these deals, compared to other deals that were going down at the same time. You did worse than most. For somebody who's supposed to be smart you sure did some dumb stuff," she digs.

Miranda remains quiet, watchful.

Kate picks up a handful of other transactions. "Deal after deal gone south, like birds in winter. You've got to have some kind of perverse talent to fuck up so consistently." She leafs though pages of documents, *tsk*ing through her teeth. "I find this interesting—for decades the Sparks family basically sat on what they had acquired in the first half of the century. But from the mid-seventies until the mid-eighties you were buying up property hand over fist, you couldn't sign the deals fast enough. And then from the late eighties until now, it's all downhill." She tosses the papers on the desk in front of Miranda. "About the time you took control of the company, it appears."

Miranda simply stares, from Kate's face to the damning evidence in front of her.

"You were going to make your mark, that's my educated guess. You were going to show this smug rich family you married into how to really make money, prove to them you're just as good as they are—better. But you overextended to the max and got the shit kicked out of you, which you couldn't face up to it like honest folks, so you paid for it with the future. The Sparks family has a lavish lifestyle, which they entrusted you to maintain. But you couldn't afford to keep it up, not with real estate plunging the way it did. Am I getting warm?" she asks, barely concealing the taunt and contempt in her voice.

Miranda looks up at her. "Yes," she chokes out.

"It still doesn't compute, though," Kate continues. "Some of these properties—several of them, in fact—were turning a profit. And yet you sold them off, one by one, at fire-sale prices. Why in the world would you do that?"

Tight-lipped: "I had my reasons."

"Yeah, I'll bet you did." She stares at Miranda, the force of her energy compelling Miranda to look away from her. "All those trips to Vegas that your husband made over the years. That must have drained you like an open wound."

Miranda turns to look at her. "How did you—?"

"I'm a detective," Kate answers, cutting her off. "I get that kind of work done before breakfast. How much money did your husband lose over the years?" she prods.

Miranda shakes her head. "I don't know."

"Ten million? Twenty? Fifty?" she asks.

Miranda looks up at her. "Maybe more," she admits.

"Year after year, selling off your assets to pay for that crap. And hating yourself every time you had to do it, I'll bet. Seeing it all go down the toilet. Didn't you ever try to stop him?"

"Of course I tried." Her eyes are blazing. "I did everything but . . ."

"Put a gun to his head?"

"Almost. Everything short of that."

"So. You can't kill the old man's gambling Jones. And you're taking a pounding in your holdings. You're losing millions, year after year. What's a woman to do? You must've spent many a sleepless night thinking about a solution."

Miranda isn't responding, but Kate doesn't care—she's on a roll, she knows what she knows and she wants Miranda to know it.

"Then it hits you. You own all that private property on the beach, which no one has access to. And you own this big ranch, with its own runway. Bring in some drugs, that's the ticket. If a kid standing on an L.A. street corner can make ten thou a week dealing dime bags, think of your possibilities."

"That's an absolute lie!" Miranda yells. "We had nothing to do with that, nothing!"

"Ah. Touched a nerve, did I? Hey," she continues, "it's easy money, and it's only marijuana, everyone smokes grass, you're not really corrupting the youth of America with coke or heroin—it's like selling bootleg booze during the Depression. The only problem is, you got caught. Rather, your front man did, your foreman. That must've been a hairy moment, when you found out they'd been caught red-handed right on your property."

"It was awful," Miranda admits, "but not because we were involved in his scheme. Surely, you can understand why we were upset."

"But of course. The family name and all that. The family name covers all transgressions, doesn't it?"

Miranda shakes her head stubbornly. "I don't know how to convince you that I had nothing to do with any of that drug stuff," she says. "But look at this: my family wants to do something with that property. Something that could be beneficial to the community and make some money for us as well, I won't deny that. Why would I take the chance of blowing it all for a boatload of marijuana? It doesn't make sense."

"You're right, except for one thing."

"What's that?"

"Greed."

"No." Adamant.

"Bullshit. That's exactly what it is. Greed and arrogance. You're the Sparks family, you can get away with anything. Drugs, sex, anything."

Miranda looks at her, her face squinted up in a quizzical expression. "What does sex have to do with any of this?"

"You don't know anything about your husband's quirky sexual peccadillos? The thousand-dollar-a-pop hookers, the private airplane flights back here. That's got to run you some hefty coin."

Miranda looks at Kate wearily. "I guess it was naive of me to think you wouldn't know about that, too."

"Quite an interesting sexual life you rich folks lead. You and the mister."

"You don't know what you're talking about."

"Not all of it," Kate admits. "But enough that if it ever came out you'd be ruined in this town."

"You think you know about us," Miranda reiterates, "but you don't. No one knows."

"I know about you. About the lovers you've had. Including Mr. Blake Hopkins of Rainier Oil"—Miranda visibly flinches—"a liaison that's been going on a lot longer than you want the world to know." She shoves her hands in her jacket pockets. "How easy was he to seduce? Easier than me? How many bottles of hundred-dollar wine did you have to ply him with to get him naked in the old hot tub?"

"All right! You know everything about me! You can stop now." She buries her head in her hands.

"Not everything." She places her hands on the desk, leaning in to Miranda, speaking slowly, clearly "Here's what I want to know. Do you love your husband? Even the least little bit?"

Miranda can't help cracking a wistful smile.

"What?" Kate asks.

"Somebody else asked me that very question not so long ago."

"One of your other multitude of lovers?"

"Yes."

"So what was the answer?"

"The answer was that I love my husband very much."

"And him?"

"He loves me, too. I'm sure of it."

"Then why? Why so promiscuous?"

"I don't need an excuse for what I do—do you?"

The woman's right about that, Kate has to agree. Who are you to pass judgment on someone else? she thinks. You're not that far off from her, not deep down.

Miranda sighs—a deep inhalation and exhalation. "My husband is a nice man," she says. "A wonderful man, in most respects. Caring, sensitive, a great father. Everything I always wanted in a man. And I was lucky enough to know, at the tender age of twenty-one, that he was special, that not every man was like that. Which is why I decided to marry him."

"That and two hundred million dollars," Kate adds.

"Oh, yes. The money was important. Crucial. I freely admit it, and he knew it. I never had any and I'd always wanted it, lots of it. And he had it, and he wanted me."

"Sounds like the perfect match."

"It was. It still is." Miranda pauses. "Except for one small detail." She pulls the center desk drawer open, takes out a crumpled pack of Virginia Slims, shucks one partway out, bends over and pulls it from the pack with her lips. "Do you mind?" As she flicks a wooden match with her thumbnail, "why am I asking permission to smoke in my own house?"

"No, I don't mind. Somehow I had the idea you don't smoke."

"I don't, hardly. I chip when I'm nervous. Like now." She offers the pack to Kate. "Care to?"

"No, thanks. I've already got enough vices, I can live without that one."

"A couple a month won't kill me." Miranda waves the match out, flicks it into a waste basket, and inhales deeply, exhaling through both mouth and nose. "Anyway. I was telling you the story of me and my perfect marriage. Perfect except for one thing."

It finally hits home for Kate. She knows what Miranda's going to say even as she's saying it.

Miranda confirms her sudden understanding. "He's impotent."

"I heard somewhere that he was gay, or maybe bi." Cecil had told her that, she assumed it was common knowledge, albeit closeted. "But not impotent," she says, still not quite believing it. "He brings in call girls here. I met one of them."

What was it the Vegas call girl had told her? That Frederick didn't fuck her, didn't fuck any of the girls. He just watched, like a kid through a peephole, in his case the viewfinder of a camera. He was saving himself for his wife, Brittany had assumed.

Miranda takes another deep drag, blows a perfect smoke ring towards the ceiling. "Think about this. What I just told you is not something you say about a man. Not a man you love. You'd say that about a man you hate, because it's the most damning thing you can say. That in the most fundamental way he's not a man at all."

"Well . . ." What a bitch. "It's weird," she hears herself saying. "So why are you telling me?"

"Because . . ." Another heavy drag, another smoke ring. "Because I've been living with it for a long time, and I need to tell someone, anyone. And Jupiter's aligned with Mars, I don't know. It's been eating me up inside, I know that."

"Shit," Kate says softly, almost to herself.

"Exactly."

"Couldn't you ever do anything about it?" Kate asks.

Miranda shakes her head. "Frederick is not psychologically impotent," she begins to explain, dropping her smoke to the floor and putting it out under the sole of her shoe. "It isn't in his head, and it isn't any type of . . . it can't be fixed through normal medical procedures. His problem is much deeper-seated. Genetically, probably. A birth defect, like a shrivelled leg or Down's syndrome." She pauses. "The poor bastard has never in his life had an erection. Not even nocturnally. He is incapable of having an erection. Under any circumstances."

"Can I ask you a question?" Kate asks after what seems to be an interminable silence.

"Sure."

"Why did you stay married?"

"Like I told you. I loved him. I still love him. I will always love him. I just can't have sex with him; which is why, I'm sure, I have it with almost everybody else, and have for the past twenty-five years. I've seen plenty of psychiatrists trying to work that one out, believe me."

Kate grunts under her breath.

"There are other reasons we stayed married, of course. I signed a prenuptial agreement, at his mother's insistence—she didn't think I loved him, she thought I was a cheap gold digger out for her baby's money."

"I heard about that," Kate acknowledges. "So if you divorced him . . ."

Miranda nods. "I'd be cut off without a cent. Although now, after all we've gone through, he and I, he'd take care of me. Like he always has. Because he loves me, too."

Kate thinks for a moment. "You've got a daughter who was not adopted," she says, "I know that for a fact. And she's the spitting image of her father."

Miranda nods. "I found a surrogate," she explains. "A man to father a child for us."

Being in group has taught her how to listen patiently, Kate realizes. It would be helpful for Miranda to be in a group. They must have groups in prison, which is where Miranda Sparks is going to wind up.

"So what did you do?" she asks Miranda. "Go to a sperm bank, one of those places that specializes in Nobel Prize–winner spunk?"

Miranda shakes her head. "I don't trust those places. For me it was going to be a man, in a bed."

"How ever did you find Sir Galahad?" Kate asks, openly curious.

"By sheer accident. I was at a conference on hunger, at Cal Tech. I was representing our foundation—donating money to a good cause, as usual. I was walking down a corridor and turned a corner and there he was. I practically bumped into him."

"How fortunate for you."

"It certainly was," Miranda responds without a trace of irony. "He was about forty, a professor at Helsinki University. Married, which was my preference—a single man might have gotten romantic, when all I wanted was to get pregnant. But the great thing, the reason I seduced that poor man out of his socks—he looked so much like Frederick it was eerie."

Kate's mind is reeling. She expects the unexpected, she sees that in her work every day, but this is weirder than anything she could have ever dreamed.

"So you lured him into your web," she says.

"Not that it took any effort," Miranda admits unself-consciously. "I guarantee you he's never forgotten it." Wistfully: "I haven't, either. He supplied the missing piece in our life together, Frederick's and mine."

"Did you ever hear from him again?"

"No."

"Wasn't he in the least bit curious?"

"I don't know, nor do I care. He was a married man, and worldly enough that it was an interlude for him, nothing more."

Kate shakes her head. "You know how to get what you want, don't you?"

"I thought I did," Miranda says, looking up. "Until now." She smiles. "You know what I remember about that weekend with the professor from Finland? What I remember most?"

"What?"

"How much he was like Frederick—not only physically, but in other, deeper ways. When my eyes were closed I was imagining he *was* Frederick. In a strange way, which I don't expect you to understand, I was making love to my husband then." She closes her eyes, remembering. "And it was wonderful."

It's quiet for a moment.

"I told Frederick, of course," Miranda continues. "Once I knew for sure I was pregnant—trying to pull an immaculate-conception scam wasn't going to cut it. He agreed to go along with the deception, although it took him a while to adjust to the reality. That Laura is his spitting image was a bonus he hadn't counted on. Frederick's a wonderful father—a much better parent than I am."

Kate rocks back on her heels. "That's a very heartwarming story," she says finally. "That and a buck eight'll buy you a cup of coffee in just about any restaurant in town."

Miranda glares at her. "You think I'm trying to soften you up?"

"Aren't you?"

"I suppose so—partly. It's . . . I know I've been a bitch. But I'm not a killer, and I'm trying to convince you of that."

Kate shakes her head. "There's too much evidence against you, lady. Way too much."

She picks up the manila envelope that contains the secret contract between Rainier Oil and the Sparks family. "This," she tells Miranda. "This is what finally convinced me. Because this really is life-and-death for you. Your only chance to recoup all those losses. Keeping this secret is worth killing for."

She paces the room, keeping her eyes on Miranda.

"I've been looking for a smoking gun," she says. "Some conclusive, irrefutable piece of evidence that proves beyond a shadow of a doubt that you were involved in the murder of Frank Bascomb, of the two in Newport, and my own attempted murder. And this," she says, brandishing the papers, "is it. This deal is worth killing for."

"No," Miranda insists. "No amount of money is worth killing for."

"That's bullshit." Kate fires back. "We all have our price, and this is a hefty load. Worth killing Frank Bascomb for, he was a liability, he would've sung like Barbra Streisand, and those two poor bastards in Orange County, too, you don't want to leave any loose ends dangling when this much money's at stake." She paused a moment—then it comes out. "And it was worth killing me for."

"No," Miranda says emphatically. "No."

"No?" Kate opens the envelope. "This is your future, right here. To get back all that money you've fucked away over the years." She leafs through a few pages, stopping at a certain part. "What was it you said at the board meeting? The mineral rights belong to the state, not the property owner, so your share will be small, a mere pittance, and what you do make you'll give back to your oceanography school? 'It's preposterous that anyone would think the Sparks family would need money.' Those were your exact words, I believe. And you uttered them with such righteous indignation." She stabs a finger at the contract. "When the smoke's all cleared, this is what it's all about. This back-door deal between you and Rainier Oil, that guarantees you a fortune in royalties. More money than the family had to begin with by the time it's all done."

She squints, reading the small, dense print. "They're not going to pay you some measly rent, a couple hundred thousand dollars a year. That's chump change. They are going to pay your family a royalty almost as big as the state's going to get, according to this top-secret document between you and them."

She holds the secret contract in front of Miranda's face with thumb and forefinger, as if it's a dog turd she's scooped off the sidewalk with a piece of Kleenex, too odious to touch.

She's super-mad now. Her voice drips with contempt.

"You duped your best friends, you whore. Your oceanography school and everything about it was merely a smoke screen, to obscure your real purpose—to give the Sparks family an out, so you could endorse Rainier's drilling scheme and make those millions under the table. Twenty million dollars every single year for the life of the lease, twenty years at a minimum, and it could be more, double that amount. That's half a billion dollars to you."

She hammers at Miranda with her voice, although it's her fists she'd like to be using, she's itching to bust up that smug gorgeous face into a thousand pieces, like they did to her. "I don't think anyone would call five hundred million dollars a pittance. More like an avalanche." Angrily, she adds, "I've known some cynical people in my time, lady, but you take the cake."

Miranda sags like a hot-air balloon shot full of holes.

"All right," she admits. "Now you know all about us, every piece of our dirty laundry. What are you going to do with it?"

"Use it to get you charged with murder."

"Lying about a business deal doesn't equate with murder," Miranda comes back at her, still arguing her position. "But it would ruin us. And all of our good projects, too. We do a lot of good in this world, whether you accept that or not."

"It's an irrelevant argument," Kate tells her flatly. "Good works don't cancel out bad deeds."

Miranda stares at Kate. She doesn't speak for a moment—the silence hangs heavy, portentous. Then, steepling her fingers and staring right into Kate's eyes, she says, "That's too bad. Because there's an awful lot of money in this." She pauses, then continues her thought. "My family's not the only ones who could get rich."

Now the air around them is really heavy, almost oppressively so—Kate consciously feels her lungs working, bellowing breath in and out. "Am I hearing you right?" she says slowly, weighing her choice of words carefully. "Are you offering me a bribe?"

" 'Bribe' is not a word in my vocabulary. I'd prefer to think of it as a partnership."

Kate nods, stalling for time. "A partnership. That has a nice sound to it. I've never been in this high-level kind of partnership before. What kind of split are you thinking about?"

Miranda traces a manicured finger around the rim of her lips. "Ten percent would be an incredible amount of money. Two million dollars a year for twenty years, maybe more."

Two million dollars a year. She can't begin to comprehend what that means. She sees the number in her head: a two followed by six zeroes. That's more money in one year than she'll ever earn in her entire lifetime, and that's if she's successful, considerably more so than she's ever been up to now.

"I would think it's worth twenty-five percent to shut me up—wouldn't you?"

Miranda cocks her head, a wisp of a smile crossing her mouth. "Fifteen," she counters.

Kate smiles back. "Twenty."

"Okay. Twenty it is." Miranda extends her hand towards the Rainier contract. "Can I have that back now?" In the snap of two fingers she's immediately calm again, as if none of what's been taking place here this morning ever happened. "And I'll want your duplicates, of course."

Kate shakes her head. Ice, she thinks. That's the only thing that runs in your veins.

"I'll hang on to it until we have a formal agreement between us—in writing," she informs Miranda, keeping the papers at arm's length.

Miranda nods. "Fair enough," she says, grudgingly. She glances at her watch. "Can we go now?"

"In a minute. There are a few more things I need to know—to round out the picture."

"Like what?" Miranda asks suspiciously. She checks her watch. "I have appointments piling up."

Kate puts the Rainier documents back into her day pack. "This won't take much longer." She takes some other papers out. "Right before that dope deal went down, you secretly sold five hundred thousand dollars' worth of foreign bonds through a Caribbean bank. Bonds that hadn't reached their full maturity. That was to pay for the grass, down in South America, wasn't it? Rent the boat, pay the crew, all those expenses."

"I don't have a clue as to what you're talking about," Miranda says.

"Oh, man, cut the shit! We're partners now, remember? I'm not going to blow the whistle on you. But I need to know, Miranda. I need closure on this case—for me, for my peace of mind."

"I'm serious. I don't know what you're talking about." She extends her hand. "Let me see that."

Kate pulls back.

"I'm not going to bite you." Miranda says. "I'm telling you the truth, I don't know what that is. And I should, if it truly is our money you're talking about."

Kate extends the papers across the desk, hands them to Miranda.

Miranda holds them, squinting. "I don't know this account," she says. "I've never heard of these bonds."

"You run the company," Kate comes back. "You know everything."

"I'm supposed to. But I don't know about this. If you don't want to believe me, that's your choice. But I am telling you the truth about this."

"It's signed," Kate points out.

Miranda turns to the back page. "That's not my signature."

Kate laughs out loud. "What—someone forged it?" She leans in close to Miranda. "Don't play me for a jerk, lady."

"Here's my handwriting," Miranda says angrily, reaching for her purse. She pulls out her driver's license, hands it to Kate along with the papers. "Here's my signature."

Kate looks from one signature to the other. She frowns.

"It's a forgery," Miranda says. "Someone forged my name."

They stare at each other.

Slowly, almost as if she were praying, Miranda touches her fingertips to her forehead.

At the exact same moment, and with as much horror, Kate shakes her head, like someone trying to get rid of her worst nightmare.

"Don't tell me you're thinking the same thing I'm thinking," Miranda says in a whisper.

"Laura," Kate replies in a voice equally low, as if the mere saying of that name is unbearably painful.

Miranda starts to crumple. She grasps the edge of the desk for support. "Oh, God," she moans. "She was in on it—the entire time."

Kate nods. "It looks that way," she has to agree.

"I believed her when she told me she was innocent. I never doubted her for an instant."

"Neither did I."

You dumb fucking ass, she rails inwardly. Don't neglect checking up on Laura, Carl had warned her. This could be a ruse, he'd cautioned her, to throw you off your client's trail.

Shit. This explains it. How Laura managed to get away. She's never been able to really come to grips with it. Yes, she had diverted their assailants, and Laura's story later had been plausible; but looking back on it now, how does a naked, frightened, inexperienced girl outrun men who if they don't find her and kill her are looking at the gas chamber, and know it?

She had buried her suspicions. This explains why Laura had set up that encounter with the phony informant. It was a trap from the get-go. And she had walked right into it with her eyes wide open.

You're an amateur. That's why Laura hired you. Laura wanted to cover her tracks, but she didn't want anything real to be found out. That's why she didn't hire a more established agency—because they would have seen through her.

"Now what?" Miranda asks.

Kate shakes her head. "I don't know."

"That forgery," Miranda says, pointing to it, still in Kate's hand. "What are you going to do with that?"

"I don't have a choice," Kate says. "I have to take it to the police."

"So bye-bye the money? You can walk away from millions of dollars? Just like that?"

"She set me up," Kate counters sharply. Her anger's directed straight into her own gut, Miranda just happens to be standing in the way. "Your daughter tried to have me killed. I can't walk away from that—there's no price tag on my life."

"There's no way I can . . . ?"

Kate puts up her free hand like a traffic cop. "No."

Miranda nods. "I guess that's it, then," she says with tired resignation.

"I guess so." Kate starts to put the forged papers back in her pack; then she hesitates. "There's just one thing," she says slowly.

"What?"

Kate rummages around in her pack, comes up with another stack of papers. She looks at them, turning to one particular page.

"What is it?" Miranda asks.

"It's a telephone bill. Rusty Lukins's phone bill, for July."

"Who's Rusty Lukins?" Miranda asks.

"The man who chartered the boat," Kate says. "Frank's accomplice. The man the police shot, trying to escape."

"How did you get . . . ?" Miranda's mouth flies open. "Those two that were murdered down in Orange County. That was at his house, wasn't it?"

Kate nods grimly.

"Were you there that night?"

Kate nods again. "I was meeting them. Wes and Morgan. I was late. By the time I arrived they were already dead." She's shaking, her body jerking spastically from head to toe. "I led the killer right to them, so I'm responsible for their getting killed," she says soberly, feeling the pain welling up inside her. "If I'd been on time, I'd be dead now, too."

They stare at each other.

"Rusty called here," Kate tells Miranda, referring to the telephone sheets. "Only one phone call, but it ties her in."

"When was that?" Miranda asks anxiously. "The date."

Kate looks at the bill. "July twenty-second."

Miranda stares at her.

"What is it?" Kate asks.

"I was out of town that day," Miranda says. "And Laura was with me," she adds, her voice rising. "We were in San Francisco, together. I can prove it—dozens of people were with us, all day long."

"He was calling Frank, then."

Miranda shakes her head. "Frank was never in this house without one of the family being here with him. This is our place," she says, "for the family only. He didn't even have a key."

"Laura could have given him one."

"Maybe. I suppose so."

All the color has drained from Miranda as she reaches into her center drawer again.

Kate's drained herself—all she wants now is to get out of here. She stuffs the telephone sheets back into her day pack.

Click.

Slowly, very slowly, she raises her eyes.

Miranda is pointing a gun at her. A .32 revolver, a comfortable gun for a woman. Easy to use, and plenty of stopping power, certainly at this range.

"Put that down," Miranda says, indicating the day pack.

Kate stands stock-still. "This is not a good idea, lady," she tells Miranda. "You do not want to do this—you don't. Trust me on this."

"I don't have a choice." Miranda nods at the day pack. "Put it down. On the desk. Slowly."

Kate places the pack on the center of the desk.

"Now step back."

Kate takes two steps back. "Are you going to kill me?" she asks.

"I've already told you—I have no choice."

"You have a choice," Kate corrects her. "Everyone always has a choice."

Miranda shakes her head. "I can't let my daughter be arrested for murder. And I'm not going to let you ruin our lives."

"You really have the guts to pull that trigger? You told me shooting wasn't your thing."

"I will do anything I have to do. You should know that by now."

"If that's the case, then you certainly could have pulled the trigger on Frank Bascomb. To order the job. And to have Wes and Morgan killed, too." Kate pauses again. "And me."

"I'm not a murderer," Miranda insists. "This is self-defense."

"Self-defense my ass." She takes a step forward.

"Don't," Miranda warns her, holding the gun steady. "No closer. I keep this loaded, and I know how to use it. I may not be a crack shot like my daughter, but I can hit a target at this distance."

"Shooting a target's not the same as shooting a real live human being."

"I don't doubt that—but I can and will shoot you." Her voice is climbing, slightly out of control. "You forced your way in here. You didn't give me an option."

"I guess the cops would buy that," Kate admits, thinking it over. "You've got them in your hip pocket anyway." She pauses. "You've done a lot of ugly things, and you've hurt a lot of people; but if you're not a murderer, then you're not going to be able to pull that trigger."

"I told you. This is different."

"Murder is murder. There is no difference." She takes another step closer. "Only the victims change."

"Don't! I will do this."

"Give me the gun." Her voice is low, soothing.

She's back in that house in Oakland again with that crazy man, Losario, and his wife and daughter, and her partner, Ray. And she isn't doing the right thing.

She isn't imposing her will on him.

That's the way it has to be. The only way to be in control, to come out alive and bring your prisoners with you. Because, she realizes with a terrifying clarity, she had never been Losario's prisoner at all. It had been the other way around. He had wanted her to take control. And she hadn't done her job.

In his perverse sickness, Eric had been right. But only about that one thing, nothing else.

Losario, in his own paranoia, had brutalized her. Eric had also brutalized her, directly, in her face. And those men up there in her secret place, those disgusting animals, they had brutalized her, too.

She wasn't going to let it happen again. No matter the outcome, she wasn't going to be the victim anymore.

Her will is so strong. As if it's the most natural thing in the world, she reaches for Miranda's gun with a slow, deliberate movement.

And the weapon slides out of Miranda's hand, into her own.

Like the wall of a dam bursting, the tension that's been gripping them both pours out of the room.

Kate cracks the cylinder of Miranda's revolver, empties the bullets into her palm, drops them into her jacket pocket.

"You aren't a killer after all," she says, feeling the weight of the world fall from her shoulders as she realizes the enormity of what she's done.

She feels good about that. God, does she feel good about that!

"At least I told the truth about something," Miranda offers in her defense. She looks at Kate. "That offer I made you—about sharing the spoils—you weren't serious, were you? About taking it."

"About as serious as you were in giving it."

"I'm glad about that."

"Oh?"

"That you're honest. I thought you were—I would have been disappointed if I really could have bought you."

Kate nods. "You already tried that, remember? It didn't work then, either."

There's nothing more to say. Kate takes her own weapon out of her pocket and points it at Miranda, motioning with her arms towards the door.

"You had a gun, all this time?" Miranda exclaims, disbelieving. "Why didn't you use it from the beginning?"

"Because it's not my style." She blows out her cheeks. "But now you've left me no choice—I can't take any more chances."

Miranda nods in mute acknowledgment.

"Let's go," Kate commands; but not harshly. She's back in control now—she doesn't have to be a tough guy anymore. She starts to pick up her day pack; again, she stops. "One more thing." She fishes a piece of paper out of her pack. "The night Frank Bascomb was arrested," she informs Miranda, "he made one phone call. To his patron, obviously, to get him out of there as quickly as possible. It's a local number: 555-5599." With a self-congratulatory smile, which she's earned (in spades), she asks the obvious question. "That's your unlisted number, isn't it?"

Miranda's face goes white as she stares at Kate—then past her with a look of unbelievable shock.

"No. That number belongs to me."

Behind her. A woman's voice. Then two loud *click-click*s: the distinctive and terrifying sound of a shotgun being cocked—both hammers.

"Put your gun on the desk," the voice commands. "Right now."

Kate hesitates for a moment. This can't be happening, she thinks. Not now, when she's finally figured it out—both the byzantine labyrinth of this case and, more importantly, how to take control of her life.

"Do it or I'll cut you in half," she hears. "Unlike my daughter-in-law," Dorothy Sparks tells her, "whose eloquence can charm the birds out of the trees, I prefer to let my actions speak for me." Forcefully: "The gun. Uncock it, put the safety on, and put it down. Both hands, where I can see them."

Slowly, carefully, Kate uncocks her gun, slides the safety up, and places the automatic on the center of the desk.

"Turn around," Dorothy commands her.

Kate turns and faces Dorothy. The old woman is dressed for the ranch, jeans over boots. She's holding an old Parker .20 gauge side-by-side, the long double barrel pointed right at Kate's gut.

You dumb bitch! Kate screams to herself: at herself. You rank fucking amateur!

The signs had been there from the beginning: the unknown dope-deal financier; Wes's bail; the building in San Francisco. The old building guard had said "Mrs. Sparks." He'd known her before Miranda had ever come into the picture—she's the one he'd dealt with, not Miranda. The signs had been there, right in her face. Why hadn't she seen them?

Because: she'd been so hell-bent on going in one direction that she hadn't bothered to read the map, to look for another road to her destination. She'd wanted to nail Miranda, and had closed her eyes and her mind to anyone else. "Get to know the family," Carl had told her, his first piece of advice on this case. She sees it all now, with the clarity of twenty-twenty hindsight.

She hadn't done a thorough enough job. Now she was going to pay for it.

Think!

Her mind starts working madly, trying to figure a way out. If there is one. Start talking. See if that distracts her. "You paid for the shipment of marijuana, didn't you?" she says.

Dorothy stares at her, her eyes unblinking. Looking at her as penetratingly as Kate looked at Miranda a few minutes ago.

"And it was your money that paid Wes Gillroy's bail."

Dorothy keeps staring. Her hands are rock-steady, holding the shotgun on Kate. Behind the desk, using it almost as a shield, Miranda watches with morbid fascination.

"And you paid off whoever killed them all. Including the men in the jail cell who murdered Frank Bascomb—and tried to murder me."

The faintest movement behind Dorothy's eyes. Then: "Yes."

"Why?" The cry is of pain, true despair.

Kate jerks her head towards Miranda, who's staring at Dorothy in anguish and bewilderment.

"Why?" Miranda cries again.

"For the money," Dorothy answers her daughter-in-law, in a tone Kate imagines she would use on a five-year-old. "We're broke." Then her voice hardens, revealing the steel beneath the civility she presents to the world.

"For twenty years you and that weak, pathetic son of mine have run our fortune into the ground. You and your grandiose schemes, him and his gambling. And I've sat back and kept quiet, because I'd turned the company over to you and the lawyers told me I was powerless to act. You had me in a bind. But I had to face facts. In a few years we would have lost everything. I had to do something."

"The building in San Francisco, where the office of the fictitious Bay Area Holding Company is, you used that for collateral to bail Wes Gillroy out," Kate says—to make sure, for herself. Not that the knowledge is going to help anything now. "You owned that yourself, outside the family's trust."

Dorothy nods. "I kept a few holdings separate, for my own protection. It's a good thing I did, as you can see."

"I didn't know about that," Miranda says, dumbstruck.

"What you don't know about me—and what I *do* know about your life and Frederick's—would fill several volumes," Dorothy states, relishing Miranda's surprise. "I've been turning a blind eye to your sexual flagrances for years, Miranda, because above all else I wanted to avoid scandal. For Frederick and Laura," she says venomously, "not for you. As for my few remaining properties, that I've held onto, you would have lost them along with all the rest, if I hadn't kept them from you," Dorothy continues. "Those were my annuities. Selling some harmless drugs—that would have sweetened the pot, given me a little more insurance. God knows I needed it."

"But we're about to make millions!" Miranda screams. "The deal with Rainier would have made us back everything we've ever lost, and more, while that stupid drug scheme of yours could have fucked the whole thing up—and for what? A couple million, maybe? We'll be making more than that every month, once the oil royalties start coming in!"

"We don't need oil developers raping our land," Dorothy says in a voice that is preternaturally calm. "That's evil, wrong. We've been fighting them for years; we shouldn't become their partners now. It's totally against everything I've stood for, all my life."

"But dealing drugs and killing people is okay?" Kate asks. This woman is crazy, she realizes. Another Losario—even worse.

"The killings were unfortunate," Dorothy answers, without a trace of remorse in her voice. "It would have been preferable not to. But once you're into something like that, you do what you have to do."

She turns to Miranda, making sure she keeps Kate in her sight. "I didn't know you were cooking up this scheme with Rainier. You've cut me out of all the decision making for years—which was a mistake, I hope you see that now."

Miranda stares at her in total disbelief.

"I knew I had to do something," Dorothy goes on. "And when Frank came along with his proposal, I thought it was a pretty good idea."

"What we have here," Kate interjects, "is a failure to communicate. Big-time."

"Well taken," Dorothy says. Then she abruptly shifts gears. "This is so unfortunate. This detective"—she indicates Kate with a head nod—"has become obsessed with her work, and despondent over having her pretty little face so mangled, it's haunted her for months. She finally got so desperate she lured you here and then, at gunpoint, threatened to blackmail you if you wouldn't pay her off. Luckily, I found out about it, and confronted her. She tried to shoot me, but I was able to beat her to the draw."

Kate and Miranda both stare at Dorothy in horror.

"You'll never get away with this," Kate tells her. She's having a hard time getting any words out, let alone speak and think rationally.

"I already have, haven't I?" Dorothy's smile is almost serene. Why not? Kate thinks. The woman is in charge; and she's crazy, gone totally round the bend.

"No. Friends know I was coming out here, and there are copies of all these documents. If anything happens to me this all goes right to the law."

"You're lying," Dorothy states.

"You don't want to find out, do you?"

"I'll take my chances. They're much better than letting you go." She motions with the shotgun. "Move over there. Away from your gun."

Kate takes one step to her left. Swiftly, Dorothy grabs the automatic off the desk and sticks it in her waistband.

"What about Miranda here?" Kate asks. "Do you think she's going to sit on this for the rest of her life?"

"She's not going to have to."

Miranda stares at her in shock. "What are you . . . ?" she gasps.

"Before I could kill your blackmailer," Dorothy explains to her, "she shot you."

"You had Frank killed," Kate says. Keep talking—keep buying time. "And you got away with it. You had Wes and Morgan killed, and you got away with that, too. And you almost had me killed, which you would have gotten away with as well—because someone else was doing it. Of course, your granddaughter might have been killed in the crossfire, but that's the price you have to pay, right? Since it wasn't your hand that was actually on the trigger you would have been clean."

She's hit a primary nerve.

"They wouldn't have killed Laura!" Dorothy erupts, her voice filling the room. Her hand is shaking, holding the shotgun. "They knew who they were after—they had their instructions!"

"That's a good one," Kate answers. "Trained professional killers, that bunch. Calm, cool, and collected. Lady," she says, taking a step forward, "you listen to me. They could've wasted Laura and they wouldn't have blinked an eye."

"No," Dorothy answers, her voice trembling. "You're wrong."

"I'm right. And you know it."

Out of the corner of her eye she sees Miranda taking all of this in: the horror, the madness, the total lack of humanity. She looks back at Dorothy. The woman has regained her self-control—the eyes are dead again.

Dorothy motions with her shotgun. "Outside. Both of you. This time I'll do it myself," she says to Kate. "So that it gets done right—finally."

Here or out there—what's the difference? Kate watches Miranda come out from behind the desk, then slowly walk through the living room towards the front door.

"Move," Dorothy commands.

She follows Miranda out. They stand on the porch, in shadow.

"Down there." Dorothy points into the yard. "Spread out."

They trudge down the steps. Miranda, then Kate, then Dorothy, a safe distance behind, but close enough that the shot from her gun won't disperse much if one of them tries to run and she has to pull the trigger.

It's late morning now, the pale yellow sun sitting high above their heads. The sky is almost colorless, as if the life has been squeezed out of it.

"I'm not doing this because I want to," Dorothy says. "I'm doing it because I have to."

"Those are comforting last words to hear," Kate states bitterly. "I guess that means your conscience is clear."

"Completely," the old woman replies. She raises the shotgun to her shoulder and takes careful aim at Kate, both barrels.

Kate dives for the gun.

The explosion is deafening.

Before Dorothy hits the ground her eyes widen with the amazed look of a woman who painstakingly prepared for everything, and still got it wrong.

Kate's head snaps around.

Laura stands fifty yards away on the hill above them, in the shadow of an oak tree. The rifle, barrel smoking visibly, hangs limp in her hand. As she starts walking towards them it drops with a thud.

Three women stand on the hard dirt ground, apart from each other, the sun so directly overhead that there seem to be no shadows. The fourth woman, the dead one, lies facedown in the center of the triangle, the back of her shirt rapidly spreading crimson.

Time is frozen.

Then it comes back to life as Miranda races to her daughter and takes her in her arms. Laura stands motionless, eyes cast down.

Kate walks slowly to them, as if moving through a quagmire. Her legs feel like they have no bones left in them.

"How did you . . . ?" Kate asks. She feels like she's going to puke her guts out and have a heart attack at the same time.

"I followed her," the girl says simply. She starts trembling, suddenly losing control over her body, feeling the reality of what she's done. "She'd been acting weird lately," she states in a low monotone, "and when you called me earlier I told her. I know you warned me not to, but I always tell her everything—things I don't even tell you, Mom," she says, looking at Miranda, who looks away, her face flushing painfully.

Laura looks at Kate again. "She was the only person who knew from the beginning that I'd hired you, which must be why she knew everything that was happening as things progressed. Like up at your private place," she adds shamefaced. "This morning I told her about your call and she freaked, it was like she'd seen a ghost. That set something off in my head, how crazed she was, so when she took off in her car I followed her. I lost her coming over the pass, but by then I knew where she was heading." She reaches out and lays a hand on Kate's arm. "You saved my life. I couldn't let her take yours."

J. F. FREEDMAN

Kate's voice is choked. "Thank you."

"You put your life on the line for me," Laura says. "I had no choice."

"It's going to be all right," Miranda consoles her daughter, trying to pull her close.

Laura shakes her head, withdrawing from her mother's arms. "No, Mom. Nothing's ever going to be all right again."

Kate comes back to life, starting to take stock of their situation. Without wasting another second she kneels down and picks up the rifle that is lying at Laura's feet. With her other hand she grabs Dorothy's shotgun, and takes her own gun from Dorothy's belt, shoving it back into her pocket. Looking at the two women standing, and the dead one on the ground, lying in a pool of her own spreading blood, she feels sick; they never understood, she thinks, that in the end, the world does not revolve around them.

Now they'll have to.

Enough sentiment. Those feelings are dangerous, there's no time for feelings. She has business to finish.

"It *may* be all right," she says, repeating Miranda's plea. "What happened here. Or it could blow up in your faces. You're going to have to do as I tell you—*exactly* as I tell you."

She grabs Laura by the shoulders. "You're going to have to pull yourself together. Can you do that?"

Miranda starts to answer for Laura, but Laura cuts her off. "Yes," Laura says, in a firm tone that states "I can take charge of my life." "I can do that."

Kate looks at her. It's a different woman she's seeing—a real woman, not a kid anymore. Out of these awful ashes a life is growing, she realizes. Something is going to come from all this pain.

She returns to the problem at hand. "And you, too," she warns Miranda.

"I will. Don't worry."

"Okay. Here's the drill. I was never here."

They both stare at her.

"That telephone call you got at the office?" she tells Miranda. "That was somebody calling to warn you that there was a problem up at your ranch. Maybe something to do with that drug deal, you weren't sure. You didn't want to come up here by yourself so you called Laura and told her to meet you here. You got here and found your mother-in-law dead, shot in the back. And you saw someone running away. A man. A tall man, athletic. You got a good look at him, you could ID him if you ever saw him again. That's the story that you're going to tell the police, and you're sticking to it. Can you do that?"

Miranda nods. "Why are you doing this?" she asks.

"You don't have to know. I'll take these with me," she says, brandishing the rifle and the shotgun. "They'll never be seen again."

She heads toward her car, then turns back. "Wait a couple of hours before you call the police. That's imperative. You got that?"

Miranda nods yes.

Kate throws the rifle and shotgun in the trunk of her car and hightails it down the road.

One more piece of the puzzle to fit in. Then it's over.

22

HAPPINESS IS A WARM GUN

She sits in her living room, waiting.

It's the first time she's been back to her apartment since she went into hiding. She's changed out of the clothes she wore up at the ranch. Now she is wearing a loose T-shirt and light silk Turkish trousers that are almost diaphanous. No bra. Her bikini underpants can be seen through the trousers. Her feet are bare, her toenails freshly painted. She has bathed and put on perfume.

The doorbell rings. She walks across the room and opens the door.

"Hello, stranger," she says.

He has come from work, where she called him, so he's wearing his uniform of sport coat, white shirt, slacks, tie. His gun is tucked into a holster clipped to his belt.

"Hello back," Juan Herrera says to her. "I've been worried about you, Kate. I tried calling, I even stopped by."

"I went to ground," she says. "After what happened down in Orange County, I was afraid . . ." She stops. "Anyway, I'm back in the open now. So come on in."

She stands aside so he can enter. Then she closes the door behind him and locks it.

The curtains have already been drawn.

"I need to see you," she told him over the phone. "I've finally gotten to the bottom of the whole rotten mess. All that Sparks family shit. I thought you'd want to hear all about it. So I can put it all behind me."

From when she hung up until the ring of the doorbell has been less than twenty minutes, which means he left his desk right away.

"You look good," he tells her. He can't help noticing her ass through the sheer pants, and her nipples showing under the T-shirt. "Real good."

"Good enough to eat?" she teases him. She reaches behind him and slips his jacket off, tossing it onto a chair.

"Yes," he answers slowly, a smile breaking out across his face. "I was going to leave for lunch in a few minutes, so I'm hungry."

"Caught you in the nick of time," she says. "Guess it's my lucky day."

They come into each other's arms, a hot, hard embrace.

"How long can you stay?" she asks when they break.

"As long as it takes," he answers. One hand is caressing a breast, the other tracing ribbons down her back.

"It could take a long time," she smiles coquettishly. Her hand is going to his belt, loosening it.

"Damn. You're frisky today," he observes.

"I'm horny."

"That's pretty direct."

"I haven't been laid for a long time," she tells him. "Ever since this." She points to her face.

"You look good," he said. "You shouldn't worry about that."

"I'm glad you feel that way. It's important to me. You know what I went through," she tells him, seriously. "More than anyone."

"Beauty is in the eye of the beholder."

"Does that mean I'm beautiful?" Playful again.

"About as beautiful as any woman I've ever known."

"What about sexy?"

"For sure, sexy."

"So am I turning you on?"

"You've always turned me on, Kate," he says, dropping the bantering tone. "From the first time I laid eyes on you."

"You mean you weren't just being a nice guy and helping out someone the rest of the department wouldn't?" she teases.

"No," he answers. "I helped you out plenty before . . ." He leaves the rest unsaid. "Because I wanted to fuck you doesn't mean I don't like you, too."

"I'm glad you feel that way. 'Cause that's how I feel about you, too."

His hand is under her shirt, caressing her bare breast. She has goosebumps all over. He is hard as she strokes him through his pants.

"So what's this important news you have for me?" he asks.

"All in good time. Let's get to the important things first."

She takes his hand and leads him into the bedroom.

"Get undressed," she orders him. "I'll be right back." She pulls her

J. F. FREEDMAN

T-shirt over her head and tosses it onto the floor, standing topless in front of him, her nipples hard, sticking straight out. "I need to get my protection. Don't go away."

He doesn't need any further encouragement—he's half undressed by the time she's out of the room.

It's warm in her bedroom. He lies on top of the covers, naked. His clothes are neatly folded, the crease in the trousers matching up, the shirt over them, then the tie. At some point he will have to shower, dress, and go back to work. Later for that. He can take the rest of the afternoon off without checking in; his time is pretty much his own at this stage in his career.

The holstered gun lies on top of the neat pile.

He hears water running briefly in the bathroom.

"Watcha doing?" he calls.

"I won't be long," she calls back from the bathroom.

He can taste her—not just her mouth where he's kissed her, but all of her. He still has that taste in his mouth's memory, from when they made love before.

"Come on," he calls again.

"This has to be right," she answers. "This is a special occasion. Everything has to be right."

She enters the room. She's wearing a white terry-cloth robe, untied, the sides folding against her hips. He can see her vagina thrust forward towards him, her breasts hanging down. The incongruity of the prosaic robe and her frank nakedness under it makes for a very erotic image.

His cock is erect, rock-hard. He extends his arms to her. "Come here," he beckons. His voice is hoarse, his throat constricted with sexual heat.

She stands at the foot of the bed, staring down at him. "You're glad to see me," she remarks, glancing at his swollen penis.

"We're both glad to see you. Now come on."

"In a minute."

She reaches into one of the pockets of the robe and pulls out some papers.

"What's that?" he asks.

"What I wanted to talk to you about."

"I thought we were going to do that later."

"I decided to do it first. So we could get it out of the way." She grins at him. "Aren't you the least bit curious?"

"No, I don't think so." He pauses. "Why—should I be?"

She nods. "I think you'll find what I'm going to tell you very interesting."

His erection is wilting. It'll come back fast enough, but he isn't in the mood to talk, or listen. Still, it's her deal. He'll make a good show of being interested, and then he'll fuck her brains out.

"You know what's really interesting?" she asks him.

"No. What?" He pushes himself up against the headboard, arms behind his back. It's more comfortable that way. If he has to talk and listen, he might as well get comfortable.

"How easily you manipulated me. And how willingly I let you."

"What's that supposed to mean?"

"Nothing. Just an observation."

"If anybody manipulated anybody, it was you," he says. "You got a ton of information out of me, stuff no one else where I work would have told you. No one else would give you the time of day," he adds.

"That's true. So I guess that makes us even, right?"

"More than even."

"Good. Oh, before I forget," she says. "What does a lieutenant on the sheriff's down here make after twenty years?"

"Why do you want to know?" he asks suspiciously. What the hell is this all about?

"This thing came up. I was talking to somebody, and it came up, I don't remember. Maybe I was talking to someone on the Oakland Sheriff's I used to work with. Asking about rates down here, in case he wanted to move."

"Sixty-six thousand a year. But tell your friend not to bother," he adds, "there's no openings. The county doesn't have any money, and there's a waiting list as long as your arm. Answer your question?"

"Sort of, but not really. The thing is . . ." She looks at one of the pieces of paper in her hand. "The reason I asked is, two days after Frank Bascomb expired in your jail you deposited $100,000 into your bank account, and there's no record where it came from. Sixty-six K is good money, but it doesn't account for a sudden windfall of $100,000. And then, a week later, you transferred the hundred into an offshore money-market account in the Cayman Islands, which is a place people hide money so the U.S. tax collectors can't find it. In impolite society it's called 'laundering,' " she adds.

He sits bolt upright. "What the fuck? Where did you find . . . what're you talking about?" he stammers. "I don't know what the hell you're talking about."

"A payoff, of course," she answers calmly. "What else could it be?"

"It could be my wife's money. Which is what it was," he says with indignation. "She and her sisters owned some property up north, which they sold, and she wanted to invest it, so I did it for her."

"So it had nothing to do with the fact that you were on duty at the jail that night," she says, pressing on. "The night Bascomb so-called hung himself, which you and I both know is bullshit. We do agree on that point, at least, don't we?"

"It was Fiesta," he points out. He doesn't like the direction this conversation is headed, not a bit. "Everyone in the department was on duty that night."

She shakes her head. "But not jail duty." She looks at another sheet of paper she's holding. "According to official records you went to the jail an hour after Frank Bascomb was locked up and volunteered to take over from another officer. You relieved him of his duty, which you didn't have to do, since you have seniority. You don't have to pull that kind of duty at all, in fact. And according to your records—" she glances down at the papers again—"you hadn't worked at the jail for over a year. Which is no surprise, since you're a detective and detectives don't normally work inside the jail."

He stares at her. "You've been a busy little beaver, haven't you?"

"You don't know how busy I've been. Not the half of it."

"Well, for your information, since you're so curious about my comings and goings, that officer had a sick wife, and he asked me for a favor. That's the reason—there's nothing sinister about it."

"Oh, good. Then I guess there's nothing sinister about the strange fact that Frank Bascomb was transferred out of a high-security cell into a common tank, either."

"It was a clerical error."

"No," she tells him. "It was deliberate."

His eyes narrow. "You sound like you're making an accusation."

She flips him a county jail computer printout. He picks it up, looks at it. As he does so he edges closer to the side of the bed, the side where his gun is sitting in its holster on top of his neatly folded clothes.

"Bascomb's arrest sheet was altered," she says. "From a major drug-trafficking offense down to a petty possession charge, barely a felony at all. Which made it easy to kick him out of his isolation cell, under twenty-four-hour watch, into a group tank. With a whole bunch of drunks who had just ten minutes before being processed and put into that cell." She stares at him intently. "The same men, coincidentally, who tried to kill me the night that phony informant set me and Laura up."

He lunges for his gun.

Hers is out of her robe pocket while his hand is a good five feet from even grabbing the holster, let alone pulling the weapon out.

"Not a cool idea," she tells him, cocking her automatic and aiming it at his pecker. "Unless you want to talk in a high voice for the rest of your life. I'm loaded up with Winchester Black Talons," she says, "you know the awful mess they make."

"You're crazy."

She pulls the robe around her, tying the cord tightly. "Peep show's over."

"You're making the biggest mistake of your life."

"No," she shoots back. "The biggest mistake of my life was trusting you, taking you into my confidence. You were in this from the get-go." Her free hand balls into a fist—a fist she'd like to smash his face in with, like hers was. "As soon as I got on this case—the first time I went down to the jail to check up on Wes Gillroy—you found out about it and called me in a flash with this bullshit story that I needed help, and you were such a sweet guy, you'd take care of me when no one else would." She stares hard at him. "You needed to know what I knew, didn't you, Juan?—so you could keep the brakes on. And like a dumb fucking idiot I played right into your hands. I kept giving you more and more information—as soon as I knew anything, so did you. Which made it pretty easy to counter my every move. Even to the point of setting me up to be murdered."

He starts to move.

"Freeze," she commands. "I will have no problem at all pulling the trigger on you, Juan. Not after what you've done to me."

He does as she tells him.

"Dorothy Sparks hired you, didn't she?" she goes on. "That was her hundred grand you banked. And there have been other payments, going back. You've been on her payroll for years. The documentation exists, it's got you nailed." She shakes her head, as if trying to shake a bad dream out of it. "You're a disgusting son of a bitch, Juan. A cop on the take. That's the lowest form of life there is."

"This is all conjecture," he spits out. "It doesn't mean shit."

"Dorothy Sparks knew Frank Bascomb had been arrested even before he got to the jail," she continues. "She was this nice old lady who was always doing nice things for the department, throwing benefits for widows and orphans, real do-gooder stuff. She even monitored police calls, a strange habit for a seventy-five-year-old heiress, but she had good reasons. She was protecting her investment. So as soon as Bascomb was booked, she made a call to her man on the inside. You, Juan. She told you to get your ass down there and fix things up so he could never put her into it. And like a good soldier, that's exactly what you did."

"No fucking way."

"Only one person knew I was going down to Newport Beach to look for Wes Gillroy. You. You were the only one I confided in, because I had to have some backup, and you were the logical choice."

Her hand is shaking, holding the gun.

"You followed me down, you shit. I led you right to them. You killed them, yes—but my hand was on the gun as much as yours, because I was the Judas goat that led those two poor bastards to slaughter."

She takes a deep breath.

"And if I had been on time for our rendezvous, I would have been dead along with them. You had already tried to have me killed once. This time you were going to make sure, you were going to do it yourself, and you sure as hell weren't going to take any prisoners."

He looks at her, trying to decide when to go for his gun.

"How long did you wait for me? Ten minutes? Fifteen? You should have waited five minutes longer, but you couldn't, you lost your nerve, so you bailed out and called the local cops, hoping I'd show and walk right into it. And I almost did. But thank God my blind dumb luck was with me a second time."

She takes another deep breath. Her nerves are shot.

"You had already killed Frank Bascomb," she says. "You personally killed Wes, and Morgan. And you would have killed me."

"You don't have proof about any of this shit," he says in answer.

She reaches into her robe pocket again and pulls out a baggie that has a bullet inside it.

"In your panic you left one of the shells behind, down in Newport Beach. It rolled under the bed, you couldn't find it like you found all the others."

She dangles it in front of him.

"This shell and your .9 mm. I'd bet my life against the hundred thousand in your secret bank account they're a perfect match."

She tosses it in her hand. "The smoking bullet. From the smoking gun."

And for the split-second she looks away to catch the baggie he has lunged for his gun and has pulled it and is turning towards her to fire.

Which is how she planned it.

The repercussive explosion from the automatic is deafening in her small apartment. The bullet enters his face in the middle of his right cheekbone, driving him back with such force he splits the headboard in half.

Later, when the coroner's crew is cleaning up, they can't find any of his brain tissue inside his cranial cavity. It's all over the back wall of her bedroom, along with the rest of his head.

The women sit in their circle. The mood is somber. It's Kate's farewell night in the group. Outside, it's raining, the first hard rain of the season.

She begins. "I got the past out of my present. That part of it, anyway. It's a great feeling, because now I can really believe I have a future. You can't hold onto things, whether they scare you or give you comfort, you have to be with them and then let them go. Whether it's your job, your kids, anything. Everything."

Everyone in the room is attentive to her. There's no fidgeting around, loud sipping of coffee, spacing out. They all know what she's gone through—it was impossible not to, the details (those Kate orchestrated and managed to control, which were the most important ones) were all over the television and newspapers. It was the biggest scandal to hit Santa Barbara in years. And she had been the catalyst, the one who had broken it open.

"Whatever I've hidden," she goes on, "I don't apologize for. In my heart I know I did exactly the right thing under the circumstances. I'd do it the same way again, that's how I know." She pauses, thinking back. "The most important thing is, I committed to a course of action, and I followed through on it. Right or wrong—flag that, there is no right or wrong in affairs such as these, that's judgmental, God give me the strength never to be judgmental again—I did what I had to do." She takes a deep breath. "And I did it for me. What was right for me. What I had to do. For me."

Everyone in the basement room sits in stunned silence.

"I thought *my* job was stressful," Maxine, the group leader, says at last. Her comment isn't meant as a joke, and nobody laughs.

"You got some *cojones,* girl," Conchita says admiringly. "You are a *woman!*"

Other voices sound out in praise, commendation, support.

Mildred Willard, the Sparks family friend who brought Kate into the case, sits silently, watchful.

Earlier, in the parking lot, the two women talked briefly. Mildred was profusely apologetic about ever getting Kate involved in such a sordid mess, especially when she already had enough troubles of her own. Kate reassured the older woman that there was no fault or blame attached; how could anyone have known what a snake pit this would become? Their friendship was intact, Kate promised Mildred. Their bond was not of the outside world but of their shared experiences here.

They hugged, hard. It was a good feeling for both of them. A cleansing.

"So," Kate concludes, "I'm rid of my demons. Some of them, anyway. The scariest ones. I'm not afraid anymore," she tells the women. "Of anything."

"God bless you," one of the other women says. "I hope I get to that place someday."

"You will," Kate assures her. She looks to Maxine for confirmation.

"We all will," Maxine states. "There is no question of that."

"That's why I'm not afraid of leaving the womb here," Kate tells the women sitting in the tight circle with her—her sisters in pain.

"Because I'm not a victim anymore."

23

PEACE

It's been a wetter-than-average winter, which means a fertile spring. Kate trudges up the hill towards her secret place, hacking away at the dense undergrowth with her machete. She hasn't set foot on this property since her near-fatal beating.

The double killings caused a monumental uproar, much greater than the brouhaha over the killing-suicide during Fiesta weekend. It dominated the front pages of the newspapers for weeks; nobody talked about anything else, from the small neighborhoods on the westside to the multi-million-dollar mansions in Montecito and all points in between.

Despite intense grilling by the police, Miranda and Laura stuck to the story Kate scripted for them: they had arrived at their ranch house to find Dorothy already dead, the assailant running away across the open fields and disappearing, heading in the direction of the highway.

As sensational as the murder of Dorothy Sparks was, it took second billing to the shooting that took place that same day in the apartment of Kate Blanchard, a licensed private detective, who had shot and killed a county deputy sheriff, a man she knew well and who was, according to everyone who knew both of them, her friend. Herrera had become obsessed with her, stalking her for months, and had come to see her on a ruse he'd made up about a case she was working on. Against her better judgment she had allowed him to bluff his way into her apartment, at which point he had attempted to rape her, then tried to kill her in the fear that she would expose him. Her killing him, she claimed, was purely in self-defense.

The two incidents converged when both Miranda and Laura Sparks identified the dead officer, Lieutenant Juan Herrera, as the man they had seen fleeing from their ranch house. They were adamant that he was the man—there was no equivocation on either of their parts.

Everything came to light after that: Dorothy Sparks's involvement in the drug trade, Juan Herrera's complicity with her in the murder of Frank Bascomb, their hiring of the men who had tried to murder Kate, and the coup de grace, the police lab matching up the shell discharged from Herrera's police automatic with bullets recovered from the bodies of the two corpses in Orange County.

After a short but extensive investigation no charges were filed against anyone. Juan Herrera was posthumously charged with the murder of Dorothy Sparks, and his death at Kate's hands was accepted as an act of self-defense by a woman who had already almost been killed under his and Dorothy Sparks's direction.

All the cases were formally closed, and it is the fervent hope of all involved that they will never be revisited again. Those who know otherwise than the official facts—Kate, Miranda, and Laura, and the women in Kate's group, who know about her and Juan but not about the rest—have taken vows of silence, which for their own personal reasons will never be broken.

*O*ne month later there was an item on the bottom fold of section B, the local news section of the News-Press. The Sparks family had decided to retire from public life. They canceled their plans to establish the oceanography school and declined Rainier Oil's generous bequest. At the same time, because of severe financial constraints, they were selling their beachfront property to Rainier, enabling the oil conglomerate to site its onshore drilling platforms on the location.

Shortly after the first of the year, Miranda Sparks filed for divorce from Frederick Sparks, citing irreconcilable differences. Her alimony request was modest; generous enough for her to live on comfortably, but not extravagantly. She moved out of town shortly after. She regained her maiden name—Tayman—and is presently thought to be liv-

ing in New York, but that is not certain. She has, for all intents and purposes, dropped completely out of sight.

Frederick Sparks is in the process of liquidating the remainder of the family's holdings. He and Laura are presently living in Paris, where they plan to take up permanent residency. Frederick will pursue fine art full-time, and Laura is attempting to start an English-language magazine that will cater to expatriates of her generation. She has never been told the story of her true parentage.

Carl X. Flaherty, one of Southern California's most legendary private detectives, passed away in February. He was eighty-three years old. He had been in ill health for some years and died peacefully in his sleep. His funeral was private; only Kate and a few members of the nursing-home staff were in attendance. He was cremated, his ashes scattered into the Pacific.

Kate reaches the swimming pool. The entire area is overgrown with weeds and vines, the pool cluttered thick with dead leaves and broken-off tree branches from the winter's storms. It will take weeks to hack enough away so that she can restore it to the way it was.

That's okay. She has time. As much as she wants.

She's put her business on hold. She finished up the few cases she had pending, closed up her office, turned off the telephone. In a few weeks she'll start taking courses at the local branch of Antioch University, with an eye towards getting a B.A. After that, maybe law school. There are other ways you can be part of the legal system and help people than being a detective. More calming, positive ways, that don't require putting your life on the line.

She sees her kids every month, religiously, sometimes making the round trip every other week. Pretty soon Wanda will graduate high school, move on to college: Stanford—she got in on a scholarship.

In a few more months Kate'll petition the court to regain custody of them. Sophia wants to live with her now.

She and Cecil still see each other, it's going well, they both want it to happen, they need to get to know each other better. The deep stuff. She hopes it'll work out—she really cares for him, and she feels ready to be with a man now, in a healthy, honest way. She knows if she keeps on getting her own shit together she'll be able to get it together with a partner.

The sun is high, midday apex. It's warm, the first day it's been truly warm this spring. She hauls armfuls of vegetal flotsam out of the pool, enough to clear the drain of scum so that the water starts flowing sluggishly. Then she strips naked.

The water isn't as cold as she expected. The thick cover of vegetation acted like a heat blanket over the winter, retaining energy.

She dips a toe in; it's bearable.

She eases in at the shallow end, taking a moment to acclimate. Then she pushes off from the wall, taking slow strokes, half-crawl, half-breaststroke, swimming and pushing gunk out of her way at the same time. As she swims she feels her muscles responding, the nice tight soreness that comes after a long layoff. She reaches the far wall, turns, and starts in the opposite direction.

Overhead, a red hawk, seeing the action below, wheels and plunges for a closer look, then soars up again when it realizes the motion is not anything it can prey upon. Up and up it climbs, until it disappears over the ridge to the north; while down below, in her own private world, the naked woman swims back and forth, swimming until she is exhausted and must climb out, gasping for breath, washed clean, to lie under the heat of the warming sun.

ACKNOWLEDGMENTS

Lynn McLaren, PI, California License #PI13155, helped me understand the philosophy and techniques of a modern detective in Santa Barbara, particularly those of a woman detective.

Richard Monk, JD, assisted in local knowledge, especially in the areas of Santa Barbara history and politics.

Jaime Raney, JD, analyzed the manuscript from a professional woman's point of view.

Each of these friends spent several hours reading the manuscript on my behalf, and to each I am grateful.

The Santa Barbara County Sheriff's Office, Jail Division, assisted in the workings of their jail. Descriptions of departmental procedure described in this book are fictitious and are not meant to reflect on the actual workings of the department, or of any sheriff's department personnel.

Shauna Clarke of Mobil Oil gave freely of her time, advice, and expertise, and I am grateful to her for helping to present the oil industry's point of view.

Creig Dolge of the Citizen's Planning Association of Santa Barbara County gave me excellent advice and editorial help in presenting the point of view of the segment of the community that is opposed to oil development in the Santa Barbara region.

David Sherman of Far West Gun & Supply assisted me in my weapons research.

Al Silverman and Bob Lescher were, as usual, supportive, enthusiastic, and encouraging.

My wife, Rendy Freedman, read the manuscript countless times, offered her advice and constructive criticism, and was supportive of the work and of what I was trying to say. As a family therapist, she was of particular help in the passages dealing with women's groups, battered women, and family problems and solutions.